BY DEFAULT

Also by David King:

Letting Paddy Fly
a short story collection published 2015 by
Ginninderra Press, Adelaide, Australia

By Default

DAVID KING

MacGregor House

Copyright © 2017 by David King

Cover photo: istockphoto/rudchenko

David King has asserted his right to be identified as the author of this work in accordance with the Copyright, Designs and Patents Act of 1988.

All rights reserved. This book or any portion thereof
may not be reproduced or used in any manner whatsoever
without the express written permission of the copyright owner
except for the use of brief quotations in a book review.

This book is a work of fiction and, except in the case of historical fact, any resemblance to actual persons, living or dead, is purely coincidental

First Printing 2017

ISBN 978 0 6480740 0 7

MH
MacGregor House Publishing
South Australia

Chapter 1

In the early days of Michael Cavanagh's acquaintance with Meredith Lomond she was simply the strange woman on the bike who turned up randomly at his workshop.

She would poise, wordless, on the threshold until Michael stopped whatever he was doing. Having captured his attention, she'd turn, depart, and for minutes afterwards, he would contemplate the empty doorway.

After several such visitations, Michael realised it didn't matter if his back was towards her, he always sensed the woman's presence. This feeling came in the form of something odd, though not a shiver, rippling down his spine. He began to think his visitor might even be a ghost.

He'd wonder why she came, what she wanted, and if it *was* something, why she always chose to leave with nothing. Once, he followed her outside, watched her pedal away down the lane on her bicycle, a bottle-green, sit-up-and-beg Raleigh with a handlebar basket and a tennis racquet holder on its forks. Perhaps, he thought, she had a whole schedule of people to visit in this mystifying way.

The bicycle was the means of their introduction. Michael had noticed her standing beside it in a lane one day, gazing about all-forlorn, as if that was how to find help in the middle of nowhere. On that occasion the tactic worked, for he could see the bike's rear tyre was flat. The woman had a puncture outfit in a little canvas bag beneath the saddle but no idea how to use it, so he did the repair for her. Not a word from her throughout, but a vague smile he took to mean thanks as he handed back the bike.

That was the prelude to her sporadic, silent visits. On the sixth or seventh of these, in Michael's reckoning, something made him call out as she left, ask what she actually wanted. She stopped, turned, surveyed him as if seeing him for the first time. Then she blinked, frowned and introduced herself formally, said she'd noticed him at the May Day Fête.

As it was the only one he'd bothered to attend, Michael knew which Fête she meant. Some years back now, though. But as soon as she announced her surname, Lomond, as in the loch with the bonnie banks, he knew who she was. He remembered her wandering around the stalls, sleeveless dress, wide-brimmed straw hat. She'd arrived at the Fête with a ramrod of a man who looked as if he belonged on horseback at Trooping of the Colour. They'd been referred to as the Lomonds, recent to the village, up from somewhere smart in the Home Counties. Mr Lomond was said to wear honourable before his name. There were whisperings of scandal too but nobody identified its nature. Honourable or not, Mr Lomond acted like a visiting celebrity, assumed control of the wellie-throwing contest and the judging for that year's May Queen.

From then on, Meredith would say 'Good morning' or 'Good afternoon', whichever suited her time of arrival, then step onto Michael's shop floor, flicking shavings and chippings aside with a delicately aimed foot.

Those feet, he observed, were small, slim and always, whatever the weather, cocooned in gleaming navy or burgundy leather. They made him too aware of his own feet: looming clodhoppers shod in rough boots with steel toecaps, fit for a carthorse. He'd shuffle them out of her sight, wish they were shiny black Oxfords or those sturdy brown brogues that country gentlemen like her possibly honourable husband wore.

Meredith's hair was a pleasant blonde-turning-grey, trimmed short so it revealed all of her handsome face, and her eyes were that clear blue that often seems cold. Hers, though, shone with an intensity that made Michael marvel. He'd delved in his mind for a suitable description, furrowing his brow as he did so. *Electric eyes* - that was the best he came up with because, as he often reminded himself, he wasn't gifted with words, only with wood.

One day, he told Meredith he was a carpenter by default. Someone said that to him once, after asking if carpentry was what he'd always wanted to do. He'd answered, "No it bloody well wasn't." When relating the incident to Meredith, he thought it best to leave it bloodless.

"Default?" Meredith said. "You mean as penance for some misdeed?" Her eyes were alight, dancing, and a vision flew into Michael's mind of a meadow of fireflies he'd seen years before in the Welsh hill country.

"Penny for them?"

Michael snapped back to reality and scrutinised Meredith's face. Was she laughing at him? He could feel the heat in his cheeks as she waited for his answer, her eyebrows raised, eyes still dancing.

"No misdeed," he said. "Apart from having the wrong parents."

Meredith's eyes flickered and for a brief moment Michael saw discomfort in them. "I'm sorry, Michael," she said. "I wasn't making fun of you, I swear."

That was the longest conversation they'd had before he met her daughter.

Halfway through an April distinguished from November by warmer rain, Michael was concentrating, head down, face-planing an oak board. He was aware of the moment Meredith came in, but didn't look up or switch off his machine until he was satisfied its work was done. As he transferred his attention, the woman he saw had Meredith's eyes but she was not Meredith.

His heart began to thump as he took in the flawless skin, pale waves of hair and the eyes, especially the eyes. She was how Meredith might have looked thirty years ago but that, he realised, was where the comparison stopped. His visitor's clothes proved this was no time warp. She wore Levis so tight he could imagine them being sewn on. Her teeshirt was even tighter. He avoided it by studying her feet. The scruffy Nikes covering them looked several sizes bigger than Meredith's dainty footwear.

When Michael dared to look up, he saw the girl's lips moving but couldn't make out what she was saying. He realised he was still wearing the ear defenders he'd put on to counter the siren whine of the planer and a heavy warmth rose up his neck, spread scalpwards until he felt that even his hair was turning crimson.

"Sorry," he said.

"I'm Daisy, Meredith's daughter," the girl said, smiling. She had Meredith's self-assurance about her as she extended her right hand towards him. Michael took it with a timid grip, after wiping his hands on a stockinette roll.

"I'm very pleased to meet you at last," Daisy said. "You've been a positive lifeline for Mummy."

Michael frowned. "A lifeline?" he said, shaking his head. "But I've done nothing." His face cooled as confusion displaced embarrassment.

"Mummy wondered if you might come up to the house? We'll take my car."

Daisy turned, made straight for the doorway, and Michael winced at the profile of a breast that strained her teeshirt as she twisted past a pillar drill. Wondering what he was letting himself in for, he pulled off his smock, brushed shavings from his jeans, rubbed a duster over his boots. He cleaned his hands with baby-wipes he kept in his workbench drawer.

Daisy's car was a blue Citroën 2CV, pockmarked and paint-shy. Michael noticed it bore French registration plates. Daisy was drumming her fingers against its roof. Her eyes raked over him.

"You'll do," she said.

Michael had glimpsed morsels of Meredith's house while passing, an elaborate bargeboard or a barley-twist chimney pot, seen through the thickness of tall oaks and ashes and dying elms shrouding the space beyond its boundary fence. Now, he braced himself, eyes focused rigidly ahead as Daisy's Citroën bucked and dodged like a rodeo pony along the narrow lanes before finally lurching up a long, winding drive, shying at potholes. After almost scraping the limbs of a stone shepherdess who tended a flock of scarlet tulips, the car crunched to a rocking halt on pallid gravel.

"At least we missed our dear lubricious Flora," Daisy said, grinning. Michael rolled 'lubricious' around his tongue, turned to see the shepherdess baring lichen-rich breasts at him. Alongside Flora's feet, prostrate tulips bore witness to Daisy's progress.

The house door opened before they reached it. A softly frowning Meredith lurked behind. Michael realised she was shorter than her daughter by several inches. This surprised him. He'd always thought her unusually tall.

Meredith smiled. "I'm so glad you could come."

She seemed preoccupied as she led the way to a sitting room that spanned the full width of the house, forty feet or thereabouts. Inside it, a man was slumped in a wheelchair. Michael recognised his face but the shrunken body had no affinity with the ramrod figure of that past May Day. Something Wagnerian blared from a serious-looking hi-fi. Meredith turned the volume down.

"Harry, this is Daisy's friend," she said. Michael looked at Daisy and she winked at him. Meredith avoided his eye.

"Daisy? Daisy? Her name is *Victoria*," Harry said, curling his lip at his wife. He retained the expression as he turned his head towards Michael. "I suppose you have a name too?" Harry's words squeezed through distorted vowels that Michael felt were intended to make him feel inferior.

"I'm Michael Cavanagh," he said, tightening his jaw and making fists behind his back. He felt someone touch him and turned to see Daisy had moved beside him. She clasped his right hand and he released the remaining fist.

Harry gave a half snort and, after his arms had tried but failed to pull himself upright, said, "So, *Mikey*, you're here to help my wife dispose of me."

Meredith's eyes pleaded with Michael.

"I'm simply here to help," he said. "You and Mrs Lomond."

Harry snorted again, louder this time. "Simply is right. Intellectus minimus," he said and Daisy squeezed Michael's hand tighter.

"Dad, don't be so bloody vicious," she said. "You're the one who refused a live-in nurse and what good has that done? You've absolutely bled the life from Mummy. She *needs* a break."

Meredith laid a hand on her husband's shoulder. "It's for a few months at most," she said. "Until I get my strength back."

"In a few months I'll be dead," said Harry.

Meredith started as if she'd been slapped. "Don't say things like that, Harry," she said. "Even in jest."

"No jest," said Harry. "And you know it. You evil... calculating... fucking... bitch."

"How dare you. How dare you!" Daisy's eyes were spitting venom and worse. Michael made it his turn to squeeze her hand. "Mummy's had to do everything for you. Everything. Lift you, dress you, wipe your arse, point your miserable dick at a pan. And all you do is lounge in that chair and feel sorry for yourself." She pointed a finger at her father. "Dead in a few months? Well, Daddy dear, I hope you're bloody well right."

Harry stared at her. His mouth opened and closed several times. He made an almost inaudible sound, the beginnings of a yelp, then his eyes screwed up.

"Oh, Daddy, I'm sorry. I didn't mean it. Only you were being so horrid."

Daisy dropped Michael's hand, rushed to Harry, knelt beside him, cradled his head against her chest. Meredith stood as ashen and motionless as Flora's statue, regarding her husband and daughter with an expression that Michael read as halfway between horror and fascination. He edged towards the sitting room door and slipped from the house, confident that none of its residents would have noticed his departure.

He trod the lanes, thought about Daisy calling him Meredith's lifeline. Judging by Harry's attitude, he could understand why Meredith might need someone to run to. But, he asked himself, Why choose me? What quality did she think she'd found?

Daisy had said they needed his help to get her father to the nursing home he'd at last agreed to go to. He'd said don't they provide an ambulance for that and she'd looked at him kindly and explained that it was a private establishment and ambulances weren't on tap, silly. Her eyes became misty then and she looked away, staring into the distance beyond the patchwork fields that surrounded his workshop. Meredith sometimes surveyed those fields in that way too and at such moments he'd imagine her high in the prow of a Viking longboat, a jewelled hand shielding her eyes as she scanned the horizon. With Daisy, although still maritime, his perception was more basic. He'd seen her as a taller, willowier Kate Winslet figure, breasting the seas from the bows of a ship more fortunate than the *Titanic*. At the high point of his vision, she had looked back at him and he'd felt as if his body was on fire.

Now, as he reached the spot where that occurred, he heard a light tapping coming from his workshop. He stiffened and his steps became catlike as he moved towards the building and peered through a pencil-thin gap where the weatherboarding had fallen away. He released a long, slow sigh then chuckled. A male blackbird, balanced on a cardboard carton, was pecking at its own reflection in the mirror of a discarded dressing table used to store wax and varnishes.

It had been a day of odd incidents. That morning, as he turned the last corner from the village on his way to work, he'd seen what looked like a mole on stilts lying in the lane. He'd got out of his van to check and saw it was a dead moorhen chick, a bundle of sooty black fluff. He'd shivered. Moorhens were unpleasant, skulking birds predisposed to murder, creatures of the shadows that made him uneasy.

Two birds, both black. He wondered if that of the morning was a warning not to get involved. Was the afternoon one, though, a sign that things might not be as bad as he feared?

The blackbird, chattering its annoyance, flew from the workshop as he entered. It landed in the canopy of a young ash that grew outside. Minutes later, he heard the bird singing.

In Michael's business mail during the following week was a letter bearing a French stamp. It bore the postmark of somewhere in Morbihan but he couldn't decipher the actual place. He didn't open the letter but took it home, placed it in a toast rack that was never used but sat on his kitchen table. He glared at the envelope as he read his morning paper. He glared at it again that evening but, as domestic correspondence gradually smothered it, it garnered increasing indifference until, some seven weeks after he'd fled her house, Meredith turned up on his doorstep again.

Michael was using his lathe which, being set against a wall left of the door, meant he did not witness her arrival. Nevertheless, he felt that familiar shimmer of expectation, and knew Meredith was there. He lifted his chisel clear of its rest, turned the lathe off.

Meredith was not alone. Daisy stood beside her. As both women stepped onto his shop floor in one synchronous movement, Michael caught his breath. They were dressed alike, in black: tailored suits, court shoes with a hard shine, leather gloves that looked softer than a baby's skin, wide hats clinging to their heads at precarious angles.

Meredith picked up the long chisel Michael had been using. "I know what this is," she said. "It's a spindle gouge."

Michael's jaw slackened as Meredith's began quivering.

"We buried Harry this morning," she said and, mewling like an injured kitten, bundled herself into his arms. All Michael could think was her suit would be covered in sawdust and stained with God knows what else. He looked over Meredith's head to Daisy, who stood as if at attention, an odd smile playing about her lips.

Meredith sobbed so violently her entire body was shaking. Michael worried about her hyperventilating. "I'm sorry, I'm sorry," she kept saying and each time, Michael hushed her and said it was okay. Then Meredith said, "I need you to come home with me. Would you come home with me?" He nodded while Daisy kept eyeing him, still with that strange expression.

Outside, a stiff breeze had brewed, strong enough to bend the ashes and hawthorns marking Michael's boundaries. They travelled in Daisy's car, but its progress was relatively sedate this time. She seemed thinner and her skin had become almost as pale as her hair. He sat in the back with Meredith. Each time he raised his eyes to the mirror, Daisy's were staring back at him.

Meredith tried to tell him how Harry died. He'd been laughing over something she didn't find funny then he stopped breathing in mid-chuckle.

"And that was that," she said.

Michael held her hands and stroked the knuckles, white mounds above taut pink skin. Harry hadn't even reached his predicted two months.

As soon as he stepped over Meredith's threshold, Michael felt as if he was treading on fine china. He wanted to remove his boots but Meredith never gave him time to stop as she hurried him and Daisy into a small sitting room left of the entrance hall. He listened to the old house as it creaked and groaned in response to the wind. He began to imagine the noises were Harry's wheelchair bumping aimlessly about the corridors.

Daisy filled fat glasses with whisky. Meredith sat alone in the centre of a sofa. She kept drawing her lower lip inwards.

"It wasn't fair to involve you," she told Michael. "We, I, had no right to do that."

"I felt like an intruder," he said. "I can't cope with family stuff."

Meredith nodded and he wondered how she'd react if she really knew why.

"You called me *Daisy's* friend," he said.

"I could hardly call you mine."

Michael thought he heard Daisy snigger and Meredith added, "I didn't mean that nastily, I'm sorry. I didn't want the bother of explaining you to Harry. It seemed easier, that's all."

"How did you manage after I left?"

"We didn't. Not for several days. Then Harry gave his ultimatum. He said..." Meredith swallowed hard several times. "He said he wanted to die where he belonged."

So, they chartered a car with wheelchair access, took Harry to Scotland. Daisy returned to France after that. Harry's return journey was by plane. Michael imagined him being conveyed in a sort of metal coolbox, men in white coats and big white gauntlets rolling it on and off a trolley at each end. Harry had asked to be interred in his family's traditional resting place ("A forlorn island in an obscure loch," said Daisy) but they'd buried him here, today, in the village churchyard.

Michael wondered why Meredith denied Harry his final wish.

Daisy micro-waved convenience food and they sank it with Harry's best whisky. By dusk, Meredith and Daisy had regained some colour and Michael began to shift in his seat. He checked his watch when he thought no one was looking.

"You can't go home tonight," Daisy said. "I'm too pissed to drive and it's too dark to walk. Where do you sleep in that barn thing anyway?"

"I don't," Michael said. "I rent a flat in town."

"Well then," said Daisy, "that's settled."

Another bottle of Harry's malt was broached and soon Meredith was talking about Jesus.

"He was a carpenter, too," she told Michael, patting him on a wrist while riveting her eyes to his. "That's one reason I chose you for *my* saviour."

"Mummy, you're drunk," said Daisy.

"I didn't mean in a holy sense. I meant you've been my saviour when Harry got me down. You were my teacup in a storm."

"It's storm in a teacup, Mummy."

"I know what I mean and it isn't that." Meredith wagged a finger at Daisy then redirected it to Michael. "I'm going to tell you a story."

Daisy snorted. Michael groaned.

"When I was sixteen," said Meredith. "I was seduced by a carpenter, and that's the other reason I chose you."

"Mummy!"

"Shhh. It's true. He was my woodwork master. One day his lessons went further than I expected. His fingers wandered inside my blouse as he taught me how to hold a chisel relative to the rest on the lathe. So, Michael, that's how I knew what a spindle gouge was."

Michael's face was burning. He looked towards Daisy for help. She shrugged at him.

"We called him Tappy," continued Meredith. "From his initials. T.A.P. Terence Arthur Parker. I'd sneak to the woodwork shop before prep and we'd do it in front of the big round iron stove that stood in the middle. It always had pots of glue warming on top. That smell still turns me on even now."

"Michael's workshop doesn't have one."

"I haven't visited Michael for sex."

"Not yet," Daisy murmured. Michael's drink chose that moment to flow the wrong way down his throat. Daisy patted his back.

"Now look what you've done, Mummy."

"What?" Meredith looked puzzled.

Although Michael and Daisy soon gave the bottle a rest, Meredith carried on drinking. She gradually became incoherent, finally sank into her cushions, closed her eyes. She began to snore like a virtuoso playing a foghorn, travelling up and down impressive scales.

"We'd best get her to bed," Daisy said.

"My saviour," Meredith half-giggled on the way upstairs but once she was on her bed she curled into a semi-comatose bundle.

Michael had been afraid Daisy might insist on undressing Meredith but she just spread the duvet over her. Then she said, "I'll show you your room."

Michael's insides quivered as he followed Daisy along a corridor whose walls were covered with stern portraits of what he assumed were dead Lomonds. He'd felt safe while Meredith was awake, even if she was drunk.

Daisy stopped outside a cream door that had floral borders painted within its panels. She wore her disturbing look again as she turned to him. "Did you get my letter?" she whispered.

"I didn't open it." Michael wondered if it was still in the toast rack.

"Just as well."

"Why?"

"I was angry with you. Among other things, it said 'Fuck you, Michael'."

"Oh."

"And that's exactly what I'm going to do now."

By Default

Daisy was gone when Michael woke, and in his half-conscious state he thought sex between him and her so unlikely it must have been some terrible, delicious nightmare. Then, in a stab of certainty, he recalled firm round breasts with belligerent nipples that stared him out as if they were an extra pair of eyes; the vee of Daisy's soft pubic hair, so neat it seemed manicured and because of that, unthreatening; and betwixt and below, Daisy's version of the mysterious folds that had terrified him since he was sixteen. His penis stiffened with each recollection but the prospect of an imminent reunion with Daisy soon provided a wilting effect.

He washed quickly at a hand basin beside the bedroom window. The taps ran only cold water and he shivered, even after he had dressed. The window faced what looked like an orchard, a long meadow with stunted trees in regular lines. Michael was about to turn away when his eye registered a human image. It was Daisy, navigating diagonal courses between the trees. He ducked behind a curtain but she was already waving at him. She reached the gravel bordering the house and was smiling to herself as she opened the door that he recognised from yesterday evening as leading into the kitchen. He gathered himself together as much as he could, palpitated his way downstairs.

Meredith was making her way through a gigantic breakfast of bacon and eggs, black pudding and sausages. "Ah, there you are, Michael," she said, as if she'd mislaid him for a moment. "Help yourself to cereals. Daisy will cook whatever else you want. You can wait for me to finish this if her cooking makes you nervous."

Daisy was leaning against a birds-eye maple counter that stretched above cream-painted cupboards and drawers. She was eating a banana, very slowly, as if savouring each cell.

"Sleep well?" she said. Michael could only nod in reply. Daisy licked the banana then keeping her eyes on his, slid it into her mouth. Heat rose in his cheeks.

He stuck to cold, thinly buttered toast. Meredith asked what work he had on and whether he needed to do any that day. When Michael said yes, he did have things he couldn't put off, Daisy seemed to find it funny.

Meredith frowned at her and said, in that case would he mind coming back afterwards because she had a proposition to put to him.

Michael mumbled assent. Daisy was contemplating her fingers, spreading them out like fans. Michael imagined a second night with her, felt himself stiffen against his jeans. He helped himself to more toast, took a while buttering it, smoothing every trace off the knife until he was satisfied it looked clean.

Daisy insisted on giving him a lift and he dreaded finding nothing to say to her. As it was, as soon as she'd started her car she began the conversation.

"Do you know what Mummy's proposition is?"

"No."

"She wants you to live with her."

"*What?*"

"I don't mean like *that.*"

"Of course not... I didn't..." Michael felt confusion shiver through him. "But isn't it a bit... soon?"

"Not to Mummy. She's had a long time to think about it."

Harry had called her evil and calculating. Michael weighed this accusation against his own experience of Meredith and decided she was guilty of nothing more than preparing for life after Harry's death. Given his illness was terminal, it seemed a sensible thing to do. Calculating perhaps, but not evil.

The car lurched as Daisy took a hand off the wheel to tap Michael's arm. "Consider," she said, "that Mummy's on her own now, vulnerable, in a thumping great house. A young man like you, strong, someone she trusts, would make her feel safe again, something she hasn't experienced since, since Dad..." Daisy stopped the car. They had only reached the bottom of the drive. She was shaking, hanging onto the steering wheel as if it was all that stopped her plummeting to disaster.

She began sobbing, her body heaving. Michael found himself pulling her away from the wheel, wrapping his arms around her, cushioning her against whatever she needed to be cushioned from.

"It's all right," he kept saying and Daisy's crying fit gradually subsided. She pulled herself away.

"But it's not all right, is it?"

"Last night was," Michael said without thinking.

"That was the worst of it," said Daisy. She clutched Michael's shoulders. "I'd just buried my father. Don't you see? I had no right to enjoy myself. No right to be so fucking selfish."

Her face was haunted, her eyes hagridden. Michael wished he had a magic balm to soothe them. "You weren't being selfish," he said. "It's a natural way of handling grief. People often turn to sex in times of stress." He suddenly felt foolish, as if he'd stepped beyond his boundaries, and added in a subdued voice, "I read that somewhere."

Daisy stared at him, expressionless at first then her face softened. "I'm glad Mummy found you," she said. She leaned across and kissed him lightly on the cheek.

The last thing she said as she dropped him off was "See you tonight."

At seven pm Meredith ushered Michael into the sitting room they'd used the day before. Despite it being June, a log fire blazed in the grate. "I felt cold," Meredith said. She poured him a large whisky. "Dinner will be half an hour."

"Is Daisy cooking?" said Michael.

Meredith frowned. "Daisy's gone, Michael. She left just after lunch to catch the Portsmouth ferry."

A spasm snatched between Michael's temples.

"*Gone?*" he said.

Meredith studied his face. "Oh no," she said. "She *didn't?*"

Michael stared at the carpet. Patterned: diamonds, chevrons, irregular circles, scrolls. And the colours: rust red, two shades of blue, a creamy beige. Everything far too complex.

"I wondered why she was so anxious to leave." Meredith sat down beside Michael and took a long breath. "Daisy's impetuous. You must have noticed that. She pleases herself and thinks of the consequences later."

Michael nodded but inside he was saying, I thought we'd sorted that out this morning.

Meredith touched his arm. "She's not for you, Michael."

"Why? Because I'm not good enough?"

Meredith shut her eyes tightly. "Daisy's married, Michael."

"She doesn't wear a ring."

"That doesn't mean she isn't married. She and Jean-Paul have a four-year-old son." Meredith looked like a doctor giving bad news.

Michael swallowed, hard. He felt Meredith pat his shoulder and he suddenly wanted her to hug him, as if he was a child in the arms of his mother. Not that his had been one for hugging. Jacinta (he could never think of her as Mum) was a stout-bodied woman with an uncertain temper inherited from Pop Delgado, her Spanish father. He recalled the one time he'd run to her for comfort. A gang of boys had peed on his legs, soaking his new grey socks. He'd flung himself against Jacinta, pressing his face on her pinafore, expecting softness, but she'd seemed armoured by steel. Years later, he discovered it was nothing more formidable than whalebone. He shivered at that memory.

"I had a son called Michael. By Tappy Parker. They made me give the baby away."

"A son?"

A wild idea filled Michael's head. He was that very baby, adopted by a half-Spaniard and her Irish spouse, come full circle back to the arms of his natural mother. His face flushed as he realised that would make Daisy his sister.

Meredith seemed not to have noticed. She was studying the fire. She reached for a brass poker, pushed the uppermost logs into the blazing remains of those below, causing sparks to spit out and singe the carpet.

"Lives in America now," she said. "Boston. Massachusetts. His new parents were professors, one at Harvard and one at MIT. The female was a distant relative of my father."

A river of disappointment flowed through Michael's fantasy, drowning it beneath dull waves. He could never be in one of those stories where the ragged beggar boy turns out to be the long-lost son of a duke.

Meredith looked up at him. Her eyes were glistening. "So, my son's a Yankee. Probably a professor himself by now."

Michael nodded because he didn't know what to say and suddenly Meredith brightened. "But he's still the son of a carpenter and you, *you* Michael, could achieve whatever you wanted to."

That seemed to be her cue to launch into her proposition – he could live there rent-free in return for the security his presence would bring. Why, there was even a barn, in better repair than the one he rented, and with her contacts, who knew what lucrative commissions might come his way? Michael listened to it all, agreed that it made sense. He didn't tell her he wasn't interested in reducing overheads or the glowing prospects she painted. He didn't explain he'd agreed because it meant he would be close to her and because of that, nearer perhaps to Daisy.

Chapter 2

Arriving home, smarting from Daisy's defection, bemused by Meredith's proposition, Michael checked the toast rack, found Daisy's letter still there. He picked it up, slit the envelope open.

FUCK YOU, Michael! I'm so BLOODY angry with you. You didn't last long when it came to it, did you? If you'd seen how devastated Mummy was, you would have died of shame. Well, we managed quite nicely without you in the end. Two feeble women struggling with an uncooperative tyrant in a wheelchair. We drove him all the way to bonnie Scotland so he could be in the bosom of his family. Funny they didn't seem pleased to see him. Anyway, he was happy, so I left him and Mummy and flew home.
If I see you again it will be too soon. FUCK YOU!
Daisy Bohec

Michael wondered why, if she never wanted to see him again, Daisy had written to him at all. And she hadn't signed herself as Victoria, so might not have been as mad with him as she made out.

Fuck you, capitalised and repeated, gained significance in his mind, especially since the words were translated into fact. It was as if Daisy meant it to happen all along.

That night, Michael had a dream in which Harry pursued him by wheelchair along tortuous, overgrown tracks, over furrowed fields, even across bridgeless rivers. The pursuit ended in a maze of corridors in a house he supposed was Meredith's. At a blank end from which there was no retreat, a sneering Harry confronted him, rising from his chair until he stood taller than he ever had in life.

"You think *you* can take my place? You're nothing, Mikey, a *minimus*, and she's an evil, calculating, fucking bitch. Don't believe a word she says."

Water then seeped into the corridor, lapped over Michael's ankles, rose rapidly up his body. He flailed and kicked his way towards Harry, making no headway, then woke to find his pyjamas pasted to his skin with cold clammy sweat, bed sheets scattered about the floor.

He tried to concentrate on Daisy, replacing Harry's invasions by a carnal frolicking so vivid it made him sit up to look at the girl that, still half locked in his dreamworld, he believed was lying beside him. A cold sadness enveloped him as he realised she wasn't there.

Michael told Meredith he'd rather leave his workshop where it was. He was used to its imperfections. She smiled and said that meant she could still cycle up to see him if that was all right with him and, he never knew, she might even bring him lunch. They shook hands as if they'd negotiated a formal treaty.

The furniture came with his flat so on the day of his move Michael had little to do but take his personal possessions. He bade a final farewell to the rooms that had made do as home for five years. There was nothing left of him there; even the furniture seemed alien. Something tugged inside his breast. How little trace we leave on the world, he thought before finally closing the door.

At Meredith's, Michael was given a bedroom with an en-suite bathroom where the hot water taps lived up to their names. It was in the front of the house. Standing before its window, he pondered Flora's grey nakedness.

He'd looked 'lubricious' up in a dictionary. It offered him 'worthless' and 'lascivious'. Flora certainly wasn't worthless - figures like her were stolen every day. Lascivious presented him with lustful, wanton, and inciting to lust. He didn't know about the first two because Flora stood

expressionless, never parting her legs. As for inciting anyone to lust –
perhaps, he thought if, like him, they desired women with hearts of stone.

He wandered into the bedroom Daisy had used, opened wardrobes,
looked through dressing tables and chests of drawers but there was
nothing of hers there. It was only a space with furniture, like the flat he'd
left behind. He moved on to the bedroom where she'd seduced him. The
stains of passion were still visible on its icy sheets. He wrapped himself in
them and masturbated.

Meredith found him asleep there hours later. "Oh, *Michael*," she said
in a voice halfway between disapproving and sympathetic.

She took him downstairs to a parlour he hadn't seen before,
rummaged in a bureau, brought out albums of photographs. She showed
him Daisy at a few weeks old; Daisy at two, three, four, five and the
subsequent years of her childhood. There were a few awkward pictures
of a gangly teenager then they were done.

"She tore up her teenage years," Meredith said, grimacing. "Those are
the few I managed to save."

Michael selected photographs that portrayed a Meredith looking as
young as Daisy was now. He arranged them on the tabletop. "You could
be twins," he said.

"If we were," Meredith said. "What would you do?"

Michael held his breath, stared at her.

"Don't look so terrified," Meredith said. "It's hypothetical. If Daisy
and I were twins, who would you choose?"

Michael lowered his eyes. "Daisy."

"Well, that was honest."

Michael looked up, saw Meredith's cheeks were flushed. How smooth
their skin still was. Her eyes seemed more intense than ever.

Meredith sighed. "You're really struck on her, aren't you?" she said.

"Yes."

"Then if you think she's worth it, go to France and get her. She won't
come back otherwise."

"What about her husband?"

"Husbands are transient."

"Transient?"

"Short-term. And that swine of Daisy's is overdue for cancellation." Meredith was looking far away now, like that Viking princess of his imagination. "I know I said she wasn't for you,' she said, 'but I'm not always right."

Michael hired a car in Cherbourg, bought yellow Michelin maps. Meredith had asked how he felt about driving on the wrong side of the road. He'd surprised her when he said he'd lived in France. "During my teens. I had to leave home," he'd said. She hadn't asked why.

Through Avranches and Dol he drove, stopped for food and a pee at Dinan then turned south for Ploermel and Vannes. He knew this area. Before reverting to type, he'd spent a summer in a café-bar in Josselin, serving croques-monsieur to chateau-hungry tourists.

He'd asked Meredith for directions to Daisy's house but she said she'd never been there. She became wry of face, gave a dismissive shrug. "I got the impression I wouldn't exactly be welcome. No matter, I have her address."

Michael's map showed him that Daisy's village was ten kilometres outside Auray. From Vannes, he took the fast dual carriageway north then turned off towards the D19. The village square was empty apart from a shit-strewn toilet near the roadside. He relieved himself in it, careful not to touch anything that wasn't his then asked for directions in a bar across the road. Old men raised befuddled faces. Nobody knew a house called Le Mazemeur but someone suggested a possible Bohec. He ended up on a dirt road in front of two cottages but the Bohec turned out to be an ancient woman unable or unwilling to understand a word of Michael's French.

Michael found a bed for the night in Auray, bought a local map and settled down beside a tall beer in a quayside bar. He discovered that the name he'd been given as Daisy's village also belonged to a commune of Auray. Scanning the area it comprised, he located Mazemeur, a sprinkling of black dots only a few kilometres from where he sat.

"Veni, vidi, vici," Meredith had said to him when he left. He mightn't have been taught Latin but he knew what that meant. So far, he'd come but he hadn't seen and he certainly hadn't conquered. Chastened by the possibility of a hostile Daisy, he left the bar, walked slowly back across the bridge and up the hill to his hotel.

Next morning, Michael waited until ten before setting off, reasoning that Daisy's husband should be at work and she'd be home with her child. Mazemeur turned out to be a mere handful of dwellings and he stopped outside a modern bungalow on the premise that it was brighter and thus more likely to contain Daisy than the other houses. His knock was answered by a fiftyish woman who shook her head when he spoke then disappeared. She'd left the front door ajar so he assumed she'd be back. After a few minutes, a pretty, dark-haired girl of about sixteen appeared. Michael asked his question again.

She answered in English. "I'm sorry Maman could not help. She will not speak French, only Breton. But that is good because I can practise my English with you." The girl pointed to a narrow road branching off the one the bungalow stood on. "Madame Bohec lives in the big farmhouse." She flicked her eyelashes then smiled shyly. "I am right in assuming you wish for the younger Madame?"

Michael hadn't bargained for a mother-in-law and Meredith hadn't warned him. He nodded. "Yes, you are right. And thank you, your English is excellent."

The girl blushed. "Your French also."

Michael parked in a circle of pines some way along the road, walked the rest of the way, keeping close to the trees. The road became a gravel track that widened into a large yard with a tall farmhouse just left of centre and a row of stone buildings at its right-hand edge. Two of the latter had baskets of scarlet pelargoniums hanging beside their doors. A sign on their wall said *Gîtes de France*.

In a grassy clearing was a child's swing. At the far end of the yard, a woman hurled white rabbits from a shopping trolley into the back of a huge estate car. Michael assumed she was Madame Bohec senior. He watched, hidden by the trunk of an ancient oak, as she squeezed the last rabbit into the car and slammed the hatch down. She drove, with a shriek of gears, out of the yard and hurtled up the lane. Michael wondered why none of the rabbits had screamed.

He approached the big house. A mass of blue hydrangeas occupied half the frontage but there was no door visible. He found one around the back of the building and, taking deep breaths, rang a brass bell that hung from the wall beside it. Eventually he heard a latch being moved. The door opened.

Daisy put a hand to her mouth. "Michael!" He thought she was about to faint but she quickly recovered and said, "You'd better come in."

She led him to a dark parlour that seemed to serve as some sort of business room, poured cognacs from a decanter she took from an ancient looking armoire. She kept staring at Michael and nibbling her lower lip. Suddenly she put her arms around his neck and kissed him.

"I love you," Michael said.

Daisy frowned. "Is that wise?" She dropped her arms to her sides, took a step back.

Michael hadn't touched his brandy. "Why did you leave? If you didn't mean it, why did you say you'd see me that night?"

"Because I did mean it. An hour later, I was running scared." Daisy gave him the unsettling smile she'd displayed on the day of her father's funeral. "I'm not as brave as I pretend to be."

"Neither am I. But when the cause is worth it I forget I'm a coward." Michael was gazing intently at Daisy, willing her not to turn him away.

She returned his gaze, holding it until he felt he'd have to blink. Then she took hold of his hand. "Come with me." She took a key from a rack, led him outside and across the yard to the gîtes he'd already seen. She unlocked the door of the left one. "You've just rented this," she said.

As she clicked the door shut behind them Michael felt a tremor sneak from somewhere in his chest to the most sensitive part of his groin. Despite the July heat, the building was chilly inside. Its ground floor was open plan with a shower room at the rear from which drifted the odd smell he recalled as being peculiar to French lavatories.

Daisy led him upstairs. At the top was a landing that also served as a bedroom and on the left, beyond a half open door, was a proper bedroom. Daisy grabbed his hand and pulled him inside.

"Fuck me, Michael," she said.

Somewhere past the middle of the day, tyres scrunched the gravel outside. Daisy flung the covers back, got out of bed. She flattened herself against the plaster beside the window then slid down in slow motion until she was on her haunches, squatting in half profile, gazing through the glass. The fingers on her right hand were bridged against the wall. They were long, what some might call musician's fingers. Her face, lit by the sun, was more seductive than ever, from electric-blue eyes to proud nose and half-open lips, generous and ripe. Her hair, unkempt from lovemaking, hung over her shoulders. The sunlight bleached that part cascading over the front to the palest flaxen, while that in the shadows became an almost lustrous brunette. The light fell in its fullness on her breasts, painting them a warm milk-white but in obedience to the coolness of the room, their nipples stood out like deep pink cones. Michael thought that nobody, nothing, he had seen before was as beautiful as Daisy at that moment.

"It's only the postman," she said, then added that she didn't realise it was so late and she had to collect Hamish from nursery class.

"Hamish?" said Michael.

"My son. Jacques to his father, Hamish to me."

Daisy pulled on her clothes as if being timed then placed the gîte's keys on the bed.

"Bring your things. Berthe will be back from market soon and then there's Jean-Paul so it might be difficult for me to see you until tomorrow."

She kissed him and with that she was gone.

After they'd made love, for that was how Michael saw it, unlike the frenzied coupling of the night she'd mounted him, Daisy, eyes glistening, asked him was that what he came for.

"I came to take you home," he said then thought how lame the words sounded.

"But I have a husband."

"Do you love him?"

Daisy's answering laugh was cheerless. Michael reached for her, but she edged away.

"He has a mistress," she said. "Thinks I don't know. She's short, dark and hairy with tiny tits. She's the least reason I don't love him. I don't want to talk about the others."

"Could you love me?" Michael wondered why she should.

"Mummy's very fond of you."

"That wasn't what I asked."

"She'd like to sleep with you." Daisy's eyes became half-closed. A smile teased her lips. Michael recalled the 'twins' question, Meredith's face when he'd made his choice.

"Perhaps," he said.

Daisy sat up suddenly. "You *haven't?*"

Michael shook his head. "*No.*"

"And you never will?"

"Never."

"Then yes, I could love you."

Daisy's expression was like a playful child's. Michael had an urge to spank her. Instead, he reached for her again.

When Michael returned from Auray, Berthe's car was outside the barn Daisy had told him was where Berthe bred rabbits for the table. For the first time, he was aware of the rank smell emanating from the building. He needed fresh air. He dumped his bag, went to investigate a track he'd noticed beside an ornate, covered well at the rear of the yard. The well had exquisite carved framework supporting a shingled roof. *1857* was cut into a cross-brace. He stopped, paid homage to the carpenter's skills then continued past unspoiled meadows to a gate beside a straight, empty road that looked as if it might go on for ever. The sequence of meadows stretched as far as he could see. He wished, for the first time in years, that he had a cigarette.

When he retraced his steps, a brown-looking man of around his years and a few inches below his height was stepping out of a big Renault. He started when he saw Michael, asked him belligerently what he was doing there but when Michael explained, pointing towards the gîte, the muscles in the man's face relaxed. "Enjoy your stay," he said and walked with a swagger towards the house. Michael resented the man's black curls and the fact that he had the right to share his life with Daisy.

She didn't come that night. Next morning, Michael took an early shower and found that it ran cold. Likewise with the hot tap. Perhaps Daisy had forgotten to switch the boiler on, wherever it was. Standing there, naked, shivering, he realised that most of the smell in the bathroom was the rabbit factory's stink wafting through the louvred window. He tried, unsuccessfully, to close it tight. Later, he ate croissants and watched Daisy's husband drive off. Daisy herself set out as he poured his coffee. A small blond head was just visible above a rear window of her 2CV. In the yard, Berthe bustled about, assisted by rustic men in blue dungarees.

Michael listened to the radio, news about the Tour de France. He drummed his fingers then boiled a kettle for his breakfast dishes. Daisy's car reappeared as he was washing a glass and he felt the latter's rim collapse beneath his fingers. When he looked down, his blood was clouding the water.

Daisy came hurrying across the yard, knocked on Michael's door. "I'm sorry. I couldn't get away." She stepped back a fraction and squinted at him. "Did you think I was avoiding you again?"

Berthe was wheeling a barrow of something and as she disappeared with it into a shed, Daisy crossed the threshold, saw the tissue wrapped around Michael's injured finger.

"Oh, Michael, what have you done? Wait."

Daisy dashed to the farmhouse and within a minute returned with antiseptic and plasters. Michael noticed Berthe glowering near the well. Daisy dressed his wound then said, "Did you mean it when you said you'd come to take me home?"

"I did."

"I can't leave Hamish behind. It won't be easy to get him away. Jean-Paul won't even let him come with me when I visit Mummy. He likes to keep a strong leash on his possessions. Hamish is his insurance policy to make sure I come back."

Daisy's lips began trembling. Michael drew her to him, cradled her head against his chest.

"Don't cry. It will be all right," he said.

He hadn't allowed for the child. He'd assumed he and Daisy would just get on the ferry and that would be that.

"We can't simply catch a ferry," Daisy said, as if she'd read his thoughts. "He'd have the police watching them, airports too. The best plan would be to drive in the opposite direction to the one he'd expect. We'll leave tomorrow. Early. Berthe does her big shop at the Continent in Vannes. We'll be well gone before anyone knows it."

When dusk was falling, Michael revisited the path he'd taken the day before. He gazed at the patchwork stretching in front of him, imagined it only stopping at the sea, no towns, no people, to intervene. By this time tomorrow, the miracle would have happened and Daisy would be his. He'd banked on a fantasy because if he'd relied on fact he'd still be moping in England.

It was dark before he made his way back and he picked his steps carefully to avoid roots and depressions. At last he saw the quiet glow of house lights and the looming bulk of the well.

As he reached this, other shapes appeared, almost liquid in their movement. Michael felt fists rain on him, something hard crack his head. He felt the ground as he met it, tasted dry soil in his mouth and the cocktail it made with his blood but he scarcely felt the boots against his ribs. He was unaware of them stopping and he didn't hear the car that bore him away. But he heard the silence afterwards.

Chapter 3

Michael heard the noise that followed the silence: a nagging, jabbing din. As he approached consciousness, he could be more specific. It was elemental, not man-made, although he couldn't have said why.

His eyes flickered, half-opened. Ahead was fuzzy, streaming greyness. The source of the noise seemed close above his head. Gradually, he realised both were related to water, and wondered if, somehow, he'd got behind a waterfall. He'd been in this situation before. He tried to remember, pressing his temples with his fingers as he did so. His head buzzed and he diverted two fingers to rub his eyes. Then he had it: the Yorkshire Dales. He and his girl... Sal, Mel...? No, her name had gone. They'd descended this rock face, edged along a narrow shelf until the waterfall veiled them. Looking from within to without, they'd marvelled at the jewelled cascade, the shimmer as the sun caught individual drops. Wonder-struck, they'd run through the liquid curtain, skinny-dipped in the pool outside. He'd been what, nineteen, twenty? It was before he married Grace, anyway. He smiled at the memory and at that moment his eyes opened fully.

He saw that he was actually inside a car and the waterfall was only rain running down the windows. What a downpour though: rapid fire, a thousand rounds a minute. The impact on the roof was deafening. He caught his reflection in the mirror. He looked like something a horse had kicked.

He turned to open a window. Jesus! Pain stabbed at him, seared his chest, his gut, everywhere above his waist. He could manage only tiny breaths and trying to compensate made it worse. He creased up, afraid to move and the events of the past days rushed into his mind like a river in spate. What was happening to Daisy? How long had he been unconscious? His watch said it was just after six twenty-five, obviously morning, but what day? The car was his hired Clio. He recognised the spot above the dash where someone had spilt something orange and sticky. He must have been driven here. But where was here?

The rain seemed lighter. He could make out dim shapes. Trees, he thought, and something rectangular and squat. He wondered if he might be able to drive but the key wasn't in the ignition.

It was definitely easing. He could see trees clearly now, and the rectangular shape was a building. He edged towards the driver's door, careful not to twist his body, gripped the window winder.

Rain raked his cheek, splashed over his shirt and jeans but it made him feel better. He forced his head out of the window. In front of the car was a low wall and below that, he could see a large expanse of water but couldn't smell the sea. There wasn't that sense of being close to living waves.

He tried to think of freshwater lakes in Brittany. There were maps in the glove box. He wished he'd thought of keeping them in the pockets behind the front seats. He reckoned he could reach those without twisting. He tried doing so, even though he knew they were empty. From the corner of an eye he saw something colourful and turned his head as much as he dared. It was the salmon pink shirt he'd worn the day he reclaimed Daisy. She'd said he looked nice in it. Along with other of his belongings, it was strewn over the back seat. He saw the edge of his luggage bag too.

So, he'd been cleared out of the gîte and dumped like so much garbage. The car keys were probably in the lake. Considering that possibility, he remembered that he'd been given two sets and he'd put the spare in a pocket of his bag.

He tried to slow his breathing, deepen it, and found the pain eased if he supported his lower left ribs with a hand. He steeled himself. One, two…

A vehicle was coming. He heard the swish of tyres first, then the engine, a diesel naturally. It was an old Citroën BX. It pulled up by the low building that he could now see housed public toilets. He pressed a hand on the horn and eventually the BX started up again and drove across to him.

Its driver stared at Michael. "Shit," he muttered.

Michael agreed. "What day is it? Where are we?"

"Saturday. Lac Guerladan."

The words were squeezed out but Michael couldn't blame the man for being reluctant. He told him he'd been mugged and needed to get his bag from the back seat. He couldn't turn round, ribs, he said. The man twisted his face as if debating whether to help or drive away. In the end he said, "Okay," turned up his collar and, donning a navy-blue workman's cap, got out of his car and opened the back door of Michael's.

The spare key was still in the bag. Michael found his mobile phone there too but it was as dead as they come and he didn't have a car charger. Still, he daren't call Daisy and he didn't know anyone else, not after all these years. He asked his rescuer which direction Auray was.

The man pointed. "South," he said and gave him directions to reach the right road. "Are you sure you don't need a doctor?"

"No, I'll be all right. And thank you. You probably saved my life."

The man shrugged, got back into his car. Michael saw him park outside the toilet block again, watched him take a mop and bucket from his boot.

Before Michael had travelled ten kilometres he knew he needed to get to a hospital. His head felt adrift and sections of whatever he was focusing on began disappearing. A vague shimmering started to distort his vision further. The only hospitals he remembered were in Vannes, so he turned off the Auray road.

The rain started again, heavier than earlier. Even with the wipers on fast, the windscreen was opaque, so it didn't matter that Michael couldn't focus on anything anyway. He slowed right down, aware of other cars screaming by in the torrent, horns blasting as they aquaplaned past. He soon stopped altogether, slurped to a halt in a village whose sign he was unable to decipher. Moments before his eyes closed, he was aware of his head slumping against the steering wheel.

Michael probably made it to hospital faster than if he'd kept on driving. He was told later the local residents objected to a drunk parking across the entrance to their bar. Luckily for Michael, two motorcycle patrolmen were close by and they recognised that drink wasn't his problem.

The neurologist said Michael was fortunate. He'd had a CT scan, x-rays, and the initial diagnosis was that he had severe concussion and a localised contusion. His skull wasn't fractured but he had cracked ribs. They didn't matter, said the doctor. The important thing was there was no sign of bleeding or clotting and no signs of lateralisation.

Michael didn't have a clue what lateralisation was but as long as he didn't have it he wasn't going to ask. He knew contusion meant a bruise and he'd had concussion lots of times. Never this bad though. Hell, once he'd fallen down a Cornish cliff and escaped with nothing worse than scratches.

He was told as long as he didn't develop worrying symptoms he could be discharged 'soon'. Was there anyone who could help him, anyone who should be informed? He gave them Meredith's address and phone number.

The policeman who interviewed Michael didn't look as if he believed him when he said he didn't know who attacked him, or where it took place. And when Michael swore he didn't remember where he'd been staying, the man's eyebrows breached the ceiling.

"I have severe concussion," Michael said. "I'm supposed to be confused."

He asked each nurse he saw if they'd contacted England. Each one said he wasn't to worry and that made him worry more and more.

On Monday, Michael saw the doctor again, who said they were concerned about his head and they might have to insert what he called a little bolt to monitor the pressure.

On Tuesday, Daisy appeared. Michael was dozing at the time but he felt the presence she and Meredith seemed able to generate. He wanted to cry out with joy at the sight of her and would have thanked God if he could. Daisy said she'd been worrying herself sick and had only just found out from Meredith where he was.

"I'll kill him for this," she said. There were dark circles beneath her eyes and a hint of a bruised cheek she swore was accidental. Her voice shook when she asked Michael how he felt. It hurt to breathe, he said, but at least his head was in one piece. He didn't mention the bolt. When Daisy asked if she was worth the pain, he said if she came close enough they'd both find out.

"Don't threaten what you can't deliver," she said but at least her eyes lit up. "Jean-Paul said you'd left on Friday as he was setting off for work. For a moment I thought you'd run out on me. Then he said you spoke excellent French for an Englishman and I knew he was lying. I'm sorry for doubting you, Michael."

"We did speak. Although it was actually Thursday afternoon. He saw me as he was getting out of his car."

"You speak French?"

Daisy's eyes were wide as Michael explained, in French, that he'd had to either learn the language or starve. He said French wasn't all he knew either. Daisy's eyes opened even more then she took Michael's hands, stroked the fingers. "What are you going to do? What have you said to the police?"

Michael breathed in too deeply. Both he and Daisy winced. "That I didn't see who attacked me, which is true. Or knew where it happened, which isn't. As for what I'm going to do, that depends on you."

"Would it annoy you very much if I asked you to do nothing?"

"Not if that's what you want." Michael rubbed his chin for a moment, gazing at Daisy. "What does Jean-Paul actually do in daylight hours?" he said. "I assume he isn't a farmer."

Daisy laughed. "He's a drug dealer. Director of a pharmaceutical company. Sells aspirin and Band-Aids to chemists."

"Berthe was watching when you brought me the plasters. That mightn't be all that she saw."

"Or invented," Daisy said. "She's always had it in for me. Jean-Paul made sure he stayed in that evening. Probably paid the three bully boys to do it. They run the used car place on the Auray Road. He fussed about Marie at the bungalow telling him you were looking for me. I asked him what he was getting at, everyone who wanted a gîte would ask for me. Then he wanted to see your booking form so I made some pretence of rummaging through papers. In the end I had to say I'd mislaid it. So, do you still have your credit card?"

Michael nodded. Daisy extracted Visa forms from her bag, made Michael complete one. She ran it through a sliding imprinter, gave Michael his copy. "This afternoon, I shall find the booking form and Visa receipt. Then I shall ask Jean-Paul if we ought to refund the unused days."

"Oh and by the way," Daisy added, pulling a face that said she wasn't best pleased about this. "Mummy's coming at the weekend to wrap you in her bosom and take you home."

"Has she told the hospital?"

"You know her, probably issued detailed instructions. Anyway, my idea is that if I become the dutiful wife. Don't even *try* to laugh, Michael. If I act whiter than white, JP has to believe he's wrong." Daisy's eyes looked pained. "It's best I don't come again. I'll miss you terribly."

Michael felt his heart leap. "I'll miss you too," he said.

"Terribly?"

"Much worse than that," he said as the prospect of losing her massed in his throat.

When Daisy left, she leaned over, kissed him full and hard. She put her tongue in his mouth and he raised more than an eyebrow. Somebody whistled.

Michael told the doctor he wanted to leave after the weekend.

Instead of threatening him with bolts in his head, the man grinned and said, "Beautiful young ladies work wonders." He recommended that

Michael see a specialist in sports injuries. "I know an excellent man. Helped many champions. Of the world, of the Tour de France, skiers too, football stars. He is expensive." He looked at Michael as if weighing his ability to pay.

Michael said he'd sell his mother-in-law if he had to. The doctor laughed and said, "Me too." Michael wondered what Meredith would think about that. Not that she was his mother-in-law.

When Meredith arrived, Michael didn't get that old buzz of anticipation at all. Head held aristocratically high, she stepped forward using precise, dancers' movements that made her seem taller than she was. Michael understood then why he'd been surprised she was shorter than Daisy.

Everyone in the ward, men and women, stopped what they were doing and stared at her. Apart from men with wistful eyes, they hadn't done that for Daisy. Meredith wore her trademark shoes and a perfectly cut buttercup yellow dress that Michael was sure must be silk. The material swished expensively when she moved. Outwardly, she looked serene but for the first time since he'd known her, he noticed lines on her face. It struck him how being bedbound allowed him to focus on things that usually passed him by.

"Lucky for you this isn't the NHS," Meredith said.

Meredith had a taxi take them to Dinard, from where they flew to Stansted. Michael was well strapped up but it didn't take much to make him wince. He caught Meredith flinching too as she watched him. At these times he'd grin, say something stupid like, "You should see the state of the other guy."

In the plane, Michael thought about Harry's final flight, wondered if this was his. Were you aware of it when the plane crashed, or would you have already shit yourself to death?

Back under Meredith's roof, Michael was forbidden from even attempting to lift a finger. With a purposeful expression, Meredith would read to him: Jane Austen, Thomas Hardy and, once, a book of modern stories by Raymond Carver. Michael liked those best, empathised with the characters because he'd been halfway there himself. Meredith would leave the books and he'd read until he fell asleep. He'd come a long way for a boy who never finished school, he thought, a long way from Bethnal Green.

Meredith phoned Daisy on the landline every week or so. She didn't want to overdo it, she told Michael, because Jean-Paul didn't like her calling. Her voice trembled when she said that. Daisy's mobile and emails were out of the question too, because Jean-Paul had a habit of policing them and you never knew if Daisy got to them first.

If it was safe, Meredith would bring the house phone upstairs so Michael could snatch a few minutes alone with Daisy, who would whisper things that made him rigid with longing for her.

During Michael's first week home, even going to the lavatory required forward planning. It took twenty minutes to progress between lying down and standing up so he suppressed his embarrassment and asked Meredith to find him a plastic funnel and an empty bottle so he could simply roll over and pee.

After two weeks, nerves bedevilled Michael constantly and he knew he'd go crazy if he lay in bed one minute longer. He ignored Meredith's instructions and avoided bed altogether during daylight hours. Sitting, he found, was as bad so he kept moving as much as possible. Each day, the pain retreated a little more.

Michael discovered that walking more than half a mile gave him backache but cycling didn't. He borrowed Meredith's roadster, pedalling it in the smallest of its three gears but found it heavy, unresponsive.

He hankered after a racer. When he'd seen that field of fireflies, with the dancing light that was echoed in Meredith's and Daisy's eyes, he'd been riding just such a machine. That was the sort of bike he'd like. In the end, Meredith borrowed a mountain bike for him, twenty-seven gears, tyres as fat as his arm. Michael loved it. It was easy to cock over its low crossbar, and its suspension forks meant he could pretty well ride anywhere he chose.

He cycled to his workshop with Meredith beside him, their lunch safe in the basket on her handlebars. He groaned at his mail heap but found he didn't care a jot about the work he was forced to turn away. Meredith said she'd help with answering letters although she hadn't typed in years. She was like an excited schoolgirl, and Michael realised how empty her life must be. At least with Harry she'd had something to occupy it, although he supposed having orders barked at you day and night wasn't exactly fulfilling. He'd been feeling guilty about freeloading but now suspected Meredith needed him to fill her day.

He asked her to help him put dustsheets over the machines. As Meredith did so, she paused in front of his lathe. Her eyes seemed glazed and she stood tall, shoulders back, chest thrust forward. Michael wondered if she was thinking of Tappy Parker all those years ago, slipping his fingers inside her blouse.

Meredith might be upwards of fifty, Michael thought, but her figure was tempting even now. At seventeen, Daisy-like, she would have been devastating. Small wonder Tappy Parker took such risks to do what he did.

Michael wondered if Tappy knew about his son. He imagined Meredith facing the inquisition, refusing to name the father of her child. She'd be good at keeping secrets, he reckoned.

A shy smile lit Meredith's face. "May I?" She pointed at the lathe. Michael picked out a length of beech, watched Meredith mark its centre and insert it between the drive and the tailstock.

Meredith selected a gouge. There were a few snatches as she rounded out the timber but she soon settled and turned a succession of curves, heights and troughs, with rings dividing them.

"You certainly remember your stuff," Michael said.

"It's been forty years," Meredith said with a little shrug, a twist of her mouth, "but I had a good teacher."

Michael would have hugged her except he knew it might hurt them both. And Daisy too perhaps.

Michael began to make a religion out of fitness. He wasn't up to weight-training yet but pounded his bike pedals for two hours every day whatever the weather and was persuaded by Meredith that yoga would speed him to full recovery.

She said it was the secret of her being well preserved. "Don't you *dare* laugh," she added as Michael grinned. He was about to compare her to a pot of jam.

So, each morning they'd exercise to a grainy video of what looked like suburban housewives contorting their bodies into impossible positions. Michael was dismayed to see how much more supple Meredith was than he, but he persevered and was soon able to complete the first programme without needing to recover for the rest of the day. The grainy housewives began to turn him on, kept his mind off the nipples pressing through the disturbing material of Meredith's leotard.

One afternoon, Meredith announced a visitor. Michael's insides fluttered. Seven weeks had passed since he'd seen Daisy.

But the visitor was a man called Peter. "Call me Pete," he said, shaking Michael's hand. He was around Meredith's age, lean and bronzed, eyes that seemed permanently half-closed, as if he only used them for peering into the blue beyond. Michael wasn't at all surprised when Meredith said he was a sailor.

"In three weeks or so," she added. "Peter is ferrying a yacht from South Brittany. If you were on that yacht, you might collect two passengers on the way." She leaned back and beamed as Michael told himself that she was mad.

"Done any sailing, Mike?" said Peter.

"A little. Dinghies years ago, crewing for a friend. And once I had a Broads cruiser for a week." Michael smiled to himself. The Broads holiday had been one of bumps and bangs, but eventually he'd got the hang of the gaff rig and asserted his rights of way over the stinkpot drivers. "It was a thank you for refitting the interior. Mahogany cabinet work."

"The Broads? I have a weekend cottage there. Don't get up very often though." Peter snapped a glance at Meredith. Michael noticed her colour had heightened.

She began to speak rapidly, said Peter knew a little harbour where Daisy and Hamish could board without anyone noticing. In England too, they'd simply come ashore as if they'd returned from a few hours up river. "Voilà," she concluded and her satisfaction filled the room.

Peter cocked an eye at Michael. "What d'you think, Mike? A crazy idea?"

What the hell? Michael thought. All the same, he wished he and Daisy could just ride off into the sunset and leave the kid behind.

As Meredith showed Peter out, Michael recalled that holiday on the Norfolk Broads. At Potter Heigham, he'd picked up a girl, a raven-haired beauty with misty grey eyes and a devastating smile, as lovely in her own way as Daisy. She was the first girl he'd dared to speak to since his wife walked out. She was one of a group of noisy Americans on a nearby motor cruiser and thought Michael's old wooden yacht was quaint. She said she was from California. Her name was Laura-May and she had a Spanish surname, nothing like Delgado though. She had perfect teeth and pleasing little breasts with extraordinarily large, deeply pigmented areolas. The combination: large within small, dark brown against alabaster-white, caused Michael to pop the buttons on Laura-May's Levis. She responded by popping his too and soon they were tearing at each other's clothes, sending them flying over the cabin floor.

Then it all went uncontrollably wrong. Laura-May spread her legs apart to reveal a lush wilderness of ebony hair and he shied away like a reluctant stallion. Laura-May's lips trembled then she started to cry. "What's wrong? What's wrong with me?"

Michael couldn't say what he'd been reminded of so he tried to hush her, say it was him not her. But although she said okay, her eyes swore she didn't believe him. He wondered now how much damage he had done, whether she still carried it inside her head. In all the years between Grace and Daisy that was the closest encounter he'd had.

Peter took Michael to the harbour where, in less than a month, they would bring Daisy home. They stepped into Peter's tender at the quayside steps then motored to his mooring a few hundred yards away.

"*Hirondelle*, the boat we're bringing back, is exactly the same," Peter said as he showed Michael over his thirty-two foot sloop, *Scallywag*. Below deck was a cabin containing a saloon, galley and a dedicated section for navigating and communications. There were two berths in the saloon and a navigator's berth aft, under the cockpit. Forward of the saloon were the heads and a wet locker, and forward again a cabin with two v-berths.

"Daisy and Hamish could snug up in there," Peter said. "It's not as comfortable as the saloon but at least she'd have privacy."

Michael cast an eye over the cabinetwork. Good but I could do better, he thought then rebuked himself for showing an interest in a trade he'd forsaken.

Peter showed him how to overcome the diesel's tantrums then got him to unfurl the jib. Michael found this didn't trouble him as long as he used his arms and not his trunk. Hoisting the mainsail though, even via a winch, with Peter at the mast sweating the halyard, had Michael hissing frustration.

They went for a sail along the river. Rather than trying to winch in the jib, Peter said the mainsheet might be easier on Michael's ribs. It was, and Michael also tried controlling the tiller with his bum. It wasn't long past high water so they didn't have the tide to fight and there was plenty of depth in the channel. Peter told Michael to keep well away from the lee shore. Although Michael's sail trimming went awry at times as the river twisted, he began to feel in tune with the wind, watching the luff of the mainsail, sheeting in or easing just enough to prevent it flapping.

They sailed to the mouth of the river for a look at the sea. As Michael saw the waves crashing over the entrance marker buoys, he wished himself back ashore. Peter pointed to a particularly turbulent area, said that was the shingle bar they had to cross. The tides ran in different directions, he explained but, as long as they maintained course for a building he was pointing to on the far shore then turned to keep the red buoy to starboard and the green to port, they should be fine.

Michael gritted teeth the first time *Scallywag* heeled but soon had a grin broader than her beam as they rode the waves.

"Quite calm today," Peter said as Michael ducked to avoid the water slapping into the cockpit. "Sea state slight, Thames coastguard said."

Michael began to adjust to the motion and found the liberating thing about the sea was that they could keep the same tack for long periods, unlike the frenzied swapping about on the winding rivers and tiny inland seas of the Norfolk Broads.

After what seemed like only half an hour Peter said it was time to make their way back. "Red to port, green to starboard this time." The tide was still on the ebb in the river and the wind had turned against them too, so Peter started the engine. He asked Michael to keep *Scallywag* head to wind while he lowered the mainsail. Michael furled the headsail himself then they motored the final few miles. Peter went forward to pick up the buoy while Michael inched *Scallywag* ahead.

"Perfect," Peter said as he signalled Michael to put the engine in neutral.

The harbour steps were now a long way below the quayside. On the quay top, only a few cars kept Peter's company. Their occupants were elderly couples, staring at Sunday broadsheets. They raised bleary eyes as Michael and Peter walked past in their bright oilskins then returned their gaze to their newspapers.

"You see?" said Peter. "Nobody will think anything of four people coming ashore here, especially if they look the part."

Chapter 4

Michael realised he was chewing his fingernails, something he hadn't done since he was a kid. In just two hours of waiting for Daisy, he'd managed to gnaw the nails almost to the quick. He closed his eyes, took himself to that long ago school playground, saw himself cowering, encircled by pointing fingers, crowing voices chanting, *Michael's Mum gets 'em out for a bob, for two-and-six she'll suck your knob.*

Why the hell wasn't Daisy answering her new mobile? It was her idea to buy the damn thing for this trip, so why didn't she answer? Having second thoughts? Doing a runner, like the morning after they'd first met? Or perhaps Bohec had found the phone, sussed out what they were up to. Well, fuck it, he'd have to phone the house. If Bohec or his mother answered, he'd pretend he was a tourist seeking a gîte.

The house phone kept ringing, no answering machine. Michael sucked his cheeks, considered his options. They amounted to one: he'd have to go to Le Mazemeur and drag Daisy out, bully boys there or not.

He walked into town to look for a car hire depot. As he reached the main street, his mobile bleeped. A text message: *Stuck at hoptl. Bert had stroke. JP weeping like baby. Sorry. Try call U 2morro LU D*

Of course - mobiles had to be switched off in hospitals. In any case, if Daisy was with Bohec he'd want to know who was calling. The big thing was she was okay. Almost as big were that Berthe wasn't around to snoop and Jean-Paul was welded to her bedside. The weather forecast, *grande houle*, meant they might have to wait a day or two anyway before sailing.

Michael wondered if Daisy's misspelling of Berthe was deliberate or merely text shorthand. He pressed Reply, decided a simple *OK* was best, just in case.

That night Michael unpacked the sailing clothes he'd bought for Daisy and Hamish. They were bright red, matching his. People might think they were a real family. How, though, could he love Daisy's child when he hadn't managed to love his own? He wondered what she was like now, that discarded daughter of his. A troubled teenager with a taste for the Gothic? Or was that out of fashion? He wondered if she ever thought of him.

It was past five before he drifted to sleep. It didn't seem much later when his phone cheeped. He stretched an arm to reach it in the cubbyhole behind his bunk. A brass clock on the bulkhead said it was gone nine. Peter wasn't to be seen.

"I'm in the gîte, on the bed where we made love."

"Daisy!" Michael sat up. "Can you get away?"

"I was only allowed in here to prepare it for an arrival. Jean-Paul wanted me to put them off but I said we couldn't do that because they'd be on the road now, somewhere between here and Paris and he couldn't expect them to arrive and then be told to find somewhere else for the night. If we did that, Gîtes de France would turf us off their books. I'm rambling, Michael, aren't I?"

"Only a little. What's the situation?"

"Berthe has some left side paralysis and is talking nonsense. By the look of her eyes she's still taking everything in, though. Jean-Paul's being an absolute arsehole. I wanted to take Hamish to nursery class, or at least pretend I was. JP, of course, said *Jacques* couldn't go to school, it wasn't right when Grandmère was so poorly. So, as soon as these people are settled in, we have to visit Berthe and I'm sunk for another day. How long can you wait?"

"As long as it takes, whether Pete has to leave or not. I don't know if he has a deadline. I suppose he has to allow for adverse weather." The last two words caught in Michael's throat. "I'm dying to see you, Daisy."

He could hear her sniffling then there was some noise in the background and she said, "I have to go, Michael. He's coming in here."

Peter was outside, swabbing the decks. "Heard the phone," he said. "Thought I'd give you some space."

Around three o'clock, Daisy called again.

"I've left Jean-Paul dog-eyed beside Berthe, said I was taking Hamish to the café. We're actually on the bus, coming to you. There's just a tiny problem. I have money and passports but we have no luggage, no clothes other than what we're wearing."

If Michael could have danced around *Hirondelle's* deck, he would have. "What do you need? There are half decent shops here. I think they have an Intermarché too."

"I'll let myself stink if I have to but Hamish will need changes of clothes and something to keep him amused. Best leave it till I'm there."

As the bus from Vannes pulled up, Michael's heart thumped so much his teeshirt seemed alive. Daisy stepped down to the pavement, clutching the hand of a small boy who had a mop of hair as pale as her own. Still holding the child, she ran towards Michael, flung her free arm around him, nuzzled her head into his chest. He kissed her hair and gazed down at the boy, who stared at them, rigid as a statue, bewilderment shrouding his face.

"Hamish, this is my friend, Michael," Daisy said. "We're going to sail in his friend Peter's boat. Won't that be fun?"

Hamish looked as if he was about to weep. Something in Michael's armour snapped. He remembered his little girl, years ago, looking back at him with much the same expression, as her mother dragged her out through the door of their dingy flat. And he had stood there, unblinking, let them go.

"Hamish," he said, crouching down to the boy's level, "I hope we can be friends too." He extended his hand. The boy, still ramrod straight, a tiny caricature of Daisy's father, stepped forward and shook it.

"How do you do?" he said, with a formal bow and not a trace of French accent.

They toured the local shops, three people hand-in-hand. Michael felt a lump in his throat the whole time. What was he doing, playing the family man, holding hands with someone else's child? He watched Daisy as she chose items she thought they'd need. She seemed carefree, conversing lightly, with little laughs thrown in, as if she were on holiday with her husband and son.

The boat rocked as they boarded it and Hamish kept trying to make it move by himself. His face fell when nothing happened, so Michael and Daisy joined in to help. They shook the boat so much that Peter popped his head out of the companionway.

He put a hand in front of his face as if to ward them off. "Oh, my goodness," he said, "Pirates!"

Hamish giggled. Michael noticed Peter's eyes glint at the sight of Daisy.

Daisy handed Michael their passports to keep safe. He was surprised to see they were British, made out to Victoria and Hamish Lomond.

"Jean-Paul keeps my French one in his safe," Daisy said, "won't allow Hamish his own. What he doesn't know is that I kept my British passport and arranged one for Hamish as soon as he was born."

Michael showed them their berths. Hamish seemed delighted they could be shut off from the rest of the boat and, when he wasn't climbing on and off the bunk, kept opening and shutting the forecabin door.

Michael showed Daisy the oilskins and lifejackets he'd bought. Hamish wanted to dress up in his right away but Daisy said, "No, they're only for when we sail."

"When will we?" said Hamish. Daisy raised an eyebrow at Michael. He raised one at Peter.

"Tomorrow perhaps," Peter said, screwing up his old salt's eyes and peering up the companionway at the sky.

"Will Papa come too?"

Daisy sighed. "No, darling. He has to stay with Grandmère."

"Don't like Grandmère," Hamish said. Daisy rolled her eyes.

After they'd enjoyed a picnic tea Daisy had bought in the town and Hamish, bleary-eyed, was tucked up in his bunk, Daisy suggested a stroll ashore. She linked arms with Michael as they walked, leaned her head against his side.

"Jean-Paul will want to kill me," Daisy said, "leaving with Berthe in that state. In fact, he'll want to kill me twice." There were shards of defiance in her eyes. "I left a note in his car, saying I regretted the timing but he should have considered the consequences of fucking his little tart. My solicitor had been considering them for some time."

"You've contacted a solicitor?"

"No, that was just for him. He thought his sloe-eyed mistress was a secret. Now he'll worry what evidence I have. Did I tell you I hired Philip Marlowe to follow them around?"

"Philip Marlowe? I must have seen The Big Sleep a dozen times."

"Me too. I suppose my private eye would be *Philippe* but he has the crumpled suit, the lived in face, the whiskey."

Daisy stopped Michael from walking. "You are prepared for trouble? You know it's going to be difficult?"

"Of course I am." Michael wasn't prepared at all but knew he'd stay in until the end, whether that was sweet or bitter. Unbidden, his old uncertainty crept in, that he was breaching his allotted boundaries. He recalled being reprimanded by a chapel-haunting Welshman when he'd whistled at a girl he knew. "How dare you. How dare you whistle at an engaged girl," his outraged acquaintance had said.

How much greater a sin then, to steal a married woman from her husband. What penance would be exacted for that?

"Daisy," he said. "How did you come to marry him?"

"Jesus, Michael! Why bring that up?" Daisy's mouth twisted as if she'd tasted something she didn't quite like.

"Just came into my head."

"I wish you'd kept it there." Daisy glared at Michael then, after a sigh that seemed more of a hiss, said, "I met him at a ski resort where I happened to be working. I've lived in France since I was sixteen."

"I ran away when I was sixteen too. To France, among other places. I told you I lived here."

"I didn't realise it was when you were so young." Daisy fingered her chin. "Anyway, who says I ran away? I was deported."

"Deported?"

Daisy's eyelashes were slung low. "Yes." She almost whispered the word. "I was expelled from school for…unsatisfactory behaviour. Mummy thought it best I didn't live at home so she sent me to her sister in Grenoble." She looked up again, frowning. "Why did you run away?"

Michael swallowed. "Didn't get on at home."

Daisy peered into his eyes. Michael felt as if she was reading all his secrets. "Jesus," she said finally, shaking her head. "We're a pair, you and I."

She linked an arm in his again. They resumed walking. Michael snapped the tip off a tree branch, twisted the leaves in his free hand.

Daisy suddenly laughed but it had no substance. "Larkin was right, wasn't he? 'They fuck you up, your Mum and Dad'."

Michael didn't know who Larkin was but sensed this wasn't the time to admit it. "I guess so. But what about Bohec? Why did you marry him?"

Daisy shrugged. "Who knows?" She frowned, snapped her arm away from Michael's. "No, I'm tired of make believe. If I'm tying my colours to yours, you should know what I'm really like. I'm not all you might hope I am, Michael."

"What do you mean?"

"I have a history you mightn't like."

"Oh."

"I managed not to get expelled from my lycée but when I graduated, I was high or low on anything I could lay hands on. I feel ashamed of how I repaid Aunt Romilly's kindness. By chance, a school friend offered me a place as her live-in nanny. Trouble was, her husband wanted to get in my pants and I very much regret I didn't refuse him. It went on for two years before my girlfriend found out. Then I heard chalet girls had lots of fun, so I applied for a job in Courchevel. A new beginning, I thought but soon I was my most fucked up. Snow, cocaine and glühwein don't mix. Jean-Paul provided the cocaine, claimed to be a rich farmer. Ha, some farmer. He proposed when he found I was pregnant but I put him off until well after the birth. I don't even know if Hamish is his." Daisy touched Michael's cheek. "I wish he was yours."

Michael wished there'd never been a Hamish. He wished he was Daisy's first and only love but he knew fairy tales didn't happen. What mattered was that she was his now and the story she'd just told him might make his own more palatable.

"My father trawled the building sites when he was sober," he said. "He left us when I was ten. And my mother was a back-street whore. We're from different worlds, Daisy."

If Daisy was shocked, she didn't show it. She was silent for a while then lifted herself on tiptoe to kiss him. "The same world, Michael. As I said before, we're a pair, you and I."

A few locks of Daisy's hair had strayed over her left cheek and her eyes had an expression of innocence betrayed, although Michael knew it couldn't be that, not now.

They turned at the road bridge over the Vilaine, retraced their steps to the marina. Peter had good news. "There's a twenty-four hour window of clear weather before us. We'll sail in the morning."

Michael stretched across his bed. An unyielding object halted his progress. He opened one eye, realised he was in his bunk and he'd been stopped by the leeboard along its open side. He opened his other eye, checked the bulkhead clock: five-thirty. He wondered if Daisy was awake.

If only the boy wasn't there. He tried to listen for Daisy's breathing but picked up only Peter's soft snores from the starboard bunk, which were augmented now and then by a carefree fart. Michael climbed out of his bunk, squeezed into the heads, closed the door.

He swilled himself in chilling water, wondered how Daisy would cope. She'd have to heat some for Hamish. He decided it was a stupid idea bringing a four-year-old on a small boat like this. Why hadn't Daisy mentioned their passports from the start? She and Hamish could have left France before anyone knew they were gone. He supposed Bohec would provide the police with photographs but nobody would watch every airport and ferry terminal in Europe, certainly not for Hamish and Victoria *Lomond*.

Michael tiptoed back to the saloon, put his oilskin jacket over his nightclothes and climbed through the hatch to the cockpit. He stood at the pushpit rails, surveying the placid river. He wished, for the second time since he met Daisy, that he had a cigarette.

A light mist played over the water's polished surface, being wisped away like promises as the sun rose. They should have kept to Daisy's original plan, driven south, Michael decided. This crazy venture was Meredith's doing. He wondered about her motives. If you threw people together in a confined space for two or three weeks, they'd end up either loving or hating each other. Maybe that was her purpose: to test the stamina of their commitment, because to be honest, apart from the sex, he and Daisy were virtual strangers. He wondered which result Meredith was hoping for.

"Couldn't sleep?"

Michael spun around, saw Peter stepping out of the companionway. "Something like that."

"Might as well get her ready to sail then." Peter began to remove the boom cover.

Sounds of movement came from below then Daisy's tousled head appeared through the hatch. She blinked as the sun lit her face. "What time are we off?" she said.

Michael grinned. "Depends how long you take to cook our breakfast."

Daisy pulled a face. "But I've only just woken."

"Ignore him," Peter said. His eyes devoured Daisy as she emerged from the saloon. "On the first day the skipper cooks and the crew wash up."

"Am I crew?" Daisy said, snapping a glance at Michael.

"Cargo," said Michael and she stuck out her tongue.

He washed up.

Michael cast off the mooring warps then Peter motored slowly astern to clear the pontoon. Several neighbouring boats had Red Ensigns furled above their transoms. Michael asked if he should put *Hirondelle's* up.

"I shouldn't. That way, French officialdom won't recognise her as foreign."

The wind was a light force three, but coming from the southwest so they had to beat downriver against it. Peter let the engine assist them and they soon reached the lock at Arzal. It was just after high water Peter said, but even so, Michael and Daisy were surprised to find they had to go upwards to reach the water on the other side.

"Spring tide," said Peter.

Daisy raised eyebrows at Michael and mouthed, "But it isn't spring."

"I should have explained," Peter said, as if he'd read Daisy's lips, "a spring tide is the combination of the highest high water and the lowest low water. The opposite – lowest high and highest low is a neap tide." He grinned. "First lesson over."

It took an hour's motor-sailing to clear the Vilaine but soon the wind backed southeast, blowing across *Hirondelle's* beam. Peter set the autopilot to maintain course. The sea was gentle and Hamish seemed absorbed in the activity on the water – plenty of small yachts like theirs, some fishing boats and once, a passenger vedette whose wash almost rocked their lunch off the cockpit table. Hamish jumped up and down and chortled at that and Michael noticed Daisy checking the boy's safety harness was secure. He was amazed how quickly Hamish became drowsy afterwards but assumed it was down to sea air and the novelty of being on a boat. After she had taken Hamish below, Daisy asked, with a timidity Michael had never witnessed before, if she might have a go at working the sails. He showed her how to use the jibsheets and he took the helm while Peter perched on a seat against the pushpit rail and coaxed Edgworth tobacco into a filthy looking pipe.

Daisy soon wore a mighty grin as *Hirondelle* creamed through the waves at speeds dependent on whether she eased or winched in the genoa and, with the continual efforts of Daisy, Michael, the autopilot, and

Peter's pipe, a happy skipper and crew reached Belle Île and anchored *Hirondelle* off Sauzon at its northern tip.

Long after Hamish was tucked in for the night, Peter stayed below while Michael and Daisy took a turn on deck. "I'll close the hatchway," Peter said. "Keep out the draught."

There wasn't much room to manoeuvre along the sidedecks between ropes and shrouds, and most of the coachroof was occupied by the liferaft, but they found a clear spot forward of the mast, where they sat and gazed at the lights on the island. Daisy stood at the prow, her hands grasping the pulpit rails. She raised her head and chest high, breathed in deeply. Michael remembered the vision he'd had on the day they first met, of Daisy in just such a position, nipples proud against her teeshirt. They were prouder now.

"I wish I could slip into your bunk tonight," he said.

"Hamish might wake. And I don't want to embarrass Peter."

Daisy pulled Michael's head towards hers, locked them together in a kiss that had him reeling, as if each atom of Daisy's passion was being transmitted through her lips to his. Oral sex suddenly took on a new meaning for him.

"It's too exposed here," Daisy said.

They made their way back over the deck, and in the cockpit well, sheltered from the night by the canvas dodgers on the guardrails, zips were unzipped, buttons unbuttoned, hooks unhooked, and sex occurred as a standing-up frenzy that had them both surprised. Michael knew he was staring at Daisy with the same primitive, wild-eyed, mouth-gaping expression that he saw on her face.

"Jesus, Michael," she said after they'd both climaxed with shouts that Peter must surely have heard below, "Is this how the cockpit got its name?"

Michael heard piping calls of "Mama, Mama," then Daisy's muffled voice. It sounded as if she was yawning. After what seemed but a second later, the forecabin door opened and Daisy shunted Hamish into the heads.

When they emerged, Michael whispered her name. She poked her head around the bulkhead.

"I love you," Michael said. Daisy cast a furtive glance at the starboard bunk. Faint snores whistled from its dark confines.

She blew Michael a kiss. "Je t'aime, aussi," she said.

He boiled water for her and Hamish to wash in then did the same for himself. By the time he emerged from the heads, they were halfway through breakfast. Peter was sitting up in his bunk, sipping tea.

They were under way by six-thirty, enjoying the same gentle southeast breeze as on the previous day. Peter said they might as well take advantage of it and instead of hugging the coast as he'd planned, run directly for Kerdonnec.

"If this holds, we'll be moored before the fishing fleet arrives. Then we can buy our dinner straight from its catcher."

The wind did hold, and they had *Hirondelle* running goose-winged before it. The mainsail was let out to starboard with a preventer rope attached to the boom to stop it from gybing, and the genoa was poled out to port. Hamish seemed to like the way the sails were set because he protested on the few occasions they had to turn onto a reach. "No, fly them the other way," he said.

Michael found himself smiling at the slant Hamish put on things. It was, well… childish, and he thought about how he'd missed out on that with his daughter. Daisy saw the tears in his eyes and hugged him hard.

"He's sweet, isn't he?" she said and Michael wanted to tell her the tears were for his child, not hers, but of course he couldn't. Not when her face was glowing like that.

Kerdonnec turned out to be a quiet little port at the head of a wide river but metamorphosed into bustling activity when the fleet came in. They bought fresh mackerel for their supper and had just returned to the pontoon when they saw a big inflatable approaching *Hirondelle.* It bore three men wearing *Douane Francaise* teeshirts.

Michael's skin turned clammy. "*Shit,*" he said.

Daisy, stone-faced, glared at the intruders. She asked them, in French: "Why do you have to turn up as we're about to cook our supper?"

One Customs man, older than his colleagues, smiled at her. "I'm sorry, but we have to do spot checks. As soon as we've seen your ship's papers we'll be off."

Make them think we're natives, Michael told himself. He resurrected his best Rennes accent, related a Breton joke he'd thought funny years ago. It was about three homesick fishermen and the catch that didn't quite make it back to port. The two younger Customs men sniggered but the oldest guffawed.

"My Dad used to tell me that," he said, "and his Dad told it to him. It's still one of the best." He was still chuckling when he was handed *Hirondelle's* papers. He barely looked at them. "So," he said, "your home port is La Roche-Bernard. It's a long time since I sailed on the Vilaine. Enjoy the rest of your cruise." He beamed at Daisy, and ruffled Hamish's hair. "Enjoy your suppers too." He gestured towards his companions, who had not uttered a word throughout the entire episode. "Come on lads, our own suppers will be getting cold by now."

They motored off with a smile and a wave. They hadn't asked for passports at all.

On her third morning at sea *Hirondelle* passed through the Raz de Sein, between the Isle de Sein and the mainland. Peter told Michael it was notorious for drowning sailors but he mustn't let Daisy know that.

The sunshine gave the Breton cliffs a deceptive red softness as they approached them. Peter pointed out some yachts coming south between a lighthouse and a large rock.

"They're on the last of the tide. It'll soon be slack water then it's our turn."

The gap looked perilously narrow to Michael, only metres wide. He grimaced and Peter caught it.

"Don't worry, Mike, we won't go through that way." Peter's face said that he wished they could.

Instead, Peter kept them well to the west of the lighthouse and a beacon beyond it. They had the benefit of the wind on their port beam and the bonus of an increasingly fair tide through the Raz and onwards to Camaret.

"This is like a holiday," Daisy said to Michael as they settled *Hirondelle* for the night, "I'm so glad we chose to escape this way."

Her face was tanning from the sea air and she seemed to have been born with sea legs, Michael thought. He'd bought sailing gloves for her but even so, Daisy's fingers were raw.

"Battle scars," she said as he kissed the broken skin. "Nothing's worth having if it's easy to get."

Day four took them through the islands extending northwest from the mainland to Ouessant. Peter planned to overnight in the little port of Abervenan, which to Michael sounded like somewhere in Wales.

Aberystwyth came into his mind because he had honeymooned there, in a sea-front boarding house lacking such basic facilities that, after an evening on the town, he'd had to pee out of the bedroom window in the middle of the night. Grace, his new bride, had looked on with a weary expression. "Men," she'd said. "You're all the same. Disgusting." Nine months after that, Anne was born.

Hirondelle's captain and crew rose very early to catch the tide but when they had a look at the morning, fog hovered above the water and the wind was non-existent. Peter wondered aloud if they ought to stay in port. Daisy's face fell. She wanted to get home, she said. Michael wondered which home she meant. Then she'd clutched his hand and, as if she'd generated a miracle, a wind appeared and the fog began to disperse.

Peter chose the Chenal du Four, close to the mainland, and their passage was calm while the islands protected them but as they neared the end of the channel, a strong Atlantic swell rolled in and *Hirondelle* bucked so much that her crew, except for Hamish, strapped to a cockpit seat, found it difficult to remain on their feet.

Peter's expression was tense as he negotiated the way past shoals and granite scimitars that sliced the waves and wanted to slice *Hirondelle* too. White fountains spurted skywards as the sea crashed against them.

Hamish pointed towards them. "Mama, can we go closer?"

"No, darling."

The boy's face fell. "Papa would take me."

"No, darling, he wouldn't."

Daisy grimaced at Michael as Hamish began to kick his feet against the cockpit sides. "I wish Papa was here," he said, and this time he spoke in French.

It was the first time Michael had heard him use the language. It reinforced a fear that the boy might cause a division between him and Daisy. He studied her now, her face as white as the spume playing off the rocks. She took Hamish down. Michael could hear her voice, sometimes pleading, sometimes hard as she spoke to the boy. Hamish's piping tones gave way to sobs then there was silence but it was a long time before Daisy's head appeared above the companionway steps.

Once they were in open water, the sea calmed. The wind veered southeast so they enjoyed an offshore breeze up to Abervenan's marker buoy. The channel took them into the wind so they motored the final leg and moored on the town's pontoon. The people at the yacht club were very friendly, offered them the use of their showers. Daisy, chronically glum-faced since Hamish's outburst, took him into the shower with her. Twenty minutes later she emerged rosy-cheeked, beaming. Hamish trotted beside her, a cherubic smile now animating his face.

"Mama let me go under the water," he said. He allowed Michael to lift him from the pontoon up to the boat.

They ate pizzas at a restaurant opposite the yacht club. As they strolled back to *Hirondelle*, Michael told Daisy he'd been jealous when she took Hamish into the shower. "I wish I could have gone with you," he said.

Daisy grinned. "There may still be time," she said. "I'll put Hamish to bed and we'll see."

But the showers were closed, the key taken home for the night.

The forecast prescribed another offshore wind and a flat sea but the wind and waves would not conform. Already a fresh westerly when they left Abervenan, it quickly brewed up to a strong one, showing an average twenty-four knots on the cockpit instruments. The tide also began to fight them. Daisy's face became increasingly grim, her eyes anxious as *Hirondelle* rode foaming white crests, slammed into ink-black troughs.

Hamish, however, wore a huge grin, squealed with delight whenever waves smothered *Hirondelle's* decks. Daisy, the wind constantly lifting her hair, clung to his harness as if she didn't trust the steel to which it was shackled.

Michael watched her spirits fragment and cursed himself for the casual way he'd agreed to this crazy voyage. He waited for Daisy to snap. It happened three hours out of Abervenan, as they passed a small inlet that Peter said was Treguelven harbour.

"Treguelven-Plage?" Daisy said and Michael knew this was her breaking point. "Can we go there, out of this? Please?" Her eyes pleaded with Michael. He cocked an eyebrow at Peter.

Peter shook his head, "Sorry. There won't be enough water for us to get in. I know a safer place further along the coast."

"How further along?" Daisy hissed the words. Michael watched Peter flinch.

"Five hours, perhaps less."

Daisy glared at Peter and at Michael then she grabbed Hamish, took him below.

Peter looked as if he'd lost a thousand ships. "What could I do? I daren't risk grounding her in this weather."

A dour blanket of cloud loomed and the wind increased to around thirty knots. Peter said they'd better deep reef. He and Michael minimised the mainsail, laced the excess along the boom. The genoa was already part-furled but Peter wasn't happy about the way *Hirondelle* was heeling in the gusts, which by now exceeded forty knots.

"I'm changing to the storm jib," he said.

He dragged a sail from the cockpit compartment and after telling Michael to maintain course, clipped his harness to a webbing line beside the coachroof and made his way forward on hands and knees along the windward sidedeck. That seemed to be a signal for the clouds that had merely threatened up to then to finally release their cargo. Horizontal hail speared Peter as he hanked the storm jib onto the second forestay and shackled it to its halyard. Michael furled the genoa then Peter transferred its sheets to the storm jib. Michael winched that up the stay and Peter crawled back to the cockpit. His face and fingers were red raw as he sat down underneath the sprayhood.

He grinned. "A little fresh up there."

The tiny storm jib made *Hirondelle* feel safer to Michael, as if she could now handle anything the weather hurled at her. As they turned more directly downwind, following the line of the coast, the waves became foothills rather than mountains and *Hirondelle's* rolling and pitching markedly less severe. Michael cast a glance at the companionway hatch.

"Tide's turning in our favour," Peter said. "I can handle things up here now."

Hamish was sitting in Michael's bunk. The safety board was inserted. He was turning the pages of a picture book. Beyond him, in the passage between the saloon and forecabin, Michael could see Daisy's legs. He heard her retch and moan, "Oh, God, not again." Her upper body was in the heads. Her arms were clutching the sides of the toilet and her head was hovering over its pan. There was a strong smell of vomit.

She stared blankly as Michael touched her shoulder then her face twisted into fury. "You can stuff yourself and Peter and your fucking boat."

"You don't mean that."

"Yes I fucking well do."

"No, you don't." Michael went to pour her a glass of water. As he passed Hamish, the boy said, "Mama said a naughty word."

"She isn't feeling well."

As Michael gave Daisy the water, Hamish began chanting, "Fucking boat, fucking boat, fucking boat."

Daisy croaked, "Hamish, stop that at once." She flashed Michael a half-smile, let him help her into the saloon.

Hamish began singing to himself. The words sounded French, but in some sort of childish code, so Michael couldn't make them out. At least someone's enjoying the storm, he thought.

"Are we going to drown today?" Daisy said.

"I don't think so. Pete says it will be easier now."

Daisy nodded. "Hold me then." She laid her head against him. Michael guessed he was forgiven. "That harbour he wouldn't take us into. We would have been safe, you know."

"But Pete said there wasn't enough water. The tide was out. It might be okay now but we'd never get back against the wind."

Daisy snuggled further into Michael. "We spent a summer there. Hamish was only two. Glorious weather, no clouds to mask the sun. Miles of sand and rocks. They'd scald if you touched them. I'm sure you could have boiled an egg. A little sailboat with a yellow hull used to pass the beach where we sunbathed. Its helmsman, he was about your height and build, even had dark hair cropped like yours, would watch me through binoculars. Jean-Paul never noticed. He was too busy clocking the tits on display."

Michael pictured the scene, only instead of Bohec, he was beside Daisy on that beach. And they didn't need to worry about Hamish because the boy had someone to look after him: a skinny girl, about fourteen, slightly freckled, auburn hair waving about her face. When he and Daisy got up to leave, Hamish and the girl ran up, breathless with exhilaration, and they both called him Daddy.

"I wouldn't have looked at anyone but you," he said. Daisy's eyes looked misty.

"Are you going to kiss Mama?"

Michael blinked. Hamish was almost falling out of the bunk in his efforts to observe them.

"Mama's not nice to kiss at the moment," Daisy said but Michael kissed her anyway.

"I thought you wanted to," Hamish said and Daisy told him he thought too much for his own good.

Michael lifted Hamish out of the bunk, carried him across the saloon to sit between him and Daisy. Between them, they worked through the pictures in his book, while Hamish read out the words beneath. Daisy flashed Michael periodic smiles while he wished this sort of thing came naturally to him. Liking children was a learned experience, he supposed, for those who had been unlikeable in their own childhood.

They sat as a working threesome for what Michael supposed was an hour or two, then they heard a brief whine of an electric motor then a mechanical clanking began behind the companionway steps, followed moments later by the untidy clatter of the diesel engine.

"I'd better go on deck," Michael said.

Peter was steering *Hirondelle* around a granite headland towards a large bay. The wind was still intent on skimming her across the sea, as a boy would a stone. White-flecked breakers hurled themselves against the lee shore. When they fell back to the sea Michael saw razor teeth exposed amongst smothering foam. But as *Hirondelle* rounded the headland, the wind was cut off abruptly, the seas stilled. Ahead was a smaller bay with a little town of white walls and steep grey roofs clinging to the sides of the rocky promontory.

Daisy clattered up the companionway. Her face was already losing its pallor. "Has the wind gone at last?"

"Not gone, but we're sheltered from it."

Peter aimed *Hirondelle* towards a vacant mooring buoy just north of the town. "This is Locquirec," he said. "We'll float here even at low water. We'll wait out the storm. Maybe stay a couple of days."

"Is there a railway station?" Daisy said.

For the first time in their voyage, the inflatable dinghy was brought from its locker, and the outboard engine that usually sat on the pushpit rails was clamped to its stern.

They ate at a quayside café. Daisy, studying a calendar on the wall, said, "It's Michaelmas Day. Your saint's day, Michael. It's an omen."

Michael frowned. He'd had enough of saints during his childhood. "What sort of omen?"

Daisy's face shone. "That we've survived the storm and things will be fine from now on."

Michael wished he could believe her, but Daisy seemed convinced. She didn't mention railway stations again.

The morning, supporting Daisy's prediction, brought cloudless skies and not a whisper of wind. Most of the space they'd crossed in the dinghy was now spotless sand, stretching to the end of the bay southeast of the town.

After breakfast they took the dinghy and pulled it up the now broad beach to a safe parking place. Nearby, small boats lay at various angles. One or two, with twin keels, sat upright. Peter went into the town while Michael, Daisy, and Hamish strolled on the beach.

Daisy bought Hamish a little bucket and spade and they watched him build sandcastles. He dug little moats around them with elaborate canals linking one fortress to another.

"Thank you for helping Hamish work through his book yesterday," Daisy said. She brushed Michael's cheek with her lips. "You'll make a father yet."

"I'm already one." Michael coloured but the words were irretrievable now.

Daisy stared at him, open-mouthed. "A father?"

"Yes, and definitely not a good one." Michael gazed along the beach, to its furthest corner. There was a green pillar, a beacon, and around it a wide ribbon of water was spilling over the sand to join the sea.

"You're married?"

"Not now."

The blueness of Daisy's eyes deepened as they ransacked Michael's. He cleared his throat.

"I'm not good at relationships," he said. "I'm the guy who never gets the girl."

Daisy drew his hands to her lips. "You have her now." She had such a look in her eyes that Michael would have made love to her right there, if only Hamish and half a dozen citizens hadn't been looking on. "What was your wife's name?"

"Grace. She was thirty-five, I was twenty." Michael watched for Daisy's reaction but her face was a mask of concentration. "We had a child, a girl. Anne. One day, Grace took Anne and left. I've never seen either of them since. The only contact we've had is by bank transfer, and that's only since the Child Support Agency caught up with me."

"Why did Grace go?"

The light from Daisy's eyes was piercing Michael now. He raised a hand to shield himself. She frowned but kept her gaze locked on him.

"Something I made the mistake of telling her about."

Daisy's eyes flickered. "Then I won't make the mistake of asking what that was. Do you ever wonder how Anne is, what she's like?"

"Not until recently. Does that seem callous?"

Daisy shrugged. "I suppose it's different for a mother. Who am I to judge?" She pulled her knees up against her chest. "Why recently?"

"Because of Hamish. Because I need to learn how to be a father, and the only experience I have is a poor thing to build on."

"You're too hard on yourself." Daisy turned on a smile that Michael read as an absolution of a sort.

Hamish had discarded his castles in favour of an open boat he was fashioning around himself, shaping the front into an imitation of a prow and curving the sides gently back towards a squared off transom. Michael caught Daisy watching him watch her son. She looked as if she was pleased about it.

"It was Hamish who changed me," Daisy said. "To feel a young life growing inside me was the most liberating experience. I was no good to my baby coked so I finally stopped punishing myself. I've never touched even cannabis since. I wanted Hamish to be mine alone, and that's why I wouldn't marry Jean-Paul. Of course, reality couldn't be fended off for ever. Hamish needed a home, security, so I finally relented. Jean-Paul was charming and good-looking in a swarthy sort of way. I soon found out he was only charming when he needed to be and he had a streak of meanness too, something I never would have guessed from the way he threw money around in Courchevel." Daisy puckered her chin, shrugged. "Mmm…"

A shout came from the townward side of the beach. Peter was waving to them. He pointed towards the sea. It was beginning to wriggle across the farthest edge of sand.

"He fancies you," Michael said.

By Default

"Hamish, darling, time to go back," Daisy said, and to Michael: "I know."

As they walked back towards the dinghy, Michael recalled someone saying that we are never happy *now*, only *then*. He thought for him it was the other way round, maybe for Daisy too. He couldn't remember ever being happy then.

Chapter 5

The next day was another benign offering, the wind dwindled to a baby's breath. Peter resorted to motorsailing. In good time for supper, they chugged up a wide estuary and berthed below an idyllic old town that, like their previous port of call, clutched the side of a hill.

Peter said this was their last day in France. "Tomorrow we sail for the Channel Islands then home to good old England. I think the occasion calls for champagne."

Hamish said, "But home is France, isn't it Mama?"

When Daisy replied, "You know Mama is English. She wants England to be our home," a frown creased Hamish's forehead. He said, "Will Papa come too?"

Daisy's eyes met Michael's. He made a show of gritting his teeth. Children adapt, said a voice in his head, but he knew from his own history that was too simplistic a statement. He was thirty-five, and still paying.

"No," Daisy said. Michael watched the colour leave Hamish's face.

He knew what was coming next: how Mama and Papa didn't want to be with each other anymore but they both love you and though you'll be living with Mama, that doesn't mean you won't see Papa too. In that, Michael was wrong, for Daisy said nothing of the sort. Instead, she hugged Hamish as if wanting to meld him into her, said he must be a very brave boy, remember that he was English long before he became French.

Hamish, face the colour of dough, stood at attention like on the day Michael first met him. He said nothing, and a few minutes later had his nose in one of his books. He turned pages and hummed what sounded like a Scottish lament.

The Lament of the Lomonds, thought Michael. He recalled Daisy mentioning her father's wish to be buried on a forlorn island in an obscure loch. According to Daisy, even Harry's own family had rejected him, perhaps to the extent that they refused to have him among their family ghosts. Was that why he'd been airlifted to England for interment?

They had the champagne, which Peter had kept refrigerated since La Roche-Bernard, but supper wasn't a success. Hamish was cocooned inside his safety shell, a tactic Michael understood too well. From Daisy's subdued demeanour, he guessed she was feeling guilty but he didn't want to provoke her.

Peter said he was going on deck to smoke a pipe or two. He looked uneasy. Michael wanted to explain how the upset with Hamish wasn't his fault but Daisy beat him to it. "I'm sorry, Peter," she said and stretched up to peck him on the cheek. "I should have told Hamish days ago."

Peter's ancient mariner eyes faltered. "He'll be all right," he said, "He has a certain stoicism about him, like his mother."

Daisy shook her head. "Oh, not like his mother," she said, grave-faced, but she was smiling as she walked back to Michael.

He guessed stoicism meant having guts.

The following morning, they were half-drifting in an indifferent wind when a purposeful-looking vessel appeared on their starboard beam. It slowed only at the point when they thought it must certainly ram them.

"Bloody show-offs," said Peter, curling his top lip. "French navy vedette. I wish we were nearer Jersey."

Two men in officers' uniforms observed them through binoculars. Daisy clung to Michael.

"Maybe I should give them something to look at," she whispered. "Like on the beach at Treguelven... the yellow cruiser?" She wore a grin but beneath it she was shaking. Michael was thankful Hamish was below.

After about five minutes the vedette suddenly veered off, accelerated towards the French coast.

Peter whistled *Farewell Spanish Ladies* and began stoking his pipe. "Probably thought we were smugglers," he said.

"We are in a way," said Michael.

Daisy pouted. "I hope you're not about to classify me as cargo again."

The incident was forgotten when a fair southwesterly appeared as if by magic. Peter claimed his whistling had brought it.

Daisy said, "That's just an old wives' tale, whistling for a wind," but her face said she half believed it.

"Old sailors," said Peter between his teeth. "Not wives."

Daisy grinned. "Aye, aye sir." Peter puffed wildly on his pipe and soon the tobacco was glowing. He said it was time they flew the red ensign.

They made St Helier by early evening. The extent of the formalities emphasised the fact that they were now on British territory. At most Breton ports they hadn't been asked for a single piece of paper beyond euros for the harbour dues.

Daisy said she wanted to go into the town to phone Mummy. She'd refused to do that from France, even on her new mobile, in case calls to Meredith's number were being traced. Michael had said she was being ridiculous but Daisy remained adamant.

Peter stayed behind to charge the batteries and refill the tanks. Michael suspected he was charging his own batteries too, depleted from the claustrophobic situation on board.

Crew and cargo followed directions to a fish and chip shop the marina office recommended.

"It's like being home again," said Daisy as they gorged on golden-battered fish and chips done just so. But try as Michael would, he couldn't image Daisy as a fish-and-chip shop habitué.

They found a phone and Daisy called Meredith. "It's ringing," she said, then, "Mummy? It's me."

Michael heard a loud "Daisy, thank God" then Meredith's tone quietened and there were several minutes of tinny cadences flavoured with Daisy's interjections. Finally, Daisy handed him the phone.

"She says put Michael on."

"Michael, you're my hero. How is Daisy really?"

"She's fine. She makes a good sailor, better than me."

"And Hamish?"

"Bearing up."

"I see. So he's been a little fractious at times?"

"Fractious?"

"Fretful, wanting his father."

"Yes."

"You're going to have to cope with that, Michael. Listen, I've just told Daisy that Jean-Paul has been here. He arrived four...five days ago... the twenty-seventh."

The day of Hamish's tantrum. "Is he still around?"

"I don't think so. Said he had to get back to his mother. He was very angry."

"Did he mention me?"

"No, only that Daisy misunderstood some business that involved him, jumped to false conclusions as usual. He said she'd left without luggage or passport so I said then she must still be in France, probably close to home. He wasn't convinced, in fact I thought he was going to hit me. He scares me, Michael."

"We'll be home soon. I'll look after you and Daisy."

"That's one reason why I wanted to talk to you. I think it would be better if you didn't bring Daisy and Hamish here, not at first."

"Where do you expect them to go?"

"I'm sorting something out. A safe house."

"Meredith, we're not up against the KGB."

"Talk to Daisy about it."

The phone chose that moment to cut him off, or it may have been Meredith's doing. Michael turned to Daisy.

"I see Jean-Paul's been busy."

"Jean-Paul? Papa?" said Hamish, who was hanging on to Daisy's coat tails. Michael wished he hadn't mentioned the name.

"Yes darling, Papa." Daisy made a face at Michael.

"Why is he busy?"

"Because he has to look after Grandmère. But he sends you his love."

"Grandmère has whiskers," Hamish said. He wrinkled his nose. "And she smells funny."

Daisy almost broke into a smile.

Peter went off seeking what he called a decent drink and Daisy and Michael sat in the saloon with the heating on, for the Indian summer seemed to have come to an end.

"I think Pete's tired of our company," Daisy said.

"Can't be comfortable playing gooseberry."

"Not when you keep touching me and he wishes he could."

Michael undid buttons on Daisy's shirt. "Perhaps I should stop."

"You'd better not."

"Do this or not stop?"

"Not stop."

Daisy lifted her arms so Michael could slip the shirt off. He unhooked her bra, buried his face in her breasts. She moaned, "Oh baby, oh my baby" as he sucked on her nipples.

There was a noise, a tiny cough. Michael jerked his head away from Daisy. Hamish was in the saloon, rubbing his eyes.

"Mama, I couldn't sleep."

Daisy took him to back the forecabin. Michael heard her say, "Mama will make you a nice drink, darling." Then, from Hamish: "Are you feeling hot, Mama? Was Michael kissing you better?" Michael missed Daisy's mumbled response.

She was blushing as she returned to the saloon, a condition that ran down her neck and across her shoulders. She flashed Michael an unhappy glance, grabbed her shirt and, with her back towards him, struggled into it then set a kettle to boil on the hob in the galley.

"God, I wish we were home," she said after she'd delivered Hamish's drink and made sure the forecabin door was firmly shut.

"Home?"

"England."

"Meredith doesn't want us at her house."

"No, she thinks the police will whisk Hamish away."

"But his British passport's older than your marriage. I'm sure a British child can't be handed over to a French father. Not without a court's say so."

"And what if they ruled against me? Perhaps we should do as Mummy suggests and disappear."

"It's a pity. I'd like to meet Jean-Paul again."

"*Michael.* You promised."

"Not for ever I didn't. Anyway, how did he manage to drag himself from the bedside?"

"Apparently Berthe's taken a turn for the better. Or worse, depending on your point of view. From what Jean-Paul told Mummy, she's terrorising the physiotherapy department and demanding to see her grandson."

"But not you?"

"Hardly. She's often told me her son should have married a Frenchwoman. She hates the English... something to do with the war. However..." Daisy's face suddenly lightened, "talking about Frenchwomen, Mummy said a fat envelope arrived from Marlowe et Companie."

"Marlowe? I assumed you called your PI that for a laugh."

"Oh no, it's real enough. Don't know if he's a Philippe though."

"A fat envelope? If quality matches quantity you'll have Bohec by the balls."

"What if he has evidence of my infidelity?"

"He can only have Berthe's concoctions. You said you'd convinced him they were false."

"Oh, I convinced him all right. I'm being paranoid. But, and it's a big but, if he sees you with me or even alone at Mummy's he'll add one and one together and make us a pair."

An image of Bohec pumping himself into Daisy stole into Michael's head. Appalling in its vividness, it churned away inside him.

"Have you slept with him since we…?"

"*Of course.*" Daisy seemed surprised he'd asked. She peered at him. "Are you jealous?" A smile teased across her face. "You are, aren't you?"

"Maybe." Michael was red-faced now.

"It may be a cliché but it didn't mean anything, my darling. And, before you ask, he's nowhere near as good as you. But I think it best he doesn't discover our relationship." Daisy gripped Michael's hands. Her entire face seemed to frown. "You don't know what he's capable of. I said he has a mean streak, and it's really mean, believe me."

"I can get mean too. I've done awful things in my time, Daisy."

"I've no doubt you can protect us physically, Michael, but his isn't that sort of meanness. He prefers psychological torture."

"I'm not thick, Daisy, just not educated."

Her jaw fell. "Of course you're not thick, Michael. Do you really think I would have fallen in love with you if you were? What I meant was you are by nature open and honest, and that's one thing I love about you by the way. Jean-Paul is out-and-out Machiavellian, although he disguised it well enough for me to marry him. More fool me."

Michael exhaled hard, forced his breath through taut lips. "See? You say things like Machiavellian, talk about people like Larkin and I don't know what you mean. You're educated, Daisy."

Daisy hung her head. "I'm sorry. The words just come out. I can't help them." She seemed absorbed in thought then she snapped her head up, looked straight at Michael. "No, I won't measure what I say. What is education, Michael? I haven't been to university and doubt I'd be accepted by one. I have some lousy GCSEs and an unimpressive French Baccalaureat. I forget who said the greater part of our education is that which we give ourselves, but it's true. What I do is read, listen, consider. You do that too even if you won't admit it."

"A teacher told me I was gifted with wood, not words. It sort of stuck in my head."

"Bollocks, Michael. I mean about the words. I've seen you reading Jane Austen and Thomas Hardy for goodness sake, more than I can manage." Daisy gave a scarcely audible sigh, "If I ramble on about stuff you don't understand, just ask me, like you and I ask Peter about cringles and luffing. I won't bite." Daisy laughed. "Well, I might, but I promise you'd like it."

"So what about Machiavellian?"

"It's used to describe a devious, self-seeking slimeball. Machiavelli was an Italian who lived five hundred or so years ago. He wrote a book – there's a copy at Mummy's - I think it's called *The Prince* – in which he set out political principles based on self-interest rather than morality. I suppose you could call them unprinciples."

"Il Principe."

"What?"

"Il Principe. That's what The Prince would be in Italian."

"See, you know more than I do about that. So let's have no more talk about not being educated." Daisy put her hand out. "Truce?"

"Truce." Michael took her offered hand and kissed it.

Daisy gazed fondly at him. "You do the nicest things sometimes," she said.

She glanced at the forecabin door then reached out for Michael as the sound of boots clamping along the pontoon carried into the saloon. There was obviously more than one pair and they were accompanied by the discordant sound of two baritones attempting *The Wild Rover*. Moments later the footsteps separated and one set clambered into the cockpit. Voices called "Goodnight" then the hatch slid back and an expensive pair of sea boots began to descend the companionway steps. They missed the second one and tumbled to the bottom with their owner following close behind. Bottles of *Old Speckled Hen* were in his arms and during his efforts to save them one of his legs corkscrewed beneath him. Michael heard something crack.

"Thought you'd like some English beer for a change," Peter said from the floor. He stood the bottles upright one by one, grasped the companionway steps with both hands and pulled himself to a standing position, keeping the weight off the leg he'd fallen on. Then he tried to stand on both.

"Jesus Christ." Peter sank back to the floor, his face all twisted up. "I think the bugger's broken."

Michael and Daisy's mouths had been gaping throughout the episode, but now they clamped them shut, rushed to Peter's aid. As they got him onto his bunk, somebody rapped on the open hatch.

"Pete, old man, permission to come aboard?"

A fiftyish man, stocky, balding, with sailor's eyes set in a cherubic face, climbed down the steps.

"Oh, I thought Pete was alone."

His eyebrows shot skywards when he saw Peter, whose face was now permanently creased with pain.

"Crikey, old man, you're in a pickle."

Daisy sniggered. Michael counterfeited a coughing fit.

Their visitor, who'd had his back to them, turned and frowned. "He really ought to be looked at you know. The General's not far."

Daisy sniggered again. Their visitor looked perplexed.

"I'll see if I can borrow a wheelchair from A&E," he said. "Then I'll give you a hand to ship him there." He slapped Peter on the arm. "Chin up old man." He made for the companionway steps.

"Who the hell was that?" Michael said.

Daisy said, "Oh Peter, I'm sorry for laughing when you're in such pain, but he's straight from Bertie Wooster. I thought he meant his boss when he mentioned the General."

Peter managed half a grin. "He may well have done. Because he happens to be a retired colonel. His yacht's berthed on the other side of the pontoon. I met him in the pub."

Daisy found painkillers, got Michael to dampen a cloth then she fed Peter pills and soothed his brow.

"You'll make Mike jealous," Peter said. He tried to laugh but it came out more like a groan.

"Try to keep still." Daisy turned to Michael. "Go and see if there's any sign of Colonel Blimp."

The breath of autumn was strong in the night air as Michael stepped ashore. He wondered what fortune the season would bring. He admired its colours; the reds, russets and yellows but was always saddened when the leaves fell. He hated the aftermath, the dankness, the mouldy mush of rotting apples underfoot, the violent winds and lashing rain that made the countryside a quagmire. Not having all that was one good thing about living in Bethnal Green, he thought.

A figure passed a light at the far end of the pontoon and as it turned towards him he recognised it as Colonel Blimp. And he had a wheelchair.

Peter inched his bum up the companionway steps while Daisy held his hands from above and Michael stationed himself below to combat slippages. Peter then hopped under support to the guardrails, a section of which Michael had opened.

The three men, with Michael pushing Peter's wheelchair and the colonel marching in front as if leading a victory parade, proceeded (the colonel's word) to the General Hospital. Michael expected a long wait but it must have been a quiet night because, within two hours, Peter had been seen by a doctor, then by a radiographer. The x-ray confirmed that Peter had a broken ankle and he was introduced to a nurse who was an expert at plastering. His right leg became encased up to the knee. Colonel Blimp cadged some crutches and they reloaded Peter in the wheelchair.

"I'll bring it back in the morning," the colonel said.

Daisy and Michael manoeuvred Peter into his bunk. "I'm sorry, folks," he said. "Would you believe I only had three beers? Don't know what *Hirondelle's* owner's going to say. It's a good job he's a mate. Well, he is at the moment."

"I suppose we'll have to check flights," Michael said. "Although I'd rather take the chance of drowning."

"Is it really impossible for us to sail her?" Daisy said. "It seems a shame to have come this far then abandon ship. After all, you're not actually ill, Pete. You can still plot courses and do that stuff with the VHF and GPS. You can sit next to me while Michael pretends to be skipper."

Peter sucked his cheeks. "Hmm…" he said.

Michael reckoned Peter was thinking that being beside Daisy all day wasn't a bad fate at all. "It could work, Pete," he said. Daisy flashed him a giant smile.

Peter began nodding, slowly at first, then increasing speed. He stopped.

"All right, we'll do it."

Daisy went over to his bunk and kissed him. Peter's face and neck turned the red side of pink and Daisy winked at Michael.

Apart from a kiss goodnight, the wink was as close as he got towards resuming what Hamish interrupted earlier.

In the morning, Peter seemed greatly improved, whether from painkillers or Daisy's ministrations, Michael wasn't sure. He suspected a bit of the first and a lot of the last, but it meant Peter was alert and happy to give him lessons with tide tables, charts, and Breton plotters.

The first thing was to make a passage plan, Peter said. They'd be heading northeast through the Alderney Race, and the idea was to wait for a fair stream to carry them up from Jersey. Although he'd heard Peter saying things like this before, it was the first time that Michael actually appreciated why they couldn't simply set off when they felt like it.

"We have about an hour before the tide's in our favour," Peter said, "and it's best to negotiate the Race at slack water, two and a half to three hours after high water."

"Why is it called the Race? Is it like the Raz in Raz de Sein?" Daisy asked. "I remember you being worried about that."

"Not worried," said Peter, "just respectful. Yes, both mean a rapid tidal stream. The Alderney can run at up to eleven knots, a hefty tide for a small yacht like *Hirondelle* to cope with. Luckily, we've a moderate westerly today, but if you hit it the wrong way, wind against tide, the overfalls can lead to disaster."

"Overfalls?"

"Disturbed water caused by underwater obstacles."

Daisy nodded. "Will it be all right for Hamish to be on deck?" He was sitting beside her and became suddenly alert when his name was mentioned.

"I should think so."

Hamish jumped up. "I'll need my red suit, Mama." He was off before Daisy could respond and in a moment had returned with his oilskins.

Michael motored gingerly astern from the pontoon. *Hirondelle* was surrounded by floating gin palaces a mile high but only inches away. Lips pressed together, he managed to spin *Hirondelle* round as if on her own axis by using brief bursts of forward and reverse. There had been no sign of Colonel Blimp but at the last moment his rotund face and figure emerged on the deck of *Passing Clouds*, his large, very expensive-looking yacht. He waved. "Ahoy Hirondelle. Bon voyage, you chaps."

Daisy said she'd never been called a chap before.

Peter said. "Did you know he named his boat after his favourite cigarette? He was forced to give up smoking or lose a leg." He shook his head as if mourning the fact then dug around in the pockets of his startling yellow oilskins, came up with his pipe.

His tidal predictions were not wrong and they did carry a fair stream up to Alderney. It was running around four knots Peter said, although Daisy said it didn't seem fast to her. Peter pointed towards fishermen's buoys being dragged under the surface, the tide creating a considerable wash as it flowed over and around them.

"Ah, I see," Daisy said then added "Shit!" as the sea began to churn from all directions and *Hirondelle* bucked and yawed. The yacht tried to roll too but Michael controlled that with some fast mainsheet work. "Well done," Peter said then almost dropped his pipe as water surged over the foredeck and lifted the anchor as if it were balsa wood.

"Now that's what I call an overfall," he said, grinning almost as wide as the mainsail.

Daisy took Hamish below.

Following the plan they'd pencilled on the chart that morning, Michael kept *Hirondelle* heading northeast until they were clear of the Race then turned her for the approach to Braye harbour. Peter gave the order to lower sails and start the engine.

"There's the white beacon. See? On the pierhead." He pointed to something Michael could barely make out. "Keep that just open to the north of the church spire and we'll be well clear of the breakwater."

Michael's teeth were clamped together as he kept one eye on the compass, the other on the landmarks, his mind on both and the tiller too. He throttled back and finally aimed *Hirondelle* towards a mooring buoy. Daisy had already gone forward, boathook at the ready.

"You don't need me on deck at all," Peter said as they made *Hirondelle* fast. His face had a pinched look about it.

After Daisy settled Hamish down, Peter said, "I suggest it's good night for everyone. We need an early start to cross the Channel, so all hands on deck at o-four-thirty hours." He yawned widely, began to slide himself into his bunk.

Daisy tutted. "Don't be so lazy, Peter. You're not going to bed fully dressed." A gleam floated into Peter's eyes only to be dispelled as Daisy said she was going to wash up. Instead of Daisy, he found Michael helping him off and on with the clothes he couldn't manage by himself.

Daisy didn't turn around until Michael slotted Peter's leeboard into its place. She smiled then and said, "Good boy" as if praising a pet dog. Michael wasn't sure whether she meant him or Peter. He was trying to think of a witty response when Daisy took his hand and led him towards the forecabin.

"Hold me for a while," she whispered. "I'm scared but I don't know why."

In a stark change from her demeanour in the saloon, Daisy looked lost. Her eyes stared at Michael with all the innocence that the child lying in the portside berth possessed. She snuggled against Michael on her own narrow berth and within a few minutes was asleep.

All hands, barring Hamish, were on deck at the time Peter had decreed. Through the post-dawn dimness a large white yacht was visible, swinging on an adjacent mooring. Peter raised his binoculars.

"He didn't mention he was coming here."

He handed the binoculars to Michael, who read *Passing Clouds* on their neighbour's transom as the boat, like *Hirondelle*, swung round in the wind.

"I ought to thank him properly for the other night," Peter said, "but we need to get under way."

The morning was breaking to gloomy skies and the wind was a sickly north-by-northwest. Beating into it, they would take a week to cross the Channel, so they furled the headsail, motored under mainsail alone.

They'd been driving on for perhaps an hour when the VHF croaked into action. "Hirondelle, Hirondelle, this is Passing Clouds. I have you in my sights, old chap."

At the edge of their limited visibility was a smudge in the sea. The smudge gradually gained definition, a slip of white above a white wedge, then a tall triangle of sail over a ghost-pale hull. *Passing Clouds* was closing fast.

"He has far more horsepower than we do," said Peter.

And then, "Ahoy, Hirondelle," as *Passing Clouds* came alongside, ten yards off their starboard beam. Colonel Blimp waved from his cockpit, which was central in his boat. He was sitting back, almost lounging. Michael imagined him having a gin and tonic by his side, his feet resting on a burgundy leather pouffe.

Peter hopped on his crutches to the guardrail. "A thousand thanks for the other night," he called over the waves.

Michael was surprised at the volume Peter achieved. He supposed it was part of being a proper sailor, projecting oneself, as Daisy's relatives might do from horseback in the hunting fields. He wondered for the millionth time what he was doing, straying so far away from a carpenter's lot.

"Think nothing of it, old man," called the colonel in a voice Michael imagined reached the southern tip of Alderney. "Might need the favour returned." He gave what looked like a military salute, shouted something Daisy swore was "Tootle pip, old bean" then quickly left *Hirondelle* astern as he motored off.

There was a call of "Mama" from the saloon. Daisy went below. Peter watched her then said, "I wonder if he took the wheelchair back." He shook his head as if answering himself.

Michael listened to the voices below then there was silence and he knew Daisy had taken Hamish to be washed and dressed. Later came a clatter of dishes and cutlery. Finally Daisy reappeared, with Hamish dressed for seamen's work.

Peter said, "Right, now all crew are on deck, let's get down to business. We'll shortly reach the eastbound shipping lane. In theory, as we're coming from their starboard, ships should give way to us but I wouldn't count on it. It takes about forty-five minutes to cross a lane. We might see plenty of ships or none at all. It's a bit like waiting for a bus.

"Anyway, everyone needs to keep a look out. It's a pity *Hirondelle* has no radar but we'll have to live with that. The point is it's difficult to say where a ship you see in the distance is going to pass you. They'll be moving at a sight more knots than we are. So, Michael, if you, and you, Daisy, note bearings and times then I'll record them."

Michael went below for the hand compasses. He gave one to Daisy. Hamish's face began to crumple. "Isn't there one for me? I'm a crew, aren't I? Mama said."

"We only have two," Michael said, "but I'll tell you what, Hamish. You keep a jolly good look out for boats and when you see one, you can help me work the compass."

Hamish nodded, very business-like. "You'll need to show me how."

Michael didn't get the chance to show Hamish anything for a while, because almost as he opened his mouth to reply, *Hirondelle's* engine shuddered then slowed dramatically. He gave her frantic doses of reverse followed by forward but there was no improvement. *Hirondelle* would not move under power either way.

Peter pulled a face. "Propeller must be snagged. Damn it, haven't had this happen in twenty years. What sort of a skipper am I?"

"An excellent one. But you're suffering from your leg, Peter," Daisy said.

"A broken ankle's no excuse for being sloppy at sea. I should have kept a proper look out. Although rogue bits of rope are difficult to spot, floating just under the surface. They often have seaweed growing around them."

"We did go through a big patch of weed," said Michael.

"What do we do now?" Daisy said.

Peter rubbed his chin. "Three choices. One, try and sail. Two, radio for help. Three, go overboard, try to cut the rope free."

"Go overboard?" said Michael, looking at the waves. There was a short chop, nothing more.

"Don't even think about it, Michael," Daisy said. Her eyes were troubled and she was clinging to him as if he was about to dive straight into the water.

Chapter 6

"Daisy's right, Mike," Peter said. "If I were a hundred per cent I might risk it, but not as we are."

"What's involved?" Michael said and he felt Daisy pulling on his arm.

"You, and I don't mean you personally, would put on a wetsuit, facemask and ideally a helmet – too easy to bang your head down there – then with lines fixed to your harness and enough people to hold them you'd go overboard with a rope-cutting knife."

"Do we have the equipment?"

"Yes but -"

"You're not doing it, Michael," Daisy cut in.

"There isn't a safety helmet," said Peter.

"There's another alternative," Daisy said quietly. "We turn about and sail back to the Channel Islands. There might not be much of it, but the wind would be in our favour and in a safe harbour the problem could be dealt with."

"But it means another day at least," Michael said.

"A day in which you'd be alive and not drowned," Daisy snapped.

Hamish tried to put his arms around her. "Don't cry, Mama," he said, glaring at Michael. "Please don't cry."

There was a crackle from the VHF. "Hirondelle, Hirondelle, this is Passing Clouds. Come in, Pete, old man."

"Can you get it, Mike?" Peter said. "It'll take me all day."

"Wondered where you'd got to, old man," said the colonel. "Is there a problem?"

Michael explained.

"Coming to stand by, old man. What's your position?"

Michael looked wildly at the handheld GPS, the chart on the table, the log that hadn't been updated since that morning.

"Just a minute," he said, but Peter's head was already halfway down the companionway and he began relaying the readings from the cockpit instruments.

Michael, red-faced, gave the colonel their position. The message came back: "Okay, old man, I have you on radar. Don't move."

"Was he joking?" Daisy said. "Don't move – how much chance does he think we have of doing that?"

Passing Clouds manoeuvred alongside and the eyes and mouths of all three adults aboard *Hirondelle* opened wide at the same moment. At the wheel was an oilskinned figure with short, dark hair and a wholesome, warm-skinned look about her. Her face was as cherubic as the colonel's own.

The man himself was poised to board *Hirondelle*, which he did as soon as Peter had answered "Yes" to his "Permission to come aboard, sir?"

"If you fancy giving it a try," Peter said to Michael, "the odds are better now."

Daisy was aggressively mute. Michael could feel her resentment burning into him. No, not resentment, he could recognise fear easily enough; he'd spent half of his life afraid.

He squeezed into the wetsuit, slid the mask over his face and with Daisy and the colonel holding his safety lines, began to descend the boarding ladder.

Daisy refused to look at him and he wanted so much to say he'd changed his mind. But he took the deepest breath he had ever managed then descended into the English Channel.

He had expected to be immersed in a kind of foggy soup but, although it wasn't tap-water clear like he remembered the

Mediterranean, he could make out *Hirondelle's* rudder and, ahead, although dimmer, the outline of her fin keel. He didn't feel that cold either.

He began to work his way around the rudder. All the while, he was aware of Peter's warning about banging his head and he wondered what it was like to drown. He'd read somewhere that it was not unpleasant, although how anyone alive could know that was beyond his comprehension. He reached the end of the cast iron skeg behind the rudder and then saw them: wrist-thick tendrils snarled about the propeller. He opened the knife that was lanyarded to his wrist, sawed away at them.

Too soon, Michael's lungs began to protest. He concentrated on cutting the rope but his mind began to betray him too. An insidious voice said, *Let me flow in and your troubles will be over. Easy, easy, easy. Go on, on, on...* His eyes began to glaze and he was tempted. Oh, in those brief moments he was very tempted. If only it wasn't for Daisy.

Daisy! The thought of her sorrowful, grieving, snatched Michael from lethargy. He let the knife hang free. With Daisy fixed in his mind, his lungs close to surrender, he pulled himself back around the rudder and up to fresh air and the welcoming sight of the boarding ladder.

Daisy's complexion was like the grey snow Michael remembered from one hard winter in Bethnal Green. "Is it done?" she asked and seemed to turn even greyer when he shook his head.

"Just needed to catch my breath."

This time, Michael knew where he was going, although in his haste, he caught his head in an oblique blow. The collision shook rather than hurt him, made him saw at the offending rope with more vigour than he was capable of. But he refused to heed the whisperings in his head and when he had to come up for air, chose the shortest route, swimming to the side of the boat, pushing one arm against the hull as he went.

Conscious of Daisy's terrified face watching from the guardrails, Michael was determined to make his third dive the last he needed. Instead of gulping in air, he took calm, measured, breaths, filling his lungs from his stomach the way he'd learned from climbing hills on his bike.

After going under *Hirondelle's* side, straight for the propeller, he hacked off the final vestiges of rope, watched them drift away beyond the stern. With his lungs screaming that they had to breathe, he checked the propeller. It seemed undamaged and turned freely so he took himself back to the surface, side-stroked feebly to safety. Hands grabbed him as his fingers failed to grip the ladder.

"Did you have a nice swim?"

Hamish was watching Michael struggle out of the wetsuit. The boy cast coveting eyes over it, touched the neoprene with an exploratory finger.

"Yes, thank you, Hamish," Michael said, thankful to be temporarily free from the new expression on Daisy's face. It was one he hadn't witnessed before, something like hero-worship.

"I love you," she said suddenly. Michael switched his attention to her. He couldn't recall her saying those three simple words to him before, not so directly, and not with such a force of emotion.

She ran to him with a little cry. He kissed her face and hair, uttered every word of endearment in his vocabulary without considering which was which.

"Don't you ever," Daisy said. "Don't you ever pull such a stupid stunt as that again. Do you want to make me a widow before we're even married?"

Married? Michael hadn't even thought about that, hadn't dared to presume that was what Daisy might want from him. He'd supposed that after one failure each, and the example of their parents, they'd simply live together, unfettered. But of course, Daisy would want Hamish living within a stable, formal relationship. Michael saw that now, but at the same time began to imagine her relations, unknown apart from Meredith, muttering amongst themselves about their Daisy marrying beneath her. Except they would be too posh to call her their Daisy.

"Michael. Say something."

"You'd marry me?"

Daisy seemed bemused. Her brow wrinkled. "Why ever not? Unless you don't want me to."

Michael gazed down at her, at the sparkle in her eyes. "Oh, I want you to."

Hamish made a noise halfway between a cough and a sniffle. He was staring at them, his eyes tinged with what Michael read as fear. The boy turned to his mother, pressed himself against her, giving Michael an impression of ownership claimed and regained.

Above their heads, all had been quiet, as if Peter was allowing them space. Now, however, his voice carried down the companionway. "Colonel Roberts is about to leave." Moments later, they heard the diesel throb into life.

"Roberts?" said Daisy, exchanging frowns with Michael. "I much prefer Blimp."

Passing Clouds was coming alongside again, ably piloted by the dark-haired woman. Michael wished he could handle a boat even half as well.

"You haven't met my lady, have you?" The colonel beamed at each of them in turn. Michael wondered where she'd been on the night of Peter's binge. "Miranda, come and say hello."

They made *Passing Clouds* fast to *Hirondelle* and Miranda stood at the guardrails, shook hands with each member of *Hirondelle's* company. "I'm very pleased to meet you," she said. Michael was surprised to detect a note of somewhere not far removed from Bethnal Green in her voice.

"Miranda flew into St Helier the day you left," the colonel said. "That's why we were a bit behind you."

"I'm a lawyer." Miranda gave a slight grimace. "Ted and I were supposed to be having a romantic cruise before Passing Clouds comes out of the water but I had a case that ran on a bit."

Michael wondered about the compatibility of romantic and the colonel then chided himself for the thought. However eccentric the man might appear, he had been their guardian angel on two occasions now.

Daisy stood beside him. Michael could feel her mind working on something. He could see it in her face too.

"Divorce lawyer?" she said.

Miranda's face twisted into a lopsided smile. "I can be."

"I wonder could you act for me?"

Miranda frowned and looked from Daisy to Michael. "Of course, but..."

"I want to marry *him*."

"Ah, I see." Miranda's face brightened. She went into the cabin, returned minutes later, handed a card to Daisy. "My private number's on the back."

The colonel, Ted as they now knew him to be, came up to say his goodbyes.

Daisy hugged him. "You've been a real friend in need," she said.

The colonel almost glowed. "Stout girl," he said, and to Peter: "See you back in Blighty, old man. We'll keep in radio contact, just in case." He climbed over the guardrails into his own boat and he and Miranda cast off. They gave a last wave and once *Passing Clouds* was clear, Michael put *Hirondelle's* engine into forward gear.

"There goes one of the kindest gentlemen you could wish to meet," Daisy said. "I'm ashamed to think we laughed at him. Don't know about me being stout though. Does my bum look fat in these oilies?"

"Well..." Michael said.

Visibility improved to moderate and there was just one scare when, crossing a line of ships in the eastbound lane, several altered course to pass astern of *Hirondelle* but others didn't so they had to scoot between them. Michael was surprised how close together the ships were but even at *Hirondelle's* six knots it was easy to avoid them. Struggling under sail would be a different matter and for a moment he felt proud of his underwater achievement.

Passing Clouds was in their sights for most of the passage and the radio crackled several times as Colonel Ted kept contact. He was bound for the Hamble River but, on learning Peter was heading for Poole Harbour, he offered to radio his 'old chum' at one of the marinas to ensure they got a berth where Peter could be got ashore easily.

Hamish was keen to get started with the compasses and Peter rustled out a walkers' one he normally used ashore. It had a lanyard so it could be worn around the neck and when Peter said he could keep it, Hamish wriggled with pleasure. He put it on immediately and kept looking down to check it was there.

Watching Hamish, Michael recalled one of his own childhood incidents. His grandmother, his father's mother, had taken him on a trip to the zoo along with his Kentish cousins. She'd bought him a watch, only a pretend one, at one of the souvenir kiosks. For the rest of the day he flashed the coveted instrument to every passerby and checked the make-believe time just as Hamish was now checking the display on his new compass. There'd been a photo of him with his cousins, sitting high on a mechanical elephant. In it, he had the shirtsleeve on his watch arm rolled up to the elbow, his wrist turned to display the watch.

Tears occupied Michael's eyes as he regarded Hamish now. He couldn't say whether they were the product of nostalgia or empathy, but he *felt* for the boy. The difference was Hamish's new pride and joy was real, not a cheap throwaway.

Michael showed him how to align the compass needle. Hamish picked the routine up rapidly and was occupied for hours spotting ships or even seagulls and, in his own way, working out their position. He disregarded the fact that gulls moved constantly. Michael was careful to note down all Hamish's observations. The boy, deep in concentration, would correct him at times, insisting "No no, Michael, that number's wrong."

Because of their enforced stop, darkness fell long before they completed their crossing and Michael began to fret about berthing *Hirondelle* in the dark. His jaw tightened as a glow on the horizon metamorphosed at last into solid light.

"Anvil Point lighthouse," said Peter.

"About bloody time," Daisy said then began to cry.

The proximity of an English landfall seemed to invigorate Peter. His eyes brightened and the pain lining his face seemed to diminish. "I'll take the helm for the run in," he said.

Michael felt as if a great burden was lifted from him. He slipped an arm around Daisy's waist. She looked up, smiled through her tears, pulled his arm tighter against her. "Isn't it a wonderful sight?" she said. "All those lights welcoming us home."

They parted company with *Passing Clouds* as she turned towards the Solent. "Ahoy Hirondelle," the VHF said. "Home is the sailor at last, eh Pete old man? Don't forget to keep in touch."

Soon they picked up the Poole Fairway buoy. Although there were lights everywhere, on water and land, to Michael it felt as if they were traversing an inky corridor apart from the world outside.

Earlier, he had helped to work out a pilotage plan, with bearings and descriptions of the lights on the buoys they had to pass on their way into the harbour. Now, he saw the bearings he'd calculated actually *did* bring them to the buoy of their choice. He and Daisy ticked them off as Peter steered: red to port, green to starboard; No. 2, red flash every two seconds; Bar buoy, quick green; No. 10, red every four seconds; No. 9, green every five.

And then: "Oh, Michael, look!" Daisy was pointing at their wake, which was illuminated by phosphorescence. "I never thought I'd ever see it. It's spectacular."

Michael shivered. He thought it eerie, an escape from the world of ghosts.

They had to contend with two ships leaving the harbour so Peter kept inside the small boat channel beside the main Swash one. At the harbour entrance, a ferry with a flashing white light was crossing the channel. Behind it, on the starboard shore, was a bright rectangle of windows that Peter said was the Haven Hotel. "Could do with a berth there right now," he said.

Ahead were the flashing white lights of an east Cardinal buoy and to its right, those of a west Cardinal. "Think of the compass as a clock face," Peter said. "Three flashes for east. Nine for west." He steered *Hirondelle* between the two and, keeping a South Cardinal to port ("Six flashes plus one long"), took her into the reds and greens of the North Channel markers and on to the beacons of the marina and the comforts the colonel had arranged.

Michael and Daisy made *Hirondelle* fast and helped Peter to go below. Hamish was long asleep. Peter asked Michael to broach whisky from the ship's store.

"I've decided," he said. "That this is as far as Hirondelle goes."

Michael heard Daisy whisper, "Thank God."

That night, Michael dreamed he was swimming underwater amid tangles of seaweed-draped rope. Beyond them, Daisy beckoned him. She was naked but, instead of legs, had the silver fishtail of a mermaid. Her breasts were great eyes with areola irises and they transfixed him, luring him on towards the rope's source, which seemed to be her honey-brown, manicured mound of Venus. The rope unformed and reformed, made new barriers to Michael's progress as he lashed out with a knife that failed to slice a single strand. With each effort he became more feeble, his lungs begged for earth's sweet air and the blood rushed into his head until its pressure was so immense he knew his brain was about to burst.

He woke up, sweating, in his bunk. All was dark around him. For a moment he thought he was still beneath the waves.

When he realised he wasn't, he thought about the way the rope had moved in the water, a relentless uncoiling and recoiling. *Snaking*. It struck him that his subconscious was trying to warn him that the snake who had gained access to Daisy's womb, the snake who fathered her child, might be to whom she was ultimately, inevitably, in thrall.

But in the cold light of morning everything seemed less threatening. Michael relegated the tangles of rope to being a dream's habit of distorting actual experiences. He decided Jean-Paul was no more than another cuckolded husband.

A fresh southwesterly was blowing as Michael walked to the shower block. It was a wind they could have done with yesterday, he thought, as he breathed the ocean air it brought deep into his lungs. After breakfast, he booked a taxi while Peter arranged *Hirondelle's* short-term berthing.

When it was time to say goodbye to her, skipper and crew stood forlorn of face, their bags by their sides. Michael was thinking not of his acts to free the propeller but of Daisy saying 'I love you' in the way she did. He saw that she was gazing at him. Her eyes were misting too.

The taxi took them to Bournemouth, where Michael hired a car from one of the big chains.

"Straight home, I think," said Daisy. "Whatever Mummy says. Peter needs some TLC."

Peter looked for a moment as if he wished his loving care could come from Daisy but his face soon greyed and Michael knew that he had to get him away as soon as possible.

"Straight home it is," he said and waited for Hamish to say that home was in France, but the boy was unusually quiet, gripping Daisy's hand tightly.

Peter's wife turned out to be a chubby woman remarkably similar in looks to Miranda, Colonel Ted's wife.

"Right, let's have a look at you," she said in precise, bluestocking tones. Peter had telephoned her regularly of course but she seemed taken aback by the state of him as Michael helped him out of the car. "I'm calling the doctor," she added in a voice that sounded much less assured.

She took one arm and Michael the other, as they negotiated a maze of passages and settled Peter on a chaise-longue in a flowery sitting room. She stared as Daisy walked in. Then she recovered, blinking, offered everyone a drink. They learned that her name was Abigail.

"But do call me Abby," she said, as she disappeared to put the kettle on and phone Peter's doctor.

They stayed in a hotel that night, could only get single rooms. Daisy tapped on Michael's door as he wondered about tapping on hers.

"It's been ten nights," she said.

They squeezed into her bed. She held Michael against her, clasping him with her arms and legs, said that she loved him and said it again between breaths as their pace quickened. She cried it without words as she came.

Hamish stirred. "Papa?"

"Papa isn't here, darling."

"Then why were you crying?"

"I wasn't, darling."

"You *were*. Like you do with Papa."

"Oh, God," Daisy moaned.

Michael recalled Daisy admitting she'd kept having sex with Bohec. Now here was Hamish's testimony that she achieved orgasms with the man. Surely not with the boy in their room?

Daisy had switched the bedside light on and was searching Michael's eyes, ferreting deep. "Michael, don't go there."

"Can I come into your bed?" Hamish said.

"Of course, darling." To Michael she said, "I faked them."

He opened his mouth to respond then Daisy added, "But not with you."

Hamish climbed in between them. Daisy made a face at Michael. "It's only when he's feeling scared," she whispered.

Hamish was asleep again within a minute. Michael eased himself from the bed before he fell out of it. He kissed Daisy, said, "I'll see you in the morning."

For the rest of the night, Michael thought about orgasms. He wondered if any man had ever satisfied a woman.

Next morning, Daisy phoned her mother. Michael could hear Meredith's agitated state from where he sat.

"All right, Mummy, all *right*."

Daisy put her phone down suddenly. "He's been there again," she said in a subdued voice that said far more than the words.

"Give me your phone." Michael was thinking about what Meredith said when they phoned her from St Helier, that Jean-Paul scared her. "Where is he now?" he said to Meredith.

"I don't know," Meredith said, "but he won't be far away. He's staying at the village pub."

"I'll be there in an hour."

"No, Michael. Honestly, I'm all right."

"Look, I doubt he'll recognise me. He's seen me once, for less than a minute. I'm not letting him frighten you into telling him where Daisy is. In fact, it's best if she moves on right now. Did you ever do anything about that safe house?"

"You implied that it was a stupid idea, so I dropped it."

"Good, because it's best if you don't know where Daisy and Hamish are."

Michael handed Daisy her phone. She was regarding him as if she'd discovered a new dimension in him. She looked both impressed and amused.

"What?" he said.

"What are you going to do with us?" Daisy's voice and attitude were uncharacteristically submissive. Michael had the feeling she was toying with him.

"I'm taking you home," he said. "As soon as I decide where that is. You can wait at my workshop while I visit Meredith. No one will bother you there."

Michael let himself into Meredith's house but once inside, felt he ought to have knocked.

"God, I thought it was him again." Meredith stood back, appraising him. "You look disgustingly healthy, Michael. I've missed you." She emitted a little sob but something in her expression kept Michael from hugging her.

"So, about Jean-Paul? What's he been up to?"

"He's apparently searched all France, even pestered my sister in Grenoble. Daisy and Hamish *must* be in England, he said, maybe *someone*, meaning me of course, fixes things for them. He half-sneered in that way he has. No, of course you don't know it. Anyway, he said I knew where Daisy is and sooner or later, I'd *want* to tell him. I thought he was going to knock me down, search the house."

"Perhaps you should go away."

Meredith sniffed. "I'm not letting him drive me out of my home." Michael saw a glimpse of her old spark.

The rasp of tyres on gravel made them both start. When the doorbell rang, Meredith looked at Michael in the same way as when her bicycle suffered the puncture.

"I'll deal with him," he said.

There was no sign of recognition on Bohec's face. He seemed smaller than Michael remembered, carried a look of deflation too, as if a male protector for Meredith was a presence he hadn't allowed for.

"I am Mrs Lomond's son-in-law," he said, in clipped tones Michael suspected were borrowed from Daisy. "May I come in?"

"No." Michael watched him take a mental step back.

Jean-Paul's brow furrowed. "You don't understand. She will be expecting me."

"What I *understand* is that you've been harassing her."

"But I am looking for my son and wife." The accent wasn't so exact now.

Michael noted Hamish came first. "Get this into your head," he said. "Mrs Lomond does *not* know where her daughter is. Do you understand *that*? Now, piss off." Michael poked Jean-Paul in the chest. More than half of him hoped the man would retaliate.

Jean-Paul took a physical step back. "Tell her she'll regret this."

"You'll regret it more." Michael growled the words. Jean-Paul either could not or would not meet his eyes. He turned as if his heels were on pins, quick-marched to his car.

"I don't know if that was a wise thing to do. But thank you."

"Wise or not. I'm tired of pussyfooting around."

Meredith sighed and, to Michael, suddenly seemed much older than her fifty-five years. She assumed that faraway look, the one he'd extended into the fantasy of her in a Viking longboat. Right now, it made her look worn out.

He had a vexing thought. What if Bohec was even now asking at the *White Horse* about the young man at Mrs Lomond's? He was pretty sure the grapevine would have recorded that he was living there. He thought of Daisy and Hamish in his workshop, the fact that he'd said no one would bother them there.

He left Meredith gaping as he dashed across the gravel.

Chapter 7

Michael parked the hire car behind the barn so it was hidden from anyone arriving by road.

"Quick, into the loft," he said to Daisy, pointing to a door in the eastern bay. "Don't make even the slightest sound."

Daisy asked no questions. Grabbing Hamish's hand, she said, "Michael has found us somewhere new to explore."

Michael padlocked the door behind them. Almost as he did, a car drew up, a door slammed then he heard footsteps, tentative, as if their owner wondered if the proprietor might not be safely out of the way after all.

The footsteps turned decisive, crunched gravel, rang on the brick paving in front of the porch. Moments later one of the great doors creaked open.

Michael, hidden in the shadows, watched Jean-Paul finger machinery, gaze up at the great roof beams, scan the perimeters, finally settle on the door to the loft. Jean-Paul weighed its padlock in his hand then, presumably satisfied nobody could lock themselves in from the outside, released it.

Michael moved into the light.

"What is it with you, Bohec? Looking for something to steal?"

Jean-Paul's feet must have jumped six inches out of their shoes but his voice did not show it. "I am looking for what is mine. As you very well know."

"Why would *anything* of yours be here?"

"Because I know who you are."

Michael raised an eyebrow as lazily as he could.

"No doubt our friendly innkeeper's given you my life history as he sees it. In an English village, everybody knows everything about everyone else, especially the bits they have to invent."

Jean-Paul smirked. "Lady Muck's toy boy, they call you. They laughed about it."

Michael wanted to laugh too but kept his expression obscure. He performed a Gallic shrug, very much overdone.

Jean-Paul's eyes turned beady. "When they told me your name I realised we had met before. I remembered you booking one of my gîtes, although the address you gave was not here or my dear mother-in-law's. So, why should you come to Le Mazemeur if not to steal my son?"

"Because it was in the family, so to speak. I was in Brittany on business and Meredith said why didn't I give her daughter a look in, introduce myself." Michael waved vaguely at some part-finished pieces of work. "Some of my clients happen to live in Brittany. I lived there myself once." He crossed to his desk, picked up a wad of papers, shook it in Jean-Paul's face. "Check the orders if you don't believe me."

Jean-Paul's brow wrinkled. Michael slapped the papers down on the desk. "No, I won't have this," he said, through tightened lips. "What the fuck has my business got to do with you?"

Jean-Paul smiled as a snake might, if it could. "Maybe you were in Bretagne on business, Monsieur Cavanagh. But I think you came to Mazemeur as Meredith's agent provocateur, to spirit my Jacques to his aristocratic English family. And my dear, darling wife was in it up to her beautiful English neck."

He's right about one thing, Michael thought, and that's Daisy's neck. He recalled how it looked when she had her hair up, the little nape hairs running like golden silk over its delicate sculpture. He considered Jean-Paul's less appealing specimen.

He gathered up a selection of turned chair legs, put them in a cardboard box, made a show of taking it outside. Jean-Paul followed, nose down like a hound on the scent. Michael placed the box on the ground then closed and padlocked the barn doors.

"You have an over-vivid imagination, Bohec," he said.

"Have I? Then explain why my wife kept hopping in and out of your gîte the last day you were there."

"You mean the day you had me attacked?"

Jean-Paul looked like an actor who'd messed up his lines. It was as if he'd failed to connect the two events. "Don't tell me you were not hatching mischiefs." He gabbled the words.

"Mischiefs? It's a singular word. *Mischief.* See?"

Michael felt rather clever saying that, thought Daisy might be proud of him for it, but not for what he was about to do next. He spat words out like bullets, "She was there, you connard, because I'd sliced my fingers on your cheap glassware. Your wife, who obviously has far more concern for your guests than you do, hopped as you put it, to bring me sticking plaster and antiseptic."

Jean-Paul's lips had thinned at '*connard*'. Now he ranted at Michael in torrents of French. Michael recognised each term of abuse, allowed himself to resent them. He hit Jean-Paul, once, twice, hard and fast, releasing a fraction of the anger born inside him when he'd woken up in the rain at Lac Guerladan.

Jean-Paul swayed with the first blow, went down with the second. His eyes seemed opaque. Michael hadn't done anything like this since his wild and angry young-man days. *Then*, he might have kicked him into oblivion but this was now and the man's wife and son were only yards away. He knelt beside him instead.

Daisy had said that Bohec preferred psychological torture and hadn't believed that he was capable of it too. Well, she was wrong about that. Michael recalled a time in Rennes when he and a fellow sou-less vagrant, a graduate of the Sorbonne no less, tamed an unpleasant landlord by combining affable conversation with the suggestion of unrestricted violence. The main thing was to maximise the pressure. Michael hovered his face an inch from Jean-Paul's, spoke softly.

"Now, let's see. You had me attacked because I'd been sent by Meredith to steal your son? But think about it, Bohec, that *can't* be right. You didn't know I was her toy boy then. So, what was the *real* reason? Shall I guess? It was nothing to do with your son. You thought I was screwing your wife. When all that poor woman did wrong was stop me from bleeding."

Jean-Paul tried to wiggle himself upright. Michael pushed him down, hard.

"Don't," he said. "I haven't finished talking to you."

Jean-Paul regarded him with a lizard's stare but his hands were trembling.

"I spent time in hospital because of you," Michael said. "Meredith had to fly out to take me home. She had to nurse me, help me get fit again. Getting fit was important because I was determined to meet you again. Now you've saved me the trouble of finding you. Can you think of any reason why I shouldn't put you in hospital too? For six months, twelve months. *Permanently?*" Michael stroked his chin. "Now, what shall I use? A chainsaw perhaps? Hmm... does have appeal but not very subtle. Ha, I have it. Are you left-handed or right-handed?"

Jean-Paul's lizard look was replaced by blatant fear. "Right," he muttered.

Michael imagined Bohec was praying mentally to whichever Celtic saint protected him. He smiled his most beatific altar boy smile. "Then I shall run your right arm through my thicknessing planer," he said. "It's a French machine, so you should be compatible."

Much of Jean-Paul was trembling now. Michael wondered what Daisy had ever seen in this palpitating creature. He suddenly wanted nothing more than to be rid of it.

"Do you know," he said, standing up. "You're not worth the effort. Just get in your car and fuck off, Bohec. I suggest you look for your precious wife and child closer to home. And if you *ever* bother me or mine again, it won't be *one* arm you'll be missing."

Jean-Paul drove off, crunching the gears after almost stalling. Michael was grateful that the loft above his workshop had no windows.

Michael drove to Meredith's in his Transit van. Telling Daisy to stay in the back with Hamish, he dashed into the house.

"We're going out to lunch," he said to Meredith.

"I've had lunch already."

Meredith seemed brittle. Michael guessed she was huffy over his sudden desertion.

"We're going anyway."

"I'm not ready. I haven't anything to wear."

Michael sighed. "Meredith, you are never less than immaculate." He saw the glimmer of a smile curl the edges of her lips. "Daisy and Hamish are in my van."

"Why didn't you say that in the first place?"

Meredith grabbed a bag from a chair, studied her face briefly in the hall mirror then followed Michael out.

Mother hugged daughter and daughter hugged mother then grandmother hugged grandson. The latter hug wasn't returned. Michael thought he saw something glisten on Meredith's cheek.

He had no destination in mind. He drove north and east and eventually arrived at a roundabout where a road sign gave directions to the Norfolk Broads. He recalled the boat he'd worked on, his holiday there, that Peter mentioned a cottage.

That might be the perfect place for Daisy and Hamish, especially if it turned out to be accessible by water rather than road. He couldn't see Jean-Paul hiring a boat. He seemed a distinctly un-maritime creature.

Michael drove over Acle Bridge and turned off along the B-road towards Potter Heigham. He almost stopped there to check out the mooring beyond the old low bridge where he met the Californian girl all those years ago. Then he looked at Daisy, sitting beside him all sunny and golden, and felt safe. At the same time, he felt guilty about the girl, about making her cry. She'd been no harbinger of danger. She was just a girl. He wished he could tell her he was sorry.

"What are you thinking about?" Daisy said. "You've gone all strange."

"I was remembering sailing on the river here, years ago."

Daisy said nothing but she gave him one of her severe looks.

Meredith coughed. "I sailed here once. With Peter." Her face was suddenly radiant. "We shot the bridge and he couldn't get his mast up again."

Daisy burst into a rollercoaster of a laugh. It reverberated around the bare steel panels of the van.

"What did I say?" Meredith's face clouded then gradually cleared. "Daisy Lomond, I might have known. I can see what you get up to on boats."

"Mama gets sick on boats," Hamish said, wriggling on his seat. "She sticks her head down the potty and goes waaargh." He acted out the procedure with elaborate gestures.

Meredith told Hamish he was a very clever boy. He said she was a nicer grandmère than the other one. Her pleasure at this remark seemed to beam out and reflect itself from the windscreen.

They went to Hickling, stood at the edge of the Broad and watched sailing dinghies chase each other around the channel markers. Michael gazed over the fine expanse of water, at the tranquil reed beds flanking it, at the forest of masts in the sailing club just over the hedge behind them and in the dykes beyond the inn on the opposite staithe.

He smiled to himself and made his decision.

There'd been no sign of Bohec's car as they'd passed the village inn. Michael doubted the man would have the bottle to turn up at Meredith's. The light was fading quickly but nevertheless, Daisy kept her head down, snuggled Hamish against her.

At Meredith's, Michael kept the engine running. "Back as soon as I can," he said to her. "I'll take Daisy and Hamish to the hotel then there's someone I have to see."

"Why can't we stay here?" Daisy said. "You-know-who isn't likely to come. Even if you didn't totally convince him I'm not here, he hates being out alone in the dark."

Michael hummed and hawed then said, "All right. But make sure every curtain's drawn, and the outside doors locked. Call me if there's the slightest thing."

"Aye, aye, sir," said Daisy. "Who are you going to see?"

Michael couldn't see Daisy's face but guessed from her tone that, once again, she found his decisiveness amusing.

"A man about a safe house."

Michael turned the van's courtesy lights off then reminding everyone to keep silent, ushered Daisy and Hamish into the house. He waited until the door was shut behind them before switching the hall lights on.

The pleasure of having her daughter and grandson in her house seemed to increase Meredith's stature. Michael saw her resume her high-stepping walk. She looked as if she could fight a million Jean-Pauls. He felt all right about leaving her and Daisy on their own.

Abby answered Michael's knock. She frowned then her face broadened into welcome.

"Michael. Do come in. Peter's been talking a lot about you."

Peter was propped up on the same chaise longue as yesterday, a nearly full glass of malt whisky beside him. The dark green bottle, uncorked, lay close to hand.

"It will be a pleasure to let you use the cottage," he said, after Michael posed the question. "That all right with you, Abby?"

"Why not?" she said. "It's not as if we ever do."

"Meredith said she went sailing with you on the Broads."

Peter appeared to grit his teeth.

"I don't remember *that*. Perhaps it was when we lived in Surrey. Harry Lomond was a colleague of mine. Our families saw a lot of each other. Darling, d'you recall us ever sailing with the Lomonds on the Broads?"

Abby was staring out of the window. She did not respond. Peter shrugged at Michael.

"We used the cottage a great deal then. Doesn't have the same appeal now. A woman in the village there looks after it for us. I'll phone her tonight. I presume you want to move in a-s-a-p?"

Michael nodded. Abby turned around. Her expression was of someone who has had an old wound reopened.

"Mixing with the Lomonds always brought trouble," she said. "Peter, I think I might go out for a while. Do excuse me, Michael, won't you?"

"I'm sorry, Pete," Michael said after he heard the front door click shut.

Peter grimaced. "You weren't to know. And I think Abby only suspects." He pulled himself a little more upright, nodded towards a sideboard. "Get a glass for yourself."

As Michael measured out his drink, Peter said, "Meredith and I had an affair, oh, eleven or twelve years ago. I remember meeting Daisy, only once I think. She would have been away at school most of the time. She was a scared looking fifteen or sixteen, rather scrawny as I recall. Daisy *now* though, reminds me very much of Meredith *then*. You're a lucky man, Mike. Although Merry must have been in her early forties you'd never have guessed it. She looked ten, fifteen years younger. She was a woman to die for." He stared, misty-eyed, at Michael.

Michael's mind was in turmoil. Eleven, twelve years ago was when Daisy was sent to France. Did this affair have something to do with that? He looked at Peter, who was biting his lip as if anticipating disapproval.

"Meredith can still twist you round her little finger, Pete. And me too. Me too." Michael grinned and Peter relaxed, sinking back into his cushions.

As he left with the cottage keys in his pocket, Michael said, "Don't tell Meredith where Daisy is."

Michael was thinking about Peter's confession as he pulled up beside Flora, who was now custodian of mauve wands of autumn crocus. He decided Peter couldn't have known what the consequences of adultery with Meredith, or Merry, would be.

Meredith opened the door. Michael put on a broad smile, walked into the light.

"Anything to report?" he said. Meredith shook her head. She closed the door, double-checked to make sure it was shut. "Daisy's in the parlour," she said then disappeared in the direction of the kitchen. "I'll get supper," she called back.

Daisy was sitting by a crackling wood fire. Michael glanced momentarily at the thick, green velvet curtains then looked around the room for Hamish.

"He's already in bed," Daisy said. "And don't worry, we've made sure every curtain's drawn, just as you said." She smiled as Michael took Peter's keys from his pocket and jangled them before her face. "Are they for the safe house? Where is it? Quick, before Mummy comes back."

"You'll find out when I take you there."

Daisy pouted. "Would you tell me if I begged?" She came so close Michael could feel her pores seducing his.

"Not even then." Michael saw that look again: amusement mixed with something indefinable. His face flushed. "Do you find it funny, Daisy, me making decisions about our future?"

She seemed taken aback. Her jaw slackened. "No, Michael. Please don't think that. I smile because I'm pleased, not amused. It's admiration I feel. And pleasure too. Is it wrong for me to be pleased with what you're doing? That's a positive thing, surely?"

Michael could see only honesty in Daisy's eyes now. "I'm sorry," he said. "I've had too many years not deciding. The last time I thought on my feet was when I lived on the streets."

"What about when you married? You must have decided that."

"That was Grace, not me. Seemed easier to go along with it. Pathetic, I know, but I needed stability. As I saw it, I didn't have a choice."

Daisy nodded. "I know about not having choices."

After supper, Daisy opened the envelope from *Marlowe et Companie*.

Meredith said, "Do you want me to go?"

Daisy shook her head. "No, stay. You should see what your son-in-law gets up to while his wife sweats away at hearth and home."

Michael almost laughed but Daisy's expression was serious. She slid the envelope's contents onto the dining table. There were photographs, colour and monochrome, a diary with places, dates, times, even the type of weather.

"Probably charges extra for working in the rain," Michael said. Daisy glared at him. Her eyes glinted as she studied each photograph, her jaw set in a tight little knot.

"Tart," she hissed at the girl in the pictures. Michael thought the girl looked rather nice, clothed or unclothed. She had dark elfin eyes, broad cheekbones, neat brown hair just curling over her nape. She wore very smart, probably designer, clothes when dressed. He'd expected to see, if not a beard, at least the traces of a moustache but there was not a hint of either. Naked, she was no more hairy than Daisy, less in fact with that short hair. She had a trim, tanned figure with a neat derrière and pert little breasts that he wouldn't have minded...

"Stop it, Michael."

"Stop what?"

"Drooling."

Daisy's lips looked sewn together. Michael felt himself squirm.

"I wasn't."

"Pfff." That came from Meredith.

"What is it with you men?" Daisy said. "Show you a pair of tits and you go terminally silly." She shook her head, carried on sifting the evidence. There was plenty of that, both from the compromising positions Jean-Paul and what's-her-name had got into and from the written itinerary of their escapades.

Michael wondered if collecting the evidence had turned Marlowe on. The girl, who Marlowe identified as Adèle Serazin, a bank clerk, certainly turned Jean-Paul on, but there was another look in his eyes, evident in several of the photographs.

Daisy had noticed it too.

"He used to look at me like that," she said at last. Her eyes welled up and her teeth harrowed her bottom lip. "Christ, why am I crying about it?" She stared at Michael as if she expected him to know.

"Because your pride's been hurt." He hoped that was all.

"She doesn't shave her armpits," Meredith said, shaking her head. "Typical of French women."

Daisy sniffed, gave her mother a wan smile, slipped Marlowe's evidence back into its envelope. She turned to Michael. "You told me Jean-Paul thinks you're Mummy's toy boy but you haven't said why."

Michael grinned, leaned back, clasped his hands behind his head.

"Oh, they gave him the full story at the pub. The terrible scandal of the village carpenter and the posh lady from the big house."

Daisy's eyebrows rose. "No doubt with juicy embellishments," she said, laughing. "You'll never be able to hold your head up in church again, Mummy." Meredith turned very red and Daisy pointed at her. "Look in the mirror, Mummy. You really *are* a scarlet woman." Then she said to Michael: "And he didn't recognise you at all?"

"No. But the thing is, they told him my name and he remembered that from the gîte."

Daisy gasped. "So why does he think you went to Le Mazemeur?"

"To steal Hamish with your connivance. He called me Meredith's agent provocateur."

"Ha. So how did you persuade him we weren't here? How did you get him to leave?"

Michael's eyes flickered. He cleared his throat.

"I hit him."

"What?" Daisy shouted the word and Meredith croaked it out.

"He said things I didn't like, so I hit him."

"Oh, you bloody fool, Michael," Daisy said, rolling her eyes upward. "You've made it personal now."

"Do you think having me attacked wasn't personal, because it certainly felt so to me. He should be thinking he's got off lightly. Look, I said I didn't know you before I came to Mazemeur, that Meredith told me to look you up, introduce myself. The wags in the pub will have convinced him far more than I could have done. He *doesn't* connect *you* with me."

Daisy's face was like Flora's granite one now but her eyes seemed too cold for stone.

"I should never have left France," she screamed. "I wish I'd never let you bring me here. I wish I'd stayed at home with my fucking husband."

Chapter 8

"I won't let you go angry into the night," Meredith said. "She'll see sense in the morning. You must have learned by now how volatile she can be."

Michael recalled Daisy's temper during the sea storm, but tonight she'd looked as if she hated him. Perhaps she did love Bohec after all she'd said to the contrary. If so, he was surely lost.

He spent the loneliest night he could remember, reliving each moment he'd spent with Daisy, analysing whys, wherefores, nuances of each gesture, each glance, each remark. On balance, he concluded, as the dull grey of an overcast dawn filtered through his curtains, she probably *did* love him. Probably. He'd stay and see what the day brought out.

Daisy was silent over breakfast, though she ate well enough. Even Hamish seemed to have caught her mood. Meredith spoke only of nothing that mattered. Michael didn't feel hungry at all. For the third or fourth time since he'd met Daisy he craved a cigarette. He considered going out for some but knew if he did so that he would not return.

"What do we do now?" he said to Daisy. "Book your tickets to France? Or are you coming to see the place I've found you?"

Daisy wouldn't look at him but said, almost inaudibly, "See the place you've found us."

Hamish, whose ears had pricked up at the mention of France, started to say something but Daisy shushed him.

Their journey was as voiceless as breakfast. Michael drove as if helming *Hirondelle* through the shoals off the Breton coast.

Peter's cottage lay in a remote area at the end of a gravelled track that twisted between overgrown Portuguese laurels before straightening to cross a lawn dotted with alder scrub. Brick walls a shade too red supported an upper storey clad in cedar. The roof was thatched with Norfolk reed.

Daisy, still silent, held Hamish's hand, waited patiently as Michael unlocked the house door. She followed him in, staring about without comment. There was a hint of mustiness inside.

Daisy picked the smallest bedroom for Hamish, opened its windows, placed her bag in the landing outside. The two remaining bedrooms each contained a double bed. Michael chose one occupying a strategic corner overlooking drive and river. The latter was twenty yards behind the house across a patch of grass. At the river's edge was a small staithe.

Daisy appeared at the door. "Is it all right if we explore outside?" She waited for Michael's nod. He counted her words: eight. The most she'd said to him all day.

He watched them from his back window. Hamish picked up a stick and prodded things with it, tried to force it into the ground. Daisy walked to the staithe, testing the boards of its quayheading before allowing Hamish on. She stared at the river, which looked placid enough. Michael doubted that tides had much influence this far from the sea. A motor cruiser chugged past, fat, squat, long. Hamish waved at the driver, who gave a cheery wave in return. Daisy smiled.

Michael saw her disappear into a low cedar building next to the staithe. A few moments later she came running out, pulling Hamish along beside her.

"Michael," she shouted from the foot of the stairs. "Come and see." Her face was brimming with excitement. Michael hurried downstairs. Daisy was halfway towards the cedar building but waited for him to catch up.

"Look," she said, pointing into the building's dark interior.

Michael looked. He saw a yellow-hulled sailing cruiser with a grubby white superstructure. He could just about read its name, *Foxy Lady*, painted on the transom. Daisy, eyes alight, turned to him.

"Don't you see, Michael, it's the yellow sailboat from Treguelven. It's an omen, a good omen. It means everything's going to be all right."

She rose on tiptoe, kissed him. Michael marvelled at how quickly Daisy could turn from gloom to sunshine. Yet it troubled him how she often saw fantasy as reality, as if somewhere inside her head dwelt a little girl who had never had the chance to be just that.

The boat was less than twenty feet long. It had its mast and boom up, mainsheet attached, but no sails. An outboard engine was clamped to the stern. Michael tried several keys among the bunch Peter had given him and found one that fitted all the padlocks on the boat. He unlocked the hatch, slid out the washboards and stepped into the cabin. The air was stale and there were traces of mildew on the furnishings, which consisted of long cushions along the hull sides. The interior was open-plan and, apart from a few plywood shelves and lockers, uncompromising fibreglass. Only Hamish was able to stand upright, which gave him a rather smug expression for a while. Daisy retrieved a sailbag that lay beneath a glazed hatch in the forward section and discovered lockers beneath the seat squabs. In one, she found a plastic container with a seat and lid.

"Is this what I think it is?" she said, screwing her face up.

"Yes, it's called a bucket-and-chuck-it."

"Chuck it? Anyone expecting me to perch on that can do the other."

"Fuck it?" said Michael without thinking.

Behind them, Hamish began chanting, "Fuckitbuckitchuckit."

Daisy told him, "Stop that at once," but couldn't quite suppress the giggle in her voice.

"Is it something rude, Mama?" Hamish said. Daisy couldn't reply.

Michael found a light switch by the boatshed door. A bulb hanging from the ridge beam illuminated the building, dimly at first but brightening as it warmed up. A collection of boating stuff huddled in a corner: paddles, boathooks, deck swab, several buckets and a long pole Michael remembered was called a quant.

Daisy said, shyly: "May we sail this afternoon?"

Michael nodded.

As soon as they got back indoors, Daisy moved her bag into Michael's room.

Michael bought petrol. He wasn't prepared to take the boat out without an engine to fall back on. He'd already found two-stroke oil and a fuel tank and line in a cockpit locker.

Foxy Lady's decks were given a swab then Hamish stood in her cockpit and pretended he was the captain. He'd insisted on wearing his oilskins although Daisy and Michael had just taken fleece jackets.

"Ready about," Hamish said. "Helm's to lee." Then, as he frowned and puffed, pushing at the tiller, he said, "Mama, it won't go."

They walked *Foxy Lady* out of her shed and round to the staithe, to get enough space and light to bend the sails on. The sailbag contained main, genoa, jib, and a gigantic red, blue, green, and yellow affair Michael said was probably a spinnaker but he wasn't sure. Daisy found jibsheets in a cockpit locker. Michael mixed fresh fuel, connected the line to the outboard then primed the carburettor. On the second pull, the engine coughed and, on the third, started.

"I never expected it to be that easy," he said. Daisy squeezed his hand. She said she'd known it would be.

The forestay had a furling mechanism like *Hirondelle's*, though much smaller and more basic. They hoisted the jibsail, furled it, cleated the line then slid the mainsail's foot along a groove in the boom before working its head into a similar groove on the mast. They flaked the excess over the boom, secured it with bungees.

"Right, Daisy, cast off."

Michael flicked the engine into forward and *Foxy Lady* puttered upriver. Within a few miles the river opened onto a large, open stretch of water on which a few other craft, one a sailing boat with red sails and two masts, were enjoying themselves.

"I guess this is a broad," Daisy said, "like at Hickling yesterday."

Michael nodded. "Must be Barton. Pete said that was the nearest."

He motored to a clear area, turned the boat head to wind to hoist the mainsail then Daisy put the anchor overboard. She'd found it in its home near the bows but it was nothing like those on *Hirondelle*. This was a solid bell of iron. Michael said it was called a mudweight and proper anchors were taboo on the Broads.

With the main up and jib unfurled, *Foxy Lady* found the wind almost by herself and they set off on a reach that took them right to the very end of the broad.

"Ready about," Michael called then swung the tiller to the boom. *Foxy Lady* turned as if on a pin and picked up the wind again immediately. She steamed, if a sailboat could be said to steam, back along the length of the broad.

They spent the rest of the afternoon sailing up, down, across it, heeling *Foxy Lady* well over when they felt like it, just for the thrill.

The light began fading fast. Daisy checked her watch. "Do you realise," she said, displaying a huge grin. "That we've been sailing for almost four hours? Even Hamish has forgotten teatime."

They went to bed early. As they finally snuggled down to sleep Michael began to believe Daisy's prediction of that afternoon. He repeated it to himself, mouthing, as he thought, silent words: *Everything's going to be all right.*

Daisy answered drowsily, "Of course it is."

Michael didn't know whether he'd spoken aloud or whether Daisy just knew what he was thinking. Soon he heard the gentle ripple of her breathing as she lay asleep, her mouth opening and closing rhythmically with each exhalation.

He was tempted to believe her fantasy about Treguelven. He imagined himself helming *Foxy Lady* there, virtually drifting on an almost still day; he saw Daisy lying on the sun-kissed beach, Hamish and the fourteen-year-old girl playing around bald, skin-scorching rocks. His eyes focused on the girl: a gangly, eager-eyed creature, with her mother's auburn hair and his own ready grin. But at times, perhaps when a stray cloud veiled the sun, he noticed a sadness stealing over her, almost as if she didn't know it was there. He decided that he *had* to see her again. Soon.

But first there were practical things to do. Meredith had been looking after his mail during his absence and, that morning, mentioned a letter from the bank. Then there was... *What?* He couldn't remember. Probably didn't matter anyway. Time to sleep.

Around four in the morning, dead man's hour as he was accustomed to think of it, Michael found himself outstaring cobwebs on the ceiling. As his eyes followed their tracery, he remembered that the item he'd forgotten mattered very much indeed. It was the business of getting Daisy divorced. It was what he wanted. Wasn't it?

Do you, Michael, take this woman? That and all the rest of it. For better for worse, for richer for poorer, in sickness and in health, keeping only unto her until death do us part. He knew there was more but those were the bits he recalled even if some were wrong. And he'd promised those things to Grace, and Daisy had done the same to Jean-Paul, although probably in French. And those whom God has joined together let no man put asunder. For poorer not richer, not better but worse. Not until death does you part but for ever and ever and fucking ever. And thereto I plight thee my troth.

Long before six, Michael could stand this rambling cocktail no longer. He rose as softly and noiselessly as he could, eliciting no more than a faint groan and stretch of limbs from Daisy. Sliding into his clothes as he went, he tiptoed downstairs and out of the house.

The air was dank. Damp-heavy leaves drooped from tree branches that seemed to groan with their unwanted burden. Inside the boathouse, condensation glistened beneath the roof panels, spattered onto *Foxy Lady's* superstructure. Michael walked past the boat onto the staithe. He sat on a gnarled willow stump, gazed at the water slowly drifting by. The tide, for what it was, seemed to be on the ebb.

He was still there when Daisy came out. She was wearing an unseasonable dress he was certain he'd last seen on Meredith. She must have picked up some of her mother's clothes before they left. The dress was a little slack on her but still made her look as fresh and appealing as the flower that its pale-yellow colour reminded him of - a paeony he knew as *Molly the Witch*. Meredith would know the Latin name for he'd seen it growing in her garden - a wispy, beautiful heart-render whose bloom was over almost as soon as it had begun.

"What are you smiling about? Mummy's dress?" Daisy twirled the skirts. "Not too bad on me, I think."

"It's beautiful. But perhaps not warm enough for autumn."

"Well, I feel summery, not autumny." Daisy hunched up next to Michael on his tree stump. "Do you realise," she said, purring her words, "this is our first home together. It's like a rehearsal for when we're a real family."

Michael's eyes widened. "I suppose it is," he said, nodding slowly.

"Having second thoughts?"

"No, of course not."

"You were restless all night, talking to yourself."

"Did I make any sense?" Michael forced his breathing to a reasonable pace.

Daisy shook her head. "Not really. You were muttering about having forgotten something then came out with what sounded like bits of the Church of England marriage service."

"Oh." Michael could feel his face heating.

"You don't have to be scared of marrying me yet." Daisy was grinning. "The divorce will take a while."

"It wasn't about marrying you. It was about me marrying Grace, you marrying Jean-Paul and..." Michael bit his lip, stayed silent.

Daisy stood up. "Michael," she said, picking up a pebble and skimming it across the water. "I think you should tell me what you're *really* afraid of."

Michael still said nothing. Daisy trawled his eyes with a diligence that began to feel like invasion to him.

He turned away from her. She picked up another pebble, drew her arm back as if to skim it. But she let the stone drop to the ground. Michael gazed into the river. He could pick out Daisy's image clearly in the calm waters. He watched her reflected eyes lock on to his.

"Daisy," he said. "Do you think it is really possible for a woman to rape a man?"

Daisy drew in her breath. "It's possible," she said slowly. "Particularly where the victim is young and the woman has dominance... let's say a teacher over her pupil. There have been enough of them convicted for it."

"But to have *sex* he'd have to have an erection. Surely that proves desire on his part?"

"It doesn't mean it isn't rape. Violence isn't a prerequisite. As for the erection – I recall you telling me people often turn to sex in times of stress."

"Yes, but I didn't mean..."

"It could be applied to rape? Think about it, Michael. The desire, the erection, is an involuntary response. Product of an increased heart rate plus the adrenalin and testosterone our bodies churn out in response to stress. It's well documented that rape victims may become sexually aroused during the experience, women as well as men. That, of course, increases the shame and self-blame they feel.

"What we call sexual desire is a subliminal sequence of chemical and electrical processes ordered by the body to reproduce itself. Think of all those hormones dashing about, receiving, delivering, carrying messages, instructions, all with one purpose, to perpetuate the DNA. They don't care about *us*. DNA isn't even *alive*, for goodness' sake. So, your victim has an erection. So what."

A grebe chose that moment to convert their liquid images from still life to shimmering activity. Michael waited for the water to settle. Daisy's speech had sounded very authoritative, as if she'd taken time to research the subject in depth. He thought about subliminal processes. Like Trojan horses, playing the innocent, tricking you into surrender. He closed his eyes, saw the black pubic hair poor Laura May's reminded him of.

"Your question was about you and your mother, wasn't it?"

Michael waited a long time before replying, rubbed a finger slowly back and forth across his lips. They, and his mouth, felt desiccated.

"On my sixteenth birthday," he said at last. "She came into my room, said I was old enough now. She was drunk, but not that drunk. And I... I...didn't know how to stop it happening."

"Did you tell Grace? Was that why she walked out?"

"Yes."

"I wouldn't do that. Walk out on you. Not for that."

"Grace said I was a pervert. And the thing is..." Michael grimaced, took his gaze away from Daisy-in-the-water, redirected it to the whispering reeds on the opposite bank, "...the thing is, she was right."

"Why do you think that?"

"Because once it... started, it was the only thing I wanted. Like my willpower was lost in some sort of fog. She purred encouragement, eyes half-closed, dreamy, smiling. After I... after it was over, her expression changed. She spat into my face. Only then did it dawn on me what I'd done. I even went to confession, something I hadn't done in years. The priest had a fit, said I was in mortal sin. And my member, as he called it, was a vile serpent. I haven't been inside a church since, not even to get married."

"Priests!" Daisy virtually spat the word. "Celibate fools. What do they know of *real* life? It *was* rape, Michael. Be certain of that. Jesus, at that age, your emotions, never mind your hormones, would be all over the place. Ninety-nine-point-nine percent of *you* wouldn't have understood what was happening but I'm sure your mother knew exactly what *she* was doing, drunk or not." Daisy's breathing became laboured. "Well, you're not alone."

Michael stopped gazing at the reeds, concentrated on Daisy's real face. She looked as if she were seeing ghosts, or rather one in particular.

"Harry?" he said.

Daisy nodded and her eyes bore a burden that denied what she'd just said to him about guilt.

"Do you know what the worst thing was? Mummy didn't want to know, denied it was possible. But she packed me off to France all the same." Daisy was silent for a while and her breathing gradually calmed. Then she said, "How many times did it happen to you?"

"I left home before there could be a second time."

"You were lucky." Daisy closed her eyes, kept them shut for so long Michael thought they were going to stay that way. "My father came from a long line of despots," she said presently. "He was brought up to expect privilege, didn't see boundaries as applying to him. It was a time when Mummy was being ... incompliant, so he used me instead. Before, he'd scarcely given me a moment of his time. I was simply one of his possessions, an easy chair to slop into or the ewe-lamb he might kill for supper."

Michael was struck by the last metaphor. He saw Daisy, her arm pulled along by Harry's as he dragged her towards the sacrificial bed. He wore a black cloak, like a silver screen Dracula. She was dressed in virginal white and her hair was pale as the ghostly moon he could see framing it through a tall window. He screwed his eyes up.

"Yet you for*gave* him." He wished he could hide the reproach in his voice.

Daisy glared at him. "What makes you say that?"

"That first day we met and he was so unpleasant, you cradled him against you. Meredith looked horrified and I felt I was trespassing inside a closed triangle. Then after the funeral, in your car, you wept for him in a way I doubt you would ever weep for me."

"On the day I ran out on you, you mean? *Christ, Michael.* So the fact that I felt and displayed emotion means I forgave him?" Daisy's mouth was half open in a sneer. "You know what I think? I think you're jealous because Daddy got there first."

Daisy turned her back on him. He went halfway to touching her shoulder but she suddenly twisted round and faced him again. Tears shrouded her eyes.

"You might also recall I told him I wished he'd die. If you think I forgave him, Michael, you would be very, very wrong. Some crimes..." Daisy stopped speaking, shook her head, released a drawn-out sigh. "Look, we're both on edge. It's not easy re-opening wounds like ours. I'm glad you've told me what happened to you and I'm so *relieved* you now have some idea why I'm like I am. I knew there was *something* about you that I recognised in me. That's why I said we were a pair. I didn't realise how much of one we really are. We're damaged goods, Michael, but that's our strength together. We *understand.* But let's leave our ghosts and live for now. *Please.* It may be all we have."

"Mama, *mama!*"

Daisy jumped up from the willow stump as if she'd been stung. "Oh, my God, I'd forgotten Hamish. He must have woken up and wondered where he is." She ran to the house, shouting, "Mama's coming darling, Mama's coming."

Michael thought how close he'd come to disaster. *Again.* It may be all we have, Daisy had said, and that concept struck him hard. It struck his lachrymal glands too, so that for more than ten minutes he had to sit there on the stump, gazing at the water. He was thankful that Daisy was probably too busy with Hamish to notice him sobbing.

Meredith handed Michael the letter from his bank. "I didn't mean to pry. I thought it was business mail." Her voice softened into a whisper. "How are you managing for money?"

"I'm fine," Michael said.

"Well, I'm not happy with you paying for everything where Daisy is concerned. She ought to pay her way. Trouble is she never thinks of things like that."

As Michael had suspected, the letter was on the lines of *we would prefer it if you banked with us rather than the other way round.* When Meredith mentioned it he hadn't been surprised. He hadn't earned anything for some while and things like maintenance payments to Grace and rent for the workshop had kept going out. Then there was his credit card, which had borne the bulk of his recent expenses.

He screwed the letter up. "I guess I need to go back to working for my living."

"But I need you to be with *me*," Daisy said. "We can live on my conscience money." Meredith frowned and Daisy added: "Michael knows, Mummy."

"Knows what?" Meredith said. Michael detected a tremor in her voice.

"About darling Daddy using me as a spare vagina."

Blotches of high colour mottled Meredith's face and neck. Hamish, who had been studying the three adults in turn, stared at her.

"What's a va-gi-na, Mama?" he said.

Michael watched Daisy fight for a response. Her eyes darted all ways then suddenly her face cleared. She smiled gently at Hamish. "It's a little piano."

"A toy one? That I could play?"

Meredith lost her dappled look. Her mouth twitched. Michael felt a burst of goodwill towards Hamish. The boy seemed to have an uncanny instinct for knowing when to lighten the atmosphere the adults around him created.

"Perhaps when you're older," Daisy said.

Meredith allowed herself a chuckle. "You're a wonderful boy, Hamish," she said and went over to a bookcase. She returned with a fat book, flicked through pages. "Here's a picture of one. Mama didn't have the name *quite* right. It's actually called a virginal."

"Vir-gin-al," said Hamish, running a finger over the illustration. Daisy mouthed a thank-you at her mother.

Michael wondered what conscience money was. "I don't want charity," he said.

"Call it a loan if you must," Daisy said.

"But it wouldn't be, would it?"

Daisy shrugged. "Why should it matter? When you marry me you'll get the warts and all."

Meredith coughed and said while they were arguing she could at least save Michael some expense. She knew he'd refused before but why didn't he transfer his workshop to her barn. "If you're reneging on carpentry it doesn't make sense to pay rent. And if you're undecided it might as well stay here while you make up your mind." She told him she'd recovered some debts that were owed him. She took the cheques from a bureau. Michael looked at the amounts written on them.

"I let *that* much slip away?"

"You need an office manager. That could be me. Daisy can be tea-girl."

Daisy snorted: "I think you'll find I have more useful talents than that."

She looked at her watch and said they ought to be getting Michael's van from his workshop before it got too dark to walk there. They'd arrived at Meredith's by train and taxi after Michael had returned the hire car to the company's Norwich depot.

Meredith said, "Why don't you leave the van and take the car instead?"

"What car?" Daisy said.

"Harry's of course."

Mother and daughter stared at each other. Daisy was thin-lipped but then relaxed and nodded.

"It's in the garage behind the barn," Meredith said to Michael. "It'd make sense if you two used it rather than let it deteriorate."

Michael wondered why Meredith didn't just sell it but then realised people like her didn't do that with possessions. They either passed them on to the servants or held on to them for generations, until they finally fell to bits. He was surprised when the car turned out to be a modern Peugeot turbo-diesel, sleek and efficient, if a little commonplace. He'd expected old and stately: a nineteen-fifties Daimler perhaps. He wondered how he'd feel, riding in Harry's car.

"He never got to drive it even once," Daisy said as Michael slipped into the Peugeot beside her. Then she said, "You're being old-fashioned. We *ought* to use my conscience money. Daddy left me rather a lot of it."

Michael decided he didn't want to know how much but Daisy told him anyway.

Michael caught his breath. "Jesus." His savings amounted to about four thousand and that had taken him years to accumulate. Now here was

Daisy with a hand-me-down fortune. It worried him. "Does Jean-Paul know?"

"I forgot to mention it."

"I wish you hadn't told me. It complicates things."

"I don't see it makes the slightest difference to *us*. I didn't want the bloody money but Daddy apparently developed a guilty conscience after he became ill. It seems he altered his will to leave me his money and Mummy the house. Luckily, she was provided for by her parents." Daisy paused, studied Michael's face. "Oh come on, Michael. I'm the girl you slept with last night, the girl you went to France for, not knowing if she had a penny to her name. The money's nothing. It wasn't Daddy's anyway. He stole it."

Michael swallowed. "Stole it?"

"He and Peter were co-directors of a property company. An insurance company financed the developments but Mummy said a fair amount of that cash went straight into Daddy's pocket. Then, wonder of wonders, a microsecond before the property market crashed Daddy sold his shares to the insurance company at peak value. Peter was left high and dry with his valueless. *And* he'd borrowed on the strength of them." Daisy pulled a face. "So there you are, it's not *old* money. Daddy stole it from ordinary people who had taken out life policies. Does that make you feel better?"

"Not about the policyholders, but yes about the money."

Michael recalled the village rumours about the Lomonds, the murmurings of an unidentified scandal. He wondered who'd spread them. Abby perhaps? He remembered her saying that mixing with the Lomonds had always brought trouble. He'd thought she was hinting at Peter's affair with Meredith but now he reckoned she was referring to financial troubles, which Harry could have prevented by including Peter in his share deal. Was excluding him Harry's way of taking revenge for Peter screwing Meredith? Still, with a nice house, the Broads cottage and a fifty thousand pound yacht, Peter didn't meet his definition of *poor*. Perhaps, unlike for Mr Micawber, something had turned up.

Chapter 9

Grace's bank wouldn't release her address but Michael knew theirs. He checked the telephone directory for that area. There she was: *Grace Cavendish-Cavanagh*, still using the combination of her surname and his she once took so much pleasure in. "We almost rhyme," she'd said when they first met, her eyes lit like a happy child's. She was thirty-five at the time.

Michael, fighting to keep the tremor out of his voice, still couldn't help smiling when Grace said "*Michael?*" before he'd had time to identify himself. Although hesitant, she agreed he could visit them. "Come for tea."

Grace had always liked teatime. Michael had often wondered if her setting out dainty china on top of frilly doilies was the continuation of some childhood fantasy, a commemoration of tea parties she perhaps used to hold with her dolls.

He travelled to see Grace on the day of Daisy's first appointment with Miranda. Daisy had been unable to get through to Miranda's private number and, according to her office, Miranda was unobtainable. By the time Daisy was able to contact her they'd been at the Broads cottage for over six weeks.

During that time, Michael moved his workshop into Meredith's barn and, as a rebellion against Daisy's conscience money, took on limited commissions, charging what he thought were absurdly high prices but which his clients accepted without argument. Meredith had displayed yet another talent and painted a sign to hang above the barn door: *Michael Cavanagh, Carpenter by Default.*

It was meant as a joke but customers seemed to relish the idea of a reluctant carpenter creating their desires only as a personal favour. Treating it as a hobby enabled Michael to enjoy his work, and regard the money it brought in as incidental.

He began to see himself as a family man. He was reminded of his early days with Grace, how even the most basic household chore was fun when you were new to the game and freshly in love. And Hamish was an almost perfect child. The phrase 'good as gold' sprang to Michael's mind; it was a term he'd often heard when he was a boy, though never about himself.

On the days he worked, Daisy and Hamish would usually join him, the boy sitting for hours at the computer in the office Meredith had made at the front of her barn. She'd found a new life there, managing *her* customers (they were never Michael's) and maintaining meticulous records. Occasionally, she'd take a turn on the lathe and some of her work was so good Michael suggested she put it up for sale. She'd smile shyly and say, "Really?" with a glow of pleasure that seemed out of sorts with the sophistication she showed when negotiating financial matters. She'd place it on the craft stall at the next church fête.

Miranda had suggested Daisy should come alone to their initial meeting. Michael was glad of that. He felt superstitious about taking an active part in the proceedings to relieve another man of his wife. On the day, Daisy was skittish, over-emotional. Michael put it down to nerves. He kissed her outside Miranda's office then took a taxi to Waterloo, caught a train to his past.

Grace looked *old.* Blown and dowdy. Only fifty, compared with Meredith's fifty-five, she could be taken for sixty at least. Michael recalled her at thirty-five, pale thighs smooth and soft to his touch beneath white lacy petticoats and gossamer stockings. Now her legs were bare, shaped like thick puddings, mottled from lolling too close to the fireside.

"This is your father."

"My dad? You mean my *real* dad?"

Anne was almost exactly as Michael imagined: tall, slim, an attractive face that sat well with his mouth and the bright Irish eyes she'd inherited from his father. Her auburn hair had darkened though, wasn't as long as in his dream. She'd lost her freckles too. She looked from her mother to him and back again. Her expression said she only half-believed Grace's statement.

"Michael's much younger than I am."

"I can see *that.*"

Anne's lips began to twitch. She shielded her face with a hand, bolted from the room. Michael heard a tiny noise, a gulp, a sob and the sound of the girl's feet hammering on the stairs.

"She'll calm down," Grace said. She looked Michael up and down. "Well, you look as if life's treating you kindly." She laughed joylessly. "No, don't try to say the same about me."

"Do you still think I'm a pervert?"

Grace looked surprised. "That still cuts you? No, Michael, I don't think that. I've seen enough of life over the last ten years to know I shouldn't jump to conclusions. If you really want to know what upset me, it was the idea that you were using me as a replacement for your mother. After all, we were virtually the same age, she and I."

"She died. And I didn't see you in that way."

"I know. I read it in the paper. I know the other thing too. I'm sorry about both." Grace reached for a packet of cigarettes, Marlboros, took one out, offered the packet to Michael.

"No thanks, I haven't smoked in years."

Michael looked about the room, noticing it for the first time. Faded cotton upholstery in flowery fabric, worn away to holes on chair arms. Carpet an unfortunate shade of green, sporadic stains from unknown liquids. Sideboard, veneer scratched, surface littered with curios: Toby jugs, Goss ware, tinted glass, and an old German clock he remembered buying for Grace at a street market in Banbury. It was issued by a Munich bank and you had to feed pfennigs into a slot to make it work. When it was full, you were supposed to get the bank to open it and deposit the money in your account. Michael was surprised Grace had kept it. Perhaps it satisfied her yen for frugality.

There was a noise on the stairs then Anne reappeared in the doorway. "Hello," she said, as if he'd only just arrived.

They went for a walk in the park, Anne and he. When he tried to take her hand she shook him away. They passed a boating lake on which small boys and some large ones as old as or older than Michael, were playing with remote-controlled motor cruisers.

"This will do," Anne said, pointing towards a seat overlooking a bowls green on which ancient men were measuring distances from ebony woods to the jack. She flopped herself down, patted the seat beside her.

"Well, this is nice," said Michael, putting on a smile he knew looked forced.

"Why has it taken you so long to come and see me?" Anne's face was screwed up as if she was avoiding the sun, but the day was overcast.

"I didn't know where you were."

"You didn't look, did you?"

Michael shook his head. His eyes were welling. He looked desperately at the old men on the bowling green, who were casting bowls as if they had not a care in the world.

"So why now?"

He risked a glance at Anne. She didn't look angry, only curious. He decided to tell her the truth. She nodded slowly from time to time as he did and it seemed that a sort of serenity came over her.

"I'd like to meet Daisy and Hamish," she said at the end.

Anne told him little of her life, apart from the fact that she liked school and hoped to go to university. Of her personal interests, Michael learned nothing and was afraid to push her too far. She did mention several 'uncles' over the years, wrinkling her nose as she spoke. Anger briefly surged inside Michael as he considered the possibility that one or more might have interfered with her but then he thought, no, Grace would have had an eagle eye out for anything like that. All the same, he wished he had been there for Anne.

"We'd better go back," Anne said after that. "Mum's bound to have our tea ready." She grimaced and they both laughed. Behind them, two old bowlers prodded each other in the chest as they argued over whose wood was the winner. On the way back through the park, Anne let him hold her hand.

"Are you going to be a proper dad? I don't mean living with Mum or anything. Just come and see me sometimes."

A shadow seemed to flit across her eyes as she said 'sometimes' and Michael wanted to hug her and tell her he was sorry for everything and he wouldn't let her down again and…

"I'll be a proper dad," he said. "If you'll help me to learn how." Anne seemed satisfied with that and her eyes began to shine again.

After they'd endured Grace's ritual of afternoon tea, Anne saw Michael to the door. He kissed her cheek and she returned it. "Bye, Dad," she said. "Don't leave it long until next time." She smiled as he left, a gloriously unaffected smile that warmed him all the way back to Daisy.

But Daisy was in tears when Michael met her.

"Oh, Michael." She burrowed into his arms. At first he thought Miranda must have said there was no hope of a divorce but Daisy said, "It's Colonel Ted." She stared, white-faced, red-eyed, at him. "He's in a hospice. That really was their last voyage in *Passing Clouds* and they both knew it and still kept on being bloody cheerful."

Michael stared back as the facts hit him then Daisy's face began to crumple again.

They talked about Ted on the train. They had to let Peter know, Daisy said and maybe they could visit Ted at the hospice, although Miranda had said he didn't want any visitors, didn't want them to see him as he was now, gone helter-skelter downhill in a matter of weeks. It wasn't his lungs, she said in answer to a query from Michael, but his stomach, riddled with it, inoperable.

Michael tried to ask about the divorce but Daisy kept succumbing to tears. He caught people looking at them, saw them hide their embarrassment behind newspapers or magazines. One or two looked as if they were judging him, finding him guilty of making a lady cry.

Daisy had all but cried herself out when they reached their station. "I'm sorry," she said as Michael retrieved the car. "How did you get on with your daughter?"

"Much better than I expected. I think we can build a good relationship."

"Just in time for her awkward years." Daisy allowed herself a wry smile.

"She wants to meet you. And Hamish too."

"Really?"

"Really."

Daisy broke into the first genuine smile Michael had seen from her that day. He smiled back, took his eyes off the road for moments too long. Daisy screamed at him to stop. They had reached a level crossing and the lights were flashing, the barrier down. Michael had to almost stand on the brake pedal. They sat there shaking while the train thundered past. Daisy began to laugh but Michael couldn't see anything to laugh about.

"Your face," Daisy said. "You should have seen your face just then."

She began to cry again.

Someone hooted.

"Miranda wants me to start the divorce proceedings in France."

They were back at the cottage, having collected Hamish on the way. Daisy was calmer, had even become philosophical about Colonel Ted. "He probably had a damn good life for the most part. That's more than many people can claim."

Michael agreed. Then Daisy had wanted to know all about his meeting Anne and did Anne mean it about wanting to meet her and Hamish. The boy had become excited at the prospect although he didn't seem to understand about the age gap. He'd gone to bed happy anyway, so Michael supposed that was all that mattered.

"In France?" he said now.

Daisy pouted. "Even though I'm British born and bred, to qualify for a divorce in my *own* country Miranda says I have to have been living here again for at least six months. In France, I can initiate proceedings right away. Miranda is concerned that I get in first. Jean-Paul has already had two months start."

"Except he doesn't know where you are. Surely he can't proceed without notifying you?"

"He doesn't have grounds except desertion and that has to be for more than two years."

"You'll need a French lawyer. Will Miranda arrange that?"

"She'll handle it all herself. Her firm has offices in Paris. When we first met her she'd been conducting a case in Rennes. She speaks fluent French."

"What about Hamish? Can Jean-Paul sue for custody, claim you've abducted him?"

Daisy shook her head. "No, or at least not yet. But apparently I'll have to come to some accommodation with him and that pisses me off. Miranda says I have to show the arrangements for Hamish are satisfactory, or the best that can be arranged in the circumstances. The court will only make a residence order if I show them why it's impossible for us to agree."

"What about Hamish's British passport?"

Daisy shrugged. She was pensive for a few moments then said "There's one thing, but I don't think I could do it. Remember I said Hamish might not be Jean-Paul's? Well, he isn't named as the father on Hamish's birth certificate."

"Who is?"

"Harry Lomond."

"What?" Michael felt nausea rise from his stomach, clutch at his throat. "Does Bohec know… about him?"

"Christ, *NO*." Daisy looked horrified. "You're the only one, apart from Mummy. Michael, it was just a name I put down because I couldn't think of anything else. No other reason. Except perhaps it made it look as if I was Madame Lomond and not Mademoiselle."

"You could have chosen a better one."

"Do you think I haven't regretted it? Have you any idea what state of mind a woman can be in just after she's given birth?"

"A little. Grace wanted to kill me."

Amusement flitted across Daisy's face. "She had good grounds. Anyway, what I'm leading up to is Miranda's suggestion that if necessary, I claim Hamish isn't Jean-Paul's child. She asked if I'd be willing to go as far as obtaining proof."

"DNA?"

Daisy nodded.

"Even if you did, would Bohec agree to take the tests?"

"I think not, if he stood a chance of losing." Daisy touched Michael's arm. "There's just one other thing," she said softly.

There was something in the tone of Daisy's voice that caused Michael's spine to tingle, in the way it still often did when she walked into a room. "What other thing?" he said, trying to make his voice as soft as hers.

"I think I might be pregnant."

Chapter 10

My own child with Daisy. The concept, almost too heady to contemplate, sang through Michael's mind like an ode to joy, quiet in its opening phase but rising to a glorious crescendo.

Daisy seemed on the verge of crying again yet her face was radiant. "I'm two weeks late and I'm always boringly regular." Tears dampened her cheeks but she laughed through them. "Now you'll have to marry me, Michael."

Michael was thinking he should have guessed. The week they moved into the cottage Daisy was crabby and he hadn't had the sense to realise why. He counted back mentally - she *was* regular – even the boat hadn't upset her cycle although there'd been times when he'd wondered.

"What are you thinking?" Daisy had one eyebrow raised. "Why I wasn't on the pill? I ran out on *Hirondelle* and sort of forgot."

"I'm wondering if it's safe to open the champagne."

"Are you pleased then?"

"*Pleased?* I'm ecstatic. I'm filled with... God, I don't know what...love, wonder, joy, gratitude, joy. I've said that already, haven't I? Oh, and a little fear too."

Daisy's tears had given up. Her skin seemed to have an overlaying bloom, a rosy glow that exuded health. She *looks* pregnant, Michael decided.

Daisy treated him to a mischievous smile. "You know what they say, don't you?"

"Who says? About what?"

"Old wives, I suppose. And about here, this place." She waved an arm vaguely. Michael's eyes followed it, saw Peter's old furniture, odd pieces he'd probably bought in auction rooms around the county. "They say 'new house, new baby'".

They decided not to tell Hamish. "Not as things are," Daisy said.

Michael understood. Better not to include *this* in the details that were bound to emerge if reaching an 'accommodation' meant Hamish spending time with his father. If Bohec *was* his father.

The more Michael thought about that, the less likely it seemed. The boy looked even more Nordic than Daisy. He didn't want to guess how many candidates there might be because Daisy *now* was his Daisy, not Daisy *then*. She'd said they'd have hated each other and maybe she was right.

Meredith seemed in bloom too. Michael wouldn't have been surprised if she had morning sickness. Although Daisy was seldom sick in the mornings, it was usually the afternoon, and that not often. Meredith, overflowing with proprietorship, insisted that Daisy see her private doctor immediately. She sulked when Daisy said she'd rather wait to see if she missed a second period.

The period didn't come. Daisy relented. Meredith's doctor confirmed what Daisy already knew and gave her an ultrasound scan.

"I saw our baby," she said. "*Our* baby." Her face held such a fusion of serenity and wonder Michael felt he'd missed out on a miracle. He was determined that next time, he would go to the movies too.

Jean-Paul requested a meeting. As Daisy showed Michael the letter from Miranda, unquiet snatched at him.

"I don't think it's a good idea, you meeting him."

"Do you think *I'm* looking forward to it?"

Daisy's tone was sharp and her eyes flashed but she continued in a gentler voice: "I really don't have a choice. I have to at least *try* to reach an agreement about Hamish." She touched Michael's cheek. "Sweetheart, I said it wouldn't be easy."

"Yes. But I have a bad feeling about this. Let me come with you."

"*No!*"

The word came like a pistol shot, ricocheted off Michael's feelings. He was aware of flinching. Once again Daisy softened. "It's not that I wouldn't feel better with you there, because I would. But we have to maintain your toyboy image, make him believe it's all about his infidelity."

"He's bound to find out about us as soon as he sees Hamish."

"Even so," Daisy said and Michael knew she wasn't going to change her mind.

"At least let me come to London with you."

Daisy hummed and hawed then said, "All right. But while Miranda and I deal with my husband you can go and tell that daughter of yours she's going to have a baby brother or sister."

Michael grimaced inside at Daisy's reminder, intended or not, that Bohec was her husband, but he lightened at the thought of Anne's expression as he told her the good news.

"Okay, I'll do it your way," he said then a tiny ribbon of anger wound around his tongue. "But I don't trust the bastard."

"Technically, my son is a bastard."

"You know what I meant."

"Actually, Jean-Paul might be a technical bastard too." An impish smile crossed Daisy's face. "Remember me saying Berthe detests the English, something to do with the war? The official reason is that an Englishman caused the Germans to execute her father. An RAF pilot was shot down over Mazemeur and Berthe's mother, Mathilde, a saint of a woman apparently, hid him in the barn where Berthe now imprisons rabbits. When the Germans found out, her poor husband Bernard paid the price."

"Wouldn't it be more logical for Berthe to hate the Germans?"

"Her logic is often illogical."

"Official reason, you said."

Daisy's eyes flowed with mischief. "There was a story I heard from the mother of one of the geriatrics Berthe employs. She *swore* Berthe was fathered by the RAF pilot and the martyred Bernard was in fact her mother's brother. She said the pilot escaped to England. Never returned to claim his prize."

Michael nodded slowly. "Now *that* makes more sense."

"She also said 'As was the mother, so is the daughter', peering at me with a half sly, half innocent expression. Then she said 'Look for Bernard in the churchyard'. I've looked. There's only one gravestone with the right dates and it says Bernard was executed by the Germans in nineteen forty-three. His wife is mentioned too. She died the following year. Her name was Marie, not Mathilde."

"So Bohec is Berthe's *maiden* name?"

"Exactly. And I think the old crone was telling me that Berthe, like her mother, never married. Now, Jean-Paul likes to boast Mazemeur has been in his *father's* family for fifteen generations. So unless I'm wrong and Berthe married whichever Bohec inherited on Bernard's death, JP's talking rubbish. When I asked him about his father he just said he died young. I've thought of searching the records but always chickened out. In France you must prove you're a descendant although I'm sure there are ways around that."

"Couldn't you ask the old woman?"

"Not in this world. And the rest of the inhabitants are as close-tongued a bunch as you'll find anywhere, apart from young Marie at the bungalow, who rather fancies you, I believe."

"I only saw her for a few minutes. Never gave her cause to..."

Daisy's mouth was open in a broad grin. She pointed at Michael.

"Caught you. But I'd bet you'd like her to... She's very pretty."

Michael foraged in his humour bank for a suitable response but Daisy let him off the hook. "It really shouldn't matter about Jean-Paul's parentage. After all, who am I to cast the first stone? But he's so fucking *proud* of his heritage, one reason he's so keen for Hamish to be there to carry it on."

Michael drew some pleasure from the fact that, like his own, Jean-Paul's background might be little to be proud about. It gave the man a comforting vulnerability.

First there was a meeting with Miranda that had nothing to do with Jean-Paul. Colonel Ted finally agreed to a visit, but only from Peter. He didn't want that 'lovely young couple' to be distressed, so in a sense Michael and Daisy were along just for the ride. However, Miranda said Ted would love to see them and if they were actually there then he could hardly refuse. If they could stand it, Ted surely could. Their mood was sombre driving down to Peter's but his gigantic welcoming grin soon dispelled that. He said he was getting about famously on his sticks but still had another four weeks in plaster. He was going to have a bloody monster of a party to celebrate.

Abby seemed much brighter than on Michael's last visit and when Daisy announced they were expecting their first child together, she kissed them both, Daisy on her cheeks and Michael full on the lips. He wondered what he had done to deserve it. Perhaps in some perverse way she was thanking him for getting Daisy safely pregnant.

Miranda and Ted lived near Biddenden. Michael felt in familiar territory as they drove into the leafy Kent countryside. Biddenden was only a few miles from where his cousins had lived. He wondered if they were still there, if they would recognise the scraggy urchin who used to darken their holidays. Three or four years older than him, they were the daughters of his father's sister Maureen: Nancy the tomboy with red hair and freckles, Maeve, dark and pretty, with the same Irish eyes his own daughter had. He'd been a little in love with Maeve.

They drove along a narrow lane, through a five-barred gate almost relieved of its hinges, and followed a curving drive beside a plantation of young Christmas trees. They emerged onto honey-coloured gravel set between open lawns, broad swards so lusciously green they seemed painted. The house was chocolate-box pretty in carved oak, dark with age and with latticed casements whose tiny panes, Michael discovered once inside the house, bore the signatures of their makers and the seventeenth-century dates of that signing.

They had telephoned ahead. Miranda was waiting for them. Her smile was ready and generous; indeed, to Michael her face seemed made for smiling but he could detect the careworn edges. "Come in," she said, "come in," after embracing each of them in turn. She led them into a long room that had a great refectory table at its centre. Michael found himself mentally pricing the oak that had gone into its making.

They expressed their shock, their sorrow, that although they had known him but a very short time, Colonel Ted had made an indelible impact on their lives.

"He's so genuinely kind," said Michael. "Generous in the ways that really matter."

Tears glistened in the corners of Miranda's eyes. "He is that."

"We laughed at him at first," Daisy said, shame-faced.

Miranda smiled fondly. "He plays the silly old buffer well. A little act of self-effacement he feels the need to display. But I soon saw the man behind the mask and married him before he saw through me."

"Now *you're* being self-effacing," said Peter. "And I'm sure it's entirely without cause."

Miranda laughed and once again Michael was struck by her resemblance to Peter's wife. The only marked dissimilarity was in their accents. He made a mental note to ask Miranda about Bethnal Green.

The hospice was in a white-rendered single-storey building set amongst mature trees and shrubs. There was an air of tranquillity that belied the nature of what was going on within. The nurses had the kind of smiles Michael had seen on pictures of angels and for a moment he wanted to turn and flee. He clutched Daisy's hand tighter, saw she was feeling apprehensive too. Peter plodded on resolutely, brow set forward, crutches striking the floor decisively. Miranda looked serene, her real thoughts a blank.

They stayed outside Ted's room when Peter and Miranda went in. Through the open door they heard Ted's voice, feeble now, reedy, where once it was sonorous.

"Looks like it's me in a pickle now, old man. But crikey, you're gadding about like a twenty-year-old."

Daisy's eyes were near flowing and Michael wondered if coming here was a good idea. It seemed inappropriate to juxtapose impending birth with impending death. He'd more or less decided not to go in when he heard Ted ask about "those intrepid young mariners, Mike and the lovely Daisy" and before he could object, Miranda was ushering them in.

Michael was shocked at how much bulk a human body could lose in two months. But when Ted's face broke into an expression of pure delight and that thin, dry voice said, "Oh, you wonderful people" he knew it was right to come. Daisy had no inhibitions. She rushed up to Ted, flung her arms about him and kissed him. Her move emboldened Michael to hug Ted, although he was worried if the strength of his grip might injure him.

They spoke for a while about *Passing Clouds*. "That's one regret," Ted said. "That Miranda and I will never sail in her again." His eyes looked wistful then and Miranda touched his brow but otherwise he remained resolutely cheerful, as if he was only in for a holiday. Michael wanted Ted to be angry about death, to scream at it, to punch it into surrender. He wanted to implore him not to go gentle into that dark goodnight, like Dylan Thomas said in a poem he'd read in one of Meredith's books. Then he remembered how close he came to letting himself drown underneath *Hirondelle,* and understood why Ted felt able to accept the inevitable so calmly.

Ted began to tire and Miranda made signs they should go but before they did she said Michael and Daisy had an announcement to make.

"If it's a boy," Daisy said at the end, after exchanging nods with Michael, "with your permission, we'd like to name him Ted."

Ted's face seemed to glow beneath its pallor and his voice regained a few decibels of its former power. "Oh my dear girl. And my dear boy. I'd be most honoured if you did."

"That was a lovely gesture," Miranda said when they were outside.

"We decided on the way down," Daisy said.

"It will mean such a lot to Ted," Miranda said. "He's taken a genuine liking to you and Michael and Peter. I know it's on very short acquaintance but I think it's because he met you all on *Passing Clouds'* last voyage. You were the last people to know him and his ship in their prime." Her composure was lost at last. She buried her face into her sleeve, snuffling into the cloth. Michael passed her his handkerchief.

He'd expected some conversation about Daisy's divorce but it was evident that Miranda kept professional matters professional. Nothing was said about it, even by Daisy. He did, however, mention Bethnal Green during the meal Miranda insisted on giving them before they headed for the Dartford Tunnel.

"I lived just behind Cambridge Heath Station," Miranda said. She fixed Michael with what he supposed was a lawyer's look. "Hmm, Michael Cavanagh of Darley Road. Any relation to Patrick or Paddy Cavanagh of that ilk?"

"My father's name was Paddy." Michael wasn't sure what ilk meant except it was something Scottish. He'd heard Daisy refer to her grandfather as Lomond of that Ilk.

"The Paddy Cavanagh I'm thinking of ran away with my mother in nineteen-seventy-seven. After the Silver Jubilee party."

"Jesus!" Michael did a rapid recalculation of Miranda's age. "It's a small world."

Daisy looked on, slack-jawed, her face expressing disbelief. Peter looked as if he was pretending not to hear. He examined his fingernails.

"I was sixteen," Miranda said as if she could read Michael's mind.

"I'm sorry." She looks older than forty-one, he thought.

"Sorry for what your father did? It wasn't your fault. You must have only been seven or eight."

"Ten."

Miranda said he shouldn't be sorry anyway because it was the making of her. Her father parcelled her off to his sister, who'd married well and encouraged her to better herself. She buried herself in schoolbooks, ended up reading law at Cambridge. She was one of the top students in her Law Society finals and met Ted when she was twenty-five. He was a major then, recently widowed. "We had sixteen wonderful years together. Sixteen wonderful years."

Michael passed her his handkerchief again.

Before they left, Miranda said, "They're still together, you know, living in Ireland. I could give you the address."

"I don't know. I'll think about it."

"Bloody hell," Daisy said as she got into the driving seat. "What are the odds against that? Fancy Miranda turning out to be the daughter of the woman your father eloped with."

"The longer I live," Peter said from the back seat. "Life never ceases to surprise me."

"Families," Michael said, and Daisy squeezed his hand.

Michael was ensconced at a window table in a sweaty espresso bar directly across the street from Miranda's office. He was supposed to be well on his way to see Anne but curiosity made him linger. Behind him, the Italian proprietor screamed abuse at his staff. Michael recalled the days in an even sweatier bar in Rome when he'd had similar words hurled at him. Today though, they made him smile.

A girl took his order. She had a heavy accent, not Italian, maybe Romanian or Albanian.

The coffee was good. Michael sat through several shots of it and was thinking about another when a smart green taxicab drew up at the kerb opposite. The curly-headed figure of Jean-Paul emerged from it, accompanied by a grey-haired ferret of a man, grey-suited, grey-shod, and carrying a formidable looking black briefcase.

Michael reneged on the third coffee, loitered in the doorway. The men on the opposite pavement were huddled in conversation then Jean-Paul began to look about in darting movements. He didn't seem able to keep his hands still. Michael shrank back as Jean-Paul shot a glance across the road but nothing seemed to have registered because Jean-Paul quickly moved his eyes elsewhere. The ferrety man slapped Jean-Paul on the shoulder and they went into Miranda's building.

After a few minutes, Michael crossed the road, pushed through the revolving door, stood inside Miranda's foyer. He watched the indicators above the lift flash on and off. The lift reached the third floor then came down again. Its doors opened. Nobody was inside.

He felt drawn to the lift, began to walk towards it. Then a uniformed security man appeared. "Excuse me, sir. Do you have an appointment?"

Michael glared at him. The man was only doing his job, he supposed. "I don't need an appointment. I'm Miranda Roberts' brother." He walked out through the revolving door and wondered why he'd said that.

"Mum's gone Christmas shopping," Anne said as she let Michael hug her, "so I have you all to myself."

"This is my Dad," she announced to a nosy neighbour, puffing her skinny chest out as she did so. Michael felt humbled by the pride she showed in him.

Anne made him tea, the bag in a mug variety Grace would never be caught preparing. She'd sooner die, Michael thought, than let that happen.

"Tell me everything you've been up to," Anne said as she opened a pack of Cadbury's biscuits Michael felt sure she'd got in especially for him. Her eyes were expectant, bright with that Hibernian light and he wondered if he should mention her Irish grandfather and that it might be possible to meet him. Better not, for Miranda's bombshell was too fresh and he didn't know what to do about it for himself, never mind Anne. He told her about her prospective brother or sister instead, waited for her face to glow as it had in his imagination.

The news took Anne aback, Michael could see that. He heard her breath catch. But she didn't smile. She was silent for an uncomfortably long period then said quietly, "Does this mean you'll have even less time for me?"

Michael's jaw dropped. "No, no, *no*, of course not. I thought it would bring us closer. I hoped it would make us *more* of a family." A fantastic concept generated itself. "Daisy and I hoped you could come and live with us though I don't suppose Grace would let it be for good."

"*Really?*" Anne's face expanded from narrow-lipped moroseness to the broad smile Michael had hoped for.

"Really," he said, although he worried about Daisy's views on the matter. "In fact, we'd like to start by inviting you for Christmas. That is if you'd like to come and it doesn't spoil Grace's plans."

"Oh, I'll work on her. You could collect me on Friday, that's the first day of the holidays. There's a school pantomime on Thursday evening. I'm Cinderella." Anne gazed at him, suddenly shy. "Parents are expected to attend."

Michael's heart skipped. "Anne, I'd be proud, very proud, to come."

"There's one little problem." Anne was frowning although Michael could see how pleased she was underneath. "Mum will be coming too."

"I think I can survive that."

They walked arm-in-arm to the park and sat on the same bench as before. The boating lake was deserted but old men still sent woods across the municipal grass, still argued about whose was closest to the jack. Passers-by gave Michael curious glances. Anne smiled and waved to one or two. Michael wanted to shout: This is my *daughter*, you morons, but he reflected that they were right to be suspicious. He could be a Tappy Parker or worse.

Anne told him more about herself, little things he presumed she felt safe in revealing now, like her crush on Johnny Depp. When it was time for him to leave, she walked with him to the station. Just before he climbed into his train, she said, "Dad, I'm really, really pleased about the baby. I hope it's a boy. I've always wanted a little brother."

Daisy had sent Michael text messages during toilet breaks she'd engineered during the meeting. The concept of her sitting on the loo tapping into a phone amused him. Daisy's last message was to say the meeting was over. She'd give it half an hour then leave via the back door.

They had travelled down by car, parked beneath a flat owned by a colleague of Miranda. The flat was in Bethnal Green. There hadn't been time to notice much in the rush of arrival but Michael took time to study his old stamping grounds as he emerged from Bethnal Green tube station. The area looked dowdy and dirty as ever, but here and there, including the flats where he was parked, modern buildings had arisen amidst houses like that in which he'd been brought up.

Daisy wasn't back, so Michael mooched along the street in front of the apartment building. On the corner was a pub like the one where Jacinta had plied much of her trade. Across the street was a terrace of houses even more decrepit than those he remembered. He thought about revisiting Darley Road. His stomach fluttered as his head worked out directions, although he knew the way well enough. He wondered if number nineteen was still there.

Michael made his way back to the car, flopped down in the front passenger seat. Ten minutes later, a motor scooter chugged into the parking area. Two people got off: a man in a dark suit and a girl in denim jacket and jeans, like Daisy's. As they removed their helmets he saw the girl *was* Daisy. He got out of the car.

She was grinning as she walked towards him. "Beats a taxi any day," she breathed. "If JP was trying to follow me, he'd have given up long ago." She waved towards the young man beside her. "This is Simon. It's his parking space we're using."

Simon made them a cup of tea while they freshened up. Michael asked him if he knew Darley Road.

Simon pointed towards a corner of his kitchen. "Five-ten minutes that way."

"What's it like?"

Simon shrugged. "Like this street, I suppose. Someone you know there?"

"Me. I used to live there. When I was a kid."

Daisy looked worried.

"You drive," she said as they returned to the car. "Are you going there?"

"Do you think it wise?"

"That's for you to decide."

Michael decided not.

He concentrated on sweeping the Peugeot safely out of the East End, through underpasses and over flyovers that made getting out of *his*

London a lot easier than he remembered. The old saying was right, he thought. It *was* a mistake to come back. He would find no closure here.

Daisy seemed to sense his need for reflection because she kept silent until he at last asked her, as their progress came to a halt in a queue, about her meeting. She said Jean-Paul was like a wind-up toy whose spring was stuck. "As if he wanted to break free and throttle me but was promised candy if he kept to his best behaviour."

She described Jean-Paul's reaction when confronted with Marlowe's dossier. "I don't think he was expecting anything so detailed. You know how dark-skinned he is? Well, he turned almost as white as Berthe's poor rabbits, couldn't speak for yonks. When he did, he was virtually stammering and when Miranda asked if he accepted the grounds for divorce, just cranked out a 'Yes'. He gave in, and that is not like Jean-Paul."

"He could hardly claim we'd faked the evidence."

"Oh, he'd try but maybe it's because he sees his way clear to pursue his hairy tart."

Michael smiled to himself. The presence of a few wisps sprouting from the armpits of Adèle-of-the-photographs hardly justified Daisy's description of her as 'hairy'. He wondered what Daisy's armpit hair would be like if she let it grow.

"Michael, stop it."

"What?"

Daisy's colour was rising. "You know what."

"I'm sorry, but for someone who doesn't love her husband, you seem overly bitter about his mistress. You should be glad he's in love with her."

"You understand pride, don't you, Michael? I want him to *pine* for me. You would, wouldn't you?"

"Don't push your luck."

Daisy laughed, very lightly, pushed her hand slowly along Michael's thigh. "Don't push what?"

"Daisy, behave." Michael began to laugh too. "You'll have us off the road."

"We're not moving."

Someone hooted. In the lane to their left, a van driver grinned at them. His right hand extended out of his window towards them, thumb pointing skywards. Daisy took her hand off Michael's thigh, raised its middle finger to the van man, who grinned even more.

"What did you decide about Hamish?" said Michael, as the jam freed and they left the van behind.

"Ha. JP lost his cool. He demanded *Jacques* be returned to him immediately but after a few sharp glances from his lawyer, a weasel with a nose like De Gaulle's, he resorted to smouldering. The weasel proposed *Jacques* should alternate between us. I said I wanted any agreement formalised because I didn't trust Jean-Paul to return my son. And I said the name on his birth certificate was Hamish, not Jacques."

"How did that go down?" They were at last on the M11, heading north.

"JP went incandescent. *Jacques* was his baptismal name, he said and if anyone couldn't be trusted, it was me. I was the one who abducted his son, the one who sent her mother's lover to arrange it. The law should *make* me return *Jacques* right away. He was French and had the right to live in France."

"So, I got a mention. At least it proves he doesn't know about *us.*"

"*Yet.*" Daisy sighed. "Miranda stepped in then. She said Hamish had a British passport virtually from the day of his birth. Jean-Paul seemed shaken by that. She pointed out that he and I didn't marry until Hamish was six months old and that he was not registered as the father on the boy's birth record. 'What are you alleging?' the weasel said. Miranda said she was *alleging* nothing, these were verifiable *facts* a court might consider. She was splendid, Michael. It would be better, she suggested, if Jean-Paul demonstrated an ability to allay his wife's concerns and not make impossible demands. She proposed that supervised visits should be arranged initially."

"What did he say to that?"

"He agreed. Begrudgingly."

"When's the first?"

"In the New Year, date to be arranged."

"So he'll find out about us then."

"Perhaps. It won't be long before I'm showing."

Michael imagined Daisy 'showing', a deliciously smooth, curved belly, the bloom on her skin even more beguiling. This time it was he who reached across and touched a thigh.

Daisy leaned back in her seat, smiled. "You want me, right now, don't you?"

"Yes."

"When we reach Mummy's, we'll make an excuse and go straight home."

She pressed Michael's hand and he tried to concentrate on the road.

"Miranda raised the question of property and maintenance," Daisy said. "The weasel piped up and said Mazemeur was not Jean-Paul's but his mother's and only the marriage's specific property could be discussed. His client was willing to pay an appropriate allowance from his salary and the small profits from the gîtes. I said I wanted nothing except my clothes and personal possessions. I said I'd scrub floors if necessary. JP laughed and said I'd never scrubbed a floor as long as he'd known me. Which was a blatant lie. I've scrubbed his bloody gîtes within an inch of their lives and when he first met me I was scrubbing chalet floors."

"I could never think of you as a scrubber, Daisy," Michael said but the pun seemed lost on her.

"A sum was mentioned and I said that's fine. Jean-Paul raised his eyebrows. I think he expected me to fight. Miranda said she'd set out everything we'd agreed and send it to Monsieur Delavarenne. He's the weasel. It's a good job JP doesn't know about the conscience money." Daisy puckered her mouth, shrugged. "So there you are. How did you get on with Anne?"

"She thought a new baby might result in her newfound dad deserting her again."

"You didn't desert her in the first place."

"Perhaps Anne doesn't see it that way. Anyway, I invited her to stay for Christmas."

"*What?*" Daisy bristled then relaxed. "Well, I suppose it's the best time but I haven't even thought about Christmas. When is it?"

"Next week. Wednesday. Anne wants me to attend a school pantomime this Thursday. She's playing Cinderella. It's the last day of term. I said I'd bring her up to Norfolk the following day. So I'll have to stop over."

"With Grace?"

"No fear. I'll book a hotel room."

Daisy's smile was curious. Michael could almost swear she was jealous. "Are you sure this isn't a ruse of Anne's to get her Mum and Dad together again?"

"She isn't like that, Daisy. You'll see when you meet her."

"Oh, I trust you anyway," Daisy said.

But she still wore that smile.

Chapter 11

"I suppose you could stay here," Grace said after Michael tried the last hotel within a thirty-mile radius. "I could have told you they'd all be booked. It's Christmas you see."

"Yes, I *know*. Only there wasn't *time* to book earlier. Not with me only being told about the concert on Monday."

"Pantomime."

Michael wanted to swipe the smugness off Grace's face. He walked over to her weary sofa instead, patted its cushions. "This will do fine. Thanks, Grace."

"Don't be silly, Michael. You can use the spare room."

Grace flopped her way out and up the stairs. Michael followed, his spirits sinking in inverse proportion to each step. Bedrooms had not been happy places in their marriage.

The spare room was directly above the hall and barely large enough for the single bed it contained. There was no wardrobe but a shelf in the space above the stairs provided a platform on which Michael could store his bag. He extracted his suit and best shirt, safe inside protective plastic covers, hung them on a picture rail above crimson-flocked paper reminiscent of a Chinese restaurant. He accepted that the maintenance he provided meant Grace had to economise but her taste was surely the greater sin. It didn't help, he thought, that she refused to take a job, even part-time. He wondered what would happen to her once Anne left home. Did the law say he had to support Grace for ever?

They found little to say to each other. When conversation dwindled, Grace filled in the gaps by extracting photograph albums from a drawer in her downcast sideboard. Michael was reminded of the evening Meredith did much the same, albeit from lovingly polished Georgian mahogany in a very different room. Still, he wouldn't have missed this collection for the world.

He saw Anne, *his* Anne, travel through her childhood in black-and-white and faded colour that touched him with a poignancy that made him ache for what he had missed. There was one particular portrait that must have been taken soon after Grace took Anne away from him. An earnest, infant face stared through saucer-like eyes that seemed to hold thoughts of immense depth that belied the subject's age. If he could have just one photograph of Anne, this would be his choice. Grace, watching him holding it, looked surprisingly sentimental. "The second after the shutter closed," she said. "Anne burst into tears."

She showed him Anne's school reports, essays, stories, poems and, last of all, her paintings, in pastel and watercolour. Grace seemed to blossom as she brought the latter out. Many of Anne's early works, childish daubs really, included a tall, daddy figure who seemed peripheral, never quite part of the picture's substance. Around the time she was seven or eight, he disappeared altogether. Her next phase eschewed human figures, being mostly landscapes wild rather than pastoral, with tortuous streams, dark chasms and stunted, wind-strafed trees. The last, and current, period reverted to human form, drawings and paintings that didn't hide the blemishes. There was an unflattering full-length study of Grace, and several self-portraits in which Anne stared back at her alter ego, often with a wry expression but always with something guarded in her eyes, even on the rare occasions she was smiling. Michael felt emotion rise inside him. He was disturbed by the messages the pictures were sending him but there was one thing certain, Anne had a rare talent.

"What do you think?"

Michael heard the pride in Grace's voice. He couldn't begin to explain what he felt. "They're wonderful," he said eventually. "I had no idea…"

"Of course you didn't." Grace sounded remarkably sympathetic.

"She's a great kid. A credit to you."

The last four words burnt Michael's tongue.

"Making her was one thing we got right," Grace conceded. She yawned, stretched her arms. The buttons on her blouse came under strain and the bottom of it lifted, leaving a gap between it and Grace's skirt. Michael was treated to folds of flesh sprawling over the waistband.

He was saved from further observation by tinny Bach tones coming from his mobile phone.

"You made it all right?" said Daisy's voice.

"Fine, no problems."

"How's your room?"

"Pretty basic but then it's very close to Christmas. There isn't much choice."

Grace waddled out of the room. Michael heard the stairs protest as Grace climbed them.

"I love you, Daisy," he said.

"You sound as if you're missing me."

"That's because I am."

"I miss you too. And so does Baby. Wish Anne luck from us. Oh, from Hamish too."

It was the first time Michael had heard her refer to the new life in her womb as 'Baby' and for some reason he didn't understand, he wanted to cry.

Anne's school was within walking distance. Michael felt eyes watching from netted windows as he and Grace stepped out; he in his only suit, Grace in a flowery two-piece that looked too frail to contain her. Still, she had dragged a burgundy raincoat over it, although the rain had thoughtfully stopped.

The auditorium was almost full, only the front few rows offering seats. Funny, Michael thought, how everyone always wanted to sit at the back. Again he felt under surveillance, especially when Grace took advantage of his arm as they twisted past occupants to reach two vacant seats.

The audience hushed as a black-suited woman with impossibly high heels and a giant clipboard proceeded down an aisle formed between the files of seats. She stopped in front of the stage and faced the audience.

"Ladies and gentlemen," she projected in clear, careful tones. "Parents, friends and students."

Flicking her clipped papers as each section was completed, she gave a synopsis of the plot, read out the names of the cast (Michael experienced a great swell in his throat at 'Anne Cavanagh as Cinderella'), followed by thanks to all who had contributed in any way to what she was sure would be a great success for the school. Feet shuffled and throats coughed. Finally she snapped her clipboard shut and walked, head and body high, back up the aisle.

"Anne's drama teacher," whispered Grace.

Michael looked down at her and smiled. He noticed she was wearing stockings.

The lights dimmed, the curtains swung aside, the performance began. Michael was mesmerised as Anne, in carefully tattered clothes, swept the floor, fetched the coals, and slaved with panache for her ugly sisters. He had his fingers crossed as she spoke her first lines but he needn't have worried, she was word perfect throughout both in memory and enunciation. Received Pronunciation was one worthwhile asset she'd had from Grace; better to have that if she was to get on in the world than his own East End vowels, however modified.

What struck him most was Anne's confidence, the assured way she moved about the stage, commanding it as her own. She had *presence*, and the slight gawkiness she displayed in her schoolgirl persona was gone, transformed into lissom elegance. Whereas before, he'd thought her pretty, when he saw her standing tall in her emerald green gown he realised she was beautiful. They'd done something with her hair, spangled it so it shone, gold-red, gossamer-soft, framing her already fine eyes and endearing smile. Her face glowed with exuberance. Michael told himself she was going to break a lot of hearts. He blinked, realised his eyes were damp.

The pantomime was over too soon. Along with the rest of the audience, Michael cheered, clapped and stamped his appreciation of the performance. The cast emerged from the wings onto the stage, bowed, went off and came back three more times before the curtains finally closed.

The aftermath was a study in disorder with parents hanging around in corridors while players appeared and disappeared, half-dressed in stage clothes, half in their own. Parents hunted children and children avoided parents until at last they merged and scurried off into the night.

Anne bounced up to Michael and Grace with a cohort of friends, all girls, in her wake. "This is my Dad," she announced. Michael felt Grace's eyes sear his back and neck as she stood behind him, ignored and silent. Of course, he told himself, they already knew her, whereas he was a novelty.

"Hello, Anne's Dad," the girls said in unison, flashing eyes, pushing out chests, wiggling hips, preening themselves. Half with innocence, half with design, Michael thought, because they know I know they don't mean it. He laughed and they ran away, giggling, to their own parents.

"You were wonderful," Michael said, taking Anne's hands in his. He searched her eyes for what her self-portraits had concealed but it wasn't there. They sparkled back at him with unfettered joy and he was treated to a much prettier version of his own smile.

"You think so?"

"You were perfect, darling," said Grace.

Anne let go of Michael's hands, moved between her mother and him. She linked her arms in theirs.

Later, as he lay awake in Grace's spare room, soft footsteps sounded outside his door. He felt pinned down, as if he was in that section of his boyhood nightmares where the evil witch had come to claim him and he couldn't move a muscle to save himself.

But it wasn't Grace.

"I knew you'd be awake, Dad. Thanks for coming tonight," Anne said in a curiously small voice. She kissed him lightly on the forehead, tiptoed out of the room.

Grace was tearful as she and Anne exchanged gifts and wished each other Happy Christmas. "Take care of her," she said to Michael. She planted a tiny kiss on his cheek, handed him a small package wrapped in festive paper.

"Oh, I'm sorry, I didn't..."

"It's all right. I didn't expect one."

Something in Grace's eyes confused Michael. For one crazy moment he wondered if he should invite her as well. No, Daisy would kill him.

"Will you be all right on your own?"

Grace, surely not the Grace he knew, *simpered*. "I won't be here. I'll be at Barnes as usual. Mummy expects it."

Michael remembered that big old house in Barnes, its cold furniture and even colder reception. He was astounded no one had murdered Mummy in the last ten years. He recalled how her nose twitched with disdain, her perpetual reminders that her daughter had married beneath her, like 'No, no, Michael, milk in *second*' and 'A gentleman *always* stands when a lady enters a room'.

"Give her my love," he said.

Daisy ran to greet them. She flung her arms about Michael then did the same to Anne.

"How pleasant to meet you at last," Daisy said then stood back to appraise the girl. "You're even lovelier than Michael described you."

Anne blushed.

Hamish had followed Daisy outside. He stood behind her formally, waiting to be introduced. He wouldn't take his eyes off Anne, as she equally wouldn't take hers off Daisy. Michael stepped in, took his daughter's hand. "Meet your brother to be."

They approached each other warily, then Hamish's stiffness left him and his face broke into a smile that broke Anne's reserve too. She held out her arms. "Come and make friends." Within minutes they were walking hand-in-hand.

"How are you?" Daisy said as she and Michael embraced again. He felt the need to hold her extra tightly.

"I slept at Grace's, couldn't find a hotel room at all."

"I knew *that* last night. But I'm glad you told me." She poked him gently in the chest, laughed lightly. "As long as that's all you have to confess."

Anne's face lit up when she saw her room. "Wicked, I've never slept in a double bed." She moved about, stroked Peter's old furniture, picked up the ornaments he'd dotted around, then finally went to the window, which looked directly onto the river. "Awesome," she said.

It rained overnight. In the morning, the ground was decidedly squelchy and in a few sections the river was outgrowing its banks. Michael had heard stories about water reaching three feet up walls.

"Never had a problem with the old place," Peter had sworn when Michael asked. The old woman who came in to clean had a different tale. She claimed in some years boats had been rowed along the village street.

Still, the forecast was dry for the next few days and they were leaving for Meredith's on Christmas Eve. If they were cut off by road, there was always *Foxy Lady.* Michael checked she was secure. He wondered if Anne would enjoy a sail.

He took a mop and, dipping it in the river, swabbed cobwebs off the boat's deck and flanks. True to her declaration she'd always wanted a brother, Anne had taken to Hamish and he to her. Despite the age difference, she seemed able to reach the child to an extent that he, and even Daisy, could not. And at dinner last night, Anne proved herself capable of conducting an adult conversation in a way he could never have dreamed of when he was fourteen. Michael supposed she'd had to grow up quickly, being fatherless. At least he'd had a father of sorts. Until he was ten.

He finished swabbing, put the mop away. He felt his eyes moistening. What was this? Weakness creeping in? He needed to feel the wind in his hair, blow his own cobwebs away. He'd take *Foxy Lady* out at full revs, no sails, sod the speed limit.

On Christmas Eve, laden with bright parcels, they drove to Meredith's. Hamish, with a sly glance at Anne, ran to his grandmother, lodged himself in her arms.

"Well, *there's* a welcome," a radiant Meredith said. "And you must be Anne," she added, turning to her. "Hamish, darling, let me say hello."

Anne, colouring, stared at Meredith. "Are you my pretend Gran?" she said, suddenly childlike.

Meredith, laughing softly, said, "Yes, I suppose I am." She released Hamish and stepped towards Anne, welcoming her with a kiss to both cheeks.

A Norway spruce dominated the sitting room. Tinselled packages lay beneath it and Daisy and Michael added theirs. Anne hesitated. "Apart from mine from Mum, I only brought one. It was for Dad really."

"I'm sure he'll let us share his pleasure." Meredith stretched a hand towards the tree and smiled encouragement.

"What about me?" said Hamish. "I want to put one there."

"You can help me with these." Anne let him carry one of her parcels and they arranged them among the others. Meredith winked at Michael.

"Dad, there's a *bathroom* in my room," Anne said, wide-eyed, after Michael came to make sure she didn't feel too intimidated by Meredith. "She's lovely," Anne said when he asked what she thought of her. "Not a bit like my Grandma in Barnes."

Michael confessed that her Grandma in Barnes scared him too.

"You know her?" Anne looked puzzled then her face cleared. "I was forgetting. Yes, of course you do."

Michael, dowsed and drowsy from a gargantuan dinner and the dwindling stock of Harry's malt, sprawled on one of Meredith's sofas. Here he was in the midst of a family he didn't have last Christmas or the Christmases before that. Daisy, his own adorable Daisy, was snuggled beside him on the sofa; and Anne, his gorgeous, artistic, thespian - was that the right word? - *genius* of a daughter, was playing on the carpet with his flaxen-haired proxy son. And there was Meredith the matriarch, the handsomest mother-in-law in creation, snoring blissfully in her deep armchair; and last but definitely not least, growing in Daisy's womb, was Baby, whether Edward or Ted or...with eyes screwed up Michael searched his memory bank of girls' names and ended up with Daisy junior. He gave Daisy senior's belly an affectionate pat.

"What?" said its owner, yawning.

"I'm a very contented man."

"You're a very *drunk* one." Daisy curled up closer to him.

"Correct. Drunk *and* contented."

Even Grace wasn't as bad as she pretended to be. The little package she'd pressed into his hand contained the photograph of Anne that had so moved him. She'd put it in an antique silver frame, one of a set she used to keep pictures of her mother in.

Anne's gift to him was one to treasure. It was a painting of them sitting together on the bench in the park. She'd captured him perfectly, God knows how, she must have a tremendous memory for detail, and she was looking up at him as if he was the only person in the world she wanted to be with. She must have worked day and night over the few weeks she'd had to get it done.

"It needs framing," Anne said, anxious-eyed as he separated the picture from its wrapping paper.

He'd hugged her, his eyes streaming, "It's perfect, darling, absolutely perfect." Even Daisy had bitten tears back and he'd suspected Meredith's weren't far off.

Yes, he was a very contented man and it didn't do any harm to be drunk at a time like this.

A phone rang. Michael's head jerked up, sank again. Meredith's snoring broke for a few seconds. Daisy sighed gently. "Go away," she murmured.

The phone rang on.

"They're persistent," Daisy said. She sat up, stretched. "Probably one of the Lomond crowd. The Monarch of the Glen himself perhaps." She walked over to the telephone, checked the caller display. "International.

Must be Aunt Romilly from Grenoble." Smiling, she picked up the phone. "Hello Romilly, it's your favourite niece, Merry Christmas." Michael heard the buzz of the caller's voice then watched Daisy drop the handset, which struck the table below and landed on the floor.

Daisy stood swaying, grasping her stomach. Michael, drunkenness discarded, helped her back to the sofa. "It's him," she said in a strangled voice.

"I'll deal with it," he said. Daisy glanced anxiously at Hamish.

"Hear him out first," she whispered. "For you-know-who's sake."

Michael nodded. He brought the fallen phone to the sofa. "Yes," he barked into the handset.

"Monsieur Cavanagh?"

"What do you want?"

"I would like to wish my son a happy Christmas. Surely that is allowed?"

"What makes you think he's here?"

"Oh come, Monsieur Cavanagh, even English families get together at Christmas. I guessed he'd be with his grandmère and new grandpère. Besides, unless I'm very much mistaken, it was my wife who first picked up the phone. May I speak to my son, please?"

Michael had almost choked at 'grandpère'. He called to Hamish, "It's Papa. On the phone."

"Papa?" Hamish sat up from the board game he and Anne were playing. "Wait for me," he said to Anne.

"Don't try any tricks," Michael hissed into the mouthpiece. "This is being recorded." He handed the phone to Hamish.

"Heureux Noël, Papa."

"Recorded?" whispered Daisy as Michael sat down. She pulled a face.

"As long as he thinks so."

Michael's teeth were grating. He listened for anything the boy might let slip. The conversation was conducted in French, to judge by the few words Hamish uttered, mostly 'Oui' and 'Non', accompanied by nods or shakes of the head. Then Hamish began to list the presents he'd received and from whom. When his own name was reached, Michael held his breath. He wished he'd brought the handset in from the hall. Hamish was silent for a few moments, frowning as he listened to Jean-Paul, then he said, "Michael is going to…"

Daisy got to the phone before Michael did.

"Jean-Paul, you asked if you could wish Hamish a happy Christmas and you've done that. Now we're guests of Mummy and Michael and we're in the middle of our dinner. We've kept everyone waiting long enough. … No, I'm not giving you our address… Yes, I suppose you could send it here. Hamish, say au 'voir to Papa, darling."

"Papa's sending my present," Hamish said as he handed the phone to his mother. "I knew he wouldn't forget."

"What if he's here?" said Daisy, looking anxiously about her. "What if he's in the village right now?" She and Michael were walking in a wavering direction through the orchard.

"Relax. The call was international. Even he must travel the way we mortals do."

"He wouldn't last five minutes on Hirondelle." Daisy was half smiling then she switched to a frown. "I wonder what Hamish was about to tell him."

Michael grimaced. "I can guess. Oh, by the way, I told Anne not to tell Hamish about the baby. I said I didn't want him to feel pushed out, me not being his real father. She understood, having felt that way herself at first."

"Can you rely on her to keep quiet?"

"She's had to be tight-lipped about many things over the years."

"And she's very loyal to her Dad. I've watched her face when she looks at you."

Michael suddenly stopped walking, grabbed Daisy by the hands. "Do you know why I said I felt contented? Because all the people I love are here with me and it feels so good."

"Is Hamish included?"

Michael frowned. "Of course he is. Why ever not?"

"But there was a time when he wouldn't be."

Daisy was scrutinising Michael's face. He sighed, conscious that she'd see any gaps in the truth of what he said.

"At first," he said. "Yes, I wished it could just be you and me. And when I met Hamish, when you brought him to *Hirondelle*, I doubted we'd get to like each other. But the voyage made the difference, with us thrown together like that. Hamish grew on me, as they say, grew on me a lot. I like to think I've grown on him a little."

"Oh more than a little. When you're not with us it's Michael this and Michael that and Michael said. I think it really confused him when Jean-Paul phoned. I think he was going to tell him you were going to be his Daddy."

"That's what I thought too."

"The thing is." Daisy gulped as if there was something she was finding hard to swallow. "The thing is I have to face the prospect of letting him stay with his father."

"Well, Anne will have to go home to Grace but I'm determined to have her back as soon as I can."

"I meant permanently."

"Never. No court, even a French one, is going to award custody to Jean-Paul."

Daisy stared at the ground. "He's up to *something*. I heard it in his voice. God, I lived with him long enough to be able to tell that. I just wish I knew what it was." When Daisy looked up again her face was full of dejection.

Michael stared at the frost-damaged grass and the half-eaten Bramleys the blackbirds had ignored. Daisy was volatile, he knew that well enough, but she had lapsed into paranoia because of one ten-minute phone call.

Then Daisy's face assumed what Michael interpreted as token serenity. "If the worst happens," she said, "we'll still have Baby. We need to be strong together for Baby's sake."

That's it, thought Michael. He remembered the moods Grace used to get. Torrents of tears, and tantrums, like the time she threw her mother's Doulton shepherdesses against the wall. Yes, Daisy's mood swings were antenatal depression caused by hormone imbalance, nothing to worry about at all.

Chapter 12

Peter phoned the day after Boxing Day. Meredith was outside somewhere when the phone rang. Daisy refused to answer it. She said to Michael, "You're the official resident" but he knew it wasn't because of that.

He'd tried phoning the cottage, Peter said. He had two legs again and was looking for takers for his party, New Year's Eve.

"Oh."

Michael looked for Daisy but she was no longer in the room.

"Something wrong, Mike?"

"We're really keen to let the New Year in at the cottage. Being our first home together, we thought it might bring good luck for… well, you know what. Besides, my daughter's staying with us and there's Hamish of course and it isn't fair to dump them on Meredith…"

"So you're saying you can't make it?"

"Sorry, Pete."

"That's okay, we'll have a houseful as it is. Does that mean Merry will be on her own? Although I don't think Abby would be too pleased if I invited her."

"We were going to invite Meredith to see the New Year in with us."

"I thought she wasn't supposed to know where you're living." An odd tone, cautious, crept into Peter's voice. "So, she's been there already - how did she react?"

"She still doesn't know where we're living. She'll find out when she gets there. Secrecy doesn't matter so much now events are moving on. What do you mean, 'how did she react'?"

"She might have a shock. She and I spent a week together at the cottage in ninety-one."

The sound of a handset dropping echoed through the receiver. Michael heard the clatter coming from the hall too. He'd thought there was a lot of noise on the line. The hall door opened.

"Pete, I have to go."

Daisy came in, her face already asking the questions and, from what Michael could see, working out the answers too.

"Did you *know* about him and Mummy?" Daisy's face was twisting up and Michael did not want to be on the receiving end of her anger.

"He let slip that they had a brief fling. That's all I know, Daisy, no details, nothing else. How was I to know if you knew or not? Mothers and daughters share secrets in a way fathers and sons never do. I didn't think it was any of my business to bring it up."

Daisy's anger abated a little, at least with him. "Well, I *didn't* know. But I accept your reasons for not mentioning it." Her eyes narrowed. "Nineteen-ninety-one is *branded* on me. Does he *know* about my father fucking me?" Daisy had boiled up again, was pounding her fists on the back of an armchair.

"He mentioned seeing you, only once he thought, 'a scared-looking fifteen or sixteen, rather scrawny'. There was no other connection. You know Peter. It would have shown on his face."

"Maybe. Scrawny indeed. The scared he's right about. Does Abby know about the affair? She's looked daggers at me each time I've seen her."

"She certainly doesn't like Lomonds but from what you've told me of Harry's business ethics that's understandable. I don't know if she knows."

Daisy's face contorted into frowns and grimaces. "Was this affair some kind of revenge? Is that why she packed me off to France? For taking her husband?"

"No, it wasn't."

By Default

Judging from her splintered expression Meredith had been listening for longer than Daisy's trilogy of questions.

"It wasn't revenge, Daisy. It happened *after* you'd gone to Grenoble and I sent you *there* because in my stupid head it was the only way to keep you safe. Peter just helped me pick up some of the pieces."

"So it was compensation," Daisy snapped.

Meredith coloured. "If you want to call it that, I suppose I deserve it. Do you think I haven't crucified myself a thousand times? Is there no remission for my sins?"

Daisy opened her mouth to respond but at the same moment, youthful voices reverberated in the hall. Anne and Hamish came tripping into the room, flush-faced. "It's snowing."

Outside, scattered flurries drifted downwards. Michael took the children's hands, led them back outdoors.

Something seemed to have been settled by the time they came back in, for Daisy and Meredith were talking civilly to each other, acting as if nothing was wrong.

They left for the cottage on the thirtieth. The rain began before breakfast and bucketed all the way. At times Michael was sure the car was aquaplaning. It was dark long before their journey ended and he wondered how far the river had advanced.

Rain rattled the windows as they clustered around the wood-burner, snug from the hardwood waste Michael had ferried up from his workshop. They played Scrabble, argued over the words, ate roasted pistachios and drank, Meredith and Daisy choosing red wine, Michael bitter beer, until long after the children were abed. Nobody mentioned Meredith's affair.

Her eyes had not so much as flickered as she walked through the front door. Michael suspected Daisy had warned her about the cottage. A sign of forgiveness, he supposed.

By morning the rain had stopped. Michael was outside early. Halfway to the staithe, he had to paddle through an inch or so of water. The ground rose towards the house. He weighed up the distance and height the river still had to go.

After breakfast, everyone walked to the village, Meredith arm-in-arm with Anne and Hamish, Michael lagging behind with Daisy. Joy encompassed him as he watched his daughter and Daisy's son strolling as if they were out with their grandmother. As one of them was of course, he reminded himself. And in half a year or so there would be a third child, uniting the blood that ran in the girl and boy. This, in Michael's mind, would draw all three neatly together. His right arm encircling Daisy's waist, he pulled her closer to him.

She smiled up at him. "Are you thinking what I'm thinking?" She nodded towards the trio ahead of them.

"Yes." He hoped it was the same thought.

They had lunch at the village pub. As Michael ordered, he overheard a conversation about water levels. "Just like the year we had to row ourselves to church," said one. "How would yew know?" said another, "Yew never bin there since the day yew was christened." There was more like that. Michael decided not to mention it to Daisy and the others.

There was no rain forecast that night and, long before midnight, Michael had forgotten the locals' tales of doom. Meredith had brought *Veuve Cliquot* and the bubbles went to the women's heads. Michael stuck to beer. They played an American board game, *Aggravation*, and the language from mother and daughter was often blue. Michael was accustomed to hear it from Daisy but Meredith surprised him. He passed a few anxious glances towards Anne but it seemed to pass her by.

It was everyday language among the young, Michael supposed, meant nothing to them. But he, brought up with prissy working class ethics, didn't expect a lady to swear. Even in her most drunken state, he'd never heard as much as 'bloody' from Jacinta. He laughed. How ridiculous could you get? To be purse-lipped about swearing but ready to drop your knickers for anyone with the price to buy you a drink.

Daisy looked up from the board. "That must have been a good one. Care to share it?"

"I was thinking about my mother." Michael laughed again, shaking his head at the same time.

Daisy frowned. "Are you sure you're all right?"

Michael said, yes he was and it was about time too. Meredith rolled her dice. "Oh fuck," she said.

At two minutes to midnight, the women made Michael go outside with a piece of coal Hamish had found in an outhouse, a mince pie, and a shining new two-pound coin.

"It has to be a tall, dark stranger," said Daisy.

"What about handsome?" said Michael.

"Well you can't have everything," said Daisy.

"I know why dark," chipped in Meredith. "It's a legacy from when blond strangers at the door were apt to be Vikings bent on rape and pillage." Her voice faltered on 'rape'. Michael remembered Harry Lomond had once been blond.

Daisy seemed not to notice Meredith's discomfort or make the connection. "All right," she said. "You can be handsome."

Michael shivered outside the front door, strained his ears for the sound of Big Ben on the radio. He'd already rapped the knocker and was wondering if he'd freeze to death before they let him in. At last he heard cheering then a feminine giggle and the welcome sound of the bolt being drawn back. Anne opened the door.

"It's a tall, dark, *handsome* stranger," she called to two shadows in the background.

"What does he want?" said Daisy's voice.

"I bring good luck," said Michael. "And fuel and food and money to buy more. Happy New Year."

"I suppose you can let him in," said Daisy.

"You haven't brought any good luck yet." Daisy was scowling at the rain. It began almost as soon as everyone was up, which was late, but not as late as Michael expected. His head felt as if it was back at sea, rolling in rhythm with the waves.

"There's probably a waiting list."

The rain eased through that day but, before dawn, started again with intent. Everyone watched the inexorable progress of the water as, unable to drain into the swollen river, it formed ever-expanding puddles, filled pockets and hollows, crept steadfastly up the rising ground towards the house.

Michael discovered some wellingtons beneath the stairs. Size eleven. He presumed they belonged to Peter. He walked along the lane towards the village. A hundred yards beyond the cottage's gates, the road dipped to cross a shallow valley, either of a tiny stream or a man-made dyke, Michael didn't know which. What he was certain about was that for a distance of thirty feet or so the road was under water by at least twelve inches and probably four feet or more where the dip was. There was no way they could drive out. "Bugger," he said.

He returned to the house, checked *Foxy Lady*, splashing through standing water to the boathouse. The water inside was a good six inches above the walkways. He'd have to lower the mast to stop it catching the crossbeam at the gable end. That was if they decided to leave that way. The more he thought about it, the more risky it seemed. Downstream there were open, reedy banks and no way to tell where those banks were, especially on bends. And there were all sorts of hazards, sunken posts and the like, to sink a little ship. Upstream would be easier, with tree-lined banks, but once they got to Barton Broad, what if the channel marker posts were submerged? He couldn't risk it, with only three lifejackets for five people. Two and a half lifejackets, he reminded himself, and *six* people, with Daisy pregnant.

"Looks as if we're stuck here until the water goes down," Michael said on his return to the house.

"Well surely that's not so bad," said Daisy. "We've plenty to eat and drink, plenty of firewood. The roof doesn't leak. Who wants civilisation?"

Meredith gave her a quizzical look but Anne's face lit up. "Does that mean I don't have to go home on Saturday?"

"Possibly," Michael said.

"Super," Anne said then her aspect changed to thoughtful. "I don't really want to miss school though."

Michael marvelled at her. He would have killed for the chance to stay away from school. "The water will go down quickly enough," he said. "We just need a few days without rain."

For that day at least, the water continued to rise. At half-past four, Daisy went into the kitchen to sort out something for dinner. "*Michael,*" she called, with a tremor in her voice.

He dashed in, with Meredith in his wake. Water was spreading over the tiles in a widening pool.

Michael phoned Peter. "I'm on my way," Peter said. Michael imagined his old salt's eyes narrowing as he peered mentally across East Anglia towards the narrow river.

"There's nothing you can do today. It'll be better in daylight. I just thought you ought to know for the insurance and such. We'll sit it out upstairs."

Peter didn't seem too sure. "Okay Mike," he said at last, "I'll see you in the morning. One way or the other."

By seven pm the ground floor was submerged by five or six inches. As the only person with wellingtons, Michael cooked the dinner. Virtually at the moment he finished, there was a loud crack and the power supply failed. The lights had stayed on though, so it seemed the culprit was rising water shorting out the sockets. Michael, hoping the house had modern split circuits and not some ancient radial horror, checked upstairs. Yes, both power and lights were working there and the supply came in overhead to a distribution board on the landing. Michael checked the fuses: one blackened, blown, the remainder white, intact.

Everyone huddled around a convector heater in Michael and Daisy's bedroom.

"Do you realise," Daisy said to Michael, "this is the first meal you've cooked for me? And it isn't half bad."

Michael grinned. "Wondered how long I'd get away with it."

"Of course," Daisy said. "You've had to cook for yourself for years since..." She bit her lip, glanced at Anne.

"Since Mum left him, you mean?" Anne said. "It's all right to say it, it won't upset me."

Daisy laughed. "Anne," she said, "I think I like you very much indeed."

Michael went downstairs to fetch tins of fruit salad. "Bring a kettle too," Daisy shouted to his back. "Don't forget to fill it."

"It's like Swallows and Amazons," said Anne, when Michael returned and set the kettle to boil. "Like when the D's camped in that hut in the middle of the wood. The Picts and the Martyrs."

"I suppose it is a bit," Michael said. "Although at least we have electricity." He had cause to regret his words because no sooner had he said them than the lights went out.

"I don't know about a waiting list," Daisy moaned. "I think our luck's run out."

"It's only weather," Michael said. "It isn't personal."

"Isn't it?" Daisy said gloomily and Michael was reminded how easily she could be persuaded that fate had its mucky hand in everything.

Hamish began to cry. "I can't see," he wailed. "Mama, I can't see."

"I've seen candles and matches in the kitchen dresser," Daisy said. "Michael, could you?" She cooed her way across to Hamish.

Michael, thankful Daisy's attention was now focused on her son's welfare, was already on his way. He bumped himself occasionally then his eyes began to adjust to the twilight. He paddled across the hall to the kitchen, fumbled through dresser drawers. He found two dozen candles, a box of cook's matches, and a small flashlight that didn't work.

They stuck candles in the necks of empty wine bottles and the room gradually acquired a warm glow but what heat remained was quickly dissipating.

"I was thinking on the way up," Michael said. "There was no bang this time when the electricity went off."

With Anne holding a candle, he checked the fuses again. Only the original one was blackened, the rest remained white. Michael turned the main power switch off and on - nothing. "Must be the overhead lines," he said to Anne. He saw that Daisy had come out to watch. She had Hamish in her arms.

"I'm putting him to bed," she said. "He'll be warmer there." Michael nodded and while Anne lighted Daisy's way, he went downstairs, phoned the power company. A recorded message said they were aware of a fault affecting consumers in the area and engineers were dealing with it. Supplies were expected to be restored within six hours. Michael went back upstairs to relay the news.

"So we'll have no heat up here until tomorrow," Daisy said. "That coal you brought must have been stale."

"Let's hope Peter can get through and rescue us. We'll have to move out anyway when the water goes down, so the damage can be made good."

"I suppose so." Daisy's face fell. "But this house has been special for us."

"It has." Michael put an arm around her. "But we'll be back."

Daisy looked up at him. Tears were forming in the corners of her eyes. "I don't know. Something's changed. I don't mean you and me. I just feel our time here is over." For more than a moment, she looked lost.

The lights came on at four am and woke Michael. Daisy didn't stir. He went to the bathroom for a pee, swilled his hands, left the toilet unflushed. Hamish's light was on too, and Anne and Meredith's. He checked on the boy, his bedcovers were as unruffled as when Daisy tucked him in. Faint snores came from the other room. Meredith, he thought. He put the lights off.

He thought he understood what Daisy meant about the cottage. It was only borrowed, like time. They needed somewhere that was truly their own.

"Where have you been?" Daisy murmured as he slipped back into bed.

"Bathroom."

Michael knew Daisy wasn't really awake. She didn't answer, just snuggled against him, warm and soft, dispelling the chill coated on his skin by the night air.

Outside, only the boatshed gave an indication where the actual river was, for a sheet of water extended from the house to well beyond where Michael knew the far bank of the river to be.

Peter phoned to say he was only a few miles away. The main roads were fine, he said but many riverside places were flooded.

"How on earth is he going to get in when we can't get out?" Daisy said.

Michael shrugged. "He knows the area better than we do. He did say he'd come in by boat if he had to. I thought of us getting away upriver on Foxy Lady but didn't fancy hitting sunken posts on the Broad."

"Foxy Lady?" said Meredith, who hadn't been near the boatshed. "Is Foxy Lady still here?" Her face was a study in mixed emotions, excitement changing to embarrassment when she caught Daisy scowling at her.

"You've already done everything here, haven't you? There's nothing new for us."

Meredith stared at the floor. Michael noticed her shoes were scuffed. Daisy turned her head away from her mother and he felt compelled to break the mood. He whispered into Daisy's ear. "She didn't make a baby here."

Daisy's scowl dissipated. "No, she didn't, did she?" Her eyes showed triumph as she looked back at her mother.

Meredith was frowning. "Didn't what?" she said and when Daisy shook her head, added, "I only went in the boat once. We sailed to Horsey. Peter couldn't get the mast up the second time after we went under Potter Bridge. I told you that. You thought it was funny then."

"It still is," Daisy said. "So it was only the one trip. I bet you never even learned how to trim a sail."

Meredith's mouth twisted as if she thought her daughter's mind had gone. "Why would you need to trim one? Surely they're already the right size."

Daisy laughed, it was almost a growl. She began to say something but stopped as the clatter of a diesel engine sounded outside. Moments later, a large four-wheel-drive ploughed through the water surrounding the house, came to a halt outside the porch. Michael pulled on his boots.

Peter grinned from the driver's seat. The door was open and he was easing wellingtons on. Thick mud clung to the car's tyres and was wedged inside the wheel arches, spattered over the blue bodywork.

"Pete, you're a bloody Superman," Michael said.

Daisy and Meredith stood together on the bottom tread of the stairs. Daisy glowered at Peter, curling her lip.

Michael heard her mutter something like "Back at the scene of the crime". He went over to her, clutched her hand. "Not now," he said. She gave him a vexed look but kept her lips closed.

Peter shook his head at the liquid invasion. "Jesus wept."

"It wasn't Jesus," Meredith said. "It was the rain."

Peter laughed. "Hello, Merry." He adopted the wistful expression he'd used on Daisy aboard *Hirondelle*. Meredith reddened. Michael felt Daisy squirm.

Peter said he'd tried the lane but had to turn back at the place where Michael had seen it flooding. He thought the stream must be blocked near the river. The flooding in the village was about the same as here, with water reaching a few metres into the churchyard immediately behind the parish staithe. He'd reversed up the lane to the farm whose land surrounded the cottage. After getting permission from the farmer, he'd driven over some of his fields to reach them. "Six knots in a short chop. Like crossing the channel," he said, with a wink at Daisy. She didn't move a muscle in return.

They packed clothes and essentials. Michael and Peter put them in the boot. One by one, Michael carried Hamish, Anne, and Daisy to the car. Meredith insisted on taking her shoes off and walking. She giggled like a young girl as the water met her naked feet.

Chapter 13

"Did you know Johnny Depp's five years older than I am?" Michael said. They'd just watched a DVD of *Chocolat*. Anne's eyes were dreamy.

"He's still hot though. All my friends fancy him."

Michael heard Grace tut behind him.

"You shouldn't fill your heads with such nonsense."

Grace's attitude reminded Michael of the parents in *Billy Liar*. He imagined Anne spraying her words back as bullets.

"It matters to them, Grace."

It occurred to Michael his reappearance had brought Anne out in a way that Grace found threatening. She was a woman happy in a world of genteel practices, hence her predilection for afternoon tea, the preparation and pouring of which was a civilised ritual, unlike the exchanging of body fluids. During the latter activity Grace had often pursed her lips. "Can't you at least pretend to take part?" he said to her once during a particularly soulless bout of non-reciprocal sex. She'd accused him of "being filthy". Now, he watched her manoeuvre her mild vexation with Anne into full blown annoyance with him.

"Her education is what matters," she snapped. "But I don't expect *you* to understand that."

"I understand more than you expect, Grace."

"Pshaw!"

Anne said, "*Stop it*. Come on, Mum, Dad. It's New Year, a new beginning. Why not make a resolution to *try* and like each other? You were close enough once to create such a wonderful creature as me."

Anne's eyes were filled with passion. Michael's heart leapt for her but Grace melted immediately, laughing softly, a laugh he hadn't heard since they were 'courting' in leafy Metroland.

"When the Irish in you shines out, Annie," Grace said. "I don't have the will to fight it." She turned to Michael. "I'm sorry. That was a mean thing to say. Friends?"

"Friends."

They sat together then and Anne related her version of Christmas. Grace's ears pricked up. Michael suspected her Christmas was cheerless.

"Daisy's lovely, *really* lovely. And Meredith, that's Daisy's Mum, is even posher than Grandma, although she doesn't wear it like a badge in the way Gran does."

Grace's mouth tightened then suddenly relaxed and spluttered into laughter. "She does rather, doesn't she?"

Michael found himself almost liking her.

"Water was everywhere..." Anne gave a vivid account of the flood, making them castaways on a remote island with only a tiny ship to save them from storm-tossed seas. She embellished her words with actions, her face dreamlike throughout. Then her expression cleared. "It wasn't like that really but it *was* an adventure. I felt quite brave in a way. And soon – is it all right to tell, Dad?"

Michael nodded.

"And *soon* I'm going to have a baby brother or sister." The smile on Anne's face then would have lit a city. "Isn't that wonderful?"

"Congratulations," Grace said but Michael saw fear cross her face.

A friend of Anne's called not long after that, one of the girls who'd been with her at the school pantomime. She breezed into the room.

"Happy New Year, Mrs C. Oh, and Mr C too."

She flashed eyes at Michael then she and Anne ran giggling out of the room. Moments later, loud rock music pulsed through the ceiling.

"I hope there'll still be room in your life for Anne," Grace said.

"Of course there will. Daisy and I want her to be a *real* sister to our child, not just a name that's mentioned now and then. Besides, Anne and I have a lot of years to make up."

Grace lowered her eyes. "I suppose that's my fault."

"Mine as much as yours."

Grace gazed at Michael through sad brown eyes in an old-before-its-time face. If anyone had asked him before, he wouldn't have been able to say what colour they were.

"She can stay with you at half-term. Maybe some weekends too. I'll have to see."

Michael smiled. "Thank you, Grace." He wished he had more than that for her.

There followed awkward silences, broken by banal pleasantries. Michael prayed for Anne to come downstairs but when she did, it was to ask if she could go round to Caroline's for tea. "I hope you don't mind, Dad."

"Of course not." Michael yawned and stretched his limbs. "I should be setting off anyway. It's a long drive home."

Anne kissed him. "See you soon, Dad."

Caroline waved. "Bye, Mr C." She blew a kiss.

"I hope you didn't do anything special for tea," Michael said to Grace.

"No, of course not," she said, although Michael knew she would have.

Safe in the car, he stared up at Grace's windows. They were shut tight against the world, apart from Anne's room, which had the casement open as far as it would reach. Snow began to flurry and a few flakes landed on Anne's windowsill. Grace's face appeared. She looked at the snow, and possibly at him, for a few moments before pulling the window shut.

Two and a half hours later, Michael brought the Peugeot to a sliding halt beside Flora. Parked on her other side was a black car, a Golf. It had Morbihan number plates. Thin-lipped, he scattered gravel as he strode towards the house.

A hubbub of voices came from the sitting room. Michael flung its door back so hard it banged against the wall inside. Heads turned. Daisy was squatting on the carpet beside Hamish; Meredith was situated, straight as *Foxy Lady's* mast, on a ladder-backed chair. Jean-Paul occupied the sofa, the girl of Philippe Marlowe's photographs beside him.

"What are you doing here?" Michael was aware his voice was shaking.

"Ah, the gigolo." Jean-Paul looked amused.

Michael clenched his fists.

Meredith seemed to spring from her chair. "Michael, *darling.*"

She moved swiftly towards him, assuming a dramatic smile, winked at him moments before she kissed him full on the lips.

"I didn't expect you back so soon," she said.

Daisy stood up.

"Mummy, *leave it.*"

With a high-tilted glance at Jean-Paul, she came over to Michael and, wrapping her arms around his neck, smothered his lips with hers. When she was finished she slipped an arm around his waist, smiled her triumph. Michael could feel the blood thumping through her veins.

Jean-Paul hid his resentment well but Michael caught it for the nanosecond it was revealed. It was followed by an unctuous leer.

"So, Mister Cavanagh, it seems you are not a gigolo after all." To Daisy he said, "That's a beautiful ring you are wearing. I've been admiring it ever since we arrived."

Daisy tried to smile the remark away but Michael knew she was furious. The ring was one she'd seen and coveted in a jeweller's window on the way to her first meeting with Miranda; it had warm red rubies and sparkling diamonds clasped in white gold. He'd gasped at the price but still skipped off to London one morning and bought it for her. She'd slipped it on the third finger of her left hand, a place she'd previously declared barren to such things.

"What am I doing here, you ask. It is of course to bring my Jacques his present. The English post is unreliable at the best of times. Even more so at Christmas. And as Adèle is now no secret, I thought it would do no harm to introduce her formally."

He's brought her along for protection, Michael thought. He wanted to ram Jean-Paul's supercilious expression into his head and out the other side. He wanted to tell him he and Daisy had fucked each other's brains out right under his nose. But he couldn't do that, not with Daisy there, and Hamish, and especially the girl on the sofa.

The photographs didn't do her justice. Daisy called her short and dark but there were surely less than two inches between them. Adèle had chestnut brown hair, so not *that* dark, and her skin was no more tanned than Daisy's. Her brown eyes were striking, vibrant, perfectly placed in a face perhaps wider than average but with every feature pleasingly proportioned. Her lips were provocatively plumped and her nose was, like Daisy's, imperceptibly aquiline. Michael noticed a tiny freckle on the right side of its bridge.

Adèle smiled at him, exhibiting nothing more malicious than curiosity. Something snatched inside him.

Hamish had been silent since Michael's arrival. Apart from a brief welcoming smile, he'd been busy assembling what was presumably Jean-Paul's present, something that looked like a cross between Lego and Meccano. Now he looked up. "Michael. I can't do this next bit."

"Let Papa help," Jean-Paul said in French, on his way through a mad scramble off the sofa onto hands and knees to crawl along to Hamish, who looked perplexed. Michael suspected he wasn't used to Papa participating in his games.

Meredith invited Jean-Paul and Adèle to stay for supper then capped it by extending that to a bed for the night. Michael asked Daisy if Meredith had finally flipped her lid. His jaw drooped when she said, "It will do us no harm to get on Jean-Paul's good side."

"He doesn't have a good side."

Daisy laughed. "Even so," she said and he gave up.

"*She's* rather nice actually," said Meredith as Michael helped her to load the dishwasher while Daisy put Hamish to bed. It was as if she was discussing someone she'd met at a garden party.

When the adults were gathered together again, Jean-Paul said he had something to say. He puffed his chest out like a small-town mayor. "It seems to be a time for revelations. So I shall add to them in telling you Adèle and I wish to marry as soon as possible. So naturally, I will agree to whatever terms you wish to hold me to."

Adèle coloured slightly. Her right hand brushed softly against her stomach. Michael noticed the flatness it had in the photographs had been replaced by a curve, barely perceptible unless you were looking for it. He snapped a glance at Daisy's abdomen – no sign yet. Mind you, she was only just over eleven weeks. Adèle must be quite a few more.

"What about Hamish?" Daisy said.

Jean-Paul's smile looked well-rehearsed. "*Jacques.* I am willing for him to remain with you. That is what Delavarenne told me to say and I am not so stupid as to disagree. As long as he may stay with his Papa sometimes. If your Madame Roberts sets out the rules then I will sign and the papers can be passed to the judge. She and Delavarenne have found one who is sensible about divorce. And quick if he is persuaded to be." His eyes assumed the snakelike look Michael witnessed during their last encounter.

Daisy's eyes became wary. "You won't attempt to obtain a residence order?"

"No."

Adèle coughed quietly. "If you don't trust Jimpy," she said, and Daisy's eyebrows rose, "then perhaps you could trust me. I won't let him take your son from you. I promise."

The girl's eyes seemed guileless to Michael. He guessed Daisy thought the same, for she said, "Perhaps I can trust you, but you're not Jean-Paul." She turned to her husband. "Would you swear on your mother's life?"

Jean-Paul didn't blink. "On my mother's life," he said. "I will not try to take Jacques from you."

"Hamish."

Jean-Paul laughed once, short and gruff, like a bark. "Hamish," he conceded but then carried on in French. "On my mother's life I swear I will not try to take Jacques from you."

"I still don't trust him." Daisy was throwing her clothes onto a chair. Michael was already in bed.

"*She* seems all right," he said.

"That's your dick talking, darling. Although I believe she meant what she said. The trouble is Jean-Paul, *Jimpy* indeed, could manipulate his way out of Colditz. Swearing on Berthe's life is another matter though. He wouldn't dare break an oath like that."

"I think Adèle's pregnant."

"You've taken more of an interest in her than is healthy for you. Why do you think that?"

Michael told her, leaving out the bit about the photographs.

"A little bulge? Hmm..."

Daisy wriggled her knickers down, stepped out of them and, carefully reinserting a toe, flicked them into the air. They landed on Michael's head. He clapped. Daisy did a little bow then climbed into the bed. Her fingers meandered upwards through the hairs on Michael's thighs. Paralysed, unable and unwilling to move a muscle, he waited for them to reach their destination. But, abruptly, Daisy sat up.

"I think you should pay attention to my little bulge," she said.

"You sadistic, bloody, tease," Michael groaned.

"Even so," Daisy said and Michael buried himself in her soft honey hairs, his tongue flicking into the moist folds of pink skin that no longer held any terror for him. Daisy moaned softly and her pelvis began to jerk. She came quickly, then again, and again in almost seamless succession, crying out more loudly each time until she ended with a final lingering shriek. Michael thought he heard an answering call from somewhere far away, though it could only have come from a certain room along the corridor.

As Daisy pushed him down onto the warm cotton, he wondered if her sonic performance was part of some animal instinct to show her discarded mate how much more his replacement aroused her. Then he began to wonder… if… he… thought… too… much… Then he didn't think of anything except how much he loved her.

They received curious glances next morning but nothing was said except by Daisy, who asked Adèle if she'd slept well. "Yes, thank you," she said, blushing under her tan. She caught Michael looking at her stomach, coloured even more.

He felt it odd, even more so than at dinner, to be sharing a table with Jean-Paul. Breakfast was such an *intimate* meal to him. Meredith seemed out of it altogether, on another plane. She wore her distant smile.

After breakfast, Adèle asked if she and Jean-Paul could take Hamish for a walk. Michael thought her use of that name was a blatant attempt to appease. He was saucer-eyed when Daisy said, "Yes, of course."

"Their belongings are still in the house," Daisy said as they watched the trio stroll towards the village street, two dark beings with a small pale one between. "And Adèle's car is here. So, they aren't about to abduct him." Her face told a different story.

Hamish was returned, Jean-Paul and Adèle left, and Daisy's expression lightened. Michael had felt the worm of jealousy when the boy gazed at Jean-Paul with what looked like hero-worship. What right did he have to come between the man and his child, whether Bohec was the biological father or not? Grace hadn't tried to keep his from him. Well she had, he supposed, but more by default than design. The difference was Hamish was a Mummy's boy whereas Anne seemed to be Daddy's girl. That might just be novelty value though, fading to distant fondness when Anne grew older, wiser.

"Penny for them?"

He told Daisy what he'd been thinking and she told him what he already knew.

"You think too much. You don't have to apply a condition or reason to everything. Some things just *are.* You need to clutch at happiness, Michael, not consider it and maybe, just maybe, you'll keep it."

Then Daisy turned to pouting. "She was sixteen weeks on New Year's Eve. I asked her. You know what that means?"

"She'll have a baby in another, er, twenty-four?"

"It *means* she became pregnant around our first day on Hirondelle. He was fucking *her* when he should have been glued to Berthe's bedside."

Michael almost made a joke but Daisy had adopted her wronged-woman face and he could see she meant it.

"She only told him about the baby after his meeting Miranda and me. She'd come to London with him and he was pretty down when he returned to their hotel. It seemed to calm him, she said, being given another child in compensation."

"Why did she leave it so late? Didn't he notice her gaining weight? I mean, I did and that was from outside…"

"I think we'll leave your observation skills right there, thank you. She didn't want him to accuse her of trapping him into marriage. Judging by his expression in those photographs that turn you on so much, I don't know why he left it so long but Jean-Paul only proposed to her that morning, on the plane. Adèle accepted him once they were safely landed. She has a thing about planes being bad karma. That's why they used the ferry this time."

"I know how she feels…about planes that is. You two seem to have developed quite a rapport."

"We have Jean-Paul in common. I think the poor girl imagines she can tame him. It's a pity really, because she's rather nice."

Michael recalled Meredith's similar sentiment. He shook his head. How quickly the two women's opinions could turn from 'hairy tart' to 'rather nice'.

"One thing's been puzzling me," he said. "How did Jean-Paul know we'd be here? I mean, we'd be at the cottage but for the flood."

"Secret agents in the shrubbery? Perhaps it was just pot luck."

"Or the grapevine's more organised than we think. Hmm, I wonder… Ask yourself who calls here every day, bar Sundays."

Daisy's face was busy for a while. "You mean the postman? He's positively geriatric. It's all he can do to push his bike around the village."

"Yet he starts and ends at the post office."

"Ah, the nosy old biddy who runs it... You think Jean-Paul's paying her for information?"

"Village post offices find it hard going these days."

"Thank goodness we told Mummy not to readdress our mail. I must warn her. And the sooner we're away from here, the better."

But better wasn't soon because that day the first heavy snow of winter arrived, soon obscuring almost everything in a crystalline fog. By dusk, a thick layer of pristine snowflakes blanketed the ground. By morning, the air was still and a peace had fallen over the village. Not one sound of a passing vehicle, not even the scrabble of sparrows raking the roof tiles.

Michael fashioned a sled, the kind he remembered his father making for his cousins, with a stout seat top-centre, metal runners. Daisy found Hamish's sea boots and they carried him out to the sled, his legs wriggling their impatience to meet the virgin snow. Hamish was fastened in the seat then Michael and Daisy each took a rope and pulled the sled through the six acres comprising Meredith's grounds. Hamish squealed and shrieked and Michael saw a little hero-worshipping transferred to him.

Michael and Daisy built a snowman, a husband for Flora. He had the usual carrot nose and his eyes, lips, ears and waistcoat buttons were made from a selection harvested from Meredith's vegetable cupboard. They named him Pan, and a pagan marriage was performed to mark his union with Flora. The day after they made him, Michael noticed a large parsnip penis had been inserted in the appropriate position. Daisy and Meredith denied all knowledge of it and Hamish was surely too young.

"Snowmen come alive after midnight," Daisy said.

The snow stayed for seven days in all then twelve hours of rain cleared it away, leaving only an odd snowy boulder here and there and a rather large one beside Flora. Something had chewed the parsnip.

During the snow spell, Miranda phoned Daisy to say she had arranged for them to see the French judge. Jean-Paul would attend with his lawyer.

"It might be a suitable time to collect Hamish's things and mine," Daisy said to Michael. "Would you come with me?" She adopted a look

Michael suspected was only half-mocking. "It'll give you a chance to see Adèle."

"Stop it, Daisy."

"Stop what?"

"Making out I have a thing about her."

"She's very attractive."

"No more than a dozen girls in this village."

"A dozen?"

"Well, one or two, perhaps."

"Two?" Daisy was pouting but Michael wasn't in the mood to give in.

"What I meant was," he said. "Yes, it's a pleasure to look at an attractive woman but I can admire a good-looking man too, or a fine piece of furniture. Doesn't mean I want to sleep with any of them. Well, the furniture perhaps if it happens to be a bed."

"I was only joking," Daisy muttered then she flung herself against him. "Michael, promise you'll never think the worst of me." Her face was earnest, eyes imploring. Michael didn't know why she thought he'd ever think anything but the best of her.

On the day the rains washed the snow away, Daisy attended her first antenatal clinic, choosing to ignore her mother's sneers and favour the local health centre.

"I want to be an ordinary mother," Daisy said.

"But you're not ordinary," Meredith said. Daisy sniffed loudly, stuck her nose in the air. Michael, observing them both, knew she was about to say, "Even so." He smiled to himself as she did.

She caught him halfway through. "I don't know what you find so funny. I'm not having you skulking around while I do all the work. You're driving me to the hospital on Tuesday. I have an appointment for a scan."

"Suits me."

Michael's smile became almost permanent for the rest of the day, so much so that Daisy eventually frowned at him, asked what it was for.

"Because I'm going to the movies on Tuesday."

"No darling, you're going soft in the head."

Daisy's scan was at a small general hospital twenty miles away. Michael felt fatherly as they marched past people waiting in rows of beige seats. Their own destination was a specialist unit on the top of the three floors. The sonographer came to greet them as they walked through the doors. She was a pretty girl around Daisy's age, hair almost as pale, smiling grey-green eyes. Her badge said her name was Helen. She was very efficient but in a nice way, Michael thought, and when she laughed it was catching.

A mixture of emotions, love, excitement and fear, wriggled through Michael as Daisy lay on a couch and jelly was smeared over her abdomen. He thought the scanner looked like an upmarket paint roller and saw it was applied in much the same way, as Helen moved it across Daisy's still flat belly.

"Oh, Michael. Look!" Daisy's face was full of wonder, mouth half-open. Tears trickled down her cheeks. Michael caught his breath as their joint creation assumed a starring role on the computer screen. A definite, miraculous, human shape, with real arms and legs: two of each he counted automatically. He was convinced he saw fingers and toes although in reality he knew the image wasn't clear enough.

"It's all right for you to cry, too," Helen said.

Chapter 14

Daisy clutched Michael's arm as they stood in Le Mazemeur's yard.

"It's hard, coming back," she said.

"You'll get through it."

Adèle came around the corner of the house, headed towards them.

"Looks as if she's moved in already," Daisy said. "*And* she's visibly pregnant. See, she even has breasts." She looked sideways at Michael. He ignored the bait.

"Jean-Paul asked me to step in for him." Adèle's tone was diffident. "I hope you don't mind. He has to work this morning."

"Why should I mind?" Daisy said. "It's not as if I was ever the lady of the house."

Adèle frowned. "Ah, you mean Berthe is that, of course."

As if on cue, Berthe emerged from the rabbit factory with a trolley-full of victims. She wheeled it towards her ancient estate car, which was lurking beside the well. It was only as she reached it that she seemed to notice the arrivals. She stood, staring, then clumped towards them, stopped about three metres short. From that position she projected what Michael considered to be a well-rolled gob. It landed about an inch in front of Daisy's feet.

"Whore." Berthe spat the words as if they were sputum too.

Daisy tilted her head to her most aristocratic. "A poor choice of words, Berthe, given your personal history. And your mother's."

What colour there was vanished from Berthe's complexion. Michael thought she was about to suffer another stroke. Her mouth began to twitch then, face contorting, she jerked herself around, trudged back across the gravel.

"*Dieu*," Adèle said, clapping a hand to her chest. Her breathing became laboured, as if she was having trouble getting air into her lungs.

"God, what have I done?" Daisy said from the side of her mouth.

"I think you've just made it Advantage Miss Lomond."

"I wish I *was* Miss Lomond," Daisy said in a dull tone. "I wish I'd always been."

Adèle was soon composed again. Michael supposed she'd had an attack of the breathlessness he'd been warned to expect from Daisy soon.

"Jean-Paul said you would be using one of the gîtes," Adèle said. She rattled keys.

Daisy grabbed them from her. "Can you get Hamish?" she said to Michael then headed towards the gîtes.

Hamish's face was pressed to the Peugeot's window glass. He said, as Michael undid the seat harness, "Why was Grandmère spitting?"

"Because she's old."

"Grandmère Meredith doesn't spit."

Michael didn't know what to say to that but Hamish didn't seem to expect an answer. He scrambled out of the car, looked around the yard.

Adèle hovered a few yards away, looking somewhat out of her depth. Michael guessed she'd felt intimidated by Daisy's aggression. Daisy herself was unlocking the door of the gîte he'd stayed in.

"Hamish, how are you?" Adèle said at last. "Your Papa will be here soon."

Hamish gave her his old man's nod and Adèle returned it with the first real smile Michael had seen on her. He shut his eyes as he felt an unwanted stirring. When he reopened them he noticed Berthe wheeling her rabbits back to the barn. *Reprieved*, he thought in a sudden snatch of gloom, *only to die another day.*

After Michael had carried their bags to the gîte, Daisy said, "I want to get my things now, before *he* gets home." She grabbed his hand.

Hamish stayed with Adèle, who still looked uncertain as to what she ought to be doing. Michael observed that they were conversing in French, although he supposed that was natural, given where they were. Daisy flashed Adèle an imperious look, said she was going into the house for her clothes.

Adèle looked flustered. "But they are not where you leave them." Her cheeks reddened.

"Then you'd better show me where they are."

Mouth clamped tight, Daisy marched to the house, pulling Michael behind her. Hamish's legs worked at twenty paces to the dozen as he and Adèle tried to catch up.

Daisy charged upstairs and was banging doors before Michael was even halfway up. "Adèle," she bawled.

Adèle was hanging onto the banister in the hall.

"Wait, Daisy," Michael said, "she's out of breath."

Adèle rewarded him with a weary smile then began to climb the stairs. Hamish overtook her, made straight for a particular door. As Adèle reached the landing where Daisy was, she pointed to a further stair winding upwards in an angle of the outside wall.

"Up there."

Daisy's eyes became slits. "The junk room? You put my stuff in the fucking junk room?" She banged her fist against the banister rail. Too hard, Michael realised from the badly concealed wince she gave.

"Not I," Adèle said, voice shaking, but Daisy was already on her way. Michael heard her cursing from somewhere above his head.

The stair led to a small landing. Daisy was inside a low-ceilinged room beyond it, glaring at the floor. It was littered with clothes, toiletries, books, ornaments. They looked as if they had simply been thrown there.

Daisy's lips began to quiver. "Look what they've done to me," she said.

"I'm sorry. I'm so sorry." Adèle came into the room, stood like a child about to be scolded, biting the fingernails on one hand, comforting her bump with the other.

Heavy footsteps sounded lower down the stairs. Soon Jean-Paul's florid features appeared round the door.

"It's not Adèle's fault," he said.

Daisy said nothing. She pushed her way past him, stomped down the stairs. Michael and the others followed. "Where's Hamish? Hamish, come here. *Now.*" She went into the room Michael had seen him enter earlier. "Oh, darling," he heard.

Hamish was sitting on a child-size bed, clutching a teddy bear to his chest, or rather to most of him, for the bear was larger than he was. Daisy held onto the headboard. Her chest began to heave and Michael rushed over to her before the tears began. "Steady, sweetheart, it isn't the end of the world." He held her closely until he judged she was calm again.

But Daisy was still angry. "Jean-Paul," she said. "Collect all of my things up properly or Hamish and I are leaving right now. I was trying to be halfway nice by bringing him here, because of Adèle's baby and look how you've repaid me."

"It was the day after you disappeared," Jean-Paul said. "I'd been at the hospital all night and I was tired, angry. I'd forgotten about it until I heard the commotion just now."

"The time you were busy getting Adèle pregnant, you mean? Oh don't look so shocked, *Jimpy*. I can work out dates as well as anyone."

Jean-Paul shrugged. "I apologise for treating your possessions so badly and of course I will pack them properly. *However.*" He paused and smiled. A corner of his top lip curled at the same time. "However, not everyone we know is whiter than white, Daisy. You would do *very* well to remember that. Now, what do you say? Will you stay?"

Daisy seemed instantly subdued. The cold, hard face of moments before was gone. She looked at Michael as if willing him to understand something then she turned to Jean-Paul.

"All right," she said.

Jean-Paul issued a smile that Michael thought was fully back to snake standard.

"Now where's my boy?" he said as he lifted Hamish complete with teddy bear into his arms.

"I'm going to lose him, just look at his face." Daisy and Michael were watching from their bedroom window as a palpably blithe Hamish trotted beside Jean-Paul and Adèle, adding an occasional skip or jump to his progress.

"No, you're not," said Michael, nuzzling Daisy's hair. "Don't begrudge him enjoying time with his father."

Daisy shot him a glance that said she knew he was thinking about Anne. "I know. I was just practising being neurotic."

Hamish had at last received the little homily Michael had expected to take place on *Hirondelle*, how Mama was with Michael now and Papa was with Adèle but it didn't mean he would lose out. In fact that was why they were here, so he could spend the whole week with Papa and sleep in his old bedroom with all his books and toys.

"But will you sleep in your old bedroom?"

Daisy explained that Adèle slept there now but Mama wouldn't be far away, only in the little house across the courtyard. Hamish digested her words silently and remained like a dummy for so long that Daisy asked, "Is that all right? You do understand?" He at last allowed her his blank-faced nod.

As Hamish and the two adults reached Jean-Paul's Renault, Daisy squatted on her haunches to avoid being seen, as she had done on the last occasion she and Michael were in that room. He left the window, sank into an easy chair, leaning back, arms folded behind his head as he gazed at her, remembering. There was no sun this time to highlight her beauty.

Jean-Paul, beaming with bonhomie as he held his son aloft, invited them to dinner. "To reciprocate," he said with an expansive smile, "Meredith's gesture of goodwill." Michael cringed as Daisy accepted in the same demure manner with which she accepted Jean-Paul's apology. He wondered what he had missed between husband and wife.

Adèle met them at the door. Michael glanced at Daisy to see how she felt about her husband's fiancée greeting her as a guest. If she was put out, Daisy did not show it, but stepped over the threshold and looked about her as if seeing the interior for the first time. Jean-Paul sauntered along the hall passage, holding Hamish by the hand.

"Mama, we went to the zoo," Hamish cried. "There were lions and tigers and em...em."

"Emus," Jean-Paul said.

"Emus," echoed Hamish.

If anything, Jean-Paul's geniality had magnified since morning. "Tell Mama all about it," he said then let Hamish dash along to Daisy. He drew Michael aside, said in a low voice: "Maybe we got off on the wrong feet, you and I. I should have recognised you were doing me a favour."

Michael stared at him. "A favour?"

"Clearing the field for Adèle and me."

"Ah." Michael remembered the beating he'd taken. Did Jean-Paul think it was that easy to discount?

Hamish was put to bed after a slight tantrum. "I want Mama to do it. Not Papa." Daisy reminded him that Papa had missed him so much and it was time to be with him.

"But I want you to sleep in your old bed," the boy cried. He pointed at Adèle. "She can sleep with Michael."

Adèle's eyes held Michael's for what he considered an uncomfortably long time. Then, as he prayed that he wasn't blushing, she erupted into giggles. Moments later Daisy followed her. Michael allowed himself to smile. Jean-Paul, pan-faced, scratched his brow.

It took some hugging on Daisy's part but Hamish eventually settled down. "It's just tiredness," Daisy said afterwards. "He'll be all right tomorrow. By the end of the week, he won't want to leave." She seemed bright as she said this but Michael wasn't convinced.

The dining room contained an oak table so large Michael guessed it was originally intended to seat the entire population of the hamlet. A cast-iron range seethed inside a cavernous fireplace. Above it, ominous iron hooks protruded from a smoke-blackened bressumer.

Berthe was slouched in a wooden rocking chair beside the hearth, watching the flames inside the open firebox of the range. Michael noticed she was wearing boots not far removed from those he wore before Meredith confined them to the dustbin, together with his smock.

"You're a *reluctant* carpenter," she'd said. "Official clothes are off limits. Remember, a big part of what you're marketing is image."

Michael thought about that as he studied Berthe. He wondered about the masks people wear, if you could ever *really* tell the true persona. Daisy had a wardrobe of personas, or was it personae? He'd seen a new one that day and doubted he'd seen all of them yet. And Meredith, vague-mannered, apparently harmless Meredith, was an arch-mistress of the art. Jean-Paul obviously had as many as suited him but Berthe, like himself he supposed, seemed to have just one, easily read by anyone. For a moment he felt compassion for her.

As if she had the sixth sense, Berthe turned, saw him watching her. Panic flitted across her face then her expression reverted to stolidity. Daisy had suggested Berthe's behaviour after the spitting incident was an aftermath of her stroke but Michael wasn't so sure. She had been perturbed enough by Daisy's insinuations to wheel her rabbits back to the shed. Her demeanour this evening was of someone cowed and her few utterances had been monosyllabic mumbles, far removed from the morning's venom. It must mean, Michael decided, that the story Daisy conjectured from an old woman's ramblings was true. At that moment, Berthe was giving him a dreadful, sickly smile, her attempt, perhaps, to appeal to his better nature. He kept his face deadpan, looked away, back to Daisy.

While Jean-Paul installed himself at the head of the table, Adèle came up to them. She avoided Daisy's eyes. "Why don't you sit down too? I'm just going to check on dinner." She disappeared through an open doorway at the back of the room.

"That's *my* kitchen through there," Daisy said with a wistful smile. "One thing I insisted on." She nodded towards the range, where Berthe was still ensconced in her chair. "You didn't think I cooked on that monstrosity?"

"No, of course not. You're strictly a microwave girl."

Daisy punched Michael, hard. "Bastard," she said loudly. He thought he saw Berthe start.

They were given adjacent seats towards the middle of the table. Daisy chose the furthest from Jean-Paul. "Below the salt," she murmured.

Conversation buzzed from the kitchen and the clash of cutlery on crockery could be heard. Adèle reappeared, followed by a girl Michael recognised as the one from the bungalow. Both carried laden dishes.

"Why, Marie," Daisy said. "I didn't expect to find you here." The girl seemed flustered, setting her plates down awkwardly.

"Madame Bohec." She made a slight bow of her head. Her face flushed. "Monsieur thought, with Mamselle's condition…"

"Ah, of course. Her condition." Daisy nodded slowly. "You've met Monsieur Cavanagh before?"

The girl looked at Michael, reddened even more. "Ah, oui." She scurried back to the kitchen.

"Adèle, let me help." Daisy rose from her chair. She took Adèle's arm, walked with her into the kitchen. Michael glanced at Jean-Paul, saw he was grinning.

"Women," Jean-Paul said. "Aren't they wonderful?"

Berthe clamped herself at the top corner of the table and when the others emerged from the kitchen, Daisy reclaimed her position on Michael's right. Marie took the chair opposite him, leaving that on his left for Adèle. In the brief moment it took Adèle to flatten her skirt after taking her seat, he caught a hint of smooth, tanned thighs. He looked away as if scalded, bypassing Marie to rest his eyes on Daisy. She was already watching him and she wore her knowing look.

They dined on roast duckling in a sauce based on cherries and other items that Adèle wouldn't reveal. Michael thought it was marvellous and said so. Daisy backed him up enthusiastically then kicked him hard.

Three, perhaps four, Michael wasn't counting, bottles of an excellent Burgundy were consumed and at some point, Jean-Paul began to denigrate the local wine.

The duck was followed by a Farz Breton pudding made using rum-soaked raisins. Michael had three helpings. Even Daisy, normally a picker, had two. A mountain of cheeses followed, Breton and Norman, then brandy distilled from the very wine Jean-Paul had insulted earlier.

Conversations, apart from between Michael and Daisy, were conducted in French. Michael felt himself warming to the language and it returned to him as if he'd only left France yesterday.

Only Berthe said nothing at all, spending the whole meal looking sorrowfully at her food and stabbing an occasional piece with her fork.

When coffee was served, Jean-Paul leaned back in his chair and said, "Jacques claims that you all sailed to England in a little boat. I said he was telling stories and Mama would never be so foolish as to take such a risk."

"It's true," Daisy said.

Jean-Paul was open-mouthed. "You put my son's life in danger, crossing La Manche like that? What do you know about sailing?"

"More than you at any rate. Hamish was never in danger. The little boat you refer to was built to withstand far more than the English Channel could throw at her. The skipper was an ocean yachtmaster with more miles at sea than you have on land."

"Jacques said the captain was ill."

Daisy snorted. "You expect precision from a four-year-old? The skipper sprained his ankle, that's all. Once strapped up he was fine. Besides, Michael's an experienced sailor too, well able to single-hand a yacht like that. Hamish was probably safer than in your car today."

"I agree." This was Adèle. "What about that idiot who nearly rammed us in Lorient this afternoon?"

Jean-Paul glared at her then his face softened. He nodded. "Maybe so," he said. He turned his oily smile on Michael. "It was a clever strategy, using the yacht. I'm impressed."

Apart from the merciless ribbing Michael received from Daisy that night over his alleged feelings for Adèle, after which she 'forgave' him, he and she enjoyed some idyllic days, alone together as they had never had the chance to be before.

He showed Daisy the places where he once lived and worked: Josselin and La Baule in summertime; Rennes in darker days. In return she took him to some of her favourite spots, like the wide, south-facing beach beyond the saltpans at Suscinio or the wild, whispering sea-caverns of the Côte Sauvage. "Places where I could be alone when I needed to be." Michael watched the memories flicker through her eyes. He guessed she'd needed a lot of solitude.

They took the time to simply *be*. Quiet, content, sitting together, an arm or an ankle carelessly invading the other's space, unthreatened, unthreatening. "A breathing time," said Daisy, "a recharging." Michael thought them some of the best days of his life.

Midweek, Miranda arrived to accompany Daisy to the meeting with the judge. Jean-Paul's lawyer did the same for him. Hamish stayed behind in the joint charge of Michael and Adèle.

As they waved their respective lovers off, Adèle said, "What should we do?"

Hamish piped up immediately, "I want to see Mama's little house." He went on his way. Michael hurried after him, leaving Adèle stranded in the middle of the yard.

"Is this Mama's?" Hamish was pointing to the bed on the landing. Michael told him, no, Mama's bed was through there, and pointed towards the bedroom. Hamish scuttled in and looked set to stay. "Why can't I sleep in the other bed?" he demanded in a vexed tone.

"Because you're with Papa this week. Mama explained that." Hamish went back to the landing. Michael heard him bouncing on the bed there. He moved over to the window. Adèle was not in the courtyard. Then he heard her "May I?" from below, her footsteps start on the stairs. Something fluttered beneath his ribs.

Adèle glanced around the bedroom, her bright eyes taking, Michael thought, everything in. Too late, he saw her cross to the dressing table where Daisy had placed Baby's scanned image. She caught him grimacing. Gazing steadily at him, she caressed the swelling in her abdomen. "Daisy *aussi?*"

Michael nodded, felt a chill pass through his body. Adèle picked up the picture. "Beautiful," she said and, as if she could read his feelings, "Don't worry, Michael. No one will learn of it from me. I promise."

That seemed to settle something between them. For the rest of the day they were at ease with each other, swinging Hamish along between them as they walked along the riverside at Auray. At some point during that walk, Adèle began addressing Michael as 'tu', not 'vous' and he reciprocated. For reasons he couldn't pinpoint, it made him feel as if he'd always known her. He bought her a coffee at a quayside bar-tabac then, while Hamish sat on a bench gorging on an off-season ice cream, they stood together watching the river flow under the old bridge.

Adèle said, "I envy you sailing around the Breton coast."

"Why, do you sail?"

"I used to, a lot. I'm a seaside girl. From St Pierre-Quiberon. I had a fiancé who had a habit of winning regattas. He died, not from drowning. It was almost ten years ago."

Michael stared at Adèle. *Ten years*? It's not possible, he thought.

Adèle touched his hand. "You don't have to be sorry for me. I'm over it now."

"We... I imagined you to be only around twenty-three."

"I'm thirty-two."

"You don't look it."

"I will soon." Adèle laughed, patted her bump. "And more. After this brute is born."

"No you won't."

Adèle flicked her head up, gave Michael a sideways glance. "Okay. Maybe not. Did you see the photographs?"

"Yes." Michael felt himself blushing.

"Jimpy was angry, said they were disgusting."

"Those of you weren't."

Adèle's naked image breezed into Michael's mind like an unwelcome guest. He tried, unsuccessfully, to think of mundane things.

"Ah. Thank you, Michael." Adèle seemed out of breath for a moment then said, "Is it possible for me to have one. Just of me. I'd like a reminder of when I wasn't like this."

"It will be difficult."

"But you could try?"

"I don't know."

"I did promise not to tell about Daisy's baby."

"Are you blackmailing me?"

"No, I wouldn't tell anyway."

"Okay, I'll try."

Adèle squeezed Michael's hand. "Just between you and me," she said. She gazed at him with those seemingly guileless gold-brown eyes.

Michael felt the worm of betrayal nibble at him until he reminded himself there was something between Jean-Paul and her that Daisy wasn't telling *him* about. What was the harm in giving Adèle a photograph of herself anyway?

Husband and wife returned in Miranda's car.

After he'd hugged Daisy, Michael hugged Miranda. "How are you? How's Ted?"

Miranda's face clouded. "Not good. It won't be long, I'm afraid."

"I'm really sorry." Michael wished he could think of significant words to say.

"I know you are." Miranda patted his arm. "And, God knows, so am I."

Michael hugged her again.

Hamish was full of his day. "Mama, I had an ice cream."

Daisy made a play of shivering. "What? It's the middle of winter. Didn't it make you feel colder?"

"No. It made me feel warm."

Miranda was invited to stay for dinner. Jean-Paul insisted it was the least he owed her, giving the guilty party a lift home.

"You could use the spare bed in our gîte," Daisy said.

As they tidied themselves before dinner, Daisy and Miranda reported on their adventures with the judge. "He was a bit of an old roué," Daisy said. "But we got what everyone wanted. He accepted that reconciliation is impossible. He's entered the details into the record and is sending the case to court." Miranda said Daisy should be a free woman by the end of April.

Dinner was much more relaxed than the previous evening's event. Michael couldn't decide whether this was due to Adèle's simple stew ("Easier when we weren't sure what time you'd be back,"), Miranda being present, or the fact that Berthe wasn't.

"She feels tired," Jean-Paul explained.

Before Miranda left next morning, she asked Michael if he'd thought any more about visiting his father. "Let me give you his address anyway," she urged. "I wouldn't want you to regret not having it."

Michael thought how he would have regretted not visiting Colonel Ted. He calculated his father's age: fifty-four. So a year younger than Meredith, only four older than Grace. He was too young to be dying yet but then, he reflected, so was Ted.

"All right," he said.

"Now, are you ready to meet Philippe Marlowe?" Daisy said as they watched Miranda drive away.

She had rescued her 2CV from its shed behind the house. After a quick battery charge, it started first time. Michael winced as she hurtled along the track to Marie's bungalow but his ordeal wasn't over there. Daisy wore a set grin as she drove at breakneck, for a 2CV, speeds, causing it to lean over on corners like *Foxy Lady* heeling in a gust.

She parked in a depressing underground car park and they made a precarious crossing over a busy road to reach the city centre. The office of Marlowe et Cie was above a shop in one of the less aesthetic streets.

"Madame Bohec, welcome."

Marlowe's journey across the room could only be described as ambling, Michael thought, though it had surprising pace. He was almost exactly as Daisy described, long and lean, crumpled grey suit that might once have been a lighter shade, down-at-heel brown shoes with cracks in their leather. Dark hair curled greasily over his collar. Michael ran a finger over the back of his own hair.

There were tables piled high with files and a desk bearing a sleeping computer. In a corner stood a row of tired looking filing cabinets. Daisy winked at Michael as Marlowe slid a drawer back, extracted a bottle of *Famous Grouse,* a handful of glasses.

Marlowe had a grin that stretched almost to the full width of his face, grey eyes that looked as if they laughed a lot. It wasn't a handsome face, too narrow for one thing, and considerably lined, but Michael could see why Daisy had taken to the man. He asked him about his name.

Marlowe laughed. "You'd be surprised how many people still know the Raymond Chandler books. Or maybe it's through Monsieur Bogart. Either way, it's been good for business." He poured out whisky, drew water from a dripping tap over a basin at the back of the room. "My grandpère Marlowe was from Oklahoma," he said as he handed out the drinks. "He came here in the war and sort of stayed. On and off."

"Are you a Philip Marlowe?"

"Ah, regrettably, no, but I do not discourage those who like to think so. I myself am Laurent."

Daisy outlined what the old woman told her and related her own visit to the churchyard, her subsequent suspicions and Berthe's reaction that week. "It's not much to go on," she said hesitantly, as if she'd only then realised how tenuous her evidence was.

"You'd be surprised," Marlowe said, doling out his wide grin. "If you are happy to pay then I am happy to investigate."

"Then it's settled," Daisy said and, as they shook hands to seal the arrangement, she added "And I shall call you Philippe, if it doesn't offend you."

"My pleasure," said Marlowe, raising his glass to her. "Then Philippe I am."

Chapter 15

Daisy's rescued possessions, as Jean-Paul promised, were neatly packed, although she suspected Marie had been called in to do the job. When loaded up with them, the Citroën was so crammed there wasn't room for Hamish. He kept grouching, "But I want to drive with Mama, not Michael" so in the end Michael said, "Look, *I'll* take the 2CV, though I doubt it will get as far as Cherbourg."

That earned him a slap on the wrist from Daisy. "It's never let me down," she said. "Don't be so mean."

Both Citroën and Peugeot made it to Cherbourg. At Portsmouth, Daisy fretted that they might be stopped but Customs waved them on and they arrived at Meredith's well before lunchtime. Daisy made Michael apologise to the 2CV.

Meredith played them her favourite music: the Schneiderhan recording of Beethoven's Violin Concerto. "Well," she said, "Now we can all relax."

And so it seemed. There was an Indian summer in their lives if not the weather. In midweek the snow returned in even greater volumes than last time. Once again a snowy bridegroom plighted his troth to Flora and grew a parsnip penis overnight. The sled emerged from storage and Hamish decided it was really a boat, and Meredith's snow-rippled lawns a sea over which he sailed to island beds that were now genuine islands. He gave his craft a name, *Swallow*, after asking Daisy what *Hirondelle* meant in English. That then gave them the excuse to play at Swallows and Amazons, journeying over frozen Windermere to reach the North Pole.

"And that was done with a sledge too, not a boat," said Daisy. "Because dinghies can't sail through ice."

That made it even better, Hamish said and, as he had done with *Coot Club* in the cottage on the Broads, insisted on having *Winter Holiday* read to him at bedtime.

When he learned that the sledge in the book became an ice yacht by having a sail added, he frowned. "Can Swallow be an ice yacht too?"

Michael and Daisy winked at each other and Michael set to and shaped a little timber mast and gaff while Daisy made a sail from an old bedsheet.

The snow lasted eleven days. During that time Hamish discovered the North Pole eleven times, selecting a different location each day.

They were good days, Michael felt, family days, and the mood continued when, after the snow was gone, he found a renewed inclination to indulge his clients. While he worked, Daisy and the others gathered around an old-fashioned woodburner Meredith had installed. Meredith would put pearl glue into jacketed pots to dissolve on the stove top then lean back in a chair, close her eyes, and smile.

Their Indian summer ended the morning Daisy left for her monthly antenatal. Meredith and Hamish set out to walk to the village, an exercise that usually took an hour and Michael at last had the opportunity to take Marlowe's file from its resting place in Daisy's wardrobe.

He knew which photograph he was going to choose and, secreting it beneath his jacket, he smuggled it to his workshop. Stomach churning like a felon's, he scanned Adèle into his computer then brought her up on screen. She'd called herself a seaside girl so the image was appropriate, Michael thought. She was reclining on clean silvery sand, smiling at the sky, petite breasts pert in the sea air, a neat downy triangle visible between athletic thighs that discreetly concealed anything more.

His eyes stung. He imagined Adèle stretching, rising, stepping carefully over the sand to the sea, cutting efficiently through the waves, returning, exhilarated, to wade through foot-lapping shallows back to the beach. He recalled Daisy ordering him to stop drooling at Adèle's pictures, but it was so hard to control those in his head.

He inserted photographic card into the printer, stared out of the window while the machine whooshed and did its business. When it was done, he copied the address Adèle had given him onto a sturdy brown envelope, inserted the photograph, sealed the flap.

After returning the original, he posted Adèle's copy in the next village, kept his foot hard down all the way there and back. After closing the door and checking Meredith's coat was still missing from its peg, he released a long, slow sigh. Then he remembered that Adèle still adorned his computer screen.

The phone on the hallstand began to ring. Michael ignored it, dashed to the barn, wiped the incriminating image. As he returned, he could hear, but not distinguish, the closing words of a voice message. He knew before he pressed replay that it was bad news.

Michael heard Daisy's 2CV squeak to a halt outside, then her footsteps and, a few moments later, her voice, its tone higher than usual: "Michael, what's happened?"

He was sitting, head down, on the seat by the telephone. He looked up, saw the concerned face.

"It's Colonel Ted," he said.

The words echoed lifelessly in his ears.

"I see the philanderer's already here."

Daisy glared at Peter's car, parked outside Miranda's front porch. The man himself appeared next, arm-in-arm with Miranda. He looked uncomfortable in his sober suit, black tie and formal shoes whereas Michael felt *smart*, on parade for Colonel Ted. Miranda was in black too. Michael could see she'd been crying a lot, although makeup was doing its best to conceal it.

"It's stupid," she said. "I knew it was coming but it's such a shock all the same. As if I was never really listening to anything the doctors were telling me."

"It's always a shock," Daisy said. "No matter how prepared you are. Sometimes I think it's easier when you're not."

Miranda said they'd all travel together in the official car. Michael had expected there to be family or closer friends to accompany her. Throughout the journey behind the hearse, he and Peter stared ahead, while Miranda and Daisy clutched hands.

A small bird, some sort of finch, flitted about the vaulting in the nave. Michael fancied it was Ted's soul, free to roam from that hateful box the funeral director's stout men had borne into the church. He watched the bird, ignored the parson's churchy cadences.

Why, he wanted to ask, did Ted have to die when there were so many evil people in the world? He didn't want to be told that God moves in mysterious ways or that man born of woman has but a short time to live. The only thing he could think of was 'cometh the hour cometh the man'.

It mightn't even be biblical but seemed a damn sight more relevant than the platitudes being said. Because when they needed him, Ted had been there.

Michael's mouth knotted. How unfair life was, what *empty* places churches were, even when full of prayers.

A freak gust, an icy northern blast, cut through the still air as Ted-in-the-box was lowered into cold, dank clay. The bird, Michael could now see that it was a bullfinch, stout-bodied and colourful like Ted, had followed them outside and was flying aimlessly about the clustered humans. As the coffin was finally allowed to rest, the bird soared into the air, flew south. *Ted seeking uncontaminated oceans, safer harbours.*

Two mourners, late arrivals, came forward to greet Miranda. Michael heard her address the female of the pair: "Oh, I hoped you could come." She said something to the male, who started as if someone had walked over *his* grave then looked across to Michael.

Michael recognised something in the man's eyes, the line of the jaw. Suddenly his legs could no longer bear his weight. Daisy grabbed his elbow.

"Are you feeling all right?" Concern edged her face. "There's a bench, there by the church wall, we could sit down."

"I'm fine. Just felt dizzy for a moment."

"If you're sure. I'm the one who's supposed to get giddy spells."

The man walked hesitantly towards them. "Michael? Is it really you?"

Miranda headed towards them too, bringing the woman with her. "Meet my mother," she said.

Daisy looked at Michael, back to Miranda then at the man. "Then you must be..."

"Michael's father. Patrick Cavanagh. Paddy."

After the ritual sandwiches, tea and whisky, Michael walked with his father in Ted and Miranda's winter garden. It consisted of York stone squares enclosed by beds of aromatic and colourful shrubs like arbutus, eleagnus, winter honeysuckle and viburnum growing above waving carpets of crocus, dwarf irises and snowdrops. At any other time, Michael would have thought it beautiful.

They sidestepped around what mattered. Patrick (Michael couldn't think of him as Dad) acted as if Michael was a long lost drinking buddy he'd met again after many years, accounting for the interlude with an embroidered biography spattered with bar-room jokes. Michael's part in this collusion was that now he had the chance for closure, he didn't know what to say. The futility of it wound around his head, spiralled until he felt it would burst out. It wasn't only his head; he felt it in his legs, arms, everywhere, as if each nerve he possessed was on fire.

At last he heard himself speak. "Why, Patrick? Why did you leave me with her?"

Patrick's face was uncomprehending. "Who else would I leave you with?"

Michael dug fingers hard into his palms. "You could have taken me with you. I would have been all right then."

"Ah, no, Michael. That wasn't possible." The accent had become Irish, and his father's gaze hard to pin down.

"How were we meant to live? Did you even care?"

"I cared. I sent money, regular as clockwork, when I had it. Jacinta told me she was working at the Rose and Crown."

"She *was*, as a whore."

"So I heard."

"You *knew*?"

"Not at first but it wasn't a surprise when I did. Jacinta always had a liking for the bottle and when I wasn't in work, well let's say she saw to it that she didn't go without. But she kept it in the family then. *My* family. I don't know about her own."

Michael took several deep breaths. "And there was me."

"What?"

"You heard. On my sixteenth birthday. She said I was old enough."

Patrick's Irish eyes, Anne's eyes, peered into his. Michael watched them recoil. "Ah Michael, don't say such things. It really isn't funny. She's dead, poor woman."

"Am I laughing? Didn't you understand what I said, Patrick? I *fucked* my mother."

Patrick gazed at the ground, shook his head very slowly as if he'd discovered some fault with the flagstone he was standing on. "No, you didn't, Michael. She wasn't your mother. Well she was in the sense that she brought you up but no, Jacinta wasn't your actual, your birth mother."

Michael felt an insistent ache immediately behind his eyes. "Not my real mother?"

"She wasn't that."

Michael screwed his eyes tight as emotions collided in his head. *Not guilty* screamed across *Then who was my mother*? For a time *Not guilty* won. So he *hadn't* had sex with his mother, not the one who would have loved him, hugged him when he got his new socks peed on. When he re-opened his eyes he saw his father's boring into him.

"She *promised* me she'd tell you. When you were old enough to understand, she said. Oh Michael, if I'd only known what she'd do instead."

"What would you have done?"

Patrick drew himself up. He was a full head shorter than Michael. "I would have taken you back to Ireland, Linda or no Linda. God, I knew Jacinta was volatile, it was the Spanish in her, but I never dreamed she was capable of such vengeance."

"Who's Linda? Is she my real mother?"

Patrick looked surprised. He shook his head vigorously. "Oh no, Linda's my wife. Here with me. Miranda's mum. Your real mother, Michael, was Jacinta's sister, Juanita. Look, d'you mind if we sit down?"

Patrick chose a bench beneath a winter-flowering cherry. He sank onto it with a sigh. Michael perched tentatively at one end.

"Juanita was such a girl as to turn a man's heart." Patrick's eyes assumed a kind of milky sheen. They were focused somewhere beyond any visible horizon. "She was my life's love, Michael, and she was killed on the fourteenth of November 1967, riding pillion behind me on a Velocette 350 I had then. We'd planned to marry in the spring. She was only seventeen years old and she had a face like a Madonna and a disposition to match. Did you know, you have her eyes and her smile?

"We were on the Cambridge Heath Road and a van, a red Bedford van, I can see it so clearly, came out of a side road right in front of us. I saw the driver looking straight at us but something told me he wasn't seeing us at all. I knew then that he wasn't going to stop, Michael, but there was pity all that I could do except slam the brakes on and pray to Jesus. It had been raining and the bike slewed across the road and ended up in a shop window. I picked myself up. Scraped but walking. But Juanita, my poor darling Juanita had been flung into a brick wall. A foot the other way and she might have lived. We had helmets on and all that, proper leathers but for all the good they did we might have been as naked as babes.

"You were eleven weeks old and I hadn't found out about you until just after you were born. She'd finished with me in the January. Trumped up something about me being seen with another girl and so I might have been but I don't remember it. I was nineteen, and the drink sometimes went to my head. Juanita broke my heart, Michael, but of course I didn't know she'd done it because she was pregnant and her family wanted to keep it within their own walls. The Delgados were a clanny bunch. So I took myself away, working on the buildings up north. By the time I came back to London you were being passed off to the neighbourhood as

Juanita's new brother. But it was Jacinta who told me who you really were. I still wonder sometimes about her motives.

"Well, I'd taken a drink or two and marched straight in through the Delgado's back door and asked Juanita if it was true about the baby although I didn't say how I found out. Next minute, the brothers had come in from somewhere and they and her old man started on me but I was so mad I didn't care. Juanita screamed at them and said she wasn't going to do what they wanted anymore and if they didn't stop she was leaving with me right then and taking the baby, that's you Michael. They stared at her as if she'd slapped them in the face. She was a girl who never answered back to her parents not if she didn't want a swipe from the back of Pop Delgado's hand and they just weren't expecting it, see? I got called all things of course but then the mother came down on our side and it was decided that if I asked Juanita to marry me then they'd go along with it but it had to be done properly, saving up and all. No shotgun affairs for the Delgados, they'd been nobility back in Andalusia, so they said.

"So I said I wanted to talk to Juanita on my own and after the mother had given them the nod they all trooped out and I went down on my knees and proposed. And that was Juanita and me, sweethearts again as if we'd never left off. I had money left from the buildings and Juanita already had a savings account from her job – she was a clever girl, worked at the Westminster Bank. If there was a happier man than me in all the world, I'd fight him to prove he wasn't. We'd take you in the pram to Viccy Park and sit there by the lake, holding hands. You'd be well wrapped up of course. Do you know, Michael, holding hands with the girl you love is one of the wondrous experiences of life, more intimate in its own way than any of the sweaty messy stuff?"

Patrick appeared to be waiting for an answer but Michael was so bewildered by his new history all he could manage was a croak.

It seemed enough because Patrick nodded then stood up, fingered the blossoms on a branch undulating gently above their seat. "Juanita loved these trees. Prunus...er... er... Subhirtella. There, I still have the remembering of it after all these years. Juanita said they were one of the two best things about the winter."

Michael blinked. "What was the other?"

"The back of it." Patrick laughed and his eyes danced. "She said a lot of things like that. Juanita was always the one with the sense of humour. Ah, I think I love that in a woman more than the sex."

"So how then, why, did you come to marry her sister?"

"I've asked myself that often enough but the way of it, the physical progress so to speak, was this. Mother Delgado was never going to give up her job so Jacinta had to stay at home to look after you. I was around every night after work, well most nights and I suppose it was natural that eventually I moved in and shared the bringing up of you with her. When the family suggested we ought to get married we just looked at each other and said 'Yes' at the same time. Jacinta saw it as a way of escape from them I suppose. She knew I was a soft touch and I probably saw her as a second-best Juanita, not that Jacinta was anything like her, in looks or anything else. Jacinta was hard-faced and angry at the world, always so bloody angry but I thought she would soften. In her defence, she was only sixteen and I suppose she expected some sort of life of her own, like other girls her age. I didn't know she blamed me for the loss of that. I found that out when she told me she was screwing my brother. 'You took my sister from me,' she said, 'so it's only fair.' And it's true I did lose Brendan for I've never so much as passed the time of day with him since. She took my sister's husband too, for good measure and that was the end of me and Maureen for years though we've made up now."

"No wonder Maeve and Nancy suddenly stopped inviting me."

"Ah yes, you had some grand holidays with those two fine girls. Both married now, and none the worse for it. Their dad, your Uncle Tom, worked in some office in Bishopsgate, insurance I think, and he took to travelling one extra stop on the tube to spend time with Jacinta. I don't think it had been going on that long, but she'd been doing Brendan for years and I didn't suspect a thing. It seemed only natural, him being in the house so much. It all came to a head in one almighty row. I forget how it started but Jacinta told me all that she'd been up to and the worst of it was that she told my sister Maureen. Even then I think I would have stayed with her but I happened to meet Linda. That was in Jubilee Year, 1977. Well you know that of course. Linda was organising the big party and needed a carpenter to knock up tables and the like. Someone mentioned me and I jumped right into it, as a way of forgetting what Jacinta had been up to, I guess, but I found myself telling Linda all my troubles. She was like the big sister I didn't have now Maureen was lost to me but before long I realised I was falling in love with her. It seemed ridiculous. She was more than a whisper over forty and I was twenty-nine, a slip of a lad. But, Michael, I couldn't get her out of my head and when she told me she felt the same, well we took our chance."

"If you knew Jacinta was so bad, how could you find it in you to abandon *me*?"

"Because I was so in love I would have sacrificed anyone for it. There, I've said it and I'm not proud of it. Have you never known love like that, Michael?"

"I know it now."

"With that lovely young woman? Daisy isn't it? Ah, that's grand, Michael. I'm happy for you."

Bullshit, Michael thought but Patrick wasn't finished.

"I really thought, deep down, that Jacinta cared for you. She wasn't a demonstrative woman in that way, but you were her sister's child, all she had left of her. I didn't realise she resented you too. I mean, she must have done, to do what she did. Maybe she saw you as *my* child, not Juanita's."

"I watched her die," Michael said. "They sent one of those messages over the radio. Will Michael Cavanagh, late of Bethnal Green, please go to the London Hospital, where his mother Jacinta Cavanagh is dangerously ill. I was in a pub off the Mile End Road, heard it by pure chance."

Patrick's head jerked round. His face seemed full of awe. "Jesus, and she wouldn't even tell you about your mother then, on her deathbed. God, Michael, she was indeed an unforgiving woman."

"I held her hand and I think she smiled. It was hard to tell. Perhaps she meant to tell me but her face was so swollen she couldn't get a word out."

Patrick shook his head. "Jesus," he said. Michael wondered how many times in a day he invoked the name.

"Did you know you have a granddaughter?"

Patrick's expression turned from morose, through incredulous, to delighted. "A granddaughter? You don't say. With Daisy?"

"No, someone I used to be married to. My daughter's name's Anne, she's fourteen and has your eyes and my smile. I lost ten years of her life but I have her back now. You could meet her if you like."

Tears, perhaps three or four, dripped down Patrick's cheeks. Michael suddenly felt sorry for him. The man had been childless most of his life, by choice, as he had been himself until he saw sense. "Oh Michael, that would be grand. It'd be a gas. You really mean it? You're not just saying it? Because I know it's more, a lot more than I deserve."

"I mean it. Daisy has a son, Hamish, four years old, and I had to try to get along with him. No one could have been more surprised than I was to find I'd become fond of him. Because of that, I was determined to find my daughter. Through the two of them, I've learned to appreciate the joy children can bring to our lives."

"And the pain." There was something beyond tears in Patrick's eyes now, a film of sadness that veiled the light behind. "The constant knowing you've let them down. Oh, I know what I said before about how I would have sacrificed anyone for Linda, but there have been a million times, Michael, when I've cried out for you, only for cowardice to stop me yet again from doing what I knew I should. And so the years flew and you're a grown man with a family of your own. I'm glad you got to know your daughter again before it was too late."

"You'll have another grandchild in July. Daisy's pregnant and we're getting married but not because of that. We would have been already but she happens to be married to someone else at the moment. She's applied for a divorce but I don't know which will come first, the wedding or the baptism. I'd like you to come to both if you can."

It seemed as if Patrick threw ten years off within seconds. The cloud lifted from his eyes and his mouth widened into a smile. Even the lines on his face seemed to diminish. "So you find it in your heart not to hate me then, after all I've failed you in? Michael, my son, my darling boy, I'd love to attend both if you can stand the sight of me."

"Do you want me to drive?" said Daisy.

Michael stroked his chin. The stubble felt like yesterday's, although he knew he'd shaved that morning. He thought about his birth certificate. One of those free ones, he recalled. All it gave was his name, sex, date and place of birth. Nothing about his parents. He ought to get a full one now, he supposed, but what if Patrick had been lying to him and it showed his wrong mother? No, Juanita would surely have registered his birth soon after he was born, with or without Patrick. All the same, it was something to think about, no need to do anything yet.

Michael put on his brave face. "No, I'll drive, sweetheart," he said. "It will concentrate my mind on something other than the fact I'm now a bastard. A lucky one though."

Peter had left long before, saying he had a tide to catch. Miranda's eyes misted at the remark and Michael guessed that she was recalling tides caught and missed with Ted. Patrick had become very jaunty about his new granddaughter and prospective grandchild and Linda began to snap at him. Perhaps she regretted not having any of her own, Michael thought. It was strange, how when he first saw them in the churchyard, she and Patrick had looked around the same age but now, while she was obviously Miranda's mother, an unwitting bystander might think that within the trio, Paddy and Miranda were the husband and wife.

Now, Michael drove as he had done when taking Daisy to see the cottage on the Broads, not angry this time but conscious of the precious cargo he was trusted with. He noticed every potential hazard, countered the misdemeanours of other road users without resort to the swearing he sometimes adopted. It was Daisy who took over responsibility for that, her face often pressed to the window glass, her mouth bawling obscenities.

Michael thought about that when they were safely home and he was holding Hamish joyfully aloft in his arms as Jean-Paul had done not two weeks before. He hadn't considered all that Daisy had to cope with during the day – the sad business of Colonel Ted's funeral; then Miranda's tears, for a woman seeks a woman at a time like that; him uploading his own shattering news onto her; and all this while she was working hard at carrying their child.

"Thank you, Daisy," he said and she looked up at him, frowning.

"For what?"

"For being you."

Michael recalled his old excuse that he wasn't gifted with words. Well, these didn't even approach adequacy, he knew that, but from the way Daisy's face lit up they were enough. For now.

Chapter 16

Long before Daisy was awake, Michael was in his workshop, surfacing and edging rough-sawn boards then running them through his thicknesser to square them off. By the time Daisy came to find him, he had a finished stack yards high.

"Are you all right?" she said.

"Need to get things straight," Michael said, gesturing at the timber.

Daisy swept the shavings into small heaps against the wall then came back to Michael and switched the machines off.

"Sweetheart, you don't have to deal with this on your own."

Michael rubbed a hand over his eyes. The workshop phone rang.

"Leave it," said Daisy. "I'll get it."

Moments later, Michael saw her scowling. "No," she said. "I'm not sure where he is."

"It's Peter," she mouthed to Michael then pulled a face.

"It's okay," Michael mouthed back. He took the phone.

"Hello Pete, sad day yesterday."

"Must have been traumatic for you, meeting your father again."

"I'd been working myself up to contacting him, but didn't plan it to be so soon, and not like that. Miranda had more than enough to cope with of course, but I wish she'd warned me he might be there."

"She phoned me this morning actually. I thought she stood up well yesterday, poor woman." Peter cleared his throat then said, very slowly for him, "Look, I wondered if you fancied a day out. Why not take Daisy up to the cottage, see how it's come on? I'm thinking of selling the place." Peter cleared his throat again. There followed the sort of silence that told Michael that Peter was hoping he and Daisy might make an offer.

"You still there?" Peter said at last then, somewhat hesitantly, "You're welcome to use it in the meantime of course. In fact, thinking about that, it would be better if potential buyers could see it under occupation."

Michael thought 'under occupation' made it sound as if he and Daisy were not as welcome as Peter intimated. "I'm not sure what our plans are, Pete," he said.

"Tell you what then, why don't you just go up for a sail. The forecast's good. Then you could have a quick butchers at the house, tell me what you think."

Michael looked at the piled wood shavings, stacks of timber, hand tools, machines, all the clutter. He felt a sudden need to feel the wind honing his face, raking his hair, to hear it sing in the shrouds of a small boat on open water.

"I don't want to go," Daisy said when Michael asked her to accompany him.

"It won't hurt you."

"You don't know that."

"It'll be all right, Daisy."

"I don't *want* Peter's house. I want our own. I don't want to sail his boat anymore either. Mummy's spoilt that too." Daisy was pouting but her eyes suddenly lit. "Michael, we could buy our own boat, live by the sea. The Broads are very pretty but it's like sailing on the North Circular. I want to go where there are no hullabaloos."

"You'd still get them at sea."

"Not so many, and there's much more space. You agree? We'll look for somewhere by the sea?"

Michael nodded. His home was wherever Daisy was.

"And, *and*," Daisy's face was more animated than Michael had seen it in weeks. "We could take our boat to Treguelven after Baby is born. The weather will be glorious until well into September. You can sail past and ogle me while I'm on the beach. Oh, I hope I can get my figure back quickly. I did with Hamish but I was young then."

"You're *still* young, Daisy. Anyway, you've inherited Meredith's metabolism. You'll be fine. How do you know the weather will be glorious?"

"Because I'm a goddess. We are gifted in such things."

Michael didn't know whether it was simply the bloom of pregnancy, but everything about Daisy suddenly seemed charged with a wonderful vitality. She might indeed be a goddess, he thought. And he, by default, her faun.

"Fair enough," Peter said in a dull monotone when Michael said they were spurning his cottage. Michael imagined him scratching his chin. "So, you're going to buy a boat? Funny that, the reason Miranda phoned me was to ask if I was interested in buying Passing Clouds."

"That's why he was hoping to sell us the cottage," Michael told Daisy afterwards.

"But it's Colonel Ted's boat, nobody else's."

"Perhaps Miranda needs the money."

"I doubt that very much. Maybe she simply needs to let go."

"Peter said it might mean he'd be selling Scallywag. She's exactly the same as Hirondelle."

Daisy shook her head. "Oh no, Michael, hold on. I don't want anything of Peter's. Besides, we'd have to sail this Scallywag to Treguelven and then we wouldn't be able to get into the harbour because someone would claim the water had run out."

"You haven't forgiven him, have you?"

"Maybe for that but not for him and Mummy."

There was little time for house-hunting as Daisy had to organise Hamish's second visit to his father. "It's come too quickly," she complained to Michael. "I'm beginning to regret saying he could go to France."

"You'll have to allow it after the divorce. Isn't it part of the arrangement?"

"Yes, but it's such a drag travelling there."

"Then let him come and collect Hamish."

"*No*. I must be on the scene. Just in case. I'll be all right once everything's formalised."

The visit coincided with Anne's half-term, and Michael wanted to have her to stay with him, especially since there was a new grandfather to tell her about.

"Can't you delay it a week? Then Anne'll be back at school."

"I might be showing too much by then. I can get away with it now if I wear big jumpers and baggy jeans."

"I could go with you," Meredith said. Daisy flashed her a look that said she wasn't sure.

But it was settled; they would leave on Saturday morning. "It'll be easier by plane," Meredith insisted. Michael would drive them to Stansted then go on to pick up Anne.

Daisy phoned Le Mazemeur and launched into an animated conversation. It was in French, and largely about having babies. "Adèle will pick us up from the airport," she said after she put the phone down. "When I said it was just Mummy, Hamish and me I could *see* Adèle's face fall. But she sends you her undying love."

Michael grunted something. Once the divorce was over he wouldn't have to see Adèle again. He hoped she kept tight-lipped about the photograph. He wished he'd said he'd never seen them then Adèle would have had to ask Daisy for a copy. Somehow he knew she'd never have done that.

He'd received a thank-you from her, a blank message card with roses on the front. She'd written a simple *Merci!* inside, drawn a smiley beside it but beneath was her far-too-legible signature and three kisses. He'd collected the post that morning, palpitated when he saw an envelope with his name beneath a French stamp and a Morbihan postmark. He'd shoved it down his underpants, opened it while sitting on the lavatory. He carried it out of the house the same way, shredded it in the office.

Before Daisy left for Mazemeur she had another appointment at the scanning unit. She was eighteen weeks pregnant.

"Oh," she said when they arrived. "Where's Helen?"

"She's only here three days a week," said the dark-haired girl commanding the desk. She didn't look up. "And today isn't one of them."

Michael glanced at her badge. It said her name was Nina.

"Oh," Daisy said again, tapping on the desk.

Nina looked at her for the first time. "We're all competent," she said, half-pouting. "You needn't worry."

As Nina prepared her for the scanner, Daisy said, "I don't want to know the baby's sex. You would be able to determine it today, wouldn't you?"

"Ye...s." Nina seemed to waver then she stiffened up. Michael thought he could feel the starch in the air. "Although it's not our policy to tell. However, as you prefer not to know, that suits both of us."

Michael and Daisy clasped hands. He felt electrified as they watched the screen, as if a magical current connected him to the miracle before his eyes. "Michael," Daisy said. "Baby's like a...like a *real* baby. He's *absolutely gorgeous*. Or she." She caught her breath. "Oh *look*, he's..." She turned to Nina. "He is, isn't he?"

"Sucking his thumb? Yes." Nina had a hint of a smile on her face but not in her eyes. "You see how body length is catching up with head size? And how the arms and legs are growing. Baby's twice the size as last time and putting on weight rapidly now. Probably weighs in at eight ounces, half as much again as a week ago."

Nina's eyes seemed to glaze. As if she was ticking off items on a list, she told Daisy the reasons for this scan were to check gestational age, determine placental position and ascertain there were no abnormalities obvious in the baby or problems with herself internally.

"With me? Like...growths, you mean?" Daisy looked horrified. Michael squeezed her hand.

"It's all right," Nina said, softening. "Both you and Baby are fine." She treated them to an unexpected laugh. "Just think, almost halfway there."

"I'll tell Helen you were asking after her," Nina said as they were leaving. She seemed more relaxed now. "Cheer up," she added with a grin. "It's all freewheeling now."

"I wish I believed that," Daisy said as the doors swung shut behind them.

When they were home, Meredith greeted Michael with, "Oh, there's a letter for you."

For a moment he froze. Meredith handed him a white envelope, A5, Irish stamp. He looked at the postmark: *Baille Atha Cliath.* He shrugged. "I'll stick it in the office with the others."

"It says personal on the envelope. And I've already dealt with the business mail."

"Aren't you going to open it?" Daisy said. She had a bemused expression and was studying him with intent. Michael tore open a corner of the envelope, slid his finger along the fold.

It was a letter, or rather note, from his father, written in an untidy, scrawling hand.

Dear Michael,
I thought you should have this now. It isn't very good I'm afraid, only taken with a cheap 35mil from Hong Kong but it's the only likeness I have.
Like I said, I think it should go to you now.
Your loving father,
Patrick, Paddy

Michael looked inside the envelope again and saw a small piece of card. As Patrick, Paddy, had said, it wasn't a good photograph. It was somewhat faded and crinkled at the edges too. But the girl in it might indeed be said to have a Madonna's face. She had an air of unlined innocence, as if she had yet to learn of the ways of the world. Her face was framed by gentle-looking waves of black hair that just reached her shoulders. And he *did* have her eyes and mouth, though hers were softer, feminine. The girl's lips were open in a half-smile as if she was amused with something the photographer had said but didn't want to admit it fully. Michael felt tears trickle down his cheeks. Soon they became rivers.

"It's my mother," he said, handing the photograph to Daisy. "And she's beautiful."

Chapter 17

Michael knew Daisy hated going to France without him but Anne was a priority in his life too, and he'd promised her he would be a real dad.

The smell of newly baked bread greeted him when he arrived at Grace's. It was one of the few attributes of hers he remembered with pleasure. "Nothing like it is there?" she gushed.

Anne winked at him, cut the bread and spread Irish butter on the slices. Michael relished its tang on the still warm bread, its graduation from fridge-hard to liquid as it melted.

Then Anne said something about the bathroom and went upstairs. Michael chose the moment to tell Grace he was thinking of increasing her allowance. He didn't say it only occurred to him as he walked into the living room and observed yet again how dowdy everything was.

Grace sniffed loudly. "Well, don't do it on my account."

"It's for Anne. She's at an age when she needs more...things."

"*Things*?" Grace's eyebrows and cheeks were raised. "What things?"

Michael fought the blush he could feel rising. "I *don't know*. Things fifteen-year-old girls need. I don't want Anne to lose out in comparison with her friends."

"What about me losing out?"

"That was your decision, Grace."

She sniffed again. "All right. I'll make sure Anne gets the benefit. D'you want me to tell her?"

"Not unless you think it's necessary."

Grace began to smile to herself then dropped it as Anne reappeared, wearing lipstick and eye shadow. It was modestly applied and Michael thought it kept on the right side of the line but Grace apparently disagreed. "What," she said in an acrid voice, "have you got on your face?"

"What does it look like?"

"Don't answer me back, Anne."

"*Well.*" Anne's eyes spat defiance. Her mouth seemed ready to follow.

"*Anne*," Michael said, much louder than he'd intended.

Anne's shoulders jumped. She stared at him, her jaw slowly drifting floorwards. "Sorry Mum, sorry Dad," she said and Grace rewarded Michael with a glimmer of goodwill. But then Anne straightened her face, pushed her shoulders back and Michael knew she was about to try again. "It's only a bit of makeup, Mum. All my friends are allowed. Crikey, I could be a Goth like Becky Ziebart then you'd have something to complain about."

Grace gave Michael a quick sideways glance. "What would the Lomonds think of me, letting you go out like that?"

"Anne, can you give us a moment?" Michael said. She smiled nervously, licked her lips, nodded and left the room. Seconds later, he heard her going upstairs.

"Daisy wouldn't think there was anything wrong at all," he said to Grace. "And neither would Meredith. Anne's almost fifteen, Grace. Don't try and force her to remain a child. She'll resent you for it."

He watched Grace simmer. Her top lip curled as she came to the boil. "And you've come to know it *all* in a few short months of remembering to be a father?"

"Don't throw that at me, Grace. No, I don't know it all but I do think you're making too much of this. Give Anne some leeway. She's a sensible girl, she won't let you down."

"I know that." Grace snapped the words but then appeared to reflect, biting her lips. "All right then but on your own head be it."

Four hours and a hundred and fifty miles further on, Michael at last told Anne everyone else was in France.

"So I've got my Dad all to myself. *Wicked.*" The tiny smile Anne arrived with began to grow then a gleam that matched the 'wicked' formed in her eyes. "Why didn't you mention it to Mum?"

"You saw how she was about the lipstick."

Anne's mouth opened. The beginnings of a word emerged then she closed her mouth again, clutched Michael's hand and they walked silently towards the house.

After they'd taken her bags to her room, Anne stood at the window. Like Michael and Daisy's, it was at the front of the house, in fact it was Daisy's old room.

Anne said: "Do you know the story of Flora?"

They looked down at the statue. Purple crocuses now ringed Flora's grimy feet.

"She was a prostitute before she became a goddess."

Michael suddenly wished Flora wasn't quite so naked. He remembered looking up lubricious.

"Is that what they teach you in school these days?"

Anne's face was earnest. "Not the prostitute bit. I found that on the internet. Our teacher told us Flora's Holiday was to flatter the goddess into protecting the blossoms. She didn't mention it turned into something the politicians dreamed up for getting votes, like having plays with naked actresses. People put flowers in their hair and gave gifts of small vegetables as tokens of sex and fertility."

Michael stared helplessly out of the window, fixing his eyes on the background of trees above Flora's head. Small vegetables, the *parsnip penis,* he was thinking. Yet Anne wasn't here in the snow.

"Have you mentioned this to Daisy?"

"Might have." Anne was grinning. "Have I shocked you, Dad?"

"Naa."

Michael tried a grin himself but imagined it looked like a Roman politician's. He rubbed his hands together, said, "Well, better sort out something for dinner I suppose" in an over-hearty voice that made his ears ring.

Perhaps Anne sensed Michael's unease because she suddenly changed into the girl he was accustomed to. "Can we explore the house first?" she said, with a touching shyness. "I've never dared to ask with everyone here."

"I suppose so."

Michael was going to add, "But don't touch anything in Meredith's room". Anne, however, had already dashed off, as enthusiastic as Hamish on his forays. It gave Michael a glimpse of what he'd missed and dismissed over the years. His eyes felt heavy.

Anne was in his and Daisy's room. She had the door to Daisy's dressing room open, and was gazing, long-faced, at the boxes containing the clothes rescued from Mazemeur.

"Oh, I so wanted to see Daisy's dresses," she said. Michael said he did too. On Daisy that was, but she preferred to be a jeans and tee-shirt girl.

The morning at the cottage when Daisy had worn the paeony yellow affair remained the only occasion he'd seen her in a dress. He recalled the way she'd twirled it, the shape of her legs as they were revealed, the sleek tautness of their muscles. She was the only woman he knew who combined raw sensuality with a feminine elegance that made him want to kneel at her feet. She'd probably be disturbed by that but then she was the one who called herself a goddess. The ache that had been in his breast from the moment Daisy went through the departure gate grew deeper, sharper, insisting.

He realised Anne was speaking.

"I was saying Dad, do you think Daisy might let me try some on? When she's back, I mean."

"I should think so."

Anne hovered, wearing an odd, half-daft smile. Michael knew she was hoping he might open one or two boxes. He also knew Daisy wouldn't appreciate anyone, even him, sifting through her clothes.

Anne appeared to give up. She walked over to the dressing table, picked up bottles of perfume, sniffed their contents, dabbed her wrists. Then she noticed the photograph of Baby's first scan beside them.

"So *this* is my baby brother." Anne's voice brimmed with excitement.

"Or sister."

Anne screwed her eyes up, peered at the image. "No, definitely a boy."

Michael wondered what she'd seen to give her that opinion. He thought he might prefer a second daughter but then he worried Anne might think he wasn't satisfied with the first. "A boy it is then," he said and Anne smiled his own smile back at him.

They crossed the head of the staircase, entered Meredith's room. Now Michael did tell Anne to look but not touch. She complied perfectly until he opened the door of Meredith's dressing room. Anne looked like a child given the keys to a sweetshop as she gazed at the racks of exquisite clothes and rows of gleaming navy blue or burgundy shoes. Before Michael could stop her, she was inspecting dresses and jackets, stroking their material, tracing her fingers over the labels.

"Gosh," she kept saying as she read out one famous name after another. Finally she coloured and said, "I really shouldn't be doing this."

"No," Michael said. "You shouldn't."

"Sorry," Anne said then pointed to another door on the far side of the room. "What's in there, Dad?"

"I don't know."

The door was locked but there was a key on a chest of drawers immediately beside it. Michael tried it. The lock turned. As he opened the door, the air inside seemed to rush out and strike him as if trying to force him away.

"Did you feel it too, Dad?"

Michael adopted a smile, took Anne's hand.

"Probably a build-up of air pressure with the room being shut up."

The room was empty apart from a stout steel clothes rack that had an army uniform, an officer's, hanging at its far end. Unlike Meredith's dressing room, there were no windows and no gaps, apart from the doorway, where air could have entered from outside.

Anne was examining the uniform. There were captain's pips on the shoulders but the regimental and other badges had been removed, as had the medal ribbons. Where they had been, the cloth was darker.

"Was Daisy's dad a soldier?" Anne said.

"Once. Before she was born. Before he and Meredith married, I think."

Michael recalled Harry, tall and straight, parading around the May Queen contestants in the village meadow, approving or disapproving their charms with a rapist's eyes. He recalled Harry in his wheelchair, shrunk and crooked, in the sitting room downstairs, curling his lip, despising the peasant who dared to love his daughter. He wondered why Meredith had kept the uniform while discarding everything else.

"Did you know him?"

Michael was worrying about that gust of air. He blinked and returned his attention to Anne. "I met him last year, not long before he died. He had a progressive illness, some form of motor neurone disease. I wouldn't say I knew him."

Anne suddenly shivered. "It's weird in here, Dad. I don't like it."

As Michael relocked the door he had the unsettling feeling that he'd managed to release Harry's ghost.

Anne wasn't interested in Hamish's room, which of course she knew intimately. Michael hoped they could go downstairs, as he'd already told her the guest bedrooms were merely collections of unused furniture. Anne seemed about to comply with his wishes but then she stopped. "No, I'd better have a look or I'll always be wondering what I've missed."

The guest bedrooms were accessed from the dark corridor housing the Lomond portraits that Michael had passed by on his first ever night there. Anne ignored the pictures and showed no interest in the rooms apart from looking at the view from their windows. In the last room, the one where Daisy seduced him, as Anne looked out at the denuded trees of winter Michael was seeing Daisy traverse between their fresh greenery on a cool June morning. He touched the bedcover as they left.

Back in the corridor, Anne seemed to notice the portraits for the first time.

"Who *are* these old men?" she said, frowning as she scanned their shaded rows. "Why are they hidden away here?"

"Because they're relations of Daisy's father, I expect, not of Meredith." But not discarded like Harry's other possessions, because art of course was sacrosanct to the upper classes.

Anne stopped in front of a blear-eyed man robed in scarlet and ermine. A decoration, an order of some sort, sparkled at the centre of his chest. Anne bent this way and that, absorbing every detail. "He must be a lord," she said in an awed whisper. "Was Daisy's dad one too?"

"His father was. Harry was just an honourable." *Dishonourable*, Daisy half-joked once but he wasn't going to tell Anne that.

"Gosh. Wait till I tell Grandma Cavendish. It'll be the talk of Barnes, me having connections with nobility. Is Daisy an honourable too?"

"Not in the same way."

Anne looked perplexed.

"It doesn't carry down that far. Only to the children of the peer."

"Right, you mean she's honourable in the best sense. What about Meredith's family, I bet some of hers are dukes."

"I don't know. She's never said."

"No, she wouldn't," Anne said, nodding to herself.

At last they went downstairs. Michael felt a distinct chill in the hall, even though the central heating had been on all day. He touched a radiator, withdrew his hand immediately. The water inside was scalding. He wished Daisy would phone.

Michael lit the downstairs fires. Anne wandered about, craning her neck to read titles on Meredith's legions of books, and spent much time appraising the paintings. In the parlour, Michael pointed out one of a serious country house, all Georgian red brick and tall windows.

"It's where Meredith and Daisy used to live."

Anne shivered. "All those glowering windows. I shouldn't have liked it there."

Michael had intended to open the bureau where Meredith kept the family photographs, show Anne those of Daisy as a child. But he suddenly had a curious reluctance to do so. *It was in that house*, he told himself. *It happened in that house.*

The only downstairs rooms Anne was unfamiliar with were beyond the kitchen, in the oldest part of the house. A narrow wing running at ninety degrees from the main structure, it contained Harry's study, plus the bedroom and bathroom he'd used during his illness. There were no rooms above them, only a loft.

The bedroom was now a clinical space containing pale new furniture of Scandinavian design arranged on white carpet, as if Meredith had wanted to bleach out Harry's occupation. "Boring," Anne said. "Those carpets will show every bit of dirt." She sounded like Grace and Michael had to suppress a smile.

He lingered in Harry's bathroom, wondered how Meredith managed to lift Harry in and out of the bath, on and off the lavatory. He recalled Daisy's burst of anger about that. He recalled too, medicines, syringes, related stuff. Soon after he moved in, Meredith got him to take them to the council tip. "Destroying the evidence," she'd said and laughed.

"Wow," Anne said as she encountered the dark panelled walls of Harry's study. Meredith had left this room untouched. The panelling was linenfold, made some time in the seventeenth century. Michael had been here only once before, when a tearful Daisy grabbed his hand, said she wanted to show him something of her father's. He had followed with some trepidation, wondering what further iniquity she was going to reveal. She'd gone to a drawer in a huge desk, brought out a small leather case containing a medal, a cross with a purple and white ribbon. "A Military Cross. For something he did in Aden. An award for bravery." Daisy had turned to him and he'd seen the anguish in her eyes. "How could he deserve that and do what he did to me?"

Around the walls hung instruments of death. Cavalry sabres, a murderously large scimitar, several claymores, basket-hilted highland swords. There were guns in locked cases: several rifles and a quartet of Purdeys Daisy had said was worth a mint. And Michael knew that in the desk containing the Military Cross was Harry's army revolver, complete with ammunition. He thought about the uniform upstairs, about Harry's ghost now roaming free.

Anne rattled a desk drawer.

"I don't have a key," Michael said, although he knew exactly where it was kept.

Anne surveyed the pictures, all framed photographs, on the walls. In the midst of ten other young men, all in whites, Harry wielded the bat. The central figure of fifteen rugby hearties, Harry had the ball. In mortarboard and gown, its hood richly coloured, Harry strolled with an older man and woman on what looked like a college green.

"Cambridge," Anne said, pointing to this last one.

"Cambridge?"

"It's the Senate House Green at Cambridge University. Must be his degree ceremony. And there's the football photo too. Light blue jerseys." Anne smiled at Michael. "That's where I shall do my degree."

Michael could see the intention in Anne's eyes. My daughter at Cambridge, he thought, the first graduate Cavanagh. It appealed to him very much.

"I can see why Daisy's so beautiful," Anne said after studying the photographs. "He's very handsome and Meredith's still lovely now."

Michael peered at Harry. Daisy had inherited her height from him perhaps but her facial features were an almost exact copy of Meredith's.

"I can't see him in Daisy at all," he said.

"She has his mouth. As I have yours."

Michael inspected Harry again. Daisy's mouth was soft and sweet, inviting, nothing like that supercilious example.

"Talking about inheriting mouths," he said. "I have something to show you."

Michael ran upstairs to fetch Juanita's photograph. As he reached the landing, he fancied he could hear a wheelchair running about on the bare boards somewhere. He recalled his dreams about that, told himself he was being ridiculous, that ghosts didn't exist. Yet when he went back down the stairs he made sure he took them two at a time.

Michael showed Juanita's photograph to Anne, told her everything he knew about her.

"And she died and you never knew you had the wrong Mum?" Anne shook her head. "Bloody hell. Oh, sorry Dad."

"Bloody hell indeed. So how do you feel about meeting your Granddad?"

Daisy phoned at last, soon after nine pm, and the chill in the house disappeared. It was as if, through the ether, Daisy's presence was asserting itself, neutralising Harry's ghost.

"We're at the bungalow with Marie and Augustine. There was a mini-disaster before we arrived. A hot water pipe burst when JP turned the boiler on in the gîtes and it brought the ceilings down. Serve him right for not lagging the pipes. At least we're in a friendly house now and I'm *Tante* Daisy again. Are you missing me terribly or is Anne keeping you jolly?"

"Both."

"Oh. I suppose one cancels the other out?" Daisy sounded disappointed.

Anne came in to say goodnight. She was wearing a sort of extended teeshirt that reached a little way down her thighs. Michael tried not to look at the latter, hoped Anne was wearing pants beneath. She gave him a child's kiss but as she hugged him, her little breasts pressed hard against him and he felt afraid, not of them, but of what Anne might be thinking and what she might be thinking he was thinking. He really needed to ask Daisy about this.

They offered to meet Paddy halfway between there and Dublin. Michael felt a night or two away from Meredith's might do him good and would be an adventure for Anne. Liverpool, perhaps. Michael had never been but Paddy had worked up there, and he'd been a Beatles fan. Michael recalled the songs Paddy used to play on his old Dansette: *Eleanor Rigby; Norwegian Wood; Penny Lane.* He smiled as he remembered thinking Penny Lane was a woman. It occurred to him that the recordings were from albums that came out during the Juanita years. They must have been *their* songs.

Yes, Liverpool would be a good meeting point. Anne was into sixties music too, funny how things went around. They could visit the Cavern Club, places like that, take a ferry across the Mersey, like Gerry and the Pacemakers in a film he'd seen once.

Paddy didn't seem keen.

"Liverpool? The Wirral?"

His voice sounded as if he was being awarded a prison sentence. The silence that followed was charged with something Michael couldn't figure out. Paddy said he didn't want to put them out, driving all that way, three or four hours. Wouldn't it be easier if he just caught a plane to Stansted, stayed in the village pub or something. 'Something' probably meant he was angling to stay at Meredith's but Michael refused to be conned into pressing her for her approval.

It was Anne who changed Paddy's mind. Signalling frantically for the phone, she seemed reluctant to say anything once she had it in her hand. Then, "Granddad?" very softly, her voice shaking a little. Michael heard Paddy's voice become high-pitched, and imagined him brushing away a tear. Paddy's tone steadied as Anne launched into reasons why Dad's idea was a good one and within a minute, Michael could tell that Paddy had been captured.

Chapter 18

Paddy held Anne lightly by her shoulders, stepped back half a pace. "Ah God love you. The perfect combination. The Cavanagh eyes, my Juanita's mouth and Maureen's crowning glory."

Anne's brow twisted. "Maureen?"

"He means your hair," said Michael.

"Maureen's my sister," Paddy said.

Anne shook her head. "Ah, no." She sounded Irish herself. "I have my mother's hair. That's what attracted Dad to her. Isn't that right, Dad?"

Michael nodded. That's what he'd told Grace anyway.

Paddy booked them into a hotel in Chester, said it was easier than fighting Liverpool traffic. It was a sprawling establishment built into a mediaeval Row but had the atmosphere of a small country hotel. It was humming with businessmen in dark suits, and they could only get two rooms, both doubles with twin beds. Anne was given her pick and Michael and Paddy took Hobson's choice. Paddy said he'd been there before.

"Didn't serve pints in those days. Kept riffraff like me away, I suppose." He grinned at Michael. "But here I am again and they're glad of my custom." He began tapping his feet, looked at his watch. "I wouldn't mind a walk as a matter of fact, Michael. Would you and Anne not care for a stroll? I'll show you the town."

Showing them the town consisted chiefly of pointing out the pubs. Michael guessed Paddy had been in every one. Paddy began his itinerary though, by steering them into a shopping precinct and indicating shops that contained his carpentry. He waved expansively, as if he was somehow a part-owner, yet he could not be persuaded to enter any.

When they left the precinct it was raining, shafts of near-ice driven by a northern wind. They were glad of the cover the Rows provided. Paddy led them in a dash across a busy street to what turned out to be a long, narrow inn he said used to serve a heavenly draught of Guinness. He looked plaintively at Michael.

"All right," Michael said after exchanging a glance with Anne. "Just one."

An overpowering aroma of cooking, as heavenly in its way as the Guinness, wafted from the interior. Michael's mouth watered. He realised that he and Anne hadn't eaten since breakfast. "My treat," Paddy said as they asked for the menu.

When they re-emerged into daylight, the rain had stopped. Paddy suggested they head towards the river. The *King's Head*, the *Falcon*, the *Bear and Billet*, he said at various points on the way but Michael became increasingly hard of hearing. They walked through the Bridgegate to the Groves and gazed awhile at the river, placid above its weir, its landing stages deserted. Paddy mentioned there used to be a good pub at the far end and he was wondering if it was still there. Anne winked heavily at Michael and said, "Can we walk along the city walls? I'd really like to do that."

Paddy bowed Cavalier fashion. "Of course," he said and, with the light beginning to fade, they crossed the road to a series of sandstone steps that linked different levels of the wall. "They're called the Wishing Steps," Paddy said. "You make a wish at the bottom but to make it come true you have to run all the way up then down and back up again without drawing breath."

Anne said "I'm going to try. How about you?"

"Not for me," said Paddy.

"Come on, Dad."

Michael looked at Anne's earnest face. "Go on then."

He wished for a future in which he and Daisy were free from the ghosts troubling them now. He knew happy ever after was a fairy tale so he just asked for life not to be too bad for them all: Daisy, Anne, Baby, Hamish, and himself.

Anne's face was working beside him. Michael wondered what she was wishing for. He saw her set her jaw square.

"Ready, Dad?"

Anne beat him to the top the first time and down to the bottom. He began to overhaul her on the second ascent but held back, allowed her the victory.

Anne's eyes were shining as they hugged each other, chests heaving as they fought to regain their breath.

"Wicked," Anne said. "That was something else."

Paddy, who'd remained at the bottom of the steps during the frenzied dashing, stumped laboriously up them. "Now if I was in my prime," he said, "you'd not even have seen the heels of me."

They had dinner in the hotel then Paddy was itching to go out for the evening. "We're both whacked," Michael said, after flickering eyelids with Anne. "You were right, it was a long way to drive. You go, we'll slum it here."

"What do you think of him?" Michael said after Paddy had gone.

"He's a hoot. Almost the stereotypical Irishman."

"Yet he isn't Irish, not really. Despite the accent. He's as London as I am."

Anne raised her eyebrows. "He was born in London?"

"And bred, though his parents were from Connemara. His mother's father had a farm. That's where he ran off to when he eloped with Linda. Did you know she's much older than him, about the same age difference as Grace and me?"

Anne's eyebrows lifted again. "Is this some Cavanagh trait? I hope I don't end up marrying some grisly, whiskery old man." She began to giggle and although it wasn't very funny that set Michael off too until they were both laughed out.

Paddy smelled and looked as if he'd had a pint in every pub within the city walls. He lurched into their room while Michael half-dozed in front of *Newsnight.*

"Has Annie gone to bed already?" Paddy looked all about him, even checked behind the door.

"Hours ago. Why?"

"I'm feeling guilty. I should have stayed in tonight, spent some time with her."

"You'll have all of tomorrow. I thought we'd go to Liverpool. See the Beatles' sites. Anne's got most of their albums on CD. We could go over on the ferry from Birkenhead."

"From Birkenhead?"

"Yes."

"Birkenhead. Ah." Paddy was frowning.

"What's wrong with Birkenhead? Don't the ferries run from there anymore?"

"Oh yes, they do, I believe. No, there's nothing wrong with Birkenhead. Well, other than the obvious."

Paddy seemed to withdraw into himself, slumped in a chair, his head studying his midriff. Michael switched the TV off.

"Christ," Paddy said, bursting out of his doldrums, "there's so much about you that I don't know, son."

"Whose fault is that?"

Paddy held his hands up. "I know, I know. Mea culpa. But that just makes it worse. Look at your young Annie, I've been her grandfather nearly fifteen years and neither she nor I have known it. What went wrong between you and her mother?"

"Grace. I told her what Jacinta did to me and she walked out and never came back."

Paddy's eyes flickered. "And took Annie with her?"

Michael nodded. "Grace was the same age as Jacinta. It seems she thought I'd married her out of some variation on the Oedipus complex. She called me a pervert."

"Jesus. When you really married her for her glorious red hair?"

"I actually married her because she asked me to and I couldn't see a reason to say 'No'. I was twenty and already tired of bumming around. She was thirty-five but could have been ten years younger. You ought to see her now. She's let herself go."

"Join the club. Though I wouldn't swap Linda for the world, she'll be seventy in a few years and her age is really starting to show. I think I was catching up until I met you again." Paddy suddenly straightened up, pushing his backside deep into the chair. "So we both wed older women, Michael. Why did I choose mine? I think after being stormbound with Jacinta, I was looking for fair winds and a safe anchorage, though you'd know more about that, you being a sailor." He gripped the arm of his chair, leaned towards Michael. "Now that's a tale to tell your grandchildren, son, how you captured your Daisy from the very lair of her wicked husband, whisked her away on a tiny pea shell of a boat over tempestuous seas, spitting defiance right into the eyes of old Neptune himself."

Michael shook his head, smiling at the same time. "I'm not that much of a sailor. But I like the way you tell it."

Paddy let out a loud belch. "Manners, Paddy. So son, tell me, what made you become a carpenter like your old dad?"

"I was sick of waiting on tables in France and Italy, so I came back to London, looking for I don't know what. One day I ended up in Darley Road. I couldn't bring myself to call at the house, just hung about in the street. Then Jacinta walked right past me without even a glance, headed for the Rose and Crown. I knew she'd be in there for hours so I nipped round the back of the house. As I was hoping, she'd left the kitchen door unlocked – still the same old habit. Nothing had changed inside either. Your tools were still where you left them and something made me take them with me when I left. I conned my way into a job with an old style cabinetmaker. All I knew was what I'd learned from school woodwork lessons and watching you. He soon realised that didn't amount to much but he said I had a rare feeling for wood. I learned fast, took over the business when he retired. I still have your tools."

"You don't?"

"You can have them back if you like."

"No, son, you keep them." Paddy looked deflated. "So Jacinta never threw them out. That's a surprise. I'll admit I lost a few tears when I heard she was dead. Maybe if we'd had a child together things might have been different. Goodness knows, we tried. She had..." He rolled his eyes up, counted, mouthing numbers silently, "...seven miscarriages in all. She wanted her own child more than anything in the wide world."

"No wonder she resented me. I was living proof it was her, not you. In her face every day. Perhaps it turned her mind. Perhaps she resented Juanita too. For producing a child when she couldn't. Then for dying and leaving her with the reminder."

Something kindled in Paddy's eyes, enlightenment or hope, Michael wasn't sure. "You know son, that makes more sense than anything I've conjured up over the years. Oh, sweet Mother of God, I wish I'd taken you away with me."

"But you didn't."

"No." Paddy scratched an ear for a few moments then fingered the slack skin under his jaw. "But then you'd never have met your lovely Daisy, or your first wife for that matter and so there'd be no Annie. So perhaps that feller was right, the one who said all things were for the best. If we dwell on maybes, Michael, we'll drive ourselves mad."

Michael, looking at the confusion of lines etched on the face of this father-come-lately, experienced something approaching affection for him, drunken old sod that he was. In between the rhetoric and the blarney there was a dram or two of solid sense. He smiled and patted Paddy on the shoulder. "Pangloss," he said.

"Pan what?"

"Pangloss. He claimed that to say all is right was nonsense because the truth was that all is for the best."

Paddy stared, open-mouthed, at his son. "You've inherited your mother's brain for sure, Michael, not mine. Juanita was always the one with the facts to dress the words. Where did you get hold of stuff like that?"

"I read it in a book. I had a lot of time on my hands."

"Of course. In a book. D'you know, Michael, I don't believe I've read one in my life."

"You do all right on it." Michael stretched and yawned. "Now, do you plan on staying up all night or can I go to bed?"

"No, you go ahead. I'm about to turn in myself. Goodnight, Son."

When Michael checked a few minutes later, Paddy was bent forward, elbows resting on his knees. He seemed in a trance, staring at the wall, but then he turned his head slightly and Michael saw that he was crying.

"Are you all right, Dad?" There, he'd said it. Dad. It didn't sound so terrible.

Paddy wheeled round. "Sorry, son. I was just thinking about someone. You go to sleep." Michael hoped he was thinking about Juanita.

They motored into the Wirral, opting for the Deeside road because Paddy said he'd like to see Parkgate again.

Michael had imagined Parkgate as a place of pleasantly proportioned trees and rolling green sward but the only green prominent was a mass of salt marsh that stretched out from the sea wall as far as he could see. It seemed to touch the Welsh coast on the opposite side of the Dee. A small motorboat passing slowly along its tip was the only clue there was water out there. And as for sand, you'd be a long time looking for it.

"This was once the main port for sailing to Dublin," Paddy said. "And then it became a bathing resort."

"They'd have a job of either now," said Michael.

On the landward side of the road were old houses, a few inns, and an ice-cream parlour. Paddy licked his lips. Michael guessed it wasn't at the thought of a Knickerbocker Glory.

Anne sat on the sea wall, her feet dangling over it. "Don't the Welsh hills look beautiful?" she said.

"That's Moel Famau over there," said Paddy, pointing to the largest lump. For a moment, his eyes were like Michael remembered Peter's, searching distant horizons. Then Paddy sighed and his eyes seemed veiled. "I used to come here a lot." He cast a wistful glance at an inn across the road. "For old times' sake?" he said to Michael.

While Paddy was in the inn, Michael and Anne strolled to the end of the promenade and came upon an unbounded area of marsh. Here they were the only humans in a world belonging to wading birds.

Anne clutched Michael's hand. "Sometimes," she said, "I wish I could find a wild place like this, where you and I and Mum could be together."

Michael felt his heart pumping. He wondered if that was what Anne asked for at the Wishing Steps. He wanted to say it was the last thing he wanted.

"Take the panic off your face, Dad," Anne said. "I know it can never be, not with you and Mum, but sometimes I wish the past had not been the past."

Michael hugged her to him. "Me too, darling. Me too."

After they collected Paddy, Michael drove to Birkenhead. They bought tickets for the ferryboat and walked down to the floating landing stage. A squat little vessel with a stubby funnel was approaching from somewhere to port.

They did Matthews Street first. Paddy stared at the bronzes of the Fab Four above the Beatles shop. He became tearful. Michael guessed he was having a bout of nostalgia for those old albums he had shared with Juanita.

"What's wrong, Granddad?" Anne said.

"Nothing," Paddy said, wiping his eyes. "Not now."

He and Anne sang all the way from the Cavern Club to the Albert Dock: *Love me do* and *Please please me*, shaking their hair in the way the Beatles used to do, although there wasn't much of Paddy's to shake. Passers-by grinned. "Aw right der la?" a man about Paddy's age said and Paddy said, "Aw right" back. It sounded like a foreign language to Michael. He suddenly felt out of place.

Anne, arm-in-arm with Paddy, had a grin wider than the cat from across the Mersey. A twinge of jealousy nagged Michael. At the Albert Dock though, Anne switched allegiance. They visited the Beatles Story and the Maritime Museum then had tea in a restaurant overlooking the tranquil water before heading back to the Pierhead for the ferry.

In Birkenhead, Paddy asked Michael if he'd mind driving into the town. There was a house he remembered.

He directed Michael into a criss-cross grid of humble streets. They drove up and down, Paddy's face hugging the window glass. "This is it," he said several times, only to decide it wasn't. At last he told Michael to give up. "I can't remember. I can't remember." His face was set in a glum attitude all the way to Chester.

That evening, after Anne had gone to bed and Paddy couldn't escape him, Michael said, "What was that business in Birkenhead about?"

"Business?" Paddy was trying to look confused.

"You know exactly what I mean."

Paddy's expression changed to shifty. "A girl I knew lived there, in one of those streets."

"Must have been quite some girl."

Paddy shrugged. He sat down, his back rigid, and when he spoke again his voice had a hoarse element to it. "She wasn't actually. But you see, Michael, considering I was working up here so far from home you might expect I'd get lonely once in a while, seek a bit of feminine company."

"I get the feeling there was more to it than company."

"I suppose you could say there was more, yes."

"How much more?"

"Well, you might have a sister."

A nerve snagged Michael's brow. He kept his face as straight as he could. "How do you mean, *might*?"

"I mean you do have. Unless...you know..." Paddy was wriggling, trying not to look at him.

"Unless she's dead?"

Paddy cleared his throat. "Exactly, that would be what I meant."

"What's the name of this sister of mine?"

"I sort of left in a hurry. Ronnie, Veronica that is, hadn't got around to choosing names."

"You ran away?"

"I might have ended up dead if I'd stayed."

"Her father threatened you?"

"Brother. He was the reason I had false teeth at nineteen." Paddy stroked his jaw as if it was still tender.

"It went like this, Michael. I was an apprentice with a big brewery. They were refurbishing their pubs and sent me to work on some up here. Anyway, this Saturday in March the year before you were born, I'd been to Anfield, watched Spurs lose to Liverpool. One nil, as I recall. My lodgings were in Birkenhead and I caught the underground back, ended up in this pub full of empty faces. It was there I noticed Ronnie. Not my type at all. I bought her a drink or two and that led to, well you know what. And before you say it, yes I was being unfaithful to Juanita and I'm not proud of that but it was an odd class of day.

"I saw Ronnie for a few months then I was called back to London. Next thing, the brewery sold the pubs off and I got the sack. Only a few weeks before Christmas too. Then, with my head still reeling from that, Juanita gave me the push. You know why now, of course. Anyway, I decided nobody in London wanted me so I headed up here again, got the job on the precinct. A gang of us used to visit that pub in Parkgate. We'd pile into our old Trannie, hide it round the corner. My London accent, I'd moved it a bit upmarket, gave me one up on the locals and many a time I was taken home to meet Mummy and Daddy. I used to pretend I was a property developer."

Michael shook his head. Paddy's accent was Irish now, with scarcely a trace of London. Was that developed to sweet-talk Dublin girls when Linda's charms began to pall? How many more skeletons were in Paddy's cupboard? He watched the far-away look on Paddy's face then supposed the story wasn't so surprising. What about himself? What if he'd actually *done* it with that Californian girl, Laura-May? She could have had his child and he'd never have known.

Paddy appeared to be ruminating, elbow resting on the arm of his chair, fist supporting his chin. "A bloke I'd known in Birkenhead mentioned that Ronnie had had a kid," he said. "I didn't believe it could be mine but when he told me the child's age I decided to check for myself.

"I mooched up and down her street, eventually knocked on her door. 'What do *you* want?' she said. I said I was just wondering if she needed help. 'Jesus, Mary and Joseph,' she said. 'A year since I seen you and only now you come offering help. You're a fucking joke, Jonesy.'"

"Jonesy?"

Paddy reddened. "Ah. The morning after that first time, she said I hadn't told her my name. George Jones, I said, reading it from a record album in a stack of them behind her. I couldn't tell her my real one, Michael, couldn't risk Juanita finding out."

"You devious bugger."

Michael would never be able to listen to George Jones again without thinking of Paddy and his urchin girlfriend.

"Anyway, Ronnie hissed 'Not here! Round the back.' So I went down the entry. She was waiting in her yard. I handed out fivers, watched her count them. 'Can I see the kid?' I said. She snorted. 'You think two hundred lousy quid'll give you access?' she said. 'Piss off and count yourself lucky.'"

"But I wasn't lucky. Her brother walked in as I was walking out. 'Who the fuck's this?' he said but she didn't need to tell him. Her face said it all. 'You fucking cockney bastard' he kept saying. I said I might be a bastard but I wasn't a fucking cockney and he hit me then, kicked the bloody lights out of me. Somebody took me to hospital but I wasn't going to stay there. I walked out, managed to get to the station and catch a Chester train. As soon as I could walk without falling over I came back to London. A few months later I bumped into Jacinta and she told me about you."

"And you've never felt the need to find out about this daughter of yours?" Stupid question, Michael thought, when he never felt the need to find out how I was doing. Any more, he chided himself, than I did about Anne.

Paddy opened his mouth then closed it. Michael watched it tighten into a hard little knot then gradually relax. "It wasn't as if she really existed. Not in my head."

"So why make me drive up and down those streets today?"

"Ah, now there you have me, Michael, caught in my own trap. Isn't it obvious? Because there's always a part of a man that makes the rest of him a liar."

Paddy was slumped forward as if the weight of all his transgressions had descended on him. Michael thought about what Paddy had just said, and it led him to consider his own sin, how he'd allowed the fact that Jacinta was only his aunt to diminish it. What matters, he decided, is that I *believed* she was my mother. And I have to accept that, live with it.

He sat down beside Paddy, who glanced at him then reverted to staring at his feet. "Dad, you were just a boy when you were up here. Irresponsible and stupid at times, like all boys. Like I was. Well I've decided I won't judge myself and I'm certainly not judging you. So you stop judging yourself."

"I had. Well at least I'd shoved it to the back of my mind. But it suddenly became important again this afternoon. When there was a chance she might be no further from me than a step across the pavement."

"You know her surname? Ronnie's?"

"Lancelot."

"Unusual. She must have registered the birth."

"I've thought of that. Never had the bottle to take it further."

"I could do it for you. When I get back home. I think you can do it on the internet."

"Technology, where would we be without it?" Paddy sighed loudly, his breath almost whistling. He leaned his head back and gazed up at the ceiling. "I don't know son, I really don't know."

"It'll just be a name, Dad. You don't have to do anything with it if you don't want to. She won't know. Would you like me to look for her?"

When Paddy looked back at Michael, his eyes were still unsure but his voice was saying yes.

Chapter 19

Michael had tried Daisy's mobile unsuccessfully while they were away. As soon as he and Anne reached Meredith's, he scrolled through the messages on the house phone. His heart raced as he heard Daisy's voice.

"Only me," it said, as if she wasn't the most important person in his life. "It's Tuesday night and I'm missing you. Hope you and your father haven't come to blows. I've been thinking how hard it must be for you both after all these years. *Michael* (Daisy's voice became excited), I've so much to tell you but it will have to wait till we can talk properly. I'll call you tomorrow evening or you could try me on Marie's number if you're back before then. Here it is..."

Michael dialled.

A young voice.

"Marie?"

Hesitantly, "Monsieur Cavanagh?"

"Michael, please. Is Daisy there?"

"Un moment."

Michael heard footsteps on tiles then women's voices, muffled. There were more footsteps. Even at this distance he recognised them as Daisy's, ringing, decisive.

"Michael, darling, you're back."

"We're back. I was beginning to worry, couldn't get through to your mobile and didn't want to phone the house and get Jean-Paul." Michael

234

half expected Daisy to say he might have struck lucky and got Adèle. She didn't.

"My phone's useless," Daisy said. "Won't hold a charge. Anyway, now I've got you I *still* can't talk properly. I'll just say I've had *very* interesting information from Philip Marlowe. You'll have to wait until Saturday to hear it. Now, tell me about your trip. How did Anne react to having a new Granddad?"

Michael gave a résumé, leaving out bits that might give Daisy an unfavourable view of Paddy, but couldn't prevent himself mentioning the possibility of his having a sister.

"A sister?" Daisy was almost in falsetto. "Michael, I swear your family has more skeletons than mine. Are you sure you can you handle this? Do you want me to come back? Mummy can bring Hamish home."

Daisy putting him before Hamish? This was unprecedented. Michael experienced a sudden flush of pleasure. "I'm fine. I think Dad's more shocked at revealing it."

"Oh, *Dad* is it now? You really must have got on." There was a shine in Daisy's voice. "I'm *really* pleased for you, Michael."

She went on to tell him what she and Meredith had been up to, the little she'd seen of Hamish and that there'd been no invitations to Jean-Paul's dinner table this time. Then her voice lowered until she was virtually purring. "Tell me all the disgusting, depraved things you're going to do to me when I get back home."

Michael checked that Anne wasn't in the hall. He heard her music playing upstairs: *Love, love me do, you know I love you...* He clicked the sitting room door shut and was grinning as he picked up the phone again.

With everyone back, Meredith's house bubbled. Hamish ran Anne as if she was his personal possession but she participated with a ready smile. Michael, for one, was grateful to see her being a child again.

He got Daisy to himself after dinner. They walked in the crisp evening air, hand-in-hand around the orchard in the pale light of an almost full moon.

"I couldn't say over the phone because it concerns Marie and Augustine," Daisy said. "Marlowe confirmed Berthe's father *was* the English pilot. He has his name, rank, everything. But the really interesting fact is that Augustine is a Bohec too, the daughter of Berthe's Uncle Bernard, the one the Germans executed. It's a sad tale: she was born after he died and giving birth to her also killed her mother. But what matters is that legally, Mazemeur belongs to Augustine. *That's* why Berthe is so terrified, in case anyone finds out."

"Wouldn't Augustine know that?"

"Berthe's mother, Mathilde, brought her up so who knows what Augustine's been told? Mathilde had de facto control of everything after Bernard was executed. That there's a relationship is no secret, that's why Marie calls me *Tante* Daisy, but it's always been made out to be more distant than it is."

"What are you going to do about this?"

"Keep it in reserve in case Jean-Paul reneges on his promises."

"Don't you think Augustine and Marie ought to be told?"

"I wouldn't want them to build up false hopes. Augustine isn't the brightest Breton button and Marie's only a kid. Jean-Paul and his mother would entangle them with legal wool. I've no doubt the deeds are securely locked away with the evidence of all the other ill-gotten gains. What we need, darling, is a safe-breaker."

Michael laughed. "I knew one once. Lived next door to us when he wasn't in Wormwood Scrubs."

He thought it wasn't very fair on Marie, being a skivvy in a house she had the ultimate right to call her own. Daisy though, for whatever reason, wanted to keep Jean-Paul sweet until the divorce was completed. After that, the idea could be planted in Marie's head. Poor girl, she couldn't have much of a life stuck in the sticks. He counted the years back to the war.

"Augustine must have been getting on a bit when Marie was born."

"She married late. She was over forty but her husband was sixty-odd, a butcher from Ploermel. How on earth two people like that managed to produce such an intelligent and lovely girl as Marie is a miracle."

"Perhaps a fairy left her on their doorstep. What about Jean-Paul's father? Did Marlowe winkle him out?"

"Not yet. Our marriage certificate gives his name as Jean Bohec, mariner, of Mazemeur but there's no record of any Jean Bohec being born there during the appropriate period and no record of Berthe marrying anyone, Bohec or not. Philippe thinks he might be a ringer."

"The choice of mariner is interesting."

"Instead of farmer? Perhaps it's a clue. There's a naval base at Lorient. Perhaps Berthe spent a lot of time there in the summer of nineteen sixty-four, although Jean-Paul was actually born in the Limousin. Maybe she was sent there to avoid wagging tongues."

They'd circumnavigated the orchard. Michael touched Daisy's arm. "Shall we walk round again? There's something I want to ask you."

Daisy started to roll her eyes suggestively then caught the look in Michael's. "Oh," she said. "I get the feeling this is something serious."

They linked arms, set off again. Michael tried to explain his problems in coping with Anne's sexuality.

Daisy listened intently. When Michael had finished she said, "Of course she's aware she was making contact with you, if I can put it like that. It's part of her growing up, becoming a woman. My advice is, don't hold off and go all distant and formal as if she's got a disease or something. Just relax. Act as if the body parts you're uncomfortable about aren't there. It will get easier, honestly. She's a bit of a late developer your Anne and that's not a bad thing when you see what some girls her age have turned into. Does that help?"

"Enormously," Michael said. Daisy leaned her head against him.

"Please don't read anything about me and Harry into that," she said. "I learned at a very young age never ever to tease him."

"I won't."

Daisy ran a hand up and down Michael's thighs. "I feel cold," she said. "I think these should be in a warm bed between mine."

Grace confronted Michael as soon as he stepped into her hall.

"What's all this," she said, arms folded and resting on her waist, "about Anne having a new Granddad?"

"I texted Mum," Anne said, her face broadcasting apologies. "I didn't think it would be a problem."

"And I don't see why it is." Michael glared at Grace. "He's my father. You can't shovel him under the carpet as if he doesn't exist. Anne has a right to know him, just as she has a right to know your mother. You don't hear me objecting to Anne seeing her."

Grace coloured. "But I don't know anything about *him*. And it's funny how he's turned up out of the blue like this."

"It isn't funny at all. He's the stepfather of Daisy's solicitor and we met again at her husband's funeral. Ted, Colonel Roberts, was a very dear friend of ours. My father and I had a long talk and I told him about Anne and about Daisy and the baby. He lives near Dublin and seeing I had Anne staying with me I invited him to fly over and meet her. He's a businessman, Grace, not some diddicoy."

"Well, I do think you should have told me." This was delivered in a more conciliatory voice. No doubt sweetened by 'solicitor' and 'colonel', Michael thought.

"Why? What difference would it have made?"

"I'd have *known*. That's what difference." Grace kept transferring her weight from one foot to the other as if there were hot coals beneath them instead of worn Wilton.

"Oh, Mum, stop being so grumpy," Anne said. "Granddad Cavanagh's a charming man. Daisy certainly thought so. By the way, did you know her father was an honourable? He was the son of a peer. They have a huge estate in Scotland, castle and everything."

Michael had to stop himself from gawping. Even he didn't know anything about the Lomonds' family seat, although Anne might have asked Daisy he supposed. Judging from Grace's bluster, it looked as if she was unaware he and Anne had been alone together whether in Meredith's house or a Chester hotel.

"A peer?" Grace's eyes fluttered. "Is this true, Michael?"

"Daisy keeps it quiet. She doesn't like to make capital out of it."

"No, no, of course not."

Michael could see Grace trying to decide how she would break such news to the dowager of Barnes. Probably announce it over cucumber sandwiches and Lapsang Souchong at a nice tea party, best Royal Doulton of course.

"I think the title goes back to the fourteen hundreds," he said, although he had no idea of its antiquity at all.

"Really?"

Grace's eyes became beady. Michael guessed she was calculating Anne's enhanced prospects in the marriage market. Over my dead body, he thought then wondered if this might be an opening to have Anne with him on a more permanent basis.

"So, I believe. Although the family's always vague about such matters."

"Well," Grace said, smiling at last. "Why don't we all have a nice cup of tea and a cake? I managed to find chocolate éclairs on special offer this morning." The question of Michael's father seemed to be forgotten.

When they'd seen him off at John Lennon airport, Paddy invited them to stay with him in Ireland: "I have a grand place. Far too big for Linda and me. It'll be yours one day. It's in Killiney, off the Vico Road. Come in summer, there's miles of beautiful beach and from Monday to Friday scarcely a soul on it."

Michael had imagined Paddy living in one of those decaying old Dublin houses he'd seen in films like *The Commitments* but according to Paddy, the Vico Road was very smart. "I've done all right for myself you see, son. Built up a good business over the years. Got in the restoration game when it was just about to take off. And I mean proper *restoration*, period stuff, not loft conversions or flat-pack kitchens. It would be nice to have someone to hand it on to."

Michael had felt his body tense, his neck and back begin to cramp up.

"I don't mean come to Ireland and work with me," Paddy said. "But what I'd like to do is this. I'm going to change the company's name to Cavanagh and Son, and I'll give you shares in the business. Put them aside for Anne if you like. No commitment from you, no need for you to do anything at all except maybe forgive your old dad for his past transgressions."

Now, as Grace poured tea (Michael's connection with nobility had apparently merited the use of the Royal Doulton) Michael said, "So have we settled that it's all right for Anne to see her grandfather?"

Grace looked up sharply and almost splashed a crisp white doily. "Grandfather?" she said. "Why ever not?"

The month they were now in, in Daisy's view the last of winter and in Michael's the first of spring, was the time, for her, that the world went crazy.

What she didn't like, and was increasingly voluble about, were the war drums beating from post-9/11 Bushland and New Labour Britain. She became addicted to news bulletins, waking up to *Today* on Radio Four, followed by *Breakfast* on BBC1, during which she ate marmaladed toast and drank sugarless tea. After that she would switch to *News 24* then back to BBC1 for *News at One*. Michael wondered why she bothered to change channels. The content was always the same: warnings, ultimatums, wild talk of weapons of mass destruction. The only glimmer of hope, as Daisy saw it, came from the country that had been her home for the past eleven years and which she had latterly been anxious to renounce.

On the day the invasion started, Michael found her sobbing in the study, Harry's Military Cross on the desk in front of her.

"Oh sweetheart," he said.

"How many mothers' sons did he slaughter to earn this?" Daisy said, fingering the medal. "Daughters too? What's the going rate for the fucking thing now? Ten? A hundred? A thousand?"

"Daisy, don't torture yourself."

"Torture *myself*? What of the torture these megalomaniacs are storing up for our children, the hatred that's being engendered? What of that, Michael? How can they be so blind?" Daisy stood up, clutched Michael by his shirtsleeves. "Is it right for me to bring a child into such a world?"

"Hamish is in it."

"It was different when he was born."

"And it won't always be like this. We *have* to have hope, Daisy. Where would either of us be today if we hadn't had that?"

"Dead. And maybe the better for it."

At no other time since he had known her had Michael felt so powerless to influence her. He felt the passion inside him yet his voice and argument came out flat.

At the time they were due to take Hamish to Mazemeur again, Daisy flashed a hand at her belly and declared: "I'm not going. He mustn't see me like this. He *mustn't*. I'll tell him Hamish is ill. Or I am."

Next time, Michael thought, the divorce should be final and Daisy's bump won't matter. He didn't see why it should be an issue now but Daisy had got it into her head that it was, so what could he do but indulge her.

"*You'll* have to take him," Daisy said and Michael's stomach tightened. "At least he'll be in a country with a mind of its own. Collect him at the end of the week. You don't have to stay. In fact I don't want you to. I need you here."

"I could bring him back."

They both stared at Meredith. She wore a smile that, disconcertingly, kept switching on and off.

"I'm meeting Romilly next week," she said, "for a few days in Paris. I could fit in a detour."

Daisy sucked a thumb. Her gaze alternated between Meredith and Michael.

"All right," she said.

Hamish, in a switch from his usual attitude, viewed the prospect of travelling without Daisy as a great adventure. "I'm a big boy now, Mama," he said, chest pushed out and head high. From the look on Daisy's face, Michael suspected she would weep a lot after they had gone.

They travelled by taxi from Vannes to Mazemeur. Michael told the driver to wait. Bohec's Renault was missing but, it being a weekday, he had expected that. It meant he had to face Adèle alone. Daisy had teased him yet again before he left: "I like Adèle," she said, "So it's all right for you to like her too. You can kiss her but not too much."

Berthe materialised near her rabbit shed, gave Michael the sickly smile she'd offered two months before. He nodded. She drifted back into her warren.

Adèle looked comfortably pregnant. "Hamish," she gushed. The boy ran into her outstretched arms and leaned himself against her belly. Adèle's greeting to Michael consisted of a smile, lingering, expectant.

"I have the taxi waiting," he said.

"Oh, but I hoped you might stay for a meal. A coffee at least. Please?" Adèle's eyes glistened and she tuned up her smile until Michael could feel his resolve melting.

Adèle set a cafetière to bubble on the stove and doled out cakes to Hamish. She patted her bump. "How is Daisy coping with hers?"

Michael nodded frantically towards Hamish, who had his back to them. He put a finger to his lips. Adèle frowned. "Ah," she said. She took Hamish's hand, led him out of the room. "Come and see what Papa's got for you. I'm sure he won't mind you having it before he gets home."

Adèle returned, shut the door carefully behind her. She poured two black coffees. "You haven't told him yet?"

Michael shook his head.

"And is Daisy really ill?"

"No."

Adèle looked pensive then her eyes clouded. "Maybe she knows best. But you don't need to worry. I've kept and will keep my promise. As you kept yours." Something else filled her eyes then, a hint of mischief perhaps, Michael wasn't sure. "Thank you again for my picture. An interesting choice, but a good one I think. Very flattering. Who says the camera never lies?" She cast her eyes downward, over her body, transferred them to Michael's, let them wander lazily upwards.

Michael felt his penis stir, was sure Adèle would have noticed. He took an urgent sip of his coffee, grimaced as it seared his throat.

"Too hot for you?"

Adèle took Michael's cup, blew gently across the surface of the liquid. "Try it now."

Outside, a car horn brayed.

"My driver's getting impatient."

Adèle's lips brushed Michael's cheeks. "À bientôt, Michael. Another time perhaps."

During breakfast on the morning after Michael got home, Daisy suddenly switched the television news off and said, "Let's drive to the coast and find our house."

"Which coast?"

"Whichever's nearest."

"There isn't much in it."

"You decide then."

He headed for the harbour where Peter kept his yacht. They walked down its cobbled street to the river where he and Daisy should have come ashore from *Hirondelle*.

"Which is his?" Daisy shielded her eyes with a hand as she scanned the boats. Michael pointed to where he thought *Scallywag* lay but there were several that might have been her. *Passing Clouds* had, he presumed, not yet arrived.

"That one, or maybe that over there. I should have brought binoculars."

The warm weather had unleashed scores of sightseers. Daisy scowled at them, clung to Michael's sleeve.

He drove westward.

"No," said Daisy time and again, "Not here."

They motored down to the mouth of a river ("Too bleak") and through a seaside town that had Daisy tight-lipped, gripping her seat. As they skimmed the outskirts of an industrial town she clamped her eyes shut, wouldn't open them until Michael swore there was no evidence of the place to be seen.

They were rewarded by glimpses of another river as the road took them close to it then, tantalisingly, veered inland to follow higher ground beyond thick belts of trees fringing the water. At last they reached the tip of the land and there, at the confluence with another river, was a splendid vista. To their left, on the far bank of the river they had been skirting, was a great quayside with gigantic ships alongside, decks bearing regiments of containers. Ahead, a streamlined ferry, a catamaran, left a terminal on the far side of the other river and headed out to sea. Sailing yachts dipped and rolled in the harbour chop. Way out, on the open water, they could see white sails passing like spectres.

Michael was enraptured but could *feel* Daisy resisting.

"I don't know," she said eventually. "It would be like a million constellations at night, at too close quarters."

So, they turned, drove west. The road led them through beguiling villages and Michael could see Daisy smiling. They stayed overnight in one but set off next morning for the south coast.

Daisy had decided she would be happier where she could see France, or at least face it. "Not Dover," she said as they entered Kent. He aimed the Peugeot roughly towards Miranda's house and ended up at the Sussex coast.

They visited Rye, where he saw Daisy torn between the prospect of living in such a beautiful town and its popularity making it impossible to find a peaceful square inch. Long before he was ready, she had given Rye the thumbs down.

This verdict was repeated for each place they visited. Michael wondered what was the point of looking any further. It seemed obvious Daisy would find fault everywhere they went. Then somewhere near Chichester, she said, "I'm annoying you, aren't I?"

"A little."

"A lot, by that fed-up look in your eyes."

"It's because I don't think you know what you're looking for."

"I was hoping the place would tell me."

"Places don't do that in my experience."

"Treguelven did, and that little place where we were stormbound."

"They're both in France."

"At least they're not involved in this stupid war."

"Are you saying you want to live there again? After our efforts to get you away?"

"Away from Jean-Paul, not France."

"So you *do* want to live there?"

"I didn't say that. But it would be easier for Hamish's visits, especially since he has to start school soon. He won't be able to take a week off in every four."

"What about what's best for our child? What about Anne? It wouldn't make her visits to me easier."

Daisy bit her lip. "I'm being selfish. I'm sorry."

"There's nothing to stop you having a house in France as well as here. You could spend the whole of the school holidays there."

"Does that mean you wouldn't be with me?"

"I meant us. You was because it would be your money, your house."

"Our house, our money Michael. Warts and all, remember."

Michael sighed. "Warts and all."

They reached the outskirts of Chichester. Daisy, with a sudden decisiveness that raised Michael's eyebrows, said, "This is far enough. Let's settle here, somewhere high on the Downs. It's close to the sea and Anne."

"Are you sure?"

"No, I'm not, but it's as good as anywhere else. And isn't home what you make it? I've never tried my hand at that; it's always been done for me, even the cottage. It's time *I* built a nest."

They invaded estate agents, were handed armfuls of details, most of which didn't begin to match what they asked for. Daisy's cut glass accent became ever more acute. The assistants quaked. The houses to consider shrank to an achievable amount.

They viewed five properties, settled for a shortlist of two, both set in the steep rolling folds of the South Downs. One was Giffards, part-brick, part timber-framed, in four acres of beautiful gardens. The other was Honeypot Cottage, flint and brick, thatch-roofed. The thatch swooped to within a few feet of the ground and neat half-moon openings were sculpted in it for windows to peep through. It had eleven acres of grounds including a riverbank but only three bedrooms compared with Giffards' five. Both houses had outbuildings suitable for Michael's workshop.

Daisy set the brochures out in their hotel room. "Honeypot Cottage is very pretty."

"But?"

"Three bedrooms might be enough for us and two children but there'd be nowhere for Anne." She gave Michael a sly look, a glance from the corners of her eyes. "Or for me when you've been horrible."

"In not giving you your way, perhaps? So what you mean is that Giffards is favourite?"

"Would you mind very much?"

"I actually prefer it. Honeypot Cottage seems to want to shut you in, keep you for itself. Even the name makes me claustrophobic. I'd worry about all that thatch and how I'd look after eleven acres. Four's intimidating enough."

"We can probably get someone from the village, like Mummy does. What do you say? Shall we go for Giffards?"

"Don't you want to wait and see what else comes up?"

"No. I'd rather it was done with. Giffards is a fine place. It's in beautiful countryside, handy for the Portsmouth Ferry, only half an hour from Anne, and when we get our boat we can surely find a berth for her in Chichester harbour. There seems enough of it."

Michael smiled to himself at Daisy's capacity for instant decisions; at least this time she'd backed it with good reasons. But the asking price scared him.

"It's an awful lot of money."

"But it isn't ours, so it doesn't matter. We can thank the good policyholders."

"You'll be quite a way from Meredith."

"Close enough for me. Anyone would think you're trying to put me off. Come on, Michael, yes or no?"

He grinned. "Yes of course."

And that was the decision done. Daisy phoned the estate agent, made an offer and within an hour the owner had accepted it.

During their time away, Daisy had not read a newspaper or switched a radio or television on, and her gloominess seemed to lift and fade away in the sunshine. But virtually the first thing she did when reaching Meredith's was to turn *News 24* on.

The same faces were there: gung-ho politicians with God in their eyes and on their mutually opposing sides. Their lies were still the same too.

Michael switched the television off. "That's enough," he said. Daisy looked up at him as a chastised child might look at a parent.

She, this not-yet wife, switched into an obsequious domesticity, fussing around after him, brushing up, dusting, wiping, bringing him food and drink because "I thought you might feel hungry". Michael reasoned that she'd tire of it soon but when she brought the third offering of coffee and biscuits that evening he said in a deliberately tired voice, "Daisy, why are you doing this?"

"It's what you want, isn't it? An obedient woman?"

"No, it isn't. I want that argumentative, impossible, unpredictable Daisy, not a Stratford wife."

"Stepford."

"Whatever."

Daisy's shoulders and neck slumped forward. She drew them further in, pushing them into her chest. "I don't know where that Daisy is," she said in a tiny voice.

"She's behind whatever you're afraid of."

"I'm afraid of everything. I'm afraid the world is going to end." She began to weep and Michael held her but it seemed nothing he did could console her. He took her to bed and held her, caressed her, stroked her hair while she stared at nothing. Fatigue in the end caused her eyes to close, but his stayed open for hours after she finally drifted to sleep.

Yet next morning, Daisy was as bright as a summer dawn. She sang as she washed and when she combed her hair. She had an antenatal class that day, went to it placid and came back bubbling, full of how she had listened to Baby's heartbeat, how strong it was, and no Boys' Own politicians were going to threaten the child in her womb.

By Default

For the first time since Michael had known her, she browsed through Meredith's opera collection. The house rang with beautiful voices and fine music as she played Mozart, Donizetti, Puccini: *Cosi fan tutte*, *La fille du regiment* and *La Rondine*.

The following day, Meredith returned from France with Hamish, who looked extremely pleased with himself as he came through Arrivals into the waiting arms of Daisy.

"Mama, mama. Papa says he'll take me to Disney World in the summer. He bought me a ham...ster, but he says the men won't let me bring it here."

"No, darling, that's because it could get sick on the plane."

"What if it came on the boat?"

"It could get sick on that too."

"Papa said you were sick."

"Yes, darling. That's why I couldn't come with you this time."

Hamish sucked on a thumb. "I said it was prob...proberly with the baby."

Daisy almost keeled over. "Probably with what?" she croaked.

"The *baby*." Hamish's face said he thought Daisy was rather dense. He gave a little cough. "I said it was proberly with the baby and Papa was all quiet and his eyes went funny."

Chapter 20

Michael, glancing at Daisy as he drove, could see she was locked in a private hell, hard-eyed, tight-lipped. Meredith hardly spoke either, and throughout the journey looked as if she was afraid Daisy might suddenly turn on her. Hamish of course chattered freely and Michael was the one left to maintain some equilibrium.

"He never mentioned it on the plane," Meredith had said. "And Jean-Paul just acted as if I wasn't there."

Michael wondered how long Hamish had known. He could have overheard it from any of them. He was certain Adèle would not have told him.

By evening, Daisy had calmed enough to tell Michael why she hadn't wanted Jean-Paul to know she was pregnant.

"On the surface he might accept we're a couple but only by fooling himself we aren't *actually* fucking. Now Hamish has unwittingly let my secret out, it will eat away at Jean-Paul. Heaven knows where it will come out. I just hope his feelings for Adèle are strong enough to neutralise it."

"But what *can* he do? What aren't you telling me, Daisy?"

"Nothing. There's nothing I can tell you."

Michael felt a hard fist of anger rise inside him. He said nothing else but knew his face showed it all. Daisy looked scared. He had the awful feeling it might be him she was afraid of.

The political news improved as the year moved into April and Daisy began playing music to Baby, pressing the headphones to her abdomen. Michael found her choice was a pointer to her disposition. Beethoven's *Pastoral Symphony* meant she was feeling good, Tavener's *The Protecting Veil* that she was so-so, Elgar's *Cello concerto* that she was drifting towards moody. Once or twice, Daisy played Steve Reich and her state of mind was impossible to discern.

Michael spent time searching internet genealogy sites and discovered a possible candidate for his half-sister, a girl hobbled with the ungainly name, as he saw it, of Fionnuala. He ordered a copy of the birth certificate to be sent to Paddy's address.

As April waned, Daisy nibbled her bottom lip more than usual. Michael caught her biting her fingernails too. She stole his shirts, wore them as maternity tops, kept undoing the buttons then fastening them again. He said he preferred them undone but the humour landed on her like a dead haddock.

Anne's school broke up for Easter. Three days after that was her fifteenth birthday. Grace was organising a party and both Michael and Daisy were invited.

"You go," Daisy said. "I can't face travelling. My belly keeps itching like mad and I'm sweating like an old sow."

Michael fetched olive oil, massaged it into Daisy's bump. She lay back, looked more tranquil than she had been in weeks.

"Ah, that's heaven, sweetheart," she said. "And don't look so worried. The itch is only the skin stretching and the sweating's because Baby's taking more blood. Did you know if I went into labour this week, he'd have a good chance of surviving?"

"No, I didn't," Michael said, frowning. "And I don't want to risk anything happening. Are you sure you don't mind me going alone?"

"Heavens, Michael, you can't miss Anne's birthday. I'm sure Grace will look after you as well as I would." He pulled a horrified face and Daisy thumped him half-heartedly in the side. "You know I don't mean like that."

Anne was wearing makeup so Grace had obviously conceded that victory. Grace herself looked as if she'd lost considerable weight although that seemed impossible given the short interval since Michael last saw her. Her midriff was certainly well controlled.

She'd redecorated the spare room. The flock wallpaper had been replaced by a sun-toned New Age design. Michael slept fitfully, one eye and ear monitoring the door.

He'd imagined a sit-down affair with cakes, jelly, and china tea. There'd be him, Anne, Grace, and the dragon-queen of Barnes wearing paper hats, and grinning like ventriloquists' dummies with toothache.

The actual event was different. The living room carpet was rolled back and the floor cleared for dancing. A buffet was laid out in the kitchen. Dragon-queens were excluded.

Anne looked gorgeous, Michael thought. Her hair had been arranged into ringlets and she wore a simple, long-sleeved dress in a green so dark it was almost black. The combination made her look as if she'd stepped from a pre-Raphaelite painting. Her girlfriends came in various guises, many with bare midriffs and skimpy tops, but some wore dresses that made them, as Anne's did, look far older than their fifteen or so years. Most wore far more makeup than she did.

There were boys too; mostly tidy in jeans and ironed shirts, neat crops, though one or two had scruffy hair. Michael found himself regarding them with an aggressive resentment. He suspected most fathers of teenage girls felt like this, although they would have had a more gradual awakening than him.

He was aware of Grace watching him, so was careful to avoid eye contact with the girls' often freely displayed charms. It was all so charged, so different from the preening at the pantomime. Caroline, the girl who'd called when he was here after Christmas seemed to take that acquaintance as a licence to claim him as her own. "Come on, Mr C," she said, pulling him into the centre of the room to dance to the throbbing rhythms escaping from Grace's stereo system. He felt uncertain what to do, watched the boys, tried to follow their moves. When the music turned slow and sultry, Caroline moved in close, wrapping her arms around him as they swayed. Her breasts pushed into him, swelled alarmingly, billowing above their low-cut containers. She gazed up at him, eyes half-closed.

Anne cut in as a second slow number followed. She rested her head on Michael's shoulder as they glided away from danger. "You looked petrified," she said. "Thought I'd rescue you."

"Dad, ask Mum to dance," Anne urged as the record finished. She selected another leisurely tune, which had several of her guests groaning, commandeered a curly-headed youth to dance with her. Michael crossed the floor to Grace, who was sitting beneath self-generated clouds of cigarette smoke.

Grace was wearing a dark red dress woven in a Paisley design. As they danced, she seemed to push even closer to Michael than Caroline had done. He felt suspenders press against his thighs.

The music gained heat. Caroline reclaimed him, effervescing as she manoeuvred herself in a way that emphasised her assets even more than before. Michael begged for a rest when the next record began.

Caroline smiled, slipped an arm around his waist. "Shall we get a drink instead?" she said, nodding towards the kitchen. Michael looked desperately for Anne but she was engaged in what looked like a deep conversation with curly-head. Their faces were animated, mouths and lips moving rapidly, as if words were gushing out. He decided Grace might be his best bet for salvation but saw she was speaking on the telephone. His spirits drooped then lifted again as her eyes sought him out and one hand waved. "It's for you, Michael," she said, coming over to him, holding the instrument at arm's length. "She says it's Daisy."

Caroline looked daggers at them both, went into the kitchen alone.

"Michael? Darling, Miranda phoned me just now. It's happened. The decree came this morning but she's been in court all day." Daisy was incoherent at times, bubbling with plans. She asked for Anne, to wish her happy birthday, and when she had done that, asked for Michael again. "So, when do you want to marry me?"

Michael didn't answer; it was still sinking in.

"Michael, have you changed your mind?"

He shook his head then realised Daisy couldn't see that. "I'll marry you now. This very minute."

"The party's that bad? Is Grace giving you a hard time?"

"Not her. Anne's girlfriends. Some of them. One of them."

He heard Daisy laughing. "She's coming on to you? You should be so lucky."

"It's not funny, Daisy. I don't know how to avoid her."

Daisy laughed again. "I'd stick close to Grace if I were you. You should be safe there."

Michael wasn't so sure about that but followed Daisy's advice.

"I'm glad we're getting on," Grace said. "I wanted to ask you how you felt about something."

Alarms clanged in Michael's head.

"I've met someone," Grace said, very quietly. "We're thinking of getting married."

The alarms changed to euphoric bells. "Married? Why, Grace, that's wonderful news."

She told Michael about James, sixty, widower, chartered accountant (naturally, thought Michael), his own children grown and gone out to conquer the world. That was the problem, Grace said. James was reluctant to take on a teenage daughter, so they might have to wait until Anne went to university. They might not have a problem, Michael said. He told her about Giffards, less than thirty miles away to the south.

"You mean Anne could live with you? I don't mean permanently of course but she could share herself between us much more. I'm sure she'd love that."

"And she wouldn't have to change schools. I'd be happy to be part of the school run."

Grace smiled. "We'll put it to her tomorrow. It will be like an extra birthday present."

Michael felt as if a kindly light had entered his life. He danced with Caroline a few more times but her flirting didn't bother him now. She tried to kiss him and he stopped her in mid advance, pushed her gently down by her shoulders.

"Caroline," he said. "I'm Anne's dad. How would you feel if she was kissing yours?"

Caroline pouted at first but then smiled. "Fair enough," she said. "Though nobody would want to kiss *my* dad." Later, Michael noticed her wrapped around a scruffy-haired youth.

He danced with Anne too. His heart sang to see her so happy. Most of the time though, he spent with Grace. He wondered how, the last time they met, neither had found anything to say to the other.

Anne stood on a chair and announced the last dance then got down and walked over to Michael. The music began, a slow waltz of the kind he thought had disappeared in the sixties. He took his daughter in his arms while everyone else stood aside, watched as they danced together. When the music ended, the room reverberated with cheers and clapping hands, and Anne wore a smile that made up for all their missing years.

Anne's face had lit up at the prospect of living with Michael and Daisy. She wasn't happy that Grace would be selling her house and moving in with James, though. Not because she was that fond of the semi-detached she'd grown up in but, as she said, it was at least familiar.

"What about living in Sussex?" Grace said in a bruised voice. "That won't be familiar."

"No, but Dad and Daisy and Hamish are."

Grace then said that James would be too. Anne said that could be taken the wrong way. Michael was treated to the rare sight of Grace blushing.

Anne said she was only teasing and what she really meant was James lived on the outskirts of town whereas here she was only minutes away from friends like Caroline.

"But it won't stop you seeing them. I'm sure James will be only too glad to drive you over."

"He'll do it to get a few hours peace," Michael said. That earned him a smile of gratitude from Grace and a dig in the ribs from Anne.

He phoned the estate agent (the owner of Giffards had already moved out) and arranged for someone to meet them at the house. As he drove down, he wondered how Daisy was enjoying her first day as a single woman. He was thinking about the date, and realised it was the anniversary of the day they met. It was one that needed marking with something more substantial, he knew, but instead of going to straight to Giffards, Michael carried on to Chichester and ordered flowers for delivery to Daisy that afternoon. The accompanying card was to say: *Congratulations on being Miss Lomond again. And thank you for coming into my life one year ago today.*

"Oh, Dad, wow," Anne said when she saw the house. Grace stared without comment but Michael could see that there was plenty going through her mind. The girl from the agency shook hands, smiled a lot. She had much to smile about, Michael thought, considering the amount her firm was about to realise. "You know your way about," she said, although in truth he could scarcely remember, and left them to their own devices while she fiddled with her mobile phone.

Anne said "Ooh" and "Ah" while Grace quietly contemplated. Michael guessed she was counting rooms, noting size and state of decoration, assessing the health of Daisy's bank balance, for she knew it could not be his that could afford a place like this. Still, if things went as planned, Grace would soon have her own little Eden, for James must have more than loose change in his pocket. Chartered accountants didn't come cheap.

That afternoon, Michael's mobile rang.

"Darling, they're beautiful."

"So you got them?"

"No, I was fantasising. Of course I got them, silly, and thank you. So, it's twelve months since you walked out on Mummy and me? I knew it was in April but I'm hopeless with dates and wasn't exactly rational back then."

Michael told Daisy about taking Anne to see the house, didn't mention Grace had come too.

"What did she think of it?"

"Can't wait to choose her bedroom." He told her about Grace's marriage plans, how it could mean Anne would be able to spend a lot more time with them.

"You mean she'd alternate between living with us and Grace?"

"Yes, that's the way I see it."

"But that's wonderful, Michael. Apart from you and Anne being happy, Hamish will be over the moon, having his big sister there."

"You don't mind then?"

"Mind? Of course not, I'm very fond of Anne. And it'll be no bad thing to have another female in the house. We can gang together when you won't do what we want." There was a little flow of banter then Daisy said, "I've had news from France. On Saturday there'll be a new Madame Bohec. We didn't receive an invitation."

"Should we send a card?"

"Definitely not. I don't want him to think about me. I just hope she keeps him satisfied."

Michael thought about a scalding cup of coffee, Adèle's eyes impaling him as she blew softly across its surface.

Anne was to stay with Michael for the next six days then return to spend the last week of the holidays with Grace. As he drove with Anne beside him, Michael caught his reflection in the mirror. He hadn't realised he was smiling.

Anne played Beatles CDs and sang along to them. Michael's head was full of plans for the new home he and Daisy would have. He would make the furniture himself, he decided and, with uncanny timing, *Norwegian wood, isn't it good* rang from the car stereo, although that would not be the material he'd choose. Still, it felt like a good omen, Daisy would certainly have thought so.

In Meredith's drive he rally-drove around the potholes but as Flora came into view his right foot hit the brake pedal hard. Parked by the statue's granite rump was a police car.

Without waiting for Anne, he dashed to the house. Daisy had obviously seen him coming for she had the front door open before he reached it.

"Oh thank God," they both said at the same time.

"What's going on?"

"The police are questioning Mummy." Daisy's eyes began to flood, as if she'd waited for him to come home before releasing her tears. "I knew this would happen. It's *his* doing."

"His?"

"Jean-fucking-Paul."

Anne came into the hall. "Is something wrong? Has there been a burglary?"

"I wish," said Daisy. She tried to smile. "Hello, Anne." They kissed cheeks.

"Where is she?" Michael said.

Daisy nodded towards the small sitting room. Michael opened its door, went in. Meredith was facing him and two heads turned round, one male, one female. There were three stripes on the latter's epaulettes.

"And you are?" This from the sergeant.

Michael bristled. "I live here. Are you all right, Meredith. Do you want me to stay?"

"Yes." Her voice barely carried across the room.

The sergeant ignored Michael after that.

"So, Mrs Lomond," she said. "Have I got this down right? Your husband died on the sixth (she pronounced it 'sikth') of June last year. Of motor neurone disease."

"Yes." The 's' sibilated around the room. "Amyotrophic lateral sclerosis it actually says on the death certificate. I'll leave you to get your own copy. No doubt you'll contact Harry's doctor."

"If necessary. And this Innis place where your husband is buried – is that one n or two?"

"One."

"Inis Lomond, Loch Fruin, Argyle?"

Michael caught his breath. Meredith's eyes flickered once, twice, at him.

"Yes."

The sergeant sniffed loudly, nodded at the constable. Notebooks were returned to pockets.

"Thank you Mrs Lomond. That's all for now. You've been most helpful." The officers rose, hands smoothed uniforms. "Goodbye Mr er..."

"Cavanagh."

"Mr Cavanagh," the sergeant said, nodding. "We'll be in touch, Mrs Lomond."

"Jesus," Meredith said when the police had gone. She went into the long sitting room, sank into a corner of her favourite sofa. Michael mixed her a gin and tonic. Daisy was already well into one. She said Hamish had dragged Anne away somewhere.

"Meredith," Michael said, "why were they asking about Harry's death?"

"Someone has been making allegations. That it wasn't attributable to his illness."

"And that someone is Jean-Paul?"

Daisy said, her voice acid, "It certainly wasn't the Monarch of the fucking Glen."

"*Daisy.*" That from Meredith. Her eyes were saying much more, thought Michael, but none of it to him.

"*Well.*" Daisy glared at her mother. "If I hadn't let Hamish go over there with you none of this would have happened."

"Let's be rational for a moment," Michael said. Both women stared at him but kept silent. "It doesn't look as if the police are treating this as a priority... a sergeant and constable from the local station. They were probably told to pop in if they were in the area. My guess is they'll report to their inspector and that will be that." He cleared his throat and, looking directly at Daisy, added. "Unless there's something you're not telling me."

Daisy didn't respond but she looked flushed. Michael gave up on her, turned to Meredith.

"Why did you tell the police Harry was buried in Scotland?"

Meredith screwed her eyes shut, pressed her lips together. Michael felt a flash of anger at the way the two women were excluding him.

"I don't know," she said at last. "It just came into my head and out of my mouth."

"Is there a grave in Scotland? For Harry?"

Meredith wouldn't look at him. Daisy sucked her thumb like a baby. Michael said a silent prayer for the one in her belly.

The distance between Michael and Daisy seemed to grow. It wasn't that Daisy was hostile or even mildly argumentative. Her demeanour was insipid, as if she wasn't there in spirit at all. Michael didn't know how he'd have coped without Anne's cheerful face.

Saturday came with a freezing north-easterly and Michael wondered if it was like that for Adèle's wedding. Although of course he had no idea of her wedding outfit, he pictured her wearing a scarlet coat with white blossoms attached to its lapel. When Marie phoned and said the deed had been done, Daisy, instead of chatting like she usually did, thanked her then put the phone down. She looked, as Grace used to be fond of saying, like a woman who'd lost a pound and found a penny.

The day before he drove Anne home, Michael said to Daisy: "I might stay over tomorrow night. Thought I might check on the house."

"Makes sense," Daisy said, nodding solemnly.

But that night she was anything but solemn as they lay side by side and made love for the first time in over a week, since the morning in fact that Michael left for Anne's birthday party. As he reached, too soon, an unsatisfying climax, Daisy reacted as if this would be their last time. "Don't stop," she urged, pulling him to her, moving with such vigour that he was soon resurrected.

"We're *all right*, Michael, we're *all right*," Daisy cried as she came in a series of shudders. As if impelled by them, Michael followed seconds later with a release as exquisite as any he had known.

"D'you remember *Hirondelle's* cockpit?" Daisy said when they finally lay still.

"As if," Michael said, "I could ever forget."

"Tonight ran it close," Daisy said.

And next morning, when Michael was about to leave, Daisy flung her arms around him, pressed her lips against his. "I love you," she said, "I love you more than life."

She gripped his arms as he got into the car. "Do you trust me, Michael? Oh, say that you trust me." She was like a heroine in some Victorian melodrama, eyes imploring, angst engraved over her face.

"I trust you," Michael said, returning her expression as best he could. He couldn't get rid of the feeling he was playing Heathcliff to her Catherine.

His performance seemed to compose her and she stood motionless, watching as he drove away. *No, not Heathcliff, not Catherine*, he thought as he reached the bottom of the drive. He searched his memory for a happier couple. *Darcy and Elizabeth*, he decided, but was afraid a second choice might not be allowed.

Anne was frowning, twisting her hair around a finger. "Is Daisy all right? Only she's been so quiet and now she's suddenly manic. Is it because I'm going?"

"It's not because of you, Anne. Daisy's delighted you're coming to live with us. No, this is all about her. I don't know exactly how or why, except that inside the same week, she's become divorced and her ex-husband has remarried. Now why the latter event should upset her I don't understand but it apparently has. Then there was that business with Meredith and the police. Add being pregnant to the list and – well, you've seen the result."

"Is it true that Jean-Paul sent the police?"

"Daisy thinks so."

"He must really hate her."

"Not necessarily. I think possession is more his driving force. Like a miser, he hates to part with anything he regards as his. Daisy told me that much at least."

"So he wants her back?"

"It's more a case of not wanting anyone else to have her."

"But how can he prevent that? She's a free woman. I think you should marry her straight away and put a full stop to his nonsense."

Michael thought that wasn't a bad idea. It would show the finger to Jean-Paul, and their child, like Adèle's, would be born legitimate, if that distinction applied these days. Not that Daisy would care, given she'd insisted on being single long after Hamish was born.

What if there *was* something irregular about Harry's death? What if Harry didn't have motor neurone disease at all? As soon as he considered that Michael knew it was nonsense. Eminent doctors were involved in his diagnosis and treatment. What then was Jean-Paul's secret weapon? He'd have to be really firm with Daisy when he got back, insist on her telling him.

Michael didn't stay overnight. Grace was put out, pouting as she said, "But I've just changed the sheets on your bed."

Anne's face fell too but when Michael told her he was taking her advice, going straight back to get Daisy to marry him, she grinned.

"Go for it, Dad," she said. "Awesome."

Michael drove through relentless, lashing rain, ignoring the cameras, throwing the Peugeot round bends that, for all he knew, were skid pans. He made it back by ten, faster than he'd ever done before, but he was still far too late.

Chapter 21

A raw-eyed Meredith swayed towards Michael, bumping against the walls. "Daisy's gone," she said, moments before her feet tripped over each other and she fell forward in awkward slow motion.

Michael caught her before she reached the floor. "Gone? Gone where?" he said, in a voice that didn't sound like his own at all.

"*He* came for them." Meredith stared at the floor as if her head was locked in that position. "Even had the flights booked."

"But Daisy's twenty-seven weeks pregnant, for Christ's sake. She can't fly. It shouldn't be allowed."

Shouldn't be allowed. Why was he saying that? What fucking difference did it make? *Trust me*, Daisy said, *Trust me.* She'd known then what she was going to do, Michael was certain, otherwise why would she have said it?

He gripped Meredith's head, forced it up. "You'd better tell me the story right from the beginning, Meredith. And it's the truth I want, not fiction."

Michael went into the sitting room, found whisky, he filled a glass, drained it, filled another. Meredith tottered in. He offered her the bottle.

She shook her head, collapsed onto a sofa. "I've had too much already."

"I can see that." Michael lifted his glass, stared at it, put it down again. "This is to do with Harry's death, isn't it? What does Bohec know about that, Meredith?"

"That I killed my husband."

She said it without a trace of emotion. The stark admission racked Michael, sent spasms across his forehead. "But the motor neurone disease was a fact. You couldn't fake that."

"No, of course I didn't. I simply helped it along until one day his heart gave out and he stopped breathing."

"You mean it was a mercy killing?" *Illegal, but not necessarily bad.*

Meredith laughed; a short humourless bark. "There was no mercy about it. Harry had to pay for his crimes."

"Wasn't it rather late for that?"

"The opportunity hadn't arisen before."

"And Daisy was in it with you?"

"*No*. She found out what I'd done, that's the only part she had in it. What did you expect her to do then? Run to the police? Turn me in?"

"I suppose not. And Bohec found out from her?"

"No, from me, fool that I was. Oh, he was charm itself when Harry became ill. I couldn't ask my doctor for extra morphine but what the hell, I had a son-in-law in the business. I knew he'd given Daisy drugs so thought he might do the same for me. He refused. Later though, he said he might know someone."

"Did you say why you wanted the morphine?"

"To keep Harry quiet so I could get some sleep at nights." Meredith nodded to herself then turned and squinted at Michael. "What you really meant was did I tell him what Harry did to Daisy."

"Yes."

"Then *no*, I didn't. And I doubt very much that Daisy did. Christ, if he knew about *that*, he was bound to bring it up, rub salt in the wounds."

Michael nodded. Daisy had already confirmed that anyway. "So you got the morphine from this...other party?"

"Heroin actually. I had to go to a certain phone box outside Liverpool Street Station and dial a number I'd find there for someone called Artan. I did that and was told to wait at a specific bus stop. This swarthy little man turned up." Meredith shivered. "He wasn't the sort of character I'd normally want to meet."

"There'd be no trail leading to Bohec of course."

"I doubt Jean-Paul even knew him. He'd just be a name someone gave him."

"When did Bohec start to threaten you?"

"Oh, he likes to keep his victims dangling. When I phoned Daisy to say Harry was dead, Jean-Paul came on. He asked me how it felt, murdering my husband. I swear that was the first Daisy knew of it, and she heard it from him, not me. I asked Jean-Paul what he was going to do. He just laughed and said why would he want to do anything. He said families must stick together."

"Until last week. After the divorce came the police. Why *did* you tell them Harry was buried in Scotland?"

"I didn't want them digging up his grave here."

"He has one in Scotland too?"

"Yes."

"Who's buried in it?"

"I don't know. Daisy and I stole someone's ashes from a funeral parlour."

Michael let his face show the revulsion he felt. "You're gross, both of you. What about the poor soul's family? How do you think they felt?"

"Think of it like this, their dear departed has a posh grave in the Lomond ancestral plot. Lord Lomond himself gave the eulogy."

"He thinks Harry was in the urn?"

"Yes."

"Harry was right. You really are an evil, calculating bitch. I thought I knew you, Meredith. I thought I knew Daisy too."

"You left out the *fucking* bit," Meredith snapped, then added in soft, wheedling tones: "Whatever you think of me, Michael, don't condemn Daisy. She was just being loyal to me. The ashes were my idea, not hers. I know it was bad but it seemed right at the time."

"Why didn't you simply have Harry cremated?"

"I wanted him to rot."

Michael could see why, given what the swine had done to Daisy.

"But why bring him here?"

"I wanted to keep an eye on him."

"It wasn't to deny him his last wish?"

Meredith looked up sharply. "You know, Michael, the longer I know you, the more I find to admire in you."

"I wish I could say the same about you."

Meredith shrugged. She nodded towards the clock on the mantelpiece. "It's seven hours since Daisy left. You haven't asked me what happened here."

"Is there any point? She made her choice."

"No, Michael. As she saw it, she didn't have one. What I didn't know was Jean-Paul recorded my phone conversations with him. Last Saturday, a package arrived. Inside was a rather incriminating tape. I hadn't realised I'd been so indiscreet. Of course, he'd been careful to say nothing to implicate himself, quite the reverse. Any listener would think he was trying to dissuade me.

"And on Sunday, while you were out with Anne, he phoned demanding Hamish in return for the master tape. He asked Daisy how she thought I'd cope spending my life behind bars. He said she didn't need to lose Hamish, she could live at Mazemeur, have one of the cottages if she begged him enough. Daisy said, no, she would stay here with you and he could keep Hamish. He said in that case I would still be going to prison. Daisy had no choice, Michael, but remember, when she thought she did, she chose to give up her son and stay with you."

If anything, Meredith's words left Michael with an even bitterer sting of betrayal.

"Daisy *did* have a choice," he said. "She could have told *me.* Then she and Hamish would still be here."

"And what about me?"

"What about *you*? What's your next move, more fucking compensation with Peter?"

Michael walked to the telephone, held the receiver, stared at it. He dialled Le Mazemeur, let the phone ring for ten minutes.

"I've been trying since late afternoon. And Daisy's mobile."

"What about Marie?"

"I kept getting Augustine. No sense there."

Michael dialled the number. He was about to give up when he heard a click, followed by the sound of the receiver being picked up.

"'Allo." It was Marie. She sounded apprehensive.

"Marie, it's Michael. Have you seen Daisy? Jean-Paul's apparently made her fly to France with him."

He heard the girl's sharp intake of breath. "No, there's nobody at the house. It's locked up, no lights anywhere. I was supposed to work there tonight."

"Shit."

Marie laughed nervously, or it might have been a cough. "It's almost midnight and I don't want to go out alone right now. Tomorrow, first thing, I promise."

"I'm sorry, I wasn't thinking of the time. Of course you mustn't go out. Listen, can you put me up?"

"Bien sûr."

"I don't want Jean-Paul or Adèle to know."

"D'accord, Michael."

"So you've decided to go after her?" Meredith said after he'd put the phone down.

"What else can I do? She's carrying my child, Meredith. This could cause her to go into labour. Besides that, I love her."

"What will you do over there?"

"Bring her back. I've done it before, remember."

Michael had prepared himself for long hours of staring at the ceiling but recalled nothing between slumping into bed and his radio burping into life at seven o'clock.

It took him a while to realise Daisy wasn't spending her usual hour in the bathroom but instead was God knows where in France, maybe in labour, in a ward full of babbling mamans. He kicked the duvet away.

Meredith's door was still closed. Slipperless, Michael sneaked downstairs, took the key to Harry's desk from her bureau. A quarter of an hour later, he was on his way to Portsmouth, with Harry's Webley revolver secured beneath the rear passenger seat.

He couldn't get a place on the express ferry so it was early evening before he arrived in Cherbourg. It took five hours of driving before he pulled into the bungalow's drive.

It was almost ten-thirty. A security light clicked on. Marie came out of the house, kissed his cheeks as if he was an old friend. He noticed she had been crying recently.

"Oh, Michael. It was awful."

Something near his heart jarred.

"No, not Daisy, Michael. It's Berthe. The house was still locked, nobody answering. Then I noticed the barn door was ajar. Berthe was just inside. I thought she was dead. She was staring horribly, as if she'd seen the devil. I almost fled but then I saw she was breathing. Her mouth moved but nothing emerged except spittle. I found the house keys in her pocket and phoned the ambulance from there."

So, another stroke. Michael recalled Bohec swearing on his mother's life. If she died it would be divine retribution, even he would have to believe that.

Marie went into the bungalow. Michael heard her shout something to Augustine then she reappeared, rattling keys.

At Le Mazemeur everywhere was pitch-black, not a chink of light anywhere. Michael shivered. How could Daisy have stuck living in such a place?

They searched everywhere from the damp, forbidding cellar to attics that looked, from their cobwebbed state, as if nobody had entered them in years. Only the beds in Jean-Paul and Adèle's room and in what Marie identified as Berthe's appeared to have been slept in recently. Michael dealt with Jean-Paul's belongings while Marie checked what she euphemistically called Berthe's 'lingerie'. Marie came in as he started on Adèle's. "You'd better handle these too," he said.

Downstairs in the business room, Michael flicked through papers, rifled through drawers, breaking into several that were locked. He found nothing that hinted where Bohec had taken Daisy.

He felt on tenterhooks. His gaze wandered around the dim room, resting on the heavy armoire, the desk where Daisy took bookings from would-be gîte dwellers. He poured himself brandy from the decanter she'd dispensed it from. Christ, what an age ago that seemed. So much time, so much water, literally, had run beneath them. He eyed the safe set in the wall.

None of Berthe's keys opened it. Michael wondered what they were for. There weren't that many outbuildings.

"Does Berthe have anywhere like this, somewhere she deals with her business?"

Marie scratched her brow. "The old kitchen where we all dined. That rocking chair. I think there's a chest beside it, in the fireplace."

The chest was huge, solid oak, carved, dark with age. It was covered with a heavy damask fabric with roses woven into it. One of Berthe's keys fitted the chest. Michael released a long sigh.

He pulled out papers, mostly bills and receipts, some recent, some dating back fifty years and more. There were envelopes full of photographs. He handed these to Marie, who began to look through them, fascination filling her face. He heard her whisper "*Maman*".

Deep inside the chest was a deed box, enamelled black, of which most had worn off. Another of Berthe's keys opened this. Others fitted compartments inside. They contained wills, deeds, contracts and the like, in French legalese. Michael wished he had Miranda with him.

Marie was gazing at the photographs. She showed him some of Augustine as a child with a belligerent looking girl beside her. "That's Berthe," she said. There was one of a tall woman beside a lanky man in front of the old well. "Grandpère," Marie said. "And Tante Mathilde."

"Bernard Bohec and Berthe's mother?"

Marie stared at Michael, wide-eyed. "How did you know?"

"Daisy said Bernard owned Mazemeur and your mother is the rightful owner, not Berthe." Michael patted the deed box. "I believe the proof may be in here. I think it's time to put things right."

Marie blinked several times, shook her hair out of her eyes. She looked both scared and excited. "But how can this be? What about Jean-Paul? He would never allow this."

"Bernard was Mathilde's elder brother, so his daughter, Augustine, *your* mother, should have inherited the estate. And Jean-Paul won't be in a position to allow or disallow anything when I catch up with him. I think we should have Daisy's lawyer - you remember Miranda? - look at these. That's if you agree, of course."

Marie was breathing rapidly. She now looked shell-shocked. Michael thought she'd had enough for one day.

Michael fidgeted as Marie stared at textbooks for her new school term. Michael could see her thoughts were elsewhere.

If only he could get through to Adèle. Maybe he was fooling himself, relying on his vanity, but he felt sure she would help him. And she had promised that she wouldn't let Bohec take Hamish. But she was very, very pregnant. He'd already asked Marie if she knew Adèle's mobile phone number. She didn't.

A memory drifted into his thoughts, of posting Adèle's photograph to the 'safe' house she'd given him. He screwed up his face, tried to visualise that moment. The address was definitely in Morbihan but he could have taken that for granted. He started working through the alphabet, trying each letter for associations. He lingered on 'c' for a while. Carnac, no too hard. He held onto Cézanne, something like Cézanne. No, not Cézanne. Serazin of course, Adèle's maiden name. Something similar followed. Serazin, Sarezin... Sarzeau, that was it. It was Adèle Serazin, Somewhere, Sarzeau. He remembered the three names had a similar ring, like an incantation.

"Have you a local map, one with Sarzeau on it?" he asked Marie.

She left her schoolbooks, rummaged in a bookcase. "Will this do?"

Michael traced a finger over the open map, concentrating on villages around Sarzeau. Lots of Ker-somethings but it wasn't one of them. Saints? Yes, a Saint-someone. St-Gildas, St-Martin, St-Jacques, St-Colombier, St-Servais. That was *it*. Serazin, St-Servais, Sarzeau.

"May I come too?" Marie was all eager-eyed and something else. For a moment Michael wanted to say yes. But he thought of the gun under the driver's seat and what he might have to do with it.

"I don't want to put you in danger."

Marie's face dropped. "But Tante Daisy might need a woman's help."

Michael almost smiled at *woman* but stopped himself in time. Marie was what, sixteen? Old enough to marry, so a woman physically, but she seemed younger in some ways than Anne.

"I'm sorry, but I need to do this on my own. Any other time, I'd love to have your company."

Marie's face flushed.

"Tomorrow," Michael said. "Perhaps tomorrow."

Michael stopped in the square at St-Servais. Behind him was the church. Ahead, stretching along the main street, was a long and motley row of buildings, not one younger than a hundred years. They began with the inevitable bar, sited conveniently for those escaping from Mass.

A man left the bar, headed for a battered 2CV. Michael asked him if he knew the Serazin house.

The man smiled. "Suivez," he said. He drove slowly across the square then stopped outside a villa cocooned by hedges of clipped hebes. He waved a hand at the house then carried on down the road that ran beside it.

Michael parked, slipped the gun into his jacket pocket, walked past sculpted evergreens to a stout front door. He rang a sonorous bell.

A woman, fortyish, fiftyish, short and dark, attractive, peered around the door. Michael put on his best smile.

"Madame Serazin? Adèle gave me your address."

She smiled vapidly then seemed to peel the door back. Michael realised it was hinged in its centre.

"You are a friend of Adèle?"

"Yes. I'm Michael Cavanagh."

"Ah, the Englishman. But Cavanagh, that is Irish, is it not?"

"Yes, my father's family was Irish and my mother's Spanish."

"So you're not really English at all."

This was the sort of thing Adèle herself might say.

"Perhaps not but I'm a Londoner, born and raised there. You are Adèle's sister?"

The woman smiled, not at all insipidly now. "Her mother, Héloise. But it was nice of you to say the other thing." Her eyes sparkled.

"I need to find her urgently. She isn't at home, at Le Mazemeur."

"No, she wanted to be closer to her mother for her first child."

"She's *here*?"

"In the apartment upstairs."

"And her husband?" Michael fingered the gun.

Héloise sniffed. The corners of her mouth turned down. "He's another reason she is here. He had to leave on unavoidable business. He's due to call this evening." She smiled again and this version seemed to include a degree of amusement. "I take it you prefer to see Adèle?"

"For the moment."

Héloise signalled him to follow her. Instead of going back into the house, she went to a door midway along the frontage. This opened onto a tiny hall with doors on each side, a flight of stairs at its centre. She began climbing.

She led Michael along a corridor and into a large living room. There, Adèle was propped amidst cushions on a narrow sofa. Music - cello accompanied by piano, came from a radio sitting beneath a large television. It sounded somewhat severe. Beethoven, Michael thought.

"Michael, how wonderful to see you."

Adèle's surprise seemed genuine. There was some delight too. Michael felt guilty for being pleased about that, it fitted ill with his reason for being there.

Adèle grinned. "You'll have to sit on a chair, I'm afraid. There isn't quite enough room to snuggle beside me."

Héloïse shook her head. "I'll leave you two to it." With the sort of glance that spoke of a secret shared, she left the room.

"Ignore Maman. She likes to imagine everyone is having an affair." Adèle patted her lump. "Only eight weeks to go, thank God. Now tell me, how is Daisy getting on with hers?"

"I was hoping you might be able to tell me."

Adèle frowned. "What do you mean, Michael?"

"The day before yesterday, Jean-Paul came for her, forced her to fly here. I was away at the time. It seems on Sunday, the day after your wedding, he demanded Hamish back. Congratulations by the way."

"He was in England?" Adèle's face turned wraith-pale. "But, how, *how* could he force Daisy...?"

"By threatening to send Meredith to prison."

"*Prison*? For what?"

"For murdering Daisy's father."

"*Dieu*! And did she?"

"Technically." Michael explained Bohec's part in it.

"So he is involved, what do they say – before and after the fact?"

"Except there's no proof of that."

Adèle began to breathe so heavily Michael was afraid she might go into labour. "I think I need to walk," she said. "Help me up, please."

They went into the back garden, most of which was taken up by an open-air swimming pool. As Michael gave her Meredith's account of events, Adèle paced up and down, leaning back to counter the weight in her belly. The exercise seemed to calm her. She pointed to a table and chairs behind the swimming pool screen. "Shall we sit there?"

"It's vital I find Daisy soon," Michael said. "She's only five weeks behind you. She should be at home resting, not traipsing about at your husband's whim. Have you any idea where he might have taken her?"

"I have none, but you're welcome to stay and ask him. I certainly shall. He'll be here tonight. It seems he has a window in his schedule. *Pff - window, schedule.* He even has his phone switched off." Adèle gazed at her swollen belly. "He swore that I and this child were all he wanted."

"He wants Hamish but with Daisy I think it's the letting go he can't bear."

Adèle shrugged. "Maybe." She gave a short laugh. "You know, I think sometimes that you and I…"

"Adèle don't."

"But Michael, you don't know what I was going to say."

Michael hung his head. "Adèle, I love Daisy and I'm worried out of my head about her."

"I know that. And I wasn't going to say anything terrible. Right now I hate Jean-Paul. I feel awful because I promised Daisy I would not let him take Hamish." Adèle gasped suddenly. She was looking downwards, towards Michael's waist. "Jesus, you're prepared to kill him."

Michael glanced down, saw the butt of Harry's revolver poking from his jacket pocket. "As I said, I love Daisy."

Adèle's breathing became laboured again. "I'll help you. I promise I'll help you all I can. But don't use that gun, Michael. Please don't use that gun." She tried to get up. "Take me back."

Michael settled Adèle on her sofa. He emptied the revolver's chamber, put the bullets in a pocket separate from the gun. "I'll talk to him, that's all. Then it's up to him. I need to tell him something anyway. Berthe has had another stroke."

Adèle didn't look surprised. "I wondered how long it would take. She's been heading that way ever since you were last here with Daisy. And he swore on her life not to try and take Hamish back." She touched Michael's right hand. "This will hurt him more than bullets ever could."

Around six to half-past, Michael's phone rang. "Michael? Marie. Jean-Paul's been here. When I told him about Berthe he swore at me for not letting him know. I said how could I when I didn't know where he was or how to contact him. What if there were other emergencies? I said. He scribbled a number on a post-it note then left for the hospital. Thank God I'd already slid the deed box behind the sofa. Sorry, Michael, I should have asked how you were getting on."

"Not as well as you it seems. Can you give me the number he left?"

Michael wrote it down then Marie said, "There is one other thing."

"What?"

"Meredith's arrived. She says you're running around loose with a gun."

Michael sighed. Didn't he have enough to deal with…?

"I suppose I'd better speak to her."

"Michael, what the hell are you playing at? Do you want us to end up in gaol together?"

"They don't have mixed prisons."

"Don't be facetious. You know perfectly well what I mean. How do you think Daisy would feel then? What would become of your baby?"

"What's become of it now? How do I know what he's done to Daisy?"

"He wouldn't do anything, not with Hamish there."

Meredith had a point, Michael supposed. If Hamish wasn't with Bohec then he must be with Daisy, so Daisy must be all right.

"I'll be back later," he said. "And the gun isn't loaded."

He reset the phone, called the number Marie had given him. It belonged to a bar-tabac in Carnac Plage.

"Take me with you," Adèle said. "As your hostage. You have his wife while he has yours."

Michael frowned and Adèle said, "Don't worry, I'm not about to give birth." Something in her eyes said she would enjoy playing her part. Michael supposed it was a change from the burden and boredom of humping that lump. This was meant to be her honeymoon but the bridegroom was absent.

"Okay," he said.

Adèle gave Michael her phone. In return, she insisted on parting him from the bullets, put them in her bag. "Now neither of us can start anything silly."

The bar-tabac was called *Billy's* and it was close to the sea front. Michael said he'd been told he might find Jean-Paul Bohec there. The barman frowned a little too much. Michael pointed towards Adèle. "This is his wife. We *need* to contact him. I don't think we have that long."

The barman eyed Adèle's bulge, licked his lips like a nervous puppy. Michael saw him calculating the odds of her giving birth right there, in his bar.

"Twenty-six rue Lesage, over the shop." The barman pointed towards the entrance door then made a sweeping motion to the right. "Just around the corner."

Adèle stayed put while Michael hurried to number twenty-six. It was a hi-fi shop and a door beside it was latched flat against an inside wall. A flight of stairs climbed to a small landing. Beyond that was a door with a cylinder lock and bell push set into its centre.

Michael rang the bell. At first there was no response then he heard footsteps on floorboards, childish footsteps. He pressed his face close to the door. "Hamish?"

The footsteps stopped.

"Hamish, is that you? It's Michael. Is Mama there?"

There was a short silence then he heard Hamish's voice, speaking in French. "Mama is tired. She's sleeping."

"Hamish, can you open the door?"

No reply, but Michael could hear the boy shifting about.

"Can you open the door?"

"Papa said I mustn't let anyone in."

"Hamish, I'm not *anyone*. I'm Michael. I need to come in. Open the door, please."

Shuffling, then a scratching sound as Hamish turned the lock. Michael pushed gently on the door as the catch clicked free.

"Where's Mama, Hamish?"

The flat consisted of a row of rooms off a corridor that overlooked the street. Daisy was in a room almost at the end.

She lay on a bed, above the sheets, in a foetal position. She wore her stretchy maternity trousers and above it, a shirt Michael recognised as the salmon pink one he'd worn when he first came to France to find her.

"Daisy. Darling. Wake up."

She wasn't asleep. Her eyes were open but they didn't look like hers at all. Sunk inside their lids, staring as if he was someone she didn't recognise, as if she didn't recognise anything, even the difference between night and day. Her whole demeanour was blank, uncomprehending, her pulse slower than a snail.

"Jesus, Daisy, what's he given you?"

Michael searched for her coat, whatever luggage she had brought. There was only her travelling bag. He heard a noise, a cough, and spun round, his hand automatically going towards the pocket containing the gun. Hamish was standing behind him, trembling.

"Mama wouldn't wake up."

Michael asked Hamish to collect his things.

"Papa's at the hospital. Mama needs to go to the hospital too."

"Can we go home after that?"

Michael nodded. "As soon as Mama is better."

He went into the corridor. Hamish headed into the room next door. It had a double bed that looked as if he'd been sharing it with Bohec. Hamish picked up the little bag Daisy had bought for him in la Roche-Bernard, before they boarded *Hirondelle*.

Daisy groaned as Michael lifted her. He half-carried, half-dragged her across the floor and along to the stairway. He wondered how to get her safely down to the street.

Through the window, he glimpsed a flash of colour. A racing cyclist, all lycra-clad advertising on a gleaming red and silver vélo, was riding along the street. Michael let Daisy gently down then descended the stairs three at a time.

"Help me, help me."

The cyclist braked sharply, leaped from his saddle, rushed over to Michael. Between them they manoeuvred Daisy down the stairs and round the corner to *Billy's*. Hamish followed behind, face like ash, bag over his shoulder.

The barman looked as if he wished it were his night off. Two extremely pregnant women where once there was one seemed too much for him to take in. He poured himself a drink from a dark bottle, swallowed it in one. Poured another.

Michael snatched the glass from his hand. "For God's sake, call an ambulance," he said.

Chapter 22

Michael's lips were tight as he tailgated the ambulance. Beside him, a fury arose. Adèle started off by muttering "It's just like it was with Jimpy" then escalated into screaming, "How could he do this to a pregnant woman?"

When they got out of the car, Adèle removed the bullets from her bag, slipped them into Michael's pocket. "Send him these from me," she said then her face contorted and Michael thought she was going to erupt.

But it was her waters breaking. Michael remembered reading in Daisy's pregnancy guides about it not happening like this, that it was a clichéd device used only by Hollywood screenwriters. It seemed Adèle's body hadn't read the rules.

"Quickly, quickly," Michael shouted to the nearest nurse, and as she hurried towards Adèle, he was off, Hamish clinging to him, following the men wheeling Daisy into the bowels of the hospital.

The doctor wore glasses that didn't suit her. "We're worried about the time that's elapsed since Mademoiselle Lomond took the heroin. Do you know when that was?"

Michael stared at her. "She wouldn't have *taken* it. That bastard did this to her." There was a barbed pain behind his eyes. He found it difficult to think. "His mother was brought in with a stroke. Bohec. Berthe Bohec. He's bound to be with her. Jean-Paul Bohec. Daisy is his ex-wife. Ask *him* what he did to her and when he did it."

Michael's hands were in his jacket pockets, one gripped Harry's revolver, the other clutched bullets. His feet tapped the hard, clinical floor.

The doctor signalled a nurse. Michael struggled to his feet, sat down again. He felt drunk, though he'd had no alcohol for days.

"Daisy is my Mama," a small voice said. Michael started. Hamish sat, rigid, shock-white, on the seat beside him. He'd forgotten the boy was with him.

Michael saw the doctor wince behind her professional detachment and he knew things were bad.

"How long before you can tell me anything?" he said.

"We must allow the treatment a chance to work."

There was a flurry of activity at the door, then Meredith entered, strode across the floor towards them.

"I'm going to find him."

"Give me the gun first, Michael."

They were in a private room near the doctor's office. Meredith pushed her bag across the seat.

"Look at me, Michael."

He lifted his head, took in the face, those eyes. *Daisy's* eyes.

"You can't help her from prison. Put it into my bag."

But it was definitely Meredith's voice. The face was hers now too. *To hell with the gun. I'll use my hands. Carpenter's hands.* Michael took the Webley and its bullets from his pockets, slid them into the recesses of Meredith's bag.

Then he left her sitting there.

He found out which ward Berthe was in. "My mother-in-law," he explained, hoped Daisy would forgive him that. When he got there, the nurse in charge frowned when he asked about Berthe.

"Madame Bohec has been moved to a private room," she said. "But you can't go in. She's in a coma."

"It's her son I'm looking for."

"Oh. He was here earlier but..." She glanced towards a series of glass-walled rooms against an outside wall.

Michael made his way towards them. The nurse cried "Monsieur" in his wake.

Bohec was in the third room, arguing with the doctor who was treating Daisy and with two men in suits, one of whom gesticulated with widely flapping arms. Michael crashed the door open, went straight for Bohec, who had barely time to register fear before Michael's hands reached his throat.

Long before midnight, the words came. "Monsieur Cavanagh, I'm so terribly, terribly sorry."

Michael looked through her, through this doctor who wore inappropriate glasses, through the white walls and machines and drips to a particular bed of his imagination, where a pale-haired goddess lay. Goddesses were immortal, so how could they be true, these deceiving devil words?

"We managed to save your baby but there was nothing more we could do for your fiancée."

"Baby?"

"You have a daughter, Monsieur Cavanagh. She's very tiny, just over a kilogram, but has a good chance of survival."

"I know I have a daughter. Her name's Anne. She's fifteen years old."

"This is your *new* daughter, Monsieur Cavanagh. So now you have two." The doctor looked perplexed, out of her depth.

Two daughters? So Anne was wrong, thinking it was a boy.

Michael smiled. "What does Daisy think of her? Can I see her?"

"Your daughter's in the Premature Baby Unit, Monsieur. The nurse will take you there." The doctor touched Michael's arm. He jerked it away.

"Not the baby. I don't want to see the baby. I want to see Daisy. I want to tell her I love her."

The doctor's face was streaming with tears and those stupid glasses were misting up. "Come, I'll take you to her."

Daisy lay still beneath crisp white sheets. He didn't know what they'd done to transform it from its state when he'd found her, but Daisy's smooth, beautiful skin now glowed with life, not death as these liars claimed. Her hair looked beguilingly untidy. He kissed it, pressed his lips into it, absorbed its scents and texture, the latter soft as fresh-spun silk. He kissed Daisy's lips, her eyes, her brow. He heard her stir then moan softly, as she often did before waking. He whispered "I love you" and her lips broke into a smile exclusively for him. It was then that he broke, his body heaving as he wept, his soul stretching out for Daisy's, finding it out of reach.

Someone was shaking him, pulling him gently back. He let it happen, turned to see who it could be. Meredith, of course, who else?

He'd been pulled away from Bohec too, though not gently, and not before he'd seen Bohec's face glaze into the prelude to death. If only they'd let him alone for just a few more seconds.

"The Wishing Steps," he said, gripping Meredith's shoulders, haunting her eyes. "I held my breath all the way up and down and up again. But it didn't work."

He watched Meredith's face twist then she shook her head.

"No Michael, it never does."

"It was another lie," he said, still staring at her. "One more fucking lie."

When they were back in the private room by the doctor's office, Michael took the gun from Meredith's bag, fished the bullets out, loaded the chamber, sat with the gun's barrel pointed at her chest. She stared him out.

"You think I should have used that on him, don't you?"

Michael shrugged. "What I think doesn't matter."

"I considered it. Believe me, I did. But with Hamish there, how could I shoot his father?"

Michael snapped his fingers an inch from Meredith's face. "I was that close. They had to wrench my hands from his throat. You shouldn't have taken the gun from me."

Meredith's eyes flickered. "You should thank God that I did."

"Why? God doesn't give a shit."

"Because you have two daughters who need you. What use would you be to them in a French prison?"

Michael glared at Meredith. "One daughter. I don't want the other without Daisy."

Meredith looked as if she was about to argue the point but she got up, lips and face set hard, as if they were rendered.

"I am going to see my granddaughter. Are you coming?" Meredith's eyes were blue steel, skewering him.

"I don't want to see her," Michael yelled. "Ever."

He couldn't help feeling that the child was responsible for Daisy's death, that Daisy would have lived if she wasn't pregnant. He was honest enough to blame himself too, for he put the seed in her. It made no difference the doctors swore that not being pregnant wouldn't have saved Daisy.

Meredith returned, said, very sniffily, the baby was doing well, considering. She didn't expand on 'considering'. She also mentioned Adèle had given birth to a son.

They took rooms in a hotel convenient for the hospital. There, on his new daughter's fifth day in the world, Michael heard that Adèle's child had died during the night.

Meanwhile, the perpetrator of everyone's misery was incarcerated in an undisclosed place. His mother lingered on.

Hamish's suffering was perhaps worse than Michael's, because he was too young to understand. Or maybe that made it easier, Michael couldn't decide. How do you explain to a four-year-old that his Mama is dead and his Papa killed her?

After days of tears, the boy reverted to the stiff, stately facade of Michael's first acquaintance with him. Hamish cried at night though and lately Meredith had taken him into her bed. Michael didn't know if she cried in the dark but in daylight she bustled about with a busyness oozing from her that made him want to shake her and tell her to mourn her daughter.

Miranda came to Vannes and she and Michael wept together. He didn't know why, but he felt able to bury himself in this woman's arms whereas he could not contemplate the same with Meredith.

Then Miranda said, "We're sort of brother and sister, with your Dad married to my Mum" and Michael's face broke into a smile for the first time since Daisy's death.

Miranda was the one who persuaded him to visit his new daughter, helped him fill in necessary forms. She held his hand as they entered the special baby care unit.

Regiments of monitors, cables, tubes, and neat files of plastic incubators greeted them. In one of the latter was his child, tinier than one of his hands, a bubble-wrapped, red-faced innocent who would never know her mother's milk. There was a tube in her mouth to make her breathe, one in her navel to feed her.

A tear dampened Michael's cheek. More followed. He saw fingers so thin he could see the bones inside, delicate, like those on a wren's wing.

"Have you thought of a name? She deserves to have a name."

"Victoria," he said, without thinking. "Like her mother. And, what's the feminine of Ted?"

Miranda's eyes moistened. "Oh, Michael. You don't have to..."

"I want to."

"Well, I don't know what it would be. Edwardia sounds dreadful. Edina, perhaps?"

"Victoria Edina it is, then."

They drank coffee in the hospital canteen. "It'll be months before she's strong enough to take home," Miranda said. "What will you do?"

"Stay with her." Michael didn't need to think. "I'll take Daisy home first then come back." The authorities had finally agreed to release Daisy's body.

"Where will you take Daisy? I'm thinking about Giffards ... the contracts were exchanged on the day ... I didn't know, you see."

"But the house, how can I pay for it? It was Daisy's money."

"She made a will. When she first came to see me. She wrote a note that I was to give to you in the event..." Miranda cleared her throat, "of anything happening to her."

She took an envelope from her bag, handed it to Michael.

Michael, it said in Daisy's handwriting. Inside was a single sheet of notepaper, pale blue, matching the envelope. *Warts and all, remember?* That was all she'd written. A lump formed in Michael's throat.

"So you *can* buy the house. But the point is do you want to put it on the market again?"

This is going to be as good as anywhere, Daisy had said. Michael looked up at Miranda. "Daisy wanted to make a nest there."

"I drove down to Sussex and took a look. It's a beautiful house." Miranda brushed something away from her eyes then added, slowly, "There's a very pretty church and churchyard in the village. I could speak to the vicar."

Michael stared at Miranda for a long while before he said, "Okay."

Meredith assumed Michael would go back to living with her.

"You, me and the two children. Anne could come and stay of course, in the holidays."

She was regarding him with calculating eyes. "It'll be better than before, Michael. I promise I'll make it better for you."

How could anything be *better* without Daisy? What the hell was Meredith implying? As her eyes hovered around alluring before switching to acquisitive, Michael felt palpably sick, clenched his mind against playing her games. He hadn't seen her cry for Daisy once.

"And Daisy would be there, next to Harry? I won't have that, Meredith."

Meredith's expression turned abruptly hard. "I'm next of kin, Michael. It's my decision."

"No you're not. And no, it isn't. Daisy was my wife in everything that matters."

"Nevertheless, I think you'll find you don't have any legal rights to the body."

The body? Michael hated Meredith for calling Daisy that.

"Pull that stunt, Meredith, and you'll never see your grandchildren again."

"But they're my flesh and blood. And Hamish isn't yours."

"Daisy appointed *me* as his guardian."

"She named *you*?" Meredith's mouth drooped. She frowned, fingered her chin.

Well that's something she didn't anticipate, Michael thought. Round two to Daisy.

"I came back that day," he said, 'to persuade Daisy to marry me right away. I wasn't even supposed to be at your house. Trust me, she said, whatever happens. She must have thought she knew what she was doing but she underestimated Bohec. She paid for that mistake with her life. Christ, we're all paying. But I'll never blame her."

"But you do blame me?"

"Look, we both have things we could have said and done better. Let's stop this pointless bickering, agree that Daisy's wishes are paramount."

Meredith nodded slowly, regarding Michael all the while as a cat might survey the people she deigns to associate with.

Daisy came home by air. A gleaming hearse, a Daimler, waited on the tarmac. The sight of it terrified Michael. He faltered as he stepped off the plane.

Miranda held him up. "You can do it, Michael."

He'd forgotten it was only a few short months since she'd been in his position herself. As Daisy was laid in the hearse, he set his jaw, stood to attention like Ted would have done.

Hamish tried to do the same but he was trembling too much. Michael put an arm around him. The boy pressed close, as if he wanted to weld himself to Michael's side. Poor little beggar, Michael thought.

Meredith looked anywhere but at what was happening right in front of her.

The undertaker asked Michael if he wanted to see Daisy. He knew what that meant, she'd be laid out like a wax doll in a soft gown, celestial music piped from plumbing hidden behind plush dark velvet curtains. That wouldn't be *his* Daisy; he'd already said goodbye to her in the hospital, looking as real as she had in life.

"No," he said. The man's eyebrows rose as if he was witnessing sacrilege.

The funeral was held on the type of spring day Daisy would have enjoyed. Warm, with a gentle southwest breeze. Twenty-one Celsius but to Michael it felt like zero as he followed the coffin. As with Colonel Ted, he could not accept that Daisy was inside that dreadful box with its ridiculous brass embellishments. He stared at it with an almost morbid detachment.

In contrast to Ted's funeral, no bird flew about the nave. The vicar uttered no platitudes but got on with the holy bits. Michael had insisted on speaking for Daisy himself but when the time came his legs had rubber for bones. Miranda and Anne, either side of him in the front pew, each clutched one of his arms and he managed to stay upright and make his way to the lectern, though it felt as if he were wading through quicksand. The lectern had eagle wings and Michael gripped them as if they were his last hope. He gazed, unseeing, at the assembled mourners. He swallowed hard, began to speak.

As he did, his mind conjured a vision of Daisy, so real he believed she was standing there before him, a few feet away. She smiled at him the way she did when she first told him she loved him.

He told her she lived up to her name, bright as a sunny day but shying from the rain. He said she was a spirit of the light who had the misfortune to meet a creature of the dark. He told her she was funny, sad, volatile, outrageous, kind, fiercely loyal to those she cared about. He said he counted it the greatest privilege on earth to have loved her and be the man she loved in return, and he would miss her terribly for as long as he lived.

He broke down then and Anne, his precious Anne, ran up to the lectern and helped him back to his seat. When he was able to look up, Daisy had gone.

"Oh, Dad," Anne said after Daisy was lowered into the chalky ground, after the token pieces of earth were sprinkled. She hugged close to Michael while her sorrow flowed down her cheeks. She said she'd live with him, help him look after Hamish and Victoria.

"Never mind what Mum says. She'll have stuffy old James to order about, so she'll be all right."

Peter came up to Michael, uncharacteristically taciturn but generous with tactile sympathy. And there was Marie, first time in England and on her own at that. "Oh, Michael," she sobbed, crushing her face against his chest.

Paddy had sailed to Holyhead on the Dun Laoghaire ferry, driven down from there. "Daisy was such a lovely girl, Michael," he said through copious tears, "kindness itself to me." Michael stopped himself from reminding him he'd only met her once and that was at another funeral.

Michael noticed a statuesque woman with a hint of Meredith about her. She turned out to be her older sister, Romilly. She never said a word to him all the time she was there.

There was a group of three other strangers, two willowy women and a cadaverous man, all looking to be in their sixties. They turned out to be the Lomond 'girls' and the Monarch of the Glen himself.

While his sisters smiled vaguely behind him, Lord Lomond introduced himself to Michael. "Call me Frank," he said. He seemed rather ordinary, like a small town solicitor and, unlike his brother, didn't use strangled vowels. He asked Michael what was to happen to poor Hamish. "He's the image of Harry as a boy. Though I hope to God he turns out better."

Michael said he hoped to adopt Hamish. He said he wished Daisy had lived long enough for them to marry. "But I'd need his father's agreement, I suppose."

"You're worried Bohec might try to get the boy back? Forget it. By the time that swine's released, Hamish will be a young man."

Michael noticed that Paddy managed to dry his eyes when the whiskey flowed in the village inn. While he himself stood trembling, with scarcely the will to raise his glass, he watched Paddy sink draughts that would have felled most men. With Paddy though, they were like a slow tide lapping on the shore of his senses, helping him into a dreamy-eyed affability that allowed him to engage other mourners as if each was a personal friend.

The wake carried on in Michael's hotel, which now also housed everyone else. He took the opportunity to slip away while the drink and reminiscences were overflowing. Anne joined him.

"You'll be all right, Dad," she said as she kissed him goodnight at the top of the stairs.

"Yeah. I'll be all right."

He went into his room, slid the sash window open. He stood there, breathing in the cool cloudless night, wondering which, out of the countless stars he could see, was Daisy's.

Michael was to return to France with Marie, and Meredith would take Hamish home with her. He'd have to do something about her. But right now, he thought, a child for whom *he* was the nearest blood relation needed him.

Paddy was ferrying Anne home before heading up to Holyhead. As he bid Michael goodbye, he told him he planned to visit Birkenhead en-route.

"I wrote to the address on the certificate but nobody replied. So I thought I might try ringing the bell. It's definitely her, it gave Ronnie as the mother. No father."

Michael frowned. *What certificate? Ronnie who?* Then he remembered his potential sibling.

"Why not, Dad? It's worth a try."

"Still, the chances are that she, they, left the place years ago."

Paddy looked lost in reminiscence, then he seemed to jerk and his brow furrowed. He gripped Michael's shoulders.

"Oh my boy, I'm so terribly, terribly sorry. I shouldn't be burdening you with this. The prospect of me finding your sister must be the last thing on your mind."

As Anne got into Paddy's car, she said, "Call me. Every night, Dad. Promise. You may be in France but I'm not letting you hide yourself away."

"I promise," Michael said. He pressed her so tightly against him she had to gasp for breath.

Michael was on deck for most of the crossing, virtually the only passenger there, for in contrast to the spring-like weather of the funeral, it was a perniciously cold day.

Marie seemed to relapse into her old shyness as soon as they boarded. Or perhaps she'd picked up the negative signals Michael was sure he was giving out. Whatever the reason, she only appeared three times, to check, he assumed, that he hadn't jumped overboard.

Michael stared at the water a lot. He recalled the fear on Daisy's face when he dived into the Channel. After that was the first time she said she loved him. He recalled a lot of other things but kept returning to that.

As he drove down the Cherbourg peninsula, Michael's mind wandered back to the sea storm, Daisy pleading with him to make Peter take them into Treguelven harbour.

He thought about going there, to gain an idea why it meant so much to her. Then he realised it would mean an overnight stop, impossible with Marie in the car, so after Dinan he turned south for Mazemeur.

Marie now became over-bright, chattering about inconsequential things, often those she saw from the car window: she discoursed on chaffinches; Dutch caravanners; those little passenger trains that run on the road; a fat gendarme on an anorexic motorcycle.

It began to jar on Michael and he stopped listening. He wondered about Marlowe, what progress he'd made into investigating Bohec's origins. He supposed he'd have to tell him Daisy was dead.

That last thought bit into him, reverberated inside his head: *Daisy is dead, Daisy is dead, Daisy is dead.* He screamed at it to shut up.

As Marie sat helpless, clearly aware from her expression that he was about to fall apart, Michael pulled the car onto the verge, laid his head against the steering wheel. The horn blared as he howled like a wounded dog.

"May I come too?" Marie said as Michael left for the hospital. "I'd love to meet my niece. If that's all right."

Michael grunted. Strictly speaking, Marie wasn't Victoria's aunt, anymore than Daisy had been hers. He screwed his eyes up, working it out. Augustine and Berthe were first cousins, so Bohec was Marie's second cousin, not her uncle. He supposed that, putting aside the fact they weren't actually blood relations, it made her and Victoria second cousins once removed.

What the hell, if Marie wanted to be an aunt why not let her?

"I'm going to visit Adèle too, if you don't mind. Did you know she's still in the hospital?"

"Adèle? Still there?" Michael considered the irony: Adèle alive, baby dead and Daisy...well, the opposite. He wiped tears away, gritted teeth.

"I feel sorry for her."

"I wish Daisy could trade places with her."

Marie hung her head. Something made Michael say he didn't mean it, at least not like that.

But he knew he did mean it, exactly like that.

"You could help," said the nurse. "If you would like to."

She inserted a tube in Victoria's mouth, showed Michael how to syringe milk into it. She stood aside for him to have a go but his hands became great clumsy blocks as he tried to follow her example.

He put himself in the mindset he used with a delicate piece of cabinetwork in front of him. He stopped gripping the tube as if it were something to wrestle with, let his hands gentle.

"That's it," the nurse said as the milk flowed. She added something about asking his permission. "But you weren't here."

"Permission?"

The nurse bit her lip as Michael stared at her.

"Because it's breast milk, and it's our policy to get the...parent's approval before using it. In your absence we took the decision for you. It's pasteurised, ideal for premature babies because it's more easily digested and contains antibodies that formula stuff doesn't. This just happened to come at the right time."

"Who donates it?"

"Usually mothers who produce more than their babies can use."

Michael had a mental picture of plump and jolly women on all fours, breasts connected to mechanical pumps, being milked like cows. When he peered closer he saw they had plastic faces with fixed grins. He shuddered.

"Usually? You mean this was different?"

"Not necessarily. But sometimes, it's a mother who has lost her own baby. Mostly, they're too distraught to even consider it but in those who do, I think it helps them to know they're helping another baby to live." The nurse smiled, put a finger to her lips. "You'll understand I'm not allowed to tell you which it was in Victoria's case."

She gave Michael a cotton bud so he could have a try at cleaning Victoria's mouth. Dipping the cotton into sterile water, he gently wiped it around and inside the tiny orifice. Victoria made a sound that he elevated in his mind to a gurgle. He was sure her eyes lit up. When he moved, they seemed to follow him.

"Oh, so tiny," Marie cooed when she came in. "Like a little doll. Who do you think she looks like?"

"Hard to say until her face fills out. She has Daisy's eyes so I hope she'll look more like her."

Marie stood back, appraised Michael. "I think I'd agree with that." She blushed then cleared her throat, twiddled her fingers. "Adèle wondered if you could spare a minute before you go."

"She wants to see me?"

"Yes."

"Oh, I don't know. I really don't know."

But something, the reproach on Marie's face perhaps, caused Michael to stop as they reached the hospital exit.

"Okay, point me back in the right direction."

Adèle was in a side ward, its only occupant. She didn't look twenty-three any more, could be older than the thirty-two years she admitted to. Her face was drawn, her eyes red-rimmed. But at least *she* was alive.

"Michael, thank you."

"For what? Not breaking your husband's neck? I tried to."

Adèle smiled but Michael knew it wasn't from amusement. "Not that. I'd break it myself if I could. I meant thank you for seeing me. I must be almost the last person on earth you'd want to be near. I know how you must be hurting. I'm so very sorry, Michael. Sorry I couldn't stop it happening."

"I'm sorry about your baby. You didn't deserve to lose him."

A band of pain crossed Adèle's eyes. "At least I had him for a while. I'm told yours, yours and Daisy's, is doing well."

"Victoria? Yes, though she's very tiny. They let me feed her today. Human milk they said, donated. Well it would have to be, wouldn't it? I had to syringe it into her stomach."

"Oh, that's wonderful. For her. For her and you, I mean. Bonding."

Adèle's smile returned and this time seemed surer of itself, though something in it, an enigmatic quality, suddenly caused Michael to wonder if she was the donor. He sought for the right words but they seemed too personal to ask a woman, especially Adèle. If she was the one, he couldn't decide whether he should be angry or grateful. On the one hand, it didn't seem right that a by-product of a union between Adèle and Daisy's murderer might be circulating inside Daisy's child. On the other, it may well have been the vital factor between Victoria surviving or dying at a time when he didn't even want to know she existed. He imagined Adèle, bereft in a mental wilderness, thinking of another's child as she mourned her own. Whatever her motives, he decided, selfish or selfless, the results justified them.

"Thank you," he said. "I'm very grateful."

Adèle frowned. "For what?"

"Whatever I should thank you for."

"There's nothing, Michael."

"Okay."

"Good."

Adèle stopped frowning but Michael was sure the colour rose briefly in her cheeks.

Chapter 23

Daisy's twenty-eighth birthday occurred during Victoria's third week in the world. The Giffards purchase was due for completion the same day so Michael travelled to England to deal with both events.

He felt detached from reality, hearing his footsteps ring, his voice bounce back at him as he patrolled Giffards' empty rooms.

Empty suited him.

He'd brought food, a kettle, crockery, a sleeping bag. He had water and electricity so he'd be comfortable enough. Only Miranda knew where he was and she was bound not to tell. He'd phoned Anne each evening as promised. He did it again now.

"You sound funny," Anne said. "Have you been crying?"

"Just the start of a cold."

"I don't believe you, Dad."

Michael protested, thought he did enough to persuade Anne he was fine and still in France. But as soon as he put the phone down, he felt compelled to drive up to Dorking and see her. Then he reminded himself that he *owed* Daisy this day. He would end it as he began it. Alone.

That morning, he'd bought Daisy flowers. Apart from a small-flowered narcissus, and daisies of course, he didn't know their names but they were mostly primrose yellows and soft creams-to-whites, clean colours Daisy loved, that always looked well on her. He arranged them in a planter he'd also bought that morning.

He saw the vicar once, who nodded, passed him a brief smile, saw three or four elderly ladies too, who seemed bent on not noticing him.

He stayed with Daisy for most of the day, sometimes kneeling, sometimes sitting. He felt her presence, that warmth down his spine. He told her about Victoria, how well she was doing, how he'd make their new house a home she'd be proud of, one for both her children. He said things maudlin, things silly, some that broke his heart, but they were things that had to be said for there could be no secrets between them, not now.

In return, he tuned his spirit to Daisy's, heard her voice, as clear as if she was there beside him. She told him he must not blame himself, not for anything he thought he'd done, just as she knew he didn't blame her. She said she'd feel at peace now the bad things of her life were gone if it wasn't that she missed him so much.

At that moment, Michael seriously contemplated joining Daisy. It was only her words echoing through his mind that stopped him jumping into the car, driving it flat out at the nearest immovable object.

"No, Michael, it doesn't work like that. It's not for you to decide when."

Meredith, with unaccustomed meekness that didn't fool Michael for a second, asked if she could move Hamish and herself into Giffards right away.

"He needs stability," she said. "And I think it will be better with two adults at Giffards. Just until you're settled."

Michael agreed it made sense but the voice in his head screamed that it was the wrong decision.

Meredith said she'd bring just enough of her furniture to make Giffards look something like a home and he could always send back what he didn't want.

Anne, with Grace's blessing, moved some of her things in too, though with attending school and Meredith not being a driver, she'd have to be based in Dorking until Michael brought Victoria home.

It meant that Meredith had the run of the house.

Victoria became Vicki, and when she was five weeks old Michael fed her with a bottle for the first time. At six weeks, she left the incubator. He allowed himself to think about taking her home.

Vicki weighed a smidgen over two kilograms and was beginning to look like a normal term baby. She was having three to four bottle-feeds a day, all formula now, with the rest by tube, which she always tried to pull out of her mouth. Bringing up her wind was a chore but the actual feeding gave Michael an internal glow he could only describe as mumsy.

He was briefly due home for Hamish's fifth birthday. He dreaded how the boy would react to Daisy not being there. Added to that was the looming spectre of school. Did Hamish have to attend as soon as he was five, or in the new school year starting in September?

The day before Michael left for England, he found Adèle waiting for him in the hospital lobby. He'd heard she was back home with her mother again. She waved a card.

"I wonder would you give this to Hamish?"

"I hope it's not from his father."

"No, Michael, it's from me."

"Then of course I will."

Adèle smiled so briefly he almost missed it. "Thank you. Michael. It means a lot to me not to be ostracised for what my husband did."

And she'd married the man less than two months ago, Michael reminded himself. He stared at Adèle as if studying her for the first time. Whereas once, he would have been embarrassed to be so direct, bereavement and the responsibility it brought had changed him. Adèle looked careworn, naturally, shoulders not as upright as they used to be but the eyes were still honest, behind the pain.

"Whatever he did, he did for himself," he told her. "Perhaps you thought you could change him but, goodness knows, Daisy tried hard enough. Please don't think you're to blame."

"Thank you."

Michael nodded then headed for the swing doors. Adèle followed, caught up with him outside. She touched his arm. "There are these also."

She rummaged in her bag, brought out four cassettes. "I found them in the safe deposit box he kept at the bank where I work."

"I hope Meredith appreciates what you've done for her. Thank you, Adèle."

Adèle then looked at Michael in a way that touched a nerve somewhere inside him. "I think we have an affinité, you and I," she said, hurried away before he could respond. He watched her go then stood, watching the empty space she'd left.

Affinité seemed such a deliberate choice. Michael bought a French dictionary, looked it up. He saw that, as in English, it meant a spiritual attraction between two people but apparently it also gave leave for a lie: an attraction that was *supposed* to be of this kind.

He wondered which meaning Adèle intended. It said something for the woman, he thought, that she had the power to disturb him in the time of his greatest grief.

If Hamish felt Daisy's absence, it wasn't obvious, because Anne, who'd come down for the day, made sure he didn't have a moment to reflect upon it. And this would be the last time, Michael thought ruefully, that the boy would know innocence. School would soon rob him of that.

Meredith's face lost years when Michael handed her the tapes.

"Where? How...? Thank God."

Michael knew she'd scoured Le Mazemeur for them, almost fainting when the police opened the safe in the business room.

"Adèle found them. You should thank her, not God."

"Perhaps," Meredith said then dismissed the possibility with a shrug.

Vicki was now on such a tiny amount of oxygen Michael was told she should be able to do without it very soon. That happened in the seventh week of her life, a good four short of the time she should have been born.

The nurses looked glum when Michael told them Vicki was leaving. "But we'll miss her," they pouted. One found a card and they each wrote good wishes and signed their names: *Bernadine, Colette, Anne-Marie.*

"Send us photographs. Let us know how she's getting on." They showed Michael albums full of such things.

Miranda helped Michael take Vicki home. She'd chartered a plane, brought a nurse along too. How much easier life was if you had money, Michael thought. Meredith had always had it, Daisy too even if she pretended it wasn't there, and Miranda had made her own. He supposed he had joined the club too. The difference was he and Miranda knew what life was like without it.

"Thanks, big Sis," he said. They hugged then lapsed into broad East End speech. The nurse, Belgravia rather than Bethnal Green, looked on open-mouthed, a deal of confusion showing in her eyes.

At last Michael's children and Daisy's were united under one roof. Anne did her best to combine the roles of schoolgirl, sister, and mother, but Michael could see the strain in her when her guard was down. She would play with Vicki for hours, showing her different shapes and colours. It was the colours Vicki seemed to like best, becoming sparkle-eyed, absorbed in them. Michael wondered if, like her sister, she'd become a painter. And when tiredness came, Anne's were the arms Vicki preferred. Michael supposed she thought Anne was her mother.

Hamish retreated into a stiff little shell of resentment. It might have been better if Meredith had given him more attention but motherhood obviously didn't come naturally to her. Michael wondered what would have happened if she'd been allowed to keep the carpenter's son.

His part solution was for Anne to keep Hamish amused while he did the feeds and cleaned the sweet-smelling mess from Vicki's tiny bum. His nights were fits and starts of dropping off to sleep then waking seconds later to Vicki's demands for attention. More than once, he cried out too.

While Michael was still punch-drunk from sleep deprivation, Meredith lobbed him her idea of Hamish starting at the church school in the village, although there were only four weeks of term left.

"It will give him a taste," she said.

Leaving Michael brooding at home, Meredith walked Hamish to his first day, collected him too. Hamish breezed into the house full of how the big boys let him play football with them.

"They weren't much bigger than he is," Meredith said. Michael smiled but inside he wasn't smiling at all. He was telling himself he should have been the one relating the tale.

The Monday of the last week of term was Vicki's Estimated Date of Delivery. She was twelve weeks and three days old, weighed three point one kilograms. There was a little party to celebrate, which Vicki mostly slept through.

The cake, a supermarket sponge affair, was brought in. Michael watched Daisy's first child, Hamish, safe and ostensibly happy as he mixed jelly with his cake. Michael gazed at Daisy's second child, Vicki, snoozing in her carrycot. He wished Daisy could see them.

The telephone rang. Vicki's eyes opened. She blinked several times then saw Michael. She grinned at him and burped. He grinned back at her, picked up the phone.

It was Marie. "It's Tante Berthe," she said. "She's dead."

Chapter 24

Berthe's death sparked a change in Michael out of all proportion to her influence on him in life. The fact that her son still breathed while she didn't spread in his mind like a malignant tumour until there was scarcely room left for even his own daughters.

He began to live his days as a muttering creature, finally spending the whole of one morning prone on Daisy's grave, scrabbling at the earth with his bare hands.

Someone must have reported a madman being loose in the churchyard for eventually a policeman appeared, asked Michael what he was doing.

"Fuck off," Michael said.

The constable's face clouded. Luckily for Michael, although he didn't see it like that then, the vicar came scurrying up the path. "It's all right," the vicar said. "I know this man. I'll deal with this."

The constable seemed inclined to argue the case but his radio crackled and Michael heard something about an RTA. The constable spoke into the radio and left.

The vicar held Michael's hand, looked sad. Michael said he wanted to be with Daisy, lay his head beside hers. "If you'll let me do that," he told the vicar, "then you can cover us up and everything will be all right." The vicar said he'd think about it. "Okay," Michael said then let the vicar take him home.

A doctor prescribed tablets.

As Michael read *May cause depression* on the leaflet that accompanied them, he laughed: a single, staccato "Ha". He threw the packet into a dustbin, slammed the lid down.

Recalling this moment in the future, he would claim that the particular frequency at which galvanised steel struck galvanised steel activated a similar one in his brain. Galvanised him too, so to speak.

He decided to start building Daisy's nest and the first step was to give the house its own furniture. He was a carpenter, ergo he would carpent.

He drove to Suffolk to supervise the removal of his workshop equipment and paraphernalia from Meredith's place. That done, he stared for a long time at Daisy's 2CV, which was languishing in the cartshed where the Peugeot was once kept.

When Michael left for Giffards, it was in the Citroën, with Daisy's belongings accompanying him. Meredith frowned when she saw the car but did not ask about the Peugeot.

Over the next six months, Daisy's furniture was created: tables, chairs, beds, wardrobes, sideboards, chests of drawers, bookcases and smaller pieces, all in English hardwoods. Michael carved an image of a daisy on each piece, always choosing a discreet position.

As part of his nest building, he who had never really known what it was like to have one threw himself into building his family. The most tenuous relationships were consolidated into it.

Hence what began as a throwaway remark by Miranda, that they were 'sort of' brother and sister, was crystallised into fact. Miranda seemed as ready to accept it too. Thinking about it years later, Michael realised why: that Miranda was still grieving and had far more years to get over than the single one in which he had known Daisy. Miranda needed the comfort factor every bit as much as he did.

Just as she encouraged him to make his first steps with Vicki, Miranda now accompanied Michael on his progress through the French judicial system, particularly that interminable process called *instruction*, in which the investigating judge would more or less decide the case before it reached the Court.

Although Michael was dismayed to find that Bohec wouldn't simply have a trial and be done with, as in England, Miranda persuaded him conviction was surer the French way, not subject to whims of juries or brilliance (or otherwise) of counsel.

From being a cousin by marriage to Daisy, Marie became a blood relation in Michael's eyes. Daisy had said she was joking about Marie's crush on him but it was a fact that the girl often blushed when he looked at her. Maybe Marie's blood was just abnormally close to her skin. Michael preferred the crush theory. He found it comforting to have some special worth in another human's eyes.

Although he could see Marie was desirable, what it brought him was a fondness for her, a kindly disposition. As if, categorised as a niece, she achieved a similar asexuality for him as Anne.

He engineered a friendship between the two quite shamelessly. And whenever he had to spend time in France, schools permitting, he'd use it as an opportunity to take Anne across or bring Marie back even if it meant getting a nurse to look after Vicki for a few days.

And thanks to Miranda's efforts, Marie's inheritance was secured. Augustine was proved to be the rightful owner of the houses and land comprising the Mazemeur estate. Michael pictured Bohec clawing the walls of his cell as he heard the news. Augustine though, preferred to live in her bungalow. She let Le Mazemeur itself out to the local *jardin d'enfants*, so shrill voices and the patter of tiny shoes about the yard replaced the silent screams of doomed rabbits and the clatter of their crates.

Michael cultivated his relationship with Paddy as if harvesting their missing years, gathering them all in. Paddy, for his part, appeared keen to re-establish himself in his son's eyes, or maybe, thought Michael, it was in Anne's. His father found many excuses to invade them that summer. He'd park Linda in Kent with Miranda, claim he'd popped over the border on the off chance.

Tears glistened when Paddy was allowed to hold Vicki in his arms but it was Anne for whom he reserved the bulk of his affection. If Anne happened to be out when he called, Paddy suffered bouts of finger tapping that disappeared the moment she returned. Michael knew Anne played on it, sometimes deliberately delayed her entrance to make Paddy's delight all the more effusive.

Michael was happy to let that happen, because he felt that he lavished attention on Vicki at Anne's expense. If Anne saw an injustice in this she never let it show. Michael told himself his love for her was different, that he didn't see her as a child, but as a woman, who needed appreciation, not hide and seek. And appreciate Anne he did, for the way she took on the role of surrogate mother, even wife as far as the running of the household was concerned. Yes, he appreciated Anne greatly and he told her so often, usually after he'd been crying somewhere on his own.

Eventually, on one day in August, it was actually Michael's thirty-sixth birthday, Anne said, "You don't have to keep reassuring me, Dad. I know you love me."

"But I keep spoiling Vicki."

"She's a baby, Dad. Mum says you used to spoil me at that age. You're not to feel guilty about it. Apart from the fact that she's a little darling, I know why you do it."

"Why?"

"You see Daisy every time you look at her."

As Michael stared, open-mouthed at his daughter's insight, she said, "And here's another glimpse, your birthday present."

It was a portrait, in oils, of Daisy in a pale yellow dress. The likeness was remarkable, Daisy at her most serene, goddess-like indeed.

"I hope I've got the dress right. I asked Meredith which one she'd borrowed but she wasn't sure."

"It's the right one."

"It's based on a photograph I took in the Easter holidays. Daisy posed specially."

"She knew it was for my birthday?"

"Yes, but she asked me not to show her pregnant, She said put me in a summer dress."

The paeony dress! It must have been something Daisy saw in his eyes that day she wore it. Daisy, whose bloom, like the paeony's, was over far too soon. Michael pulled Anne close to him, let his tears fall free.

"I'll keep reassuring you, as you put it, because you're the brightest light in my life, Anne. The painting is beautiful. You've captured the essence of Daisy. I shall treasure it always."

Only with Meredith did Michael maintain a distance. She had become prone to fits of silence and resentful staring. He'd never witnessed her mourning Daisy, and not once, to his knowledge, had she visited Daisy's grave. He had progressed. But she'd regressed into the role of Harry's not necessarily evil but always calculating, not necessarily fucking, bitch.

Peter had at last bought *Passing Clouds* from Miranda. Michael toyed with the idea of buying *Scallywag* but couldn't get round the fact that he'd be going against Daisy's wishes. Besides, he'd be reminded of *Hirondelle* every time he saw her.

No, it had to be a boat carrying no memories. Acting on Daisy's dream of trailing their boat to Treguelven, he bought a brand new twenty-four footer with a lifting keel. He named her *La Belle Pacquerette.*

Following Daisy's suggestion, he secured a mooring in Chichester harbour. *La Belle Pacquerette* had her maiden voyage there that autumn with Anne as crew and Hamish papered as official Ship's Boy because he'd said, "I want to be Roger in *Swallows and Amazons*". Hamish's eyes lit when Michael said the man who wrote the stories once sailed those very waters in a boat called *Lottie Blossom.*

Anne said she wouldn't play Susan because "Daisy was your mate, Dad, and one day you'll have another."

He'd stared at her as if she'd told him Daisy had died all over again.

"That's not going to happen, Anne."

Anne turned those dark Irish eyes on him. "You have to get on with life eventually, Dad. We all have to."

She sounded as if she was speaking from personal experience and Michael unhappily remembered there was a time when she'd had to get over him.

Returning home one morning after driving Anne to school, Michael found a stranger taking photographs of the furniture he'd made. A core of anger welled in his chest. He was about to grab the camera as Meredith sailed in with a young woman in her wake. Apprehension filled the latter's face. She signalled the photographer to stop.

"What the hell's going on, Meredith?"

"I mentioned your furniture to some people. Don't be angry, Michael. It deserves to be recognised."

"Well you'd better *unmention* it." Michael ignored the photographer and turned to the woman. "I'd like you both to leave. I'm sorry you've had a wasted journey."

When they'd gone, Michael said, "The furniture is *private*, Meredith, made for Daisy, not you." He shook his head, sighed heavily. "I really think it would be best if you went back home."

Meredith said she didn't think it would be best at all. "What would it do to Hamish, in his first term at school, if he were suddenly uprooted?"

"Uprooted?" Michael's eyes narrowed. "What do you mean by that?"

"Daisy's will, and particularly your guardianship, could be tested in the courts. And regarding Hamish's father, tell me, whose name is on the birth certificate?"

Michael glared at Meredith, felt her betrayal pulse towards him. "You'd do that to the boy? Claim that his father and his mother's were one and the same? You know Daisy wasn't in her right mind when she put that down."

"Nevertheless, that's what the certificate says." Meredith's gaze suddenly softened and her mouth ruffled into an appearance of concession. "Of course I wouldn't *do* any of that, do anything to hurt Hamish or you, but if you're serious about bringing the children up together, you need me here, Michael. Anne has a life of her own to make something of, not spend in drudgery. So all in all, I think I should stay. Is that all right?"

It was definitely not all right but Michael nodded anyway and cursed Meredith silently. "But no more surprises like today's."

"Of course not." Michael was treated to those electric eyes, appraising him, even mocking him.

But the photographer had done his damage. Daisy's furniture was featured in an upmarket glossy that made much of its maker being a reluctant carpenter. The result was a rash of enquiries from would-be customers. Michael wanted to tell them all to go to hell but Meredith was there, burrowing into his anger.

"It will help you to focus on something positive. Come on, Michael, we worked well together before."

As with the old ones, the new clients seemed to love having their orders accepted grudgingly. Michael supposed it satisfied some obscure need they had. Whatever the reason, he conceded that it gave him a sense of worth, in that he was successful in doing what he did best, independent of Daisy's conscience money. And Meredith couldn't make the bloody furniture even if she did know what a spindle gouge was.

Though it irked Michael to admit it, Meredith was dynamite in the office. She was the one who wielded the phone, answered emails, faxes, replied to letters. She was the one who sieved the orders, presented him with a shortlist to accept or reject. Michael often wondered about her criteria. They refused personal callers so it wasn't down to faces. He imagined it was how they phrased their words on paper or screen, or if Meredith liked or disliked the accent, the timbre of the voice. He wondered how he would fare, being judged by her. Although, he realised, he already had been, still was.

Since Daisy's death, Michael had been blind to the killings that carried on in the outside world. One, though, about seven months afterwards, had him in shreds. It was yet another suicide bombing, with the usual obscene results. What hit home, what tore Michael's heart, was a newspaper photograph of a lovely young woman. She was reported as being mischievous but caring and very excited about her future. Although she was nothing like her in looks, the same could have been said about Daisy. She was Daisy's age too, her fiancé around Michael's. The fiancé survived the bombing; the girl died.

"You were right, Daisy," Michael cried, "to despair for the world."

He wondered how the minds of these men, for they were virtually always men, could be distorted so much that they threw away their lives and took those of others for the sake of a God who, whatever his name, did not care. *Suffer little children to come unto me*, Jesus said. Suffer was right. Michael feared for the lives of his own.

Less than a month later, Christmas loomed. Michael, recalling his contentment of the last, dreaded the prospect of his first without Daisy but at least he wouldn't have to suffer Meredith's barbs for she was taking Hamish to Scotland to stay with the Lomonds.

Paddy, as if he had the second sight, invited Michael, Anne and Vicki (now eight months old and bonny as they come) to spend Christmas with him and Linda. Miranda was going too and they all travelled together.

Paddy really did live in a rather smart house. Michael's conscience flushed as he thought how he had doubted him. It was in an idyllic location, halfway up a hill, just off a tree-lined road that curved above a wide bay. Far below, glimpsed through stately trees, was a broad beach of bright sand that stretched out towards a hill-topped headland, miles distant. Michael was reminded of villas he'd seen in Italy.

"Bought the place cheap," Paddy said. "It was virtually falling down, not touched in fifty years. Must be worth a few millions now. Euros, if not your English pounds."

He took Michael on a tour that ended in the suburbs of Dun Laoghaire in front of a pair of massive gates painted an aristocratic shade of green. *Patrick Cavanagh and Son Limited* was emblazoned across them in gold, edged with black. Behind were a neat yard and a warehouse bursting with reclaimed staircases, doors, windows, chimneypieces, architraves, skirtings, floorboards, beams and the like. A door at the back opened into a workshop armed with a formidable array of machinery, more industrial in nature than Michael's.

"Not bad for poor London Irish, is it?" Pride illuminated Paddy's face.

Michael thought of the lean years of his childhood, left behind in Bethnal Green with a madwoman. His lips hardened. He turned away from his father, looked back at the thin December sun visible through the open doors.

"No, not bad for you at all."

"Well, it's officially half yours now, son."

Michael's face burned as his father handed him a certificate that proclaimed it as true.

Back home in the Vico Road, Paddy showed his guests his latest acquisition, a personal computer. "Got it for the internet. I've joined some genealogy groups."

Michael already knew Paddy hadn't found Fionnuala in Birkenhead. "Have you had much luck?" he said.

"It's early days," said Paddy, rubbing his chin, "But I'll find you a sister one day."

"I have one already."

Michael linked arms with Miranda and Paddy's eyebrows reached the ceiling. Paddy looked at Linda, back to Miranda, scratched his head.

"So you have, my boy, so you have. And me the old fool for not realising it all this time."

Linda looked on, smiling quiet satisfaction. She was a reticent woman, preferring the background, in direct contrast to her daughter's gregariousness. Yet this same woman, Michael thought, had somehow, by conjuring or commitment, turned his feckless father into a success.

Chapter 25

Jean-Paul Bohec's trial began on 2nd February. When Michael was called to give evidence, the accused had the demeanour of one controlling the proceedings. If he'd been wearing robes and wasn't in the dock, you might assume Bohec was the judge, Michael thought, as the man's eyes annexed his and the face acquired that familiar sneer.

But Michael recalled the terror in those eyes when he was oh so close to throttling the man's miserable life out. Without changing expression, he gathered every atom of malice he could muster, melded them into a white-hot javelin of ill intent, hurled it to Bohec across the court.

Bohec appeared to tremble, turned his eyes towards the floor, the walls, the ceiling, anywhere rather than directly at Michael.

Michael would have allowed himself to smile if it wasn't for the fact that he was about to stand at the *barre des témoins*, knowing he had already committed perjury.

At the pre-trial *Instruction*, Michael neglected to mention that Daisy travelled to Brittany under duress. Instead, he claimed she was adamant about accompanying Hamish for his first official visit to his father. He claimed also that because he, Michael, was unavoidably away from home, Jean-Paul agreed to come to England and escort Daisy to France.

Michael's reasoning at the time was, if Bohec accused Meredith in court of murdering Harry, then somehow Daisy would have to suffer all over again.

So, there had been some collusion between Michael and Meredith, who seemed to have the idea that Michael was protecting her. Marie, too, was a party to the deception although she didn't know how Harry died. She'd simply agreed because, as she said, she was family.

Michael knew Bohec would see the prosecution evidence, but calculated on him seeing an advantage to himself in not contesting the perjured element. Adèle would see it too, Michael assumed, although he had no idea if she was reconciled with Bohec or not.

So Michael waited for his lie to be exposed but the dreaded question never came. The only time he was thrown off tack was when the Président asked him if, to his knowledge, Mademoiselle Lomond regularly took heroin or other illicit substances.

"Of course not," Michael said fractiously. "She was meticulous about her own and our baby's health, regularly attending clinics. Daisy's medical records will prove that. Are you telling me nobody's bothered to check them?"

Michael was treated to a judicial glare. He mentally bit his tongue but his time under interrogation was over. As he left the bar he ignored Bohec but concentrated on the sour face of the defence advocate. He was glad cross-examination was not a feature of French trials.

Michael was excluded from court either side of his own appearance but Miranda was present throughout. She told Michael why he'd been asked the drug question. Bohec claimed Daisy was a heroin addict and during their marriage often injected herself. Skin-popping, he'd called it. He even tried to claim that the heroin and other narcotics the police had found in his car were commercial samples, part of his normal stock-in-trade. His employers, however, categorically denied that was so.

But the big news, the really big news that set the court humming, occurred when Bohec was asked if it was true that his mother subsequently died from the stroke she suffered on the day in question.

Bohec's face twitched. "Yes," he said.

"Is it also true you swore an oath on her life not to abduct your son?"

Bohec blanched, began to shake visibly. It was an accident, he said, a tragic accident. He then admitted injecting Daisy but not in order to kill her. It was a moment's foolishness. He was worried about his mother. She wasn't answering her phone so he decided to check on her. He thought he'd given Daisy just enough heroin to keep her quiet and expected to be away for no more than an hour, intending on his return to apply Naloxone to neutralise it. But he was so distraught upon learning of his mother's stroke that Daisy entirely slipped his mind. An act of God had lost him his mother, his home, his two sons, his wife, and had him standing in this court today, accused of a murder he never intended to commit.

Michael expected the case would end there, but Miranda said the judicial liturgy had to press on until the very last actor, the Advocat de la Defense, had his say. That took another day and a half though Miranda said the man's heart did not seem to be in the job.

At last, the Président and his assistant judges combined with the jury and found Jean-Paul Bohec officially guilty. They committed him to prison, to serve at least twenty years.

Michael wished France still used the guillotine. Bohec's head rolling into a basket seemed a just punishment to him. And that *after* the man's balls were ripped off and served to the dogs. As it was, he'd be as old as Meredith was now before he could avenge Daisy. Meredith delayed her vengeance for only ten years and she had Harry in her sights all that time.

After the trial, Michael wandered down a side street near the court and was seduced by the aroma oozing from a small coffee house. He ordered Colombian, noir. As his eyes adapted to the dim interior he noticed Adèle sitting alone. He'd seen her briefly in the vestibule of the court, before the sequestration of witnesses. She'd smiled at him briefly then kept her eyes low.

"You don't mind?" he said, as he took his coffee over to her table.

"Not if you don't."

Adèle asked about Vicki, how he was coping. He asked Adèle how she was. They both swore they were fine.

Then Adèle said, "Why did you lie about the reason Daisy was in France?"

"Because the truth would have complicated matters."

"For Meredith?"

"For Daisy. And possibly for you. I don't care about Meredith. By the way, she says thank you for the tapes."

Adèle shrugged. "If you say so, Michael. To all those things."

Something made Michael say he'd like to keep in touch. Adèle looked at her coffee cup, turned it around and around on the table. Finally, she nodded. "Yes," she said. "I think I'd like that too."

She touched Michael's hand briefly as they parted.

There had been a flurry of interest immediately after Bohec's arrest but the French press seemed interested only in fabricating a triangle of tragedy linking him, Daisy, and Adèle. Nobody wanted to know about Michael Cavanagh. Apart from an announcement in *The Times* obituaries, Daisy's death had not reached the English papers.

But now the trial was over, her history and Michael's were being probed mercilessly. The tabloids made much of variations on *The Cockney Carpenter and the Society Girl*. They'd discovered plenty of willing tongues to relate Daisy's teenage exploits but these seemed mild compared to those she'd confessed to Michael. The people who really knew were keeping their mouths shut.

An excrescence of reporters infested Giffards' doorstep. Michael sent Anne to Dorking and retreated upstairs. Meredith, jaw steadfast, guarded the front door. She fielded the questions, blocking them in their infancy or blasting them full-grown beyond the boundaries, while Michael stood at the landing window, glaring. He drummed his fingers, assigned half an ear to the proceedings. More than once, he stormed downstairs to propel a reporter's arse backwards onto the gravel.

The invaders disappeared en masse one afternoon. Meredith wore a sheen of self-congratulation as she mentioned that she'd phoned Lord

Lomond. His lordship had already been perturbed by headlines like *Peer's niece murdered by jealous ex-husband* that had appeared in the better papers. When Meredith told him what they had to put up with, he almost combusted. "Leave it to me," he said. "I'll call in some favours."

"What did he do? Slap a D notice on them?"

"Who cares as long as they've gone?"

So Daisy became last week's news and Michael went out free of cameras and men in slept-in clothes who pushed voice recorders in his face. He visited Daisy's grave. Its surrounding grass was trampled and there were footprints in the soil that covered her. When he saw that someone had removed her flowers, bile rose in his throat. He heard footsteps and turned, fists at the ready. It was only the vicar, and he was carrying Daisy's vase.

"I hope you don't mind. I took the liberty of removing this before it became a souvenir." The vicar looked at the ravaged ground, shook his head. "And they call them *gentlemen* of the press. I'll see that it's all put right again, made shipshape. They won't be back, they'll have forgotten the poor girl by now."

Michael and Adèle corresponded sporadically, posts copious with chatter but without a hint of anything that mattered. And on the occasions Michael happened to be in Brittany, ferrying Anne to Marie's, he found the time to pay his regards to Adèle.

Usually it was a coffee snatched during Adèle's lunch break but at Easter they had a whole three hours together, lunching by the quayside in Auray where, a lifetime before, they had bought Hamish an ice cream.

They commented on the weather, enthused about sailing, discussed passers-by. Adèle asked about Vicki and Hamish. Daisy and Jean-Paul were never mentioned.

They were like the occasional meetings of cousins who live at a distance. It was hardly a friendship and Michael didn't know why he kept it up except that he couldn't find a reason not to. Did that amount to *affinité*?

In mid-April, Anne turned sixteen, and a week later was bridesmaid at her mother's wedding. Grace had dropped hints about Michael giving her away, edging around the actual words.

"Impeccable timing, Dad. I'm sorry," Anne said after Michael squirmed and finally said he had too many other things to deal with.

One of these was only four days later: the anniversary of Daisy's death and also the day he was obliged to smile and laugh at Vicki's first birthday party. Yet Michael managed those things and the smiling and laughter felt good. The proof was evident on the faces of both his daughters.

Michael left the sad and lonely until what would have been Daisy's twenty-ninth birthday. He sailed *La Belle Pacquerette* alone out of Chichester harbour and along the Sussex coast until he fancied he could see the hill that Giffards sat upon. Grief knotted inside him as he hove to.

"It's a glorious day, Daisy. You should be out here with me. I can't handle her on my own." Michael wasn't certain what or whom he meant by the latter: the boat, Vicki, or Meredith. Maybe one, two, maybe all three. His state of mind wasn't helped by a letter he'd received that morning from Marlowe, addressed to him and signed *Laurent.* Marlowe expressed his sincere sympathy but there was a little matter of an outstanding account sent with his last report.

Michael had put the invoice aside to be dealt with when he paid his other bills but, on arriving home from sailing, he looked at it again. For the first time, he noticed the date it bore. He caught his breath. Daisy wouldn't have received it until the day, or at the earliest, the day before Bohec came for her.

Michael hadn't yet got around to sorting Daisy's things. But for that letter they might well have remained forever untouched, at least by him.

He recalled Daisy on that last morning, her final, never-to-be-forgotten words: "I love you. I love you more than life. Do you trust me, Michael? Oh, say that you trust me." As he thought of what he now needed to do, his eyes filled and a dull ache harassed his breast.

Michael searched three boxes of Daisy's possessions before finding the file. *Marlowe* was scrawled on it in her handwriting. His pulse raced as he saw the big buff envelope on top of Marlowe's earlier reports. It was empty apart from the original of the invoice he'd received that morning.

He drank whisky, telephoned Marlowe. Within the hour, he received an email with the missing report attached. It included a copy of an entry in the births register of a mairie in the Limousin, for a male child born on the eighteenth of September 1965. The mother was Mireille Bardinet, 16, student; the father was unrecorded. Mireille's parents were named as Paul and Madeleine Bardinet. The witnesses were the aforesaid Paul, and Max Regourd, a priest.

Marlowe included details of the child's baptism as an unhyphenated Jean Paul, and a copy of a deed by which his surname was changed to Bohec. That event was also noted in the register.

Marlowe had traced Mireille, now a married woman. At first she denied giving birth to the child. Later, she admitted it but when asked who the father was, claimed she had forgotten. She gave the baby away, no formal adoption, the woman simply wrote a receipt. She'd burned that years ago. Did she remember the woman's name? No, said Mireille, it was arranged by the father. The father? Marlowe asked. Mireille became evasive, said eventually that by father she'd meant the priest.

Father Max was long dead but Marlowe discovered he was the dean of the locality and that from July 1963 until August 1965 the actual incumbent of the parish where Mireille lived was one Jean Bohec.

Michael's heart rate soared past its threshold.

Marlowe traced Jean Bohec via St Etienne and Rennes to Rochefort-en-Terre, as being the son of a cousin of Bernard and Mathilde Bohec. In August 1965, he was transferred to an administrative job at the cathedral of St-Etienne in Limoges. In the following year, he resigned from his post. Marlowe was unable to trace his further progress.

"Jesus," Michael said, putting the report down. Marlowe hadn't commented, but the evidence suggested that Father Jean Bohec was the father of Mireille's baby. He recalled 'mariner' being on Daisy's marriage certificate. Perhaps the good Father was press-ganged and taken to sea. He wondered how Berthe was persuaded to take the child. To create her own dynasty, freeze Augustine's out? Who knows what childhood slights and jealousies might be involved. What did Augustine think about the sudden appearance of a baby? Were Jean Bohec's parents aware their grandson was living at Le Mazemeur?

Michael formed a dreadful theory. He imagined Daisy's excitement at the proof that, never mind Berthe not being entitled to the Mazemeur estate, Jean-Paul was not even her son, natural *or* adopted. Daisy must have seen that as a decisive bargaining point - her silence in exchange for both Hamish and the tapes. *That* was why she'd gone to France, to make sure she brought the tapes back with her.

Michael pictured Daisy seeing Bohec's face change as she made her fatal mistake and caused his history to confront him. The tapes' evidence would be gone as soon as they were destroyed but the same could not apply to this bombshell. Bohec could burn the proof Daisy brought but the evidence itself remained. It had been safe for almost thirty-eight years and the bastard must have thought it would go on being so if Daisy wasn't around to resurrect it. The fact that she arranged for him to come while her fiancé was away must have convinced Bohec that she'd kept it to herself. He might have seen Marlowe's name of course, but probably assumed his interest in the particulars would cease once he was paid.

How Bohec thought he would get away with murder was impossible to surmise, as was what he imagined he was going to do with Hamish. It struck Michael that Bohec either didn't know Berthe wasn't entitled to Mazemeur or he thought the evidence was safely locked away. Perhaps that was why he'd gone there that afternoon, to make sure all was well, not with Berthe, but the family treasure chest.

Michael wondered whether it was expediency or a bizarre twist in Bohec's mind that caused him to make the daughter die by the same substance that helped to kill her father. One day, he swore, he would wring the truth from him.

"Oh, Daisy," he cried, "Never mind me trusting *you*, why couldn't you have trusted *me*? I would have dealt with this. You know I would."

He poured more whisky, slopping it over the rim of the glass. "Well, happy birthday, Daisy," he said then threw the glass across the room, watched it shatter against the chimneybreast. Whisky dripped from mellow red bricks. Shards of crystal spattered the carpet. Michael stared at them until reason told him he'd best clear the mess up before someone else got hurt.

Although Daisy's Citroën was now Michael's everyday transport, it was woefully inadequate as a tow car for *La Belle Pacquerette.* To remedy this, Michael bought Colonel Ted's old car, a Land Rover Defender, from Miranda. In the last week of July, he put *La Belle Pacquerette* on her trailer, took her, Anne, Vicki, and Hamish via the Portsmouth Ferry to Cherbourg then towed her to Treguelven. Meredith invited herself and Michael could not find a valid reason to refuse.

The little horseshoe bay looked far different than from a storm-stressed sea. It had a curve of wide, white sands and the water there, as Peter had claimed almost two years before, virtually disappeared at low tide.

Michael saw the rocks Daisy enthused about, how they separated the sands into small beaches and were weathered into the most fanciful shapes: toad, elephant, camel, sphinx. Working from Daisy's descriptions, he identified the beach from which she watched the yellow-hulled sailing cruiser.

He launched *La Belle Pacquerette,* sailed her past that very place. Young women soaked up the sun; one in particular had pale-gold hair. Michael's eyes misted. He could have been watching Daisy. He swung the tiller hard across to the boom, headed towards the sea.

On a whim, he phoned Adèle, invited her to come for a few days. She didn't say she would, not definitely, but midway through their second week, a black VW Golf turned up outside the house Michael had rented. Its driver parked the car, skew-whiff, on the forecourt.

Michael, by chance, was looking out of the window. He watched Adèle as she emerged from the car. She'd grown her hair long, gathered it at the back in a loose ponytail. Her skin was tanned and she looked as if she'd been exercising seriously since Easter, the last time he'd seen her. She was wearing denim shorts cut down from jeans, a pink vest that left her midriff bare. It was obvious she wasn't wearing a bra. Michael felt the first carnal stirrings he'd had since - he winced at the memory - since the last night with Daisy.

"Just a few nights," Adèle said. "Maybe three."

"What's she doing here?" Meredith hissed while Adèle renewed her acquaintance with Marie and Hamish.

"I invited her."

Meredith adopted the look she reserved for dogshit on her sole.

"Oh, Michael. How could you?"

"It was easy. I picked up a phone, called her number."

"Don't be so flippant." Meredith looked down her nose, head so far back Michael thought it would snap. "What is it with you and Jean-Paul's wives, Michael? Some sort of fetish? It's obscene, you inviting her here."

"Obscene?"

Michael had been uneasy about including Adèle. But Adèle was a friend of Daisy and Daisy had said it was all right for him to like her too. Surely it was within the rules to invite a friend? It wasn't as if there was anything between Adèle and him. His blood began to heat.

"Oh, I get it," he said. "She happens to be the woman your son-in-law was sleeping with while he was still sleeping with your daughter, who happened to be sleeping with me at the time. So, it would be virtually incestuous if I were to do it with Adèle. That's what you mean isn't it?"

Meredith didn't respond and her expression didn't change. Michael banged his fist down on a convenient table.

"Give the woman a break, Meredith. She's here for a few days sailing, not for sex. And... *For God's sake put your bloody head straight.*" He intensified his gaze until Meredith lowered her eyes to a level with his. "*And* if it wasn't for her finding those tapes, you might not be with us today."

"So she got a few things right. She's still a tart."

"Funny, I distinctly remember you saying 'she's rather nice actually.' Are you telling me I shouldn't rely on your opinions?"

"That was a totally different situation."

"You mean she wasn't a threat then? She isn't one now" (Michael banged a fist against his breast) "to the love I'll always hold in here for

Daisy. Did you know Daisy said the same thing as you, that Adèle was rather nice? Could it be you both thought she was actually a likeable, decent sort of girl? And as for tart, what does that make Daisy and me? What does it make you and Peter? Aren't we all tarts too, by your definition?"

Meredith coloured. "There was no need to bring Peter up. It was a long time ago."

"The time is irrelevant, Meredith. What you're saying is you and Daisy and I should enjoy a different set of morals to Adèle, who has committed no crime other than adultery."

Meredith's complexion deepened. "Meaning I *have*?" Her mouth twisted into a bittersweet smile. "You know, Michael, you've turned out to be most perspicacious."

Michael's plan had been for Adèle to join in the general activities: sailing, swimming, or simply wiling away the day on the beach. Now he made a point of devoting time to her.

On the afternoon of her arrival they walked across the granite-strewn landscape to Pontdinas Point, northwest of Treguelven. Adèle had let her hair down, swapped her vest and shorts for a sleeveless blue cotton dress that reached just above her knees. She looks safer like that, Michael thought.

It was sizzlingly hot. Halfway into their walk they stopped to rest at a tall menhir Michael's guidebook called *Men Marz*. "It means Boundary Stone," Adèle said, as they sat in its shadow. "The Maz in Mazemeur is essentially the same word, so Mazemeur means the great boundary. Of what though, I don't know."

"Did he tell you that, Jean-Paul?"

Adèle shook her head. "No, it's a remnant of the Breton I learned at school. Marie could have told you the same. Did you know she has a thing about you?"

"Yes."

"I know how she feels."

Michael's pulse began to quicken. Adèle's eyes appeared to mock him.

"I meant..." she said, "that I remember what it's like to be sixteen. Dieu, I used to think our teenage years were the worst of our lives, but I was wrong. Mmm..." Adèle nodded to herself then she shrugged. "Did I tell you I've divorced Jean-Paul?"

Michael shook his head but Adèle wasn't watching him. She was staring at the cross on the top of the menhir. "I began proceedings immediately after the trial, after we met in that coffee bar as a matter of fact. Do you know what the funny thing is?"

"No."

"He never consummated the marriage. So it could simply have been annulled, I think."

Annulled? Michael checked himself from saying it had been consummated enough before the wedding. He considered telling Adèle the dreadful secret he'd discovered, wanted to ask her why she hadn't mentioned the divorce to him before. But Adèle looked as if she might break out in tears and he didn't think he could handle that, not alone with her, not out here.

When they returned to the holiday house, Meredith said to Michael in a voice that was only half a whisper, "Where's *she* sleeping?"

Adèle was only a step or two behind him.

"Not with me," Michael snapped then said he'd sort something out. He could feel Adèle's eyes burning into his neck.

"Oh, dump me anywhere," Adèle said. "Even your boat. I brought a sleeping bag."

"No. I invited you. You'll have a proper bed."

The house was a chalet-bungalow with two bedrooms upstairs, two downstairs. Meredith and Hamish had an upstairs one each, Anne and Marie shared one downstairs room, and Michael and Vicki the other. Michael decided Hamish could either share with Meredith or with him and Vicki, so Adèle could have his room.

"You choose," he said to him.

The boy sucked a thumb then said, "I want to sleep with Grandma. She tells me stories." Meredith let victory drift across her face and

Michael recalled how he used to read to the boy at bedtime. When Daisy was alive.

On Adèle's second day, Michael took her sailing. They dressed in swimming gear, Michael in bright red Bermuda shorts, Adèle in a yellow bikini that elicited a disapproving look from Meredith although it was no briefer than those Anne or Marie wore during the day. Michael noticed Adèle's armpits were shaved.

Michael had beached *La Belle Pacquerette* opposite the house although she was now afloat and swinging on her mooring warp. They walked across the sand and into the water, swimming the last few metres. There was soon enough depth for *La Belle Pacquerette's* keel to be lowered. A warm southerly breeze was blowing and Michael steered onto a course that put the wind just off their starboard quarter. The bay at the town end was crowded so he headed for the open water between the ends of its horseshoe. Reaching it, he relinquished the helm to Adèle.

"You really *do* know how to sail," he said as Adèle punched *La Belle Pacquerette* into the wind then spun her round from the close-hauled course they were on. When leaving the circle, Michael expected the boat to stall, but under Adèle's control she simply romped away as if nothing had happened.

"I told you I was a seaside girl," she said.

Adèle was grinning at him, her entire face radiant. Her eyes sparkled and she looked so...frighteningly *wholesome*, weaving the gleaming mahogany tiller gently from side to side, spray glistening on her tanned skin, too much of which was visible outside that pale yellow bikini. Daisy always looked good in that colour too. And though Daisy had the advantage above the waist, her hips never curved so voluptuously as Adèle's...

"I need to check the tides," Michael said and darted down the step into the cabin.

"We have hours yet," Adèle called behind him. He heard her laugh, light yet earthy. "But if you're worried, we'll go back."

"I'm not worried, just cautious."

"Hmm..." Adèle smiled to herself. "Well then, let's show the pleasure boaters in the bay how to sail. When we get tired we can drop anchor and take to the beach."

Michael took the tiller and tried to sail into the wind as crisply as Adèle had. He felt her eyes on him as he tacked the boat consistently through seventy degrees or so over the choppy water and back into the bay, where after an hour or so of exhilarating close encounters, he nudged her into the shallows by a sparsely populated beach.

"You're not so bad a sailor yourself," Adèle said.

"I'm learning."

"She's a good boat. Has a sense of purpose. You named her after Daisy of course?"

"Yes."

They swam ashore then lay on the sand to dry. Michael closed his eyes. When he reopened them he saw that, like several other women on the beach, Adèle had removed her bikini top. She was watching children playing near the rocks, splashing each other with water. Michael stared at Adèle's breasts. They seemed bigger than he remembered from the photographs. He supposed it was to do with the baby.

Adèle turned. "Ah, you're awake." She smiled. "You dropped off almost as soon as we got here." She stretched, raising her arms above her head then picked up her bikini top, put it back on. "We ought to get back. I think the tide has turned."

Adèle left the next morning.

"No, I'd better go," she said when Michael urged her to stay.

"Why? Because of Meredith?"

"No. Because of this."

Adèle reached up, pulled his face down to hers. She kissed him, long and hard, pressing into his lips. He returned it in kind, matching her all the way.

"Now you see," she said as she finally released him.

Michael's entire body seemed to ache as Adèle drove away.

The holiday lasted for a further week during which Meredith acted as if Adèle had never been there at all. Then *La Belle Pacquerette* was winched onto her trailer but before they left for England, Michael drove Marie home.

There was a fresher air about Mazemeur, as if a depression had been lifted. Hanging baskets, gay with scarlet pelargoniums, were evident everywhere. The big house was festooned with brightly coloured flags and the rabbit factory had been demolished, replaced by a children's playground. It felt as if the entire hamlet was on holiday. As indeed, Michael supposed, it was, for Marie told him Augustine had declared that no tenant would have to pay rent, except for the *jardin d'enfants* at Le Mazemeur itself.

Anne came along for the ride. As they got in the Land Rover to return to Treguelven, she said, "It's been a great holiday, Dad. You looked happier than you've been in ages."

Michael grunted something to the contrary and Anne said, "Dad, Daisy's been dead for over sixteen months now, longer than she was with you in life."

"You think I don't know that?"

Michael blinked a few times, looked at his watch.

"Why not drive on a little further? To Saint-Servais, perhaps."

Michael gazed at Anne's earnest face, at her limpid, Irish eyes.

"Life's not that simple, Anne." He started the engine.

"I never suggested it was." Anne turned her face away, looked resolutely ahead. "Did Adèle ever tell you how her fiancé died?"

"You seem to know a lot about Adèle."

"I don't, but Marie does. Jimpy was her cousin."

"Jimpy?"

"Jean-Pierre Bertin. He was a yachtsman, quite a local hero I'm told."

"I know that much and that he didn't drown himself."

"But you didn't know he died from a heroin overdose, or that he was Jean-Paul's best friend from their schooldays?"

"No." Michael's heart quickened.

"Adèle told Marie she'd never known Jimpy to take drugs. She didn't know Jean-Paul well but he kept coming round afterwards, consoling her, saying he would have stopped Jimpy if only he'd known. She went out with Jean-Paul for a while but they broke up. She didn't see him again for years. He was married to Daisy by then but Marie says it was months before Adèle found that out. By then I suppose Adèle imagined she was in love."

Michael was thinking back to the night they found Daisy, of Adèle saying, 'It's just like it was with Jimpy' as they followed the ambulance.

"So you see, Dad, she knows what it's like to lose someone that way."

Was that why Adèle returned the bullets? Did seeing what Bohec had done to Daisy convince her he was involved in her Jimpy's death too? How did Bohec feel about her calling him Jimpy too?

"You have to move on, Dad."

Michael checked the dashboard clock then put the Land Rover into gear. "But not to Saint-Servais," he said.

Chapter 26

Michael selected daisies from his garden, dark red chrysanthemums, bronze-red heleniums, then put Vicki into her pushchair and took her down the lane to the churchyard.

He arranged the flowers on Daisy's grave, told her about Treguelven, what happened, everything, warts and all.

Then he squatted, head cocked, but heard nothing in response. "Why weren't you there, Daisy?" he cried. "If you'd trusted me, there wouldn't be this problem now. There'd just be you, me and the children. Nobody else would matter." He held Vicki up in his arms. "Look, Daisy, here's your baby. Isn't she beautiful? Just like her mother. And it's her mother she needs. That's you Daisy. But Vicki can't have *you*, can she? Not now, not ever. So what am I to do about that, Daisy? Tell me. What am I to do?"

Tears streamed from him, some dampening Vicki's hair and brow.

"Dada no," Vicki said then began crying too, and that put a stop to Michael's own.

"Shush, darling, it's all right. Daddy got a little silly, that's all. He didn't mean to frighten you."

Michael rocked Vicki in his arms. The act, the gentle swaying motion, allowed tranquillity to return.

"There, it's all right now," he said. Vicki smiled up at him.

"Aw wight," she said.

Michael's head suddenly felt as if it might float away, like a balloon free of its confining string. A scarcely definable tingling sensation began above his ears. He heard Daisy's voice: *"You need to clutch at happiness, Michael, not consider it."*

He recalled the context in which those words were originally spoken. It was true he thought too much. It was Daisy's tragedy though, and by extension that of her children and himself, that she didn't think enough.

He took Vicki home, gazed at *La Belle Pacquerette* squatting in the yard on her trailer. He thought about returning her to the water. He thought about Treguelven.

Anne was spending a week with Grace and with Michael deprived of his protector, it seemed to him that Meredith regained some of her old poise, the quality that had mesmerised an entire hospital ward as she swished across its floor. Her eyes often had their old intensity now, as if gathering power from some source beyond the imagination.

Then, the evening before Anne was due to return, Michael, relaxing on his bed with a Roddy Doyle novel, felt a shiver, not cold, down his spine. Heart racing, he turned around.

It was not Daisy. How could he have even thought that possible?

Meredith stood there, regarding him with a proprietress's air. She came towards him, smiling, in her high-stepping way.

Jesus, she was wearing the paeony dress Daisy borrowed.

She posed, poised, in front of him, chest thrust out so far he found himself thinking of Tappy Pringle slipping his hand inside her bra. She had no right at her age to have such breasts.

"I want you to like me again," she said.

As Meredith unzipped herself from the paeony dress Michael knew the time for prevarication was over.

"Have you missed me, Dad?"

Michael looked over Anne's head at the four-square structure of James's house. It was surely Grace's suburban dream come true.

"Of course not."

"Liar."

Father and daughter hugged and Michael marvelled for the thousandth time at his good fortune that this wonderful girl actually loved him despite the years in which he failed her.

"Yeah, I reckon I've missed you," he said.

As they left Dorking, he was conscious of Anne peering at him.

"What?" he said.

"You're up to something."

"Me?"

"Don't stall, Dad. You can't fool me."

"I'm sending Meredith home," Michael said but he felt his throat gag.

"Don't go feeling guilty, Dad. Daisy would have sent her back much sooner."

"How do you know that?"

"From what she didn't say. I think it's one reason she stayed in France, why she chose a house as far south as Giffards."

Michael smiled. "You're very perceptive, Anne. And I'm well aware Meredith views me as her personal project, a sort of masculine Eliza Doolittle." And something more, he thought, but I can't ever tell Anne that.

"To her Henry Higgins? Ha. I could never imagine you in skirts, Dad. Or Meredith in trousers come to that." Anne's mouth twisted into a gleeful smile. "*Elijah* Doolittle perhaps. And Henrietta Higgins."

Michael laughed. "Henrietta Higgins suits Meredith well." It made her seem much less formidable. He needed that.

"I hate the way she tries to keep you in thrall. And how she was so nasty to Adèle. Talking of Adèle, you didn't see her tears that night after you both went sailing."

"Adèle crying? Did Meredith pick on her again?"

"I rather think it was because of you."

Michael raked teeth over his bottom lip.

"Dad, were you listening?"

Michael took his eyes off the road, smiled at Anne.

"I heard you."

"Don't let Adèle slip away, Dad. She'd be so good for you."

"Shouldn't I be the one to decide that?"

"No, you might make the wrong decision."

"Daisy wasn't one. Neither was finding you."

"Then what's stopping you now?"

"Yellow streak down my back?"

"Oh, Dad…"

A long silence followed, broken only when Anne began drumming her fingers against the fascia.

"I'm thinking of leaving school," she said.

"You can't do that, not now."

"And you can't cope on your own with two children."

"What about Cambridge? If you don't follow your dream, Anne, you'll regret it. It will tear at you. Constantly."

"If you'll follow yours then I'll follow mine, Dad. That's the deal. No compromises. You might have lost one dream but there's no rule that says you can't have another."

They'd reached Giffards by then. Michael parked in the stable yard.

"You're a blatant blackmailer, Anne," he said as he switched the engine off.

"Tough shit," she said. "But nine out of ten for alliteration."

Chapter 27

Adèle, eyes half-closed, regarded Michael with an urchin smile.

"So, Michael, you said you needed to see me. What, I wondered, could be so urgent. Should I expect good news or bad?"

"I want to carry on where we left off."

Adèle's smile deepened. "Then you'd better come in."

She skipped up the stairs of her apartment, leaving Michael to contemplate the fine lines of her calves as they pounded the treads before him.

Their subsequent kiss was intense, lingering, and that of Treguelven became but a brief sampler. Michael, eyes closed, relished the sweet taste of Adèle as their lips and tongues flexed and softened, found and wound their way against each other's.

"So, Michael, you have carried on," Adèle said at last. "Was that all you came for?" Her eyes were teasing him again.

"No, I came to find the nature of our affinité."

"Ah. You remember me saying that."

"I've never forgotten anything you've said to me. Even when I should have."

"Now there's an admission." Adèle's teasing look was replaced by serious contemplation.

"I think Daisy was aware of it too."

"And that distresses you?"

"She made a joke of it at first. But even after I stopped reacting she kept implying there was some...thing between us. It didn't seem to annoy her. She didn't seem threatened by it."

"If events went as we all expected, you and I would have seen each other rarely, if at all. But I sensed our affinité when our eyes first met. Something passed between us, something stirred me, even though I was happy enough with *him*. And when we two walked by the Auray River, I suddenly wanted it to be more than a nebulous attraction. I wanted you to look at me as a man looks at a woman. That's why I asked you to choose a photograph."

"I knew you'd never have asked Daisy."

"Did you feel guilty about it?"

"Of course. She was the one in my heart but I couldn't get you out of my head. Now though..."

"You feel different?"

"I feel different. What I need to know is how you feel."

"Michael." Adèle pressed a finger to her lips. "Time to stop talking."

He'd known it would be good. He'd seen it in Adèle's eyes, in their latent sensuality, seen it in the way she moved, heard it in the cadences of her voice.

But when it happened it was far better than good. It was transcendent. It began with the joy of being inside the woman he had desired for so long, but it was the passion in Adèle, the glow on her skin, the sight and touch and taste of every part of her urgent body that wrenched Michael from mere enjoyment, raised him to peaks of pleasure he'd thought he'd never experience again. At last he understood their *affinité*. Through all of it, he had not thought of Daisy once. That was surely a significantly good thing.

"Now you know exactly how I feel," Adèle whispered when they finally disentangled themselves and sank, exhausted, into the sticky, passion-scented depths of her bed.

Lying beside Adèle, Michael decided he could not help the feelings he'd held for her while Daisy was still with him, for such emotions came unbidden, acknowledged no bounds. Only acts of love could be confined and he had not crossed that line.

So there would be no more torturing himself and though he still missed Daisy terribly he could not, would not, live the rest of his life in unmitigated grief. This new love had come unawares and he would relish it, keep it if he could.

They chartered a boat, cruised the Golfe du Morbihan. There Michael learned more about sailing than on the entire voyage with Peter. On land, he and Adèle walked hand-in-hand and, like teenagers, snuggled together in secluded doorways. They talked in a way and of things that Michael never found uncomfortable, whereas with Daisy, he'd never quite rid himself of his notions of inferiority. He supposed it was because Adèle and he had modest backgrounds. Why, she was even a clerk in a bank, just like his mother, Juanita, had been. There were no monarchs in their glens.

On their last full day together, they strolled along the lane behind Adèle's mother's house. As they neared the sea marsh at its edge, Adèle said "So where do we go from here?"

Two youths rode by on mopeds, whistled at her.

Adèle's mouth was partly open, her eyes questioning Michael's.

He clasped her hands. "I want you to come to England."

"For how long? There's the bank...I have my job..."

But from the way Adèle's eyes were shining Michael knew that she knew what he was going to say next. Yet still he had palpitations.

"I want to marry you."

"You don't have to do that."

"It's what I want. What I've wanted for a long time but only realised at Treguelven when Meredith was so nasty to you."

"She doesn't frighten me."

"She won't have the chance. I'm sending her back home."

"Ah. Because of me?"

"Because I need to breathe again. So, what's your answer, Adèle? Will you marry me?"

"Yes, Michael, of course I will marry you."

She said it in English and, it may have been because of her accent, Michael was moved far more than he was prepared for. Emotion lumped in his throat and glistened his eyes just as the moped youths passed them again, this time returning to the village.

Adèle yelled something at them that Michael didn't catch, but it stopped their whistling, almost caused them to fall off their bikes. "Wankers," she said to Michael.

As they turned the corner from the lane, they saw a stocky man about sixty-five years old, five-feet-ten in height mooching around Héloise's garden gate. He had a tanned, clean-shaven face and frizzy grey hair that must once have been black, Michael thought, judging by the fellow's eyebrows.

"Madame Bohec?" the man said.

Adèle frowned. "I was once, but not now."

"Forgive me," the man said, bowing briefly. "I am aware you are divorced. But old concepts die hard with me."

Michael, bristling, placed himself between Adèle and the stranger. "What do you want?" he said in a voice that sounded a deal less aggressive than he intended it to be.

The man appraised Michael with eyes that looked accustomed to dealing with empty threats. "You must be Monsieur Cavanagh," he said, causing Michael's eyebrows to stand tall. "I wish to speak to both of you about something that troubles me. Troubles me greatly in fact."

A tangible sadness exuded from the stranger, so compelling that Michael felt drawn to comply with his request. He moved to Adèle's side, placed a protective arm around her shoulder.

"This must be to do with my ex-husband," Adèle said, thin-lipped. "What's Jean-Paul put you up to? What devilment is he planning now?"

"He's put me up to nothing. Neither has anyone else."

"Then what's your interest in us?"

"The truth."

"About what?" Adèle snapped the words.

The man's gaze was direct, steady, morose. "About what he has done."

"Are you a reporter?" Michael said, tightening his protective grasp on Adèle.

The visitor smiled, shook his head. "No reporter. You might say I'm the oldest friend of the Bohecs. I am concerned about the family honour."

"Dishonour, more like," Michael snorted. He clenched his free fist. Adèle then took possession of it so Michael was forced to soften his aggression, let his fingers intertwine with hers.

"Why has it taken you so long to find us?" she said.

"I have been out of France, out of Europe in fact, for many years. I came as quickly as I could." The stranger extended his hands in a gesture of supplication. "I've read the official version but wanted to hear the facts from those who suffered."

"They are not here to tell their story," Michael said in a fractured voice. "Bohec, or should I say, *Bardinet*, made sure of that."

"Bardinet?" Adèle gazed up at Michael, her expression one of confusion.

The stranger had not cocked so much as a single eyebrow. "Yet you both suffered and are very much alive," he said, his voice as calm as when he had first spoken to them.

Michael stared at him, this stranger who had intruded on a very special day, souring it by resurrecting the grief that brought them together. Michael wanted to strike him but although he searched within himself for the necessary aggression, he found none. At Michael's side, Adèle became fidgety, squeezed his hand, dug fingernails into his flesh.

"If we're to talk facts and truth then we'd better sit down," Michael said at last and Adèle stopped scouring his hand. They led their visitor to the area hidden by the screens around Héloise's swimming pool.

As their visitor padded benignly towards a taxi waiting for him in the village square, Adèle said to Michael, "Why didn't you tell me? Surely it would have helped to share the burden, the truth about why Daisy died."

"I wanted to, Adèle, but I was afraid to awaken the pain. For you as well as me. Didn't want to break the magic that made *us* happen."

Adèle drew Michael's hands to her lips.

"Oh, my poor, poor cherie," she said.

The taxi rounded the corner by the church, disappeared from sight.

"I think I know who he is," Michael said.

Adèle nodded. "The Limousin priest. One more dishonourable Bohec."

Chapter 28

Héloise planted kisses on Michael's cheeks.

"An Irish-Spanish-Breton cocktail," she gushed. "It will produce lusty men and passionate women. And the men will all be tall and strong like you, Michael." She embraced him again then started on her daughter, who was regarding her with something close to horror.

"Who said we want babies, Maman? I don't know if I can go through that again. Besides, Michael's Vicki is only sixteen months old."

"Three years is a nice age gap."

"I suppose you've worked out the exact date we should start trying."

Adèle raised eyebrows at Michael. He shrugged then they both began to laugh, collapsing onto the sofa. Héloise began talking about the wedding.

"There's so much to organise. Invitations… The church."

Adèle was suddenly stern-faced, ramrod-backed. "*No, no,* Maman, stop right there. No church. God has done nothing except kill the people we loved."

"The devil did that, cherie."

"Then why didn't God stop him? He's supposed to be omnipotent. Michael and I have a chance to wrest happiness from tragedy but we'll do it ourselves, not invoke a loving God that does not love at all."

Michael gazed at this wife-to-be, felt the energy pulsing through Adèle's words. It thrilled him. She had depth, fire, and passion, this woman, he thought.

Héloise was giving signs that tears weren't far away.

"I've given you one church wedding already, Maman," Adèle said softly. "Let this one be for me. Please? The Mairie is grand enough. Michael doesn't like churches either."

Michael reckoned it was sixty-forty against the tears. Gradually Héloise's face cleared.

"All right. But promise me you'll wear a dress this time."

Michael's face stretched into a smile as Adèle said, "*D'accord*, Maman. A dress it is."

Michael mentally ticked off the guest list: Héloise of course; Adèle's closest friends; handful of Serazins; Marie definitely; maybe Augustine. Travelling from England would be Anne and the children; Paddy and perhaps Linda; Miranda; and Meredith if she wasn't so far up her own backside.

Meredith. She was a problem he still had to deal with but he forced her from his mind until he stepped once more onto the gravel in front of Giffards.

Anne, Vicki and Hamish spilled from the house.

"Dada back," said a grinning Vicki as Michael scooped her into his arms.

Anne stood facing him, hands on hips. "Well, Dad, aren't you the lucky one?" She gave a little whoop, danced Hamish in a circle around Michael and Vicki. "Oh, I'm so happy," she cried.

Meredith was more elusive. Michael found her in the office they'd set up in a room above his workshop. She was peering at a computer screen, playing solitaire.

"Bugger," she said as she ran out of luck. "So,' she said, over her shoulder. "I see you're back."

That night in his bedroom, the night of the paeony dress, Meredith had reminded him how he'd once said she and Daisy could have been twins.

"You don't have to choose between us anymore," she said, "there's just me. And I promised I would make it better for you, Michael. I could do that now." That was the moment she slipped out of her dress, began to unclasp her bra.

"Get out," he'd yelled, leaped from the bed, propelled her from the room, thrown her dress after her. "For God's sake, Meredith, you're old enough to be my bloody mother."

"You're not exactly averse to older women," she'd snapped. "You did marry one, after all."

He waited for her to throw Jacinta in too, but no, Daisy would never have given her that ammunition. As it was, Meredith said no more, marched off, leaving the dress on the floor. Then Vicki saved him by waking up and starting to cry.

"And I see you're still here," Michael said.

Meredith whirled her chair around, faced Michael. He watched her assume a haunted expression. "Why do you hate me so much?" she said.

"You forgot to add 'after all I've done for you'," Michael said, more testily than he had meant to. "I don't hate you, Meredith but you can't pretend things aren't different between us now."

"Since the night I offered you comfort? I was only trying to help." Meredith got up, retreated from Michael until the wall prevented further progress. She watched him warily.

If he hadn't bundled her out of his room so quickly, Michael knew what would have happened next. And that would have wrecked everything for everyone, Meredith included, not just him and Adèle. He sighed, forced himself to relax.

Meredith was watching him closely. Her mouth unpursed. In a tone of cloying sweetness, she said, "You're upset, Michael, that's what it is. Let's just forget all this unpleasantness, forget it happened."

Michael sat on the desk, facing her, drew himself up. "Meredith, you need to make a decision."

"Michael, what *are* you talking about?"

"Are Daisy's children to be brought up together, or will you act against her wishes and try to break them apart? I won't be blackmailed any longer."

Meredith cupped her hands over her mouth. "Blackmailed? I never…"

"No, you're never explicit, you prefer to insinuate. Which is it to be, together or apart?"

"Together." The word was whispered. Meredith's eyes bored into Michael's, full of wounds, but he was impervious to them now.

"Together means *I* bring Hamish up, not you."

"Yes."

"I and whoever I choose to share that role. Whoever. Whether you think she is suitable or not."

"Yes." Meredith nodded, closed her eyes.

"Good. Because as you've probably guessed, I've chosen someone."

"*Her?*"

"She has a name, Meredith."

Meredith stared at her feet. Then she said, in a tiny voice Michael knew was intended to squeeze sympathy from him, "I suppose that means you want me to leave."

"You did say you'd only stay until I was settled. That was well over a year ago."

Meredith looked forlorn now, deflated. Another of her weapons, Michael thought.

"I'm not trying to push you out of the children's lives. You could sell your house, move closer."

"But not too close?"

"Closer than you know Daisy would accept."

Meredith looked up sharply. There was a hint of a smile.

"As I think I've said before, Michael, you're most perspicacious."

Michael allowed himself a smile too then got down from the desk.

"What I want is for you to be what you are, Meredith - Hamish and Vicki's grandmother. But they need a mother too. You yourself said it's not fair to put it all on to Anne. Loving Adèle doesn't mean I don't love Daisy too, for I loved her for what she was and that will *never* change, because Daisy can never change. We'll never know if we would have grown to hate each other."

"Like Harry and I did?"

"I wasn't thinking of you and Harry." What Michael was thinking was that Paddy never had the chance to grow old with Juanita.

Michael made to leave but then turned back. "There's something that's been puzzling me, Meredith," he said. "Why do you never visit Daisy's grave?"

Meredith looked as if he had struck her. "I don't *know*. Please stop torturing me," she cried. "*Please.*"

Michael touched her softly on the shoulder.

"It was only a question. I won't ask it again. You mightn't think so at the moment, but I do care for you, Meredith."

"Well, I suppose that's something."

"Yes, it's something."

Michael and Adèle had discussed bringing up Daisy's children. He'd said he didn't want her to have any illusions about what she was taking on.

"I'm worried about Hamish. I let Meredith take him over and I don't know what she's filled his head with. What I'm trying to say is I don't how he'll react to you being his stepmother."

"I'll tread carefully," Adèle said. "Hamish and I have always got along well. One day I hope he'll be able to accept me as his second mother. It should be easier for Vicki because she has never known her real one. I feel a special bond with her because she and Frédy arrived in the world at the same time and, of course, the same place."

Michael had never considered that Adèle's baby might have had a name. She'd never mentioned one and he'd never asked. He realised he should have.

"You will be Vicki's real mother in all that matters," he said. Then he recalled she might have been something of one already.

"Michael, why are you looking at me like that?"

"Like what?"

"All...strange."

"I wasn't. It's nothing."

"No, it's something. Come on, out with it."

Adèle began to prod Michael with her fingers, changing their target too swiftly for him to anticipate where they would strike next.

"Tell me," she urged with each repetition until he finally said, "All right."

Yet he remained silent.

"Go on." Adèle had a finger poised to strike again.

Michael reddened then with much hesitation said he'd been thinking about Vicki being fed with donated milk. "Your mentioning the two births reminded me. I wish I knew who the donor was." His eyes strayed to Adèle's breasts.

"Why is it so important to you?"

"Because I wish I could thank her. Her selflessness saved Vicki's life."

"Oh, Michael," Adèle said. He thought he saw tears in the corners of her eyes. "I'm sure she knows how grateful you are. But she would have only agreed on the basis that it remained a secret. If you need to thank someone, thank those wonderful nurses for persuading her something good could come out of her tragedy."

Michael thought he could love Adèle for that alone.

With Meredith dealt with, Michael returned to France to prove his status at the Mairie. He called at Héloise's first and as soon as he opened the garden gate, Adèle emerged from the house. Instead of coming towards him, she waited by the porch. Michael looked in vain for the smile with which she normally greeted him. She looked as if she didn't want to see him at all.

"He's dead," Adèle said in a voice scarcely above a whisper.

Michael did not have to ask who.

Adèle went indoors, leaving Michael to follow. He found her in Héloise's salon, flopped on a sofa. Héloise lolled in an armchair, sipped something coffee-coloured from a tall glass. In between sips, she drew on a black-papered cigarette held in a long, ivory holder, blew out the smoke in rings.

"Suicide, apparently." Héloise gestured towards a newspaper spread out on a table. She sounded as if she couldn't care less.

Bohec had been allotted a half-column. He had, at 7:10 the previous morning, been found hanging from a rope fashioned from his bedding and tied to the window bars of his cell. Prison staff tried to resuscitate him but at 9:15 he was pronounced dead by the prison doctor. The reporter said a priest had visited Bohec the previous afternoon. He speculated whether this was to hear the prisoner's last confession and suggested that the prison's classification of Bohec as not subject to 'suicide watch' was unwise. Brief details of Daisy's murder closed the report.

Adèle began to sob. With an unwelcome memory of Daisy weeping over her father, Michael tried to comfort her.

"Someone must have told him about us," Adèle wailed. "He's done this deliberately to spoil everything. How can I marry you with this on my conscience?"

Michael gritted his teeth. Reading the report, his principal thought was that he'd been cheated out of exacting revenge. It was natural that Adèle would be upset but he hadn't anticipated this reaction at all. Well, he was damned if he'd let the bastard take her from him too. He grasped Adèle's hands, transfixed his eyes to hers.

"That way, he gets away with suicide as well as murder. You can't allow that, Adèle. You owe it to yourself and Frédy, because Jean-Paul killed him as surely as he killed Daisy. Probably your Jimpy too."

Adèle's eyes revealed her torment but when they finally told him she had reached a decision Michael could see it was not the one he sought.

"I accept all you say, Michael," she said in a sunken voice. "But I can't marry you. I'm sorry."

At least Meredith will be pleased, was Michael's only witting acknowledgement. He kept his expression stiff as a corpse's, yet Adèle looked so bereft it made him soften and say, "Does that mean not ever?"

Adèle shook her head. "No, it doesn't."

"So you're still my fiancée?"

"Yes, Michael. Unless you want it different."

"It will do for now."

Michael thought he saw the birthing of a smile, quickly discarded it was true, but there nonetheless.

Walking alone down the lane where so short a time ago Adèle had agreed to marry him, Michael thought about Treguelven, Meredith accusing him of having a fetish for Bohec's wives.

Was it possible he saw Daisy and Adèle as prizes, a result of some rivalry born in him when he first saw Bohec's self-satisfied sneer?

Being beaten up and left for dead had certainly concentrated his resolve but at the moment he fell for Daisy he didn't even know she was married.

As for Adèle, he couldn't help meeting her, given that Bohec brought her to the house where he lived, but his involvement with her wasn't deliberate.

Her photographs certainly filled him with old-fashioned lust, consolidated that by seeing her in the flesh then transformed it into something more the day she made her photographs replay their part. But the fact that she was Bohec's mistress was irrelevant. She could have been the Pope's for all that it mattered.

When it came to it, in each case it was the woman who activated their relationship: Daisy by seducing him after Harry's funeral, Adèle when she kissed him at Treguelven. Left to himself, Michael knew he'd have done nothing, simply remained a pathetic loner, crippled by his past.

No fetish on his part then, and not even the admirable motive of rescuing Bohec's wives. It was they who rescued Michael Delgado Cavanagh.

And when payback time arrived and he really did have to rescue Daisy from that homicidal psychopath, when every decision and action he took truly mattered, he'd failed catastrophically. And now he had to rescue Adèle. Her life might not be in danger from Bohec but her mind was very much under threat.

Michael reached the end of the lane, looked out over Morbihan, the little sea, where he and Adèle fought treacherous tides together.

A large seabird with pale wings, a gannet, he thought, dived from a fair height into the water. Emerging with a fish clasped neatly in its beak, it flew straight out again, the whole sequence achieved in one seamless frame.

Instinct was the key to the bird's success, Michael told himself, whereas we humans worry about every possibility before acting. Was that why the Church invented Confession, to let the faithful off the hook with a few trite words?

He was surprised to hear himself whisper: *Hail Mary, full of grace; the Lord is with thee.* As he checked himself, something connected in his mind. According to Daisy, Bohec was a devout atheist, so why would he be seeing a priest?

Michael decided to act upon instinct, like the seabird. Instinct told him to present his papers to the Mairie as if the wedding would go ahead as planned. Having done that, instinct next took him to Mazemeur.

Marie's face was more flushed than usual. Her hands flew to her cheeks.

"Michael! Is something wrong?"

"Something's very wrong."

From the way they both started when he relayed the news, it was plain neither Marie nor Augustine knew of Bohec's death. A rapid conversation in Breton ensued between mother and daughter, during the course of which Augustine's face travelled through what Michael interpreted as fear and bemusement, finally reaching relief.

"And now Adèle feels unable to marry me," he said when the women were silent. Marie bit her lip.

Michael described the visit from the Bohecs' 'oldest friend'. Augustine's eyes suddenly twinkled. She said, in English: "He was here, too."

Michael stared at her. "You speak English?" He felt his cheeks smart as he tried to recall unworthy things he might have uttered before her in the past.

"Enough," Augustine said, her face creasing into a sly smile. "Marie she insist to teaching me."

Marie's face twitched but Michael saw her fighting it. "It was Anne's idea," she said. "So Maman could join in the fun when we were all together. You see, it is only French she objects to. She has no objection at all to English."

"Either the peoples or the language," Augustine said, nodding. Then she laughed and added, "Well, perhaps Meredith. She is too...too big of herself sometimes."

"Ha," Michael said. "She is certainly that."

From dismissing Augustine as a quasi village idiot, Michael at last recognised the wisdom hidden behind her dark eyes. How cocksure he and Daisy had been that Marie's undoubted intelligence could never have been inherited from her. While there were no tell-tale slogans or flags visible in her house, it seemed obvious now that Augustine was a serious Breton nationalist, not someone too stupid to grasp the French language. She was also an unusually benevolent landowner, even if that experience was only latter-day. She was a Bohec, too. As, of course, was Marie. And both very honourable.

"So, back to our visitor," he said, "I did wonder if he was Jean Bohec."

Augustine nodded. "He was indeed Jean. It was surprise for me seeing his face here. The first time in forty years."

"What did he want?"

"Adèle. I tell to him go to Saint-Servais. I say..." Augustine squinted at Michael, cocked her head. "Why did you wonder? What do you know of Jean Bohec?"

"I know he is Jean-Paul's father."

Augustine stared at Michael as if she didn't believe him. "Him and Berthe?" She shook her head. "Never."

"No, not Berthe. Berthe was not Jean-Paul's mother."

Both women gaped as Michael related what Marlowe had uncovered. When he added his own theory about the motive for Daisy's murder, Marie turned increasingly pale. She gripped his hands.

"Oh no, Michael," she said, her eyes filling as they scoured his.

Michael grimaced. "I told Jean Bohec too. He wanted to know everything we could tell him about Jean-Paul's crimes. He didn't say what he was going to do but the report of Jean-Paul's death says that a priest visited him the day before."

Behind him, he heard Augustine say, "You think this prison priest is Cousin Jean."

Michael nodded. "I'm hoping you might help me find him. I know his parents lived in Rochefort-en-Terre."

Augustine shook her head. "They are dead now, many years." She gathered in her cheeks, blew them out, scratched an ear. "There was a daughter. Older than Jean. Married..."

"She lives in Rochefort?"

"I don't know. Perhaps..."

"What was her name?"

"Monique for sure. But I don't know her other."

Rochefort-en-Terre is a town of ancient houses, straddling a wooded promontory between deep valleys. Though it was well into September its houses, walls, anywhere someone could fix a hanging basket or display a terracotta pot, were summer-bright with flowers, mainly scarlet pelargoniums.

"An idyllic place to live, you might think," said Marie.

Michael grunted.

Walking along the main street, he was over-conscious of each moment he and Marie brushed against each other. Once or twice, their hands touched and he snatched his away as if it had been scalded. Marie didn't seem to notice. Several times, he caught her reflection in a shop window. She looked happy, almost serene.

They stopped, for no particular reason that Michael could discern, outside a tabac. Its door was open. Inside he could see old-fashioned counters and cabinets, a shining symphony of mahogany. Afterwards he would claim the carpenter in him felt drawn to them but in truth he had not a thought in his head as he crossed the threshold.

The shopkeeper was a tall, thin man who wore a shiny brown suit and a contented expression. Michael and Marie were beamed at in turn. There were no other customers.

"How can I tempt you?" The shopkeeper waved a hand around his empire.

Suddenly, Michael felt foolish, wondered why he had come in. So much for instinct, he thought. He looked at Marie, his eyes imploring her to save him. She smiled and nodded back.

"We're trying to find a relative who lives or lived here," she said. "We've lost touch over the years and wondered if you might help us."

"And which relative would that be?"

"My mother's cousin. She was born Monique Bohec but I don't know her married name."

"Monique Bohec." The man's eyes widened then seemed to look into the far distance before returning to Marie. "You've certainly come to the right place. Monique Bohec was my first schoolteacher, almost as pretty as you. It must run in the family. It broke my heart when she became Madame Groussard." His expression became rueful. "I was only seven years old."

He stood poised as if waiting for applause, and when neither Marie nor Michael responded said, "She's dead now, poor woman. But her daughter Loli married my friend, Alain Bobet. They live in the Bohec house now, no kids unfortunately. It's just around the corner, the one with red shutters, on the little ridge." He looked at his watch. "You should catch Loli in about now. Now, are you sure I can't tempt you to buy anything?"

Michael chose the first thing his eyes settled on, a 400-gram box of chocolates, then grasped Marie's hand, almost dragged her from the shop. Outside, he stopped and stared at the chocolates, Marie's rapidly heating face, at her hand in his.

"Here," he said, releasing her and holding out the chocolates. "You'd better have these."

Nobody answered the doorbell, so they walked round to the rear garden. A pretty woman, petite, dark-haired, late fortyish, was watering a pot of purple and red fuchsias. She almost jumped when she saw her visitors.

"Loli?" Marie said. "I'm Marie Bertin from Mazemeur. We're cousins of sorts."

The woman's face softened. "Augustine's daughter," she said, nodding. She smiled. "We've met before, at your baptism. Heavens, you're a young woman now. Was it really that long ago?"

"Eighteen years," Marie said. Loli raised her eyebrows.

Marie handed her the chocolates. "We brought these for you," she said. "I hope that's all right."

Loli smiled vaguely. "Oh," she said. "Thank you. You are kind."

She invited them into her kitchen, made cappuccinos in an elaborate machine. Marie chatted about Bohecs, about relations Michael neither knew of nor cared about although he knew Marie was only trying to soften Loli up. When Marie started to talk about Daisy, Michael signalled her to stop.

"It's time I introduced myself," he said.

"Oh," Loli said. "I thought you were Marie's young man."

"She deserves better than me," Michael said. "And I'm far too old in any case." He knew Marie would be blushing furiously so he kept his eyes on Loli. She, wearing a quizzical expression, was now looking at Marie.

Loli said she'd read about the trial ("it was terrible what happened to your fiancée"), and yes, she knew about Jean-Paul's death too; it was reported on yesterday's TV News. "I didn't know him though I suppose I must have met him when the family was closer, before my mother died."

Michael detected no giveaway expressions in this interchange but when he mentioned the visit he and Adèle had from Jean Bohec, Loli's eyes refused to settle on his.

"The thing is," he said. "I didn't know who he was at the time. Now that I do, I need to talk to him. Is he staying here?"

"Uncle Jean? Staying with me?" Loli's voice was a tad higher-pitched now, her words a little hurried.

"Yes. Is he, was he, staying with you?"

"*No.* No, of course not."

Michael sighed. "That's a pity. Because I really need to talk to him. Can you tell us where we can find him?"

Loli's eyes were shifty again. Then she suddenly drew herself up. She stared at Michael without flinching.

"Ulaan Bator, I imagine."

Michael made a face at Marie. "Where?" he mouthed.

"It's the capital of Mongolia," Marie said.

"He lives there," Loli said. "He's a missionary of the Immaculate Heart."

More than that Loli would not say except to deny she had seen Uncle Jean at all recently or even knew he had been in the country. She stood at her door and watched Michael and Marie as they walked away from her house.

"I'm sorry I couldn't help," she cried.

Chapter 29

As they passed the tabac, Marie pulled Michael to a stop. "Let's ask if he knows Uncle Jean."

The shopkeeper was serving but took time off to grin. "Aha, you couldn't resist coming back for more."

Marie grinned back. "I have a sweet tooth." She waited until the shop was empty then asked about Jean Bohec.

"Funny you should mention him," the shopkeeper said, rubbing his chin. "He was in here, oh, some weeks ago now. He turns up every few years, sometimes more, never less. Stays a week or so. Then only yesterday, I saw him again. In the street this time. He mentioned something about buying flowers. For Loli, I suppose."

"Does he stay with her?"

"Naturally. His parents left the house to him and Monique. Her share of course passed to Loli but old Jean insisted on retaining his half. A pied-à-terre, he said, in his home town."

"So, she lied," Michael said when they were outside the shop. He kept clenching and unclenching his fists. "I'm going to ask her why."

"No," Marie said. "It's my responsibility."

Michael stared at her, open-mouthed. "Yours?"

Bright pink suffused Marie's skin, radiating upwards from her neck. "It concerns my family's honour. As I'm probably the last Bohec, it's my duty. Besides, I think Loli's more likely to confide in me."

"The last Bohec?" Michael thought about the small one he was bringing up. Although, he reminded himself, he didn't believe Hamish was a Bohec at all.

"Unless I persuade someone to marry me."

Marie looked plaintive now. Michael felt a twinge of guilt. Yet, he thought, I've never done anything to encourage her, not wittingly.

"Marie," he said, "You are beautiful, bright, and a pleasure to be with. I bet every boy in Morbihan is in love with you."

"In Auray perhaps. But they are just boys."

"And you are still a girl. Marriage should be way outside your plans. I know it's boring but I keep nagging Anne in the same way. It's something fathers do."

"And you see yourself as my surrogate Dad?"

"I suppose…in a way…I do. Yes. If that's all right with you."

Marie's expression turned wistful then her face suddenly cleared and she smiled. "Okay," she said. "But it's still my job to sort Loli out. Tomorrow. On my own. Agreed?"

"Agreed."

"Is it all right to hug your surrogate Dad?"

"I think it's obligatory."

Michael opened his arms and Marie nestled within them. He felt her heartbeat, rapid, pounding his chest.

Adèle didn't ask Michael where he had been. They spent the evening staring at TV while Héloise uttered platitudes. At ten o'clock, Héloise went to bed. Michael then told Adèle he was returning to England in the morning, that he had to be home to take Anne to school. It was her first term in sixth form and she couldn't afford to lose any time.

"If it wasn't for that, I'd stay. If you'd want me here."

"Of course I would," Adèle said, grave-faced. "But I also recognise you are stuck between…what is the English?…the devil and a hard rock."

"It's the devil and the deep blue sea but there's also a rock and a hard place. They mean the same but I like yours better."

"Am I the devil or the rock?"

"We both know who the devil is."

Adèle stared at Michael. She slowly chewed her lip then said, "And he is the rock our hope has now foundered on."

"Not my hope," said Michael.

He thought it best to sleep on the sofa. Adèle didn't demur. He walked with her to the staircase that led to her flat. She gave him a single goodnight peck, scampered up the treads. All night he waited in vain for slipperless feet creeping downstairs, Adèle's fingers unlatching the door.

The morning, however, did bring a surprise. Adèle, watching as Michael packed his bags, suddenly said, "Would you mind if I came with you? I could do with getting away from here. I've phoned work, told them I have a flu bug, that I'll be better in a few days."

When they were within a mile of Giffards, Adèle said, "I want to see where Daisy is."

She knelt beside the grave while Michael stayed back. He noticed there were fresh flowers in Daisy's vase. Bless Anne, she thought of everything.

Adèle murmured something. When she stood up her cheeks were moist. "I wanted to make my peace with Daisy. Shall I tell you what I said?"

"Only if you want to."

"I told her thank you for letting me borrow you, that she mustn't think I was stealing you from her."

"She wouldn't. Do you know, that time I brought Hamish to Mazemeur, Daisy said it was all right for me to like you. She even said I could kiss you. Now I'm not so sure it was meant as a joke. I think perhaps she could see the future."

"And I teased you. I'm sorry."

"I'm glad nothing happened. Then."

Adèle nodded slowly. "I would never have been able to forgive myself."

At Giffards, Adèle stood by the car, gazing all about her. "So beautiful," she said.

Moments later, Anne's face appeared at the sitting room window. Soon she and the children were claiming their attention.

Anne told Adèle how she'd despaired that Dad would ever pluck up the courage. Michael, rapidly turning florid, concentrated on hugging Vicki.

Hamish stood patiently waiting his turn and, when Adèle held out her arms, raced into them without a moment's hesitation. "Anne says you're going to be my new mama."

"Would you like me to be?" Adèle glanced back at Michael as she spoke. She looked apprehensive.

"Yes," Hamish said and for a moment Adèle looked as if she'd won the world.

Meredith had not appeared.

"She went off in a taxi," Anne said.

"A taxi? Well, that's a first."

Michael stroked his chin, wondered what Meredith was up to then forgot her as he showed Adèle what he still hoped would be her new home.

Adèle smiled at the sign above Michael's workshop. "Does it mean you failed to do something you should have and carpentry became your punishment?"

"Yes. I failed to make a living doing anything else."

"Ah, and you regret that."

"I used to."

"But not now."

"No."

"What did you want to be instead?"

"There you have me, Adèle. I don't actually know."

Meredith turned up halfway through dinner. It was a salad that Adèle and Anne had prepared. Meredith served herself from the dishes lining the centre of the table.

"Michael tells me you two are getting married," she said with a brittle smile. "Welcome to the family, Adèle."

Adèle blushed just enough for Michael to notice. He waited for her to tell Meredith the wedding was off but all Adèle said was, "Thank you, I'm pleased to have your good wishes."

Meredith smiled again but it looked more like a grimace to Michael. "And a huge thank you for those tapes. I'm sorry for leaving it so long." She picked at her food, kept staring at Michael then moving her eyes away when he returned her gaze. She's been crying, he thought, and that not long ago. Finally Meredith coughed a few times then said, "I put flowers on Daisy's grave this morning."

"*You* put them there?"

"I thought it was about time."

"Yes it was, Meredith."

Across the table, Anne was making faces, feigning shock. "Henrietta," she mouthed to Michael.

Meredith placed her knife and fork on top of her half-eaten food. "I think I'm full," she said and left the table.

When Michael showed Adèle around the house, she frowned at his bed, ran her fingers over the footboard, traced the patterns moulded on its serpentine edge. "*Exquis*," she said. "Anne tells me you made all the furniture."

"Just the wooden pieces."

Adèle stroked the daisy emblem. "Does this appear on each one?"

"Yes."

Adèle moved around the room, examined each piece of furniture. Finally she came back to Michael. Her eyes looked desolate.

"I shouldn't have come. I can't take her place."

"Adèle, hasn't it dawned on you yet? I don't want a Daisy substitute. I love you for yourself. You're so different from her and that difference has always attracted me."

"But if you could, which of us would you choose?"

The question was put lightly but Adèle's expression belied that. This was no hypothetical question like the similar one Meredith had once put to him, although that, he recalled, had apparently not been hypothetical to Meredith.

"I wish you hadn't asked me that."

"Then don't answer. It wasn't fair of me."

"I could lie."

"Ah, and say you'd choose me?"

"If I said I'd choose Daisy, I'd be lying too. The truth is, right now, I'd choose both of you."

"Then you are very greedy, Michael." That was also said lightly but this time Adèle was smiling.

"I could never give you up, not now. However long you make me wait."

The light that appeared in Adèle's eyes then, its mesmerising quality, tugged at Michael's emotions.

"Then I am heartened," she said.

"Does that mean…?"

"No, Michael. I'm sorry." Adèle looked mournful. "And I'm very grateful for your patience even if you insist on having two women."

"Dad, Marie told me," Anne said after Adèle had gone upstairs to read Hamish a bedtime story. "She texted me to see if you'd arrived then I phoned her. Don't be mad at her."

"Told you what?"

"About Jean-Paul. And that Adèle's called the wedding off."

"Oh." Michael gazed at his daughter, at the concern written over her face. He felt a rush of emotion.

"Dad, here, let me…" Anne produced a handkerchief and dried Michael's eyes as if he was the child and she the parent. "There now, that's better…"

Is that what you think? Michael wanted to say. He tried to smile. "Did Marie mention anything else?"

"She wants you to call her. After eight. Definitely not before, she said."

Michael glanced at his watch. An hour and a quarter to wait.

"You'll have to keep Adèle out of the way," he said to Anne. "And please don't tell her I've involved Marie."

"Of course. To both things," Anne said. Then she frowned. "Go easy with Marie, Dad."

They gazed at each other, silent, for perhaps a half minute. Neither blinked. Then Michael said, slowly, "You don't need to worry about that, Anne. She has no more illusions."

"Who has no more illusions?" Adèle said, coming into the room.

"Meredith," Michael said. "About living here."

"How did you get on?" Michael said when Marie picked up his call. "Did you persuade Loli to tell the truth?"

"Better than that," Marie said. Michael heard her talking to someone, then came an answering voice, low, deep.

The receiver crackled. "Monsieur Cavanagh? My estimable niece says you need my help."

Hearing that voice again, Michael felt hope germinate within him. How could he ever repay Marie? "Yes, I do," he said then let his concerns flow out.

"I can see why Mademoiselle Serazin might think Jean-Paul acted from spite," Jean Bohec said. "And you are correct in surmising that I am the priest who visited him. However, I'm certain he knew nothing about you and her being together. Of course you were among those I said I visited but I didn't mention that in your cases it was at the same time and place. How would Jean-Paul know anyway? He said he'd had no contact with any family or so-called friends except for a single visit from Adèle and that was to tell him she was divorcing him. I believe that was long before you and she..."

"Yes it was."

"So. Jean-Paul asked how Adèle was and I said well, considering what he did to her. He gave me a hangdog look but said nothing more. When I mentioned you, all he said was 'Did you see Jacques?' I took the liberty to say Jacques was fine. Is that true, Michael? May I call you that? Monsieur Cavanagh seems so formal."

"Of course. And Jacques is happy enough, although we call him Hamish, the name Daisy gave him."

"Hamish, yes. I shall remember in future. Perhaps I may be allowed to meet him one day."

Michael didn't respond. Jean Bohec cleared his throat.

"What I actually said was that my *grandson* was fine. Jean-Paul stared as if he was seeing Beelzebub himself. 'You are my father? My real father?' he said. When I admitted I was, he bowed his head and covered his face with his hands. After many minutes he looked up and said, 'Why are you here? Why come now?' I said I had come to hear his confession.

"And now Michael, it's time I made mine. I began this sorrowful history by bringing disgrace on a poor innocent girl. In my folly I thought I'd contained my sin by giving our son into the care of my family. Berthe and I were once... Well, you don't need to know about that. Suffice it to say I thought she was the ideal mother for him. I didn't know she and Mathilde had connived to displace Augustine and that the possession of my son was designed to perpetuate that usurpation.

"Now I spend my life with the most disadvantaged people in the most disadvantaged places of the world. I seek no reward beyond redemption but have been repaid a thousand-fold by the joy on their faces. Perhaps taking pleasure in that is another sin on my part.

"Home news rarely reaches me. It was chance that prompted Loli to tell me about Jean-Paul's trial because she had not the slightest idea I was his father. Bohec is a relatively common name and it was the Mazemeur connection that jogged Loli's memory. She recalled us having cousins there. She thought the newspaper cutting might interest me, nothing more, so kept it aside to be sent with her next letter to me.

"As soon as I received that, I knew I must come home. If I could make even the smallest thing better... That is why I sought Mademoiselle Serazin. And there in Saint-Servais, I was surprised to also find you.

"After meeting you, I returned to the village where I once betrayed the trust of a child. I called it *love* but should have been imprisoned for what I did. However, the Church looks after its own and Mireille's family was bought off. I was diverted to filing duties at the diocesan office, where they assumed I could do no further harm. I did no good either, for guilt clawed me constantly. Then one day I read about the mission societies' work and decided that would be my path to redemption."

Michael thought about paths to redemption. Committing yourself to forty years in the wilderness seemed like overkill to him. So was making yourself responsible for the acts of your thirty-nine-year-old psychopath son. In fact, Father Jean's path sounded very much like running away, something he'd done himself until Daisy helped him to live with his past. It struck Michael that he had not yet told Adèle about Jacinta. Somehow he knew she'd be all right about it.

"Michael, are you still there?"

Michael blinked, shook himself. "Sorry, I missed that last bit. The line went faint."

"I was saying that I prayed for guidance in my old church, and the answer was granted to me. It said twenty years in prison was not enough to atone for Jean-Paul's crimes."

Michael found himself murmuring, "An eye for an eye, a tooth for a tooth." He had pitched his words, he thought, too low for Jean Bohec's ears.

"An eye for an eye, you say? Exactly. Jean-Paul seemed grateful that anyone should want to see him, even a relation he'd never heard of. Maybe the fact I was a priest intrigued him and that I wanted to visit him in that category.

"Up to now I have never broken the sacrosanctity of the confessional but I believe the greater sin would be in not telling you what Jean-Paul said. Admissions poured from him as if he was grateful to be free of them. He began with Jimpy Bertin, whom the delightful young lady of this house tells me was the son of her father's brother. Jean-Paul said he killed that poor young man out of jealousy, because Jimpy had the adulation of the community and the prettiest girl in the district too. Jean-Paul couldn't have the first but was determined to have the second. However, he tried too soon and she ended the relationship. The girl, as I imagine you know, was Adèle and he could not believe his luck when he got a second chance with her, a second chance to pretend he was Jimpy."

So Adèle was closer to the truth than she knew, Michael thought. He'd asked her why she called Bohec Jimpy and she said it began as a slip of the tongue, that one day she called him Jimpy by accident. Bohec had liked that so Adèle let it stick. She'd reflected that it couldn't hurt the real Jimpy and perhaps made Jean-Paul feel as if his friend was somehow still alive.

Jean Bohec's voice was droning in Michael's ear and he realised he had lost track again: "...he joined the set who infest the Riviera in summer and the ski slopes in winter. On the latter, of course, he met Daisy, the granddaughter of an English earl."

"Scottish," Michael said. "A Scottish earl."

"As you say. Jean-Paul decided to marry her. Pregnancy and cocaine were the means he chose to bind her. Even so, he had a hard job to persuade her and hadn't anticipated the hostility he would receive from her father. He could not do much about that while the man was alive but...well you know all about the later unpleasantness.

"Daisy died for the reasons you hypothesised, Michael. You were wrong though if you thought Jean-Paul knew he and Berthe were not entitled to Mazemeur, or that she was not his real mother. He said Daisy's revelations came as a total shock. They made him panic, act impulsively. Daisy did not deserve to die, he said and God knew he loved her once. But the worst thing about killing Daisy... Remember, these are Jean-Paul's words, Michael, not mine. The worst thing about killing Daisy was the fact that he terrified one son so much the boy refused to have anything to do with him, and he had effectively slain his second, newborn one."

"Frédy," Michael said. "The baby's name was Frédy."

"Is that so? A good, honest name."

"Adèle chose it. I don't think she told Jean-Paul."

"No, I expect not." There was a heavy sigh, then the priest continued, "I asked my son if he was truly repentant. He said yes, for all his crimes, for Daisy, Jimpy, his baby son, and the terrible loss and pain he inflicted on Jacques and on Adèle. I regret that he didn't mention you, Michael."

"No matter, but he should have mentioned depriving a baby girl of her mother. It was only by the slenderest chance Vicki wasn't added to his killing list."

"Daisy's daughter? I should have remembered. I don't think Jean-Paul registered her existence. Though God would have had her in mind."

I doubt she was in God's mind, Michael thought but it occurred to him that killing Vicki had been very much in Bohec's mind. Perhaps that was too monstrous a sin to confess.

"...I said absolution for such sins came with a most heavy price. Then I quoted the text we discussed before, Michael: An eye for an eye, a tooth for a tooth. Jean-Paul did not flinch. 'When you said you would hear my confession,' he said, 'I assumed you meant my last. Although it is also my first for over twenty years. What do you want me to do?' Your duty, I said, as I have done mine.

"So, Michael, is that what you wanted from me? Appallingly melodramatic, the stuff of a bad opera but it happened. But, oh sweet Jesus, ordering your own child's death is the hardest cross to bear."

There was a long pause. Michael heard Marie in the background, making comforting sounds. Then Jean Bohec came on again.

"I'm sorry," he said. "Now, I am told you don't wish Adèle to know about our conversation so I shall phone in perhaps half an hour and ask directly for her. I took the precaution of telephoning Adèle's mother and was told her daughter was in England. She wouldn't say where so I also have Marie's permission to say that she suggested Adèle might be staying with you. Be assured that I shall only say what should set Adèle's mind at rest. God be with you both."

"And also with you, Father," Michael said in spite of himself.

Adèle came back from the telephone looking thoughtful but not untroubled. She sank into an armchair, laid her head against the backrest. "It was Maman," she said. "Checking if I was all right."

"And are you?" Michael asked.

Adèle said, somewhat crossly, "Why shouldn't I be?"

Michael decided not to push his luck. He was set for an uncomfortable evening of being desperate to know what Adèle was thinking while being unable to reveal he was party to Jean Bohec's revelations too.

Anne, obviously aware of the tension, brought out the *Aggravation* game that was last played when she, Michael and Daisy were marooned in the Norfolk Broads. A tear or two invaded his eyes but they were dispelled as everyone became locked into shrieks of laughter and frustration, and the shouting of more than a few expletives in English and French.

For all that, Michael slept alone.

Next morning, Adèle asked Michael if she might spend the day with Vicki. "Just her and me."

"Of course," he said, while disallowing himself any hope regarding Adèle's motive. She might simply feel sorry for the child.

"What will you do?" Adèle said.

"Oh, I'll be in my workshop. Plenty waiting for me there. It'll do me no harm to get into the habit again."

In fact there was nothing waiting, with courting Adèle in mind, Michael had frozen all commissions. He sat at his computer, idly staring at the screensaver, and it came to him that Adèle had remarked on there being no dressing table in his bedroom. He'd said he hadn't seen the need just for himself. She'd given him an odd kind of smile.

She'd called it a coiffeuse. Funny that, the French calling a dressing table a hairdresser. Still, Michael supposed, it was principally for dressing the hair so their logic wasn't far out.

In his head, he designed a coiffeuse for Adèle. Hepplewhite with a touch of Empire, echoing both England and France. He pictured Adèle gazing into its mirror as she combed her hair, her eyes concentrating as she ordered each chestnut strand into place.

She had once told him that Adèle meant 'noble' so in the place he reserved for his trademark, Michael mentally carved a coronet, a noble's crown. There should be something to signify a seaside girl too. Not a mermaid, for he would always associate them with Daisy. He settled on a dolphinet who carried more than a hint of Adèle's smile.

Michael switched to a vision of Adèle playing peek-a-boo in the house with Vicki. It was a promising scene and he was allowing himself to develop it further, making Adèle so totally captivated by Vicki that she couldn't bear to leave her, when he caught a movement from the corner of an eye. He swung his chair around, rejoined reality.

Meredith was poised in the doorway. If Michael didn't know her better he'd have said she was embarrassed.

"You used to stand on the threshold of my old workshop like that. Then walk out without saying a word."

"That was because I felt out of my depth."

"With me?"

"With everything."

Meredith came into the room. Her colour was so high Michael wondered if she was running a temperature.

"That morning you and I met," she said, "I'd just given Harry his first instalment. I didn't even know I had the puncture until you offered to help. Each time I visited you after that, I'd dosed Harry a little more."

"Jesus, Meredith!" Nausea filled Michael's gullet. "Who the hell did you think I was? Your confessor?"

"My lifeline, Michael. I told you that. You were my breath of sanity. Watching you make things that were beautiful, yet had solidity, like yourself, sustained me more than you'll ever know."

"Solidity? I was more hung up than you were."

"But I didn't know and you didn't show it. That was what mattered. I've been selfish, Michael. With Daisy gone, I wanted you all to myself again, like it used to be. I'm sorry I tried to seduce you. That was very wrong of me. I accept that now. I'm glad you've found love again. I won't come to the wedding if you don't mind but I wish you and Adèle the greatest joy together. Truly."

"Thank you."

A coy smile played over Meredith's face. "Would you like to know where I was yesterday?"

"That depends."

"There's a little house that's taken my fancy near Arundel. I wondered if that was too close." There was a catch in Meredith's voice as she said 'too close'. "I thought I might learn to drive Harry's car too. Don't worry, I've no intention of being a nuisance. I just thought I should broaden my horizons."

"That's a good idea, Meredith. That's really good."

Michael allowed himself to hold her in a loose embrace. She'd had her hair cut, it felt bristly against his chin. He hoped she took a long time to pass her driving test, years preferably. He was thinking that Adèle would surely look after the office. If she ever married him. After all, she did work in a bank. It should be second nature to her.

When Meredith had gone, Michael spent another hour daydreaming. Then he heard Adèle's voice in the workshop below.

"We thought we'd come and see how you are getting on. It's long past lunchtime."

Adèle was at the bottom of the stairs, hand-in-hand with Vicki. Michael raced down them two at a time.

"I've missed you both terribly," he said.

"It's only been one morning," Adèle said but Michael could see she was pleased. She brushed her fingers over a stack of cherry boards. After tomorrow, he thought, I face God knows how long without her.

"This is beautiful wood, Michael."

Vicki stroked the cherry boards too, mimicking Adèle. She rattled off a string of made-up words, addressing Michael and Adèle in turn, with accompanying facial gestures. Then she giggled. Adèle picked her up and cuddled her.

"Maman," Vicki said.

Cherry wood, Michael thought, I shall make the coiffeuse from cherry wood.

Adèle had said 'Au revoir' to the others. As Michael put her bags into the car she asked would he walk with her for a while. "It seems too abrupt simply driving away," she said.

They strolled to the edge of the lawn, gazed across the Downs towards the sea. Lazy clouds drifted in a kindly sky and, somewhere in the trees that marked Giffards' western boundary, a blackbird sang to his love. A lump began to form in Michael's throat. This could have been a perfect September evening.

The blackbird left the trees, scuttled about on the grass a few feet from them. They watched it spear the soil, turn fallen leaves to select its supper. Michael envied the bird for its uncomplicated life.

Beside him, Adèle suddenly breathed in sharply. "Do you remember when you came looking for Jean-Paul," she said softly, leaning into him. "How you stopped me saying something, even though I said it wasn't anything terrible."

"I remember."

"It was this. I think sometimes that you and I are just outsiders. Excluded from the inner circle, left to guess what's really going on."

"Was that what you were going to say?"

"Yes. And it's only just come to me that the circle is now broken, that we're no longer outsiders. That there are no secrets to fear anymore."

Michael held his breath. He wasn't sure what Adèle meant exactly but he sensed something significant had just occurred, a pivotal change in their relationship. Perhaps the blackbird's song was the catalyst. He recalled another blackbird singing, long ago, on the day he first met Daisy. That had heralded a pivotal change in his life too, one that led relentlessly, pas à pas, via cause and effect, to this moment.

"So then why am I doing this, Michael? Leaving? I don't want to go. I don't have to go."

"What about your job?" Michael said, and wished he'd chosen something more pertinent.

"It's just a job." Adèle made a face, a demi-pout. "So what do you say, Michael? May I stay? Until you take me back to marry me?"

"Marry you when?"

"October twenty-third. Michael, I *know* you took your papers to the Mairie." Adèle smiled. "Sarzeau is a small town, news gets around."

On hearing those words, Michael felt a lightness of mind, almost palpable, as the burden of his distress fell away. He wanted to sing out but chose to smile instead.

"There's something else," Adèle said. "That phone call the other night was not from my mother. It was Jean Bohec."

"Oh, really?"

"Oh really, you say? *Oh? Really?* You knew that already, you…you carpenter by defeat."

"By default," Michael said. Adèle was grinning at him now and Michael's answering one was so wide he thought his face would split. "Well," he said. "I suppose I'd better tell Anne to lay an extra place for dinner."

They retrieved Adèle's bags from the car, re-crossed the lawn. The blackbird flew past them, settled on the finial over the porch gable. As they neared the house, the bird cocked its head, as if gauging their approach. When they were less than a yard away it began to serenade them.

They stopped and listened to the song. Adèle pressed her body into Michael's. "We're the insiders now," she said. "And he's welcoming us home."

Even in the fading light, her smile and her eyes were hypnotic. Michael lost himself willingly in their magic. He was filled with a quiet exhilaration, a confidence in his future with Adèle that he'd never experienced with Daisy.

www.ingramcontent.com/pod-product-compliance
Lightning Source LLC
Chambersburg PA
CBHW050616110726
47899CB00001B/126